CARAVAN OF
SPECTERS

Published by St. Petersburg Press
St. Petersburg, FL
www.stpetersburgpress.com
Copyright ©2024

Design and composition by St. Petersburg Press and Isa Crosta
Cover Art by Gabe Palma
Cover design by Isa Crosta

Hardcover ISBN: 978-1-940300-96-2
Paperback ISBN: 978-1-940300-97-9
eBook ISBN: 978-1-940300-98-6
First Edition

CARAVAN OF SPECTERS

BY CARLOS GARCÍA SAÚL

20 June 1765, aboard the royal frigate *El Águila*.
To His Majesty Don Carlos Sebastián de Borbón, King of Spain and the Two Sicilies:

The origin and principal cause of the backwardness of Puerto Rico lies in the people…These men are worthless and lazy, they possess no implements, have no knowledge of agriculture, have no one to assist them in the work or aid them in clearing the forest; therefore, how could they advance? To encourage such laziness, there is also a balmy climate…

Alejandro O' Reilly
Major General and Special Commissioner to the Indies

*****

August 5, 1910
What if these people were merely innocent victims of a disease, modern only in name? What if the brand placed by the Spaniard, the Englishman, and the Frenchman in olden times upon the "jíbaro" of Porto Rico were a bitter injustice? The early reports savor strongly of those touristic impressions of the island which from time to time crop out in the press of modern America, in which "laziness" and "worthlessness" of the "natives" are to be inferred, if, indeed, these very words are not employed to describe a sick working man, with only half the blood he should have in his body.

Bailey K. Ashford, Major, U.S. Army

A Note on Spelling Conventions

The United States Government officially changed the name of Puerto Rico to Porto Rico in 1899. I have retained the original Spanish spelling in the narrative text and dialogue, but utilized the official 1899 spelling in written exchanges between the characters, or where actual documents are quoted. The name reverted to Puerto Rico in 1933.

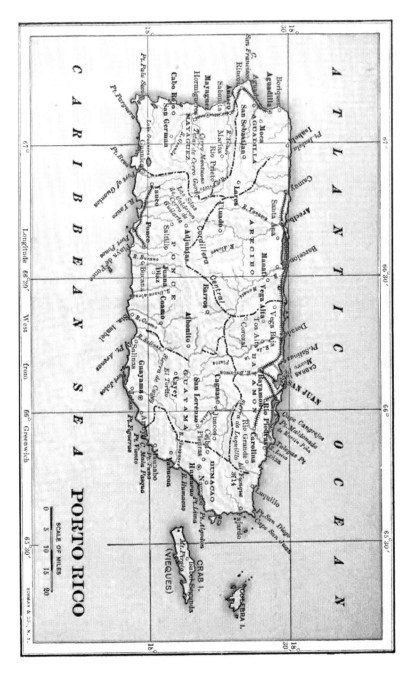

Puerto Rico, 1903. At the time, the island was divided into 69 municipal districts named after their principal city or town, as shown above in small bold type.

San Juan

Puerto Rico, circa 1900

1 Fort El Morro
2 Fort San Cristóbal
3 Ballaja Barracks
4 San Juan General Hospital
5 Casa Blanca
6 Cathedral
7 Cristo de la Salud Chapel
8 La Fortaleza
9 Carmelite Convent
10 María Asunción's House

LA PUNTILLA

CITY WALL

CRISTO ST.

FORTALEZA ST.

SAN SEBASTIAN ST.

SAN JOSE ST.

CRUZ ST.

SOL ST.

SAN JUSTO ST.

TANCA ST.

SAN FRANCISCO ST.

RECINTO SUR ST.

RECINTO DE ST.

O'DONNELL ST.

Cecilia Ortega

Contents

Chapter One

AN INVISIBLE SCOURGE

T he killer started life as a fertile egg in the soil, a microscopic oval sac of nutrients and genetic instructions. It was destined to become the agent of a deadly disease when conditions proved right. Even under a powerful microscope, it would have appeared bland and nondescript, without a hint of movement or detail within its thick, dark coat. But after only two days, nurtured by the warmth and humidity of the rich black soil, the egg began a subtle change. That same microscope would now reveal the jelly inside the oval to be slowly taking shape, dividing into the first manifestations of an embryo. First along its length, then along its width, the structure acquired the form of the tiniest mulberry, and within a few hours, the embryo lengthened and streamlined into the unmistakable shape of a worm. With each shedding of its outer skeleton, the minuscule animal transformed itself slightly, cycling through three juvenile stages, until the tiny creature reached its final, or filarial stage. The transformation from embryo to filaria had taken only ten days.

The tiny animal next underwent a complex ritual of development and migration, one in which human hosts played a central role. Nature had endowed the filarial larva with the unusual ability to penetrate human skin. No other being held its interest. The wiggling, blind worm, light gray in color and scarcely half a millimeter in length, was able to detect the faintest cues emanating from human skin. Carbon dioxide, humidity, skin flakes, sweat—all oriented its tiny head like a light in a tunnel and led the animal to its one goal: a skin pore bearing a hair shaft. There, in the slight indentation where the tiny hair punctured the skin, it searched tirelessly for a vein. Any unlucky juvenile which failed to find its vessel was condemned to months of aimless wandering. To a trained eye, these lost larvae could just barely be seen beneath the victim's skin as small comma-shaped entities, shifting position slightly from day to day and producing an otherworldly itch that its unfortunate hosts called *la piquiña*, but otherwise did little harm.

By contrast, the luckier filaria eventually found a tiny vein and, using its piranha-like teeth, punctured the vessel wall to enter the lazy, nutrient-rich flow. It became a passive explorer of the bloodstream, drifting aimlessly past the heart toward the capillaries of the lungs, where it became stuck. Then, the tiny animal again deployed its razor-sharp teeth to cut its way into one of the hundreds of millions of air sacs leading to the trachea, a welcoming pathway with its warm, slimy mucus. Higher and higher up the airway the juvenile progressed, gaining two inches a day with a relentless determination to reach the throat.

A person might notice a slight urge to cough, or possibly feel nothing at all—but, in a most casual reflex and without a second thought or warning, the victim swallowed the worm and became its host. The filaria soon entered a hospitable environment within the small intestine, amidst millions of microscopic, blood-rich, finger-like villi. With an instinct honed during millions of years of evolution, the lucky juvenile bit into the intestinal lining, provoking a flow of blood which it lapped up like a hyena at a waterhole. Only now could the larva dispose of its outer skeleton for the last time and acquire the characteristic hook-like shape that gave it its common name.

Safely settled within the small intestine, male and female worms engaged in a sort of primitive orgy as they fed on a seemingly endless supply of blood. Fertilized females, gorged to bursting, underwent complex biochemical processes which allowed them to produce a near-endless stream of fertilized eggs—twenty thousand every day. Billions of eggs traveled through the many thousands of hosts, to be evacuated at a propitious time and restart the cycle, multiplying the numbers of viable eggs by three or four orders of magnitude.

In the same way that the damp, rich, and finely particulate soil of Puerto Rico provided an ideal environment for the bountiful harvest of sugar cane, coffee, and tobacco, it also provided, tragically, the conditions for an equally rich crop of killer hookworms.

Chapter Two

TAMPA, JULY 1898

The young lieutenant stood at attention. Buzzing around in the oppressively sticky air, two giant horse-flies circled his nose looking for a landing spot. Facing him, post commander Hunter Liggett sat behind a beat-up desk, barely able to contain his pleasure.

"Ashford, after twelve weeks of waiting, you and I are finally pulling out."

"The orders came through?"

Captain Liggett beamed. "At long last, this pimple-in-a-swamp will soon be a memory for both of us. I have been assigned to Cuba, and you, to Puerto Rico."

Lieutenant Bailey K. Ashford looked puzzled. "Puerto Rico? Could you check the orders one more time? I thought the fighting was in Cuba, where this whole mess started."

Liggett looked down at the papers once more. "Yes, Ashford. Your orders say Puerto Rico."

Most people only knew Puerto Rico as the far smaller and poorer sister colony of Cuba, and nothing more.

Ligget shrugged. "There must be something going on over there."

Ashford replied with a half-smile, "Well, any place is better than this, Captain. *Good ol' Fort St. Philip!* Spending a muggy summer in a third-rate camp at the mouth of the Mississippi isn't my idea of practicing medicine."

Liggett regarded Ashford closely. The lieutenant was a slender man, slightly under six feet tall with fine sandy hair only just beginning to thin and attractive features anchored by intelligent blue eyes. He had developed a reputation as a good clinician, a God-fearing, bible-toting Southerner, direct and soft-spoken until his volatile temperament was aroused, at which time his mouth veritably dripped with venomous irony. Liggett thought that Ashford's tongue had kept him marooned in that forsaken Louisiana bayou while many of his medical colleagues were already seeing action in Cuba.

"So, what happens now?" The young lieutenant asked.

Liggett arose from his desk. "You will depart from New Orleans bound for Tampa. There, you'll get all the details you might need."

Ashford could not hide his enthusiasm. "Tampa, sir? It must be an invasion force, then."

Liggett nodded. "Highly probable. Rumor has it Miles and Schwan are commanding. Who knows? You may even find yourself some real shooting, more than what you're doing with the squirrels here, anyway."

Ashford smiled distractedly as his mind drifted away, trying to process the news. Here he was, twenty-five years old and a brand-new member of the Army Medical Corps, bound for Florida and potentially the adventure of a lifetime. He had never even been out of the South, but it appeared that now he was going to war far away in the Caribbean.

Ashford was brought back to earth by Liggett's crisp salute. "Lieutenant, you should be ready to depart by this evening, at the latest."

"Yes, Captain."

Liggett extended his hand. "Here are your orders; you are hereby relieved. Good luck, Ashford."

The lieutenant raised an open hand to his forehead. "Thank you, sir."

His head bowed in thought, Ashford walked slowly from his commander's office toward the barracks as his best-loved Old Testament verse echoed through his brain:

And the LORD, he it is that doth go before thee;
He will be with thee, he will not fail thee, nor forsake thee:
Fear not, neither be dismayed.

In a barely audible voice, he responded to himself, "Amen."

But even with the great uncertainties of going to war, he was overjoyed to leave that accursed place. The Army post at Fort St. Philip, in the marshy lowlands of Louisiana, consisted of a few gun emplacements and exactly one ramshackle wooden house, which simultaneously served as a headquarters, quartermaster's store house, dispensary for the sick, and sleeping quarters. Not only was the place cramped and hot, but the gargantuan mosquitoes carrying malaria meant wearing heavy clothing, buckskin gloves, boots, and a sombrero with a net draped over it. The only relief came from the untold barrels of Budweiser shipped weekly from New Orleans, sixty miles upriver. Ashford had no doubt that whatever Puerto Rico had to offer, it would be better than this.

In half an hour, he had gathered his belongings and said goodbye to fellow soldiers, most of whom could barely contain their jealousy. By the time his orders arrived, the war was rapidly approaching a climax, and Ashford was impatient to join the fray. Moreover, the Spanish were taking a licking and the conflict could well be over before long, which in his mind would surely spoil his chances for glory.

When Ashford left that evening on the camp's tumbledown flatboat, ahead of him stretched four days of battling the muddy current. He felt pressured for time, already somewhat behind schedule and fully aware that trains in the South chronically ran late. The fleet was due to sail in one week, on July 20, 1898, and Ashford knew he was cutting it very close. Not surprisingly, when he arrived in New Orleans his train had already left, resulting in an additional twelve-hour wait for the next one. At last, orders in hand, an impatient Ashford boarded and proceeded down the long line of rickety coaches, searching for a cabin with a window to moderate the crushing heat.

The journey proved oppressive, the train crossing endless stretches of the Deep South baking under the relentless midsummer sun. Ashford found the air in the coach thick and sticky, the poor ventilation contributing to a perpetual recycling of the more pungent odors of humanity. Only the late evening, with its cooler temperatures, provided some token of relief. As the train rocked lazily through endless plantings of cotton and sugarcane, Ashford gradually succumbed to exhaustion, still clutching his orders in his sweaty right hand. He awakened abruptly to a shrill whistle from the train—and blinked repeatedly to spot his precious orders fluttering out of the window and landing in one of the fields swiftly receding away. Ashford felt his heart drop. In his stupor he had released his grip on the papers, and now they might as well have been on the moon. Those papers proved his identity and described his mission; now he was going to have a hard time explaining his presence in a military embarkation port. Ashford's mood soured, and for the rest of the journey he remained awake, consoling himself by chain-smoking his way through Mississippi, Alabama, and into Florida. *I really should quit these darned things before my lungs turn into chunks of coal,* he thought with disappointment.

After twenty long hours, the train pulled into Tampa. The city of ten thousand souls near the Gulf Coast was prospering from a robust boom rooted in the curious juxtaposition of endless phosphate deposits and quality cigars. Ashford found his way to the port area and walked among the busy piers, past merchant and fighting ships of diverse tonnage. Toward the northern apex of Hillsborough Bay were ferries slated to transport the soldiers to several large troop ships, anchored five hundred yards from the wharves. Ashford took it all in with a fascination born from the unfamiliar. He had not yet been to sea, his only experience on the water limited to skiffs and yawls on the lower Potomac.

After making a few inquiries, the lieutenant physician reported to his immediate superior, Colonel Robert O'Reilly, Chief Surgeon of the expedition. After exchanging a few pleasantries, O'Reilly pointed him to the commanding general's office, located 200 yards away across a field of dusty palmetto trees. As he walked, Ashford took in the disagreeable features of the enormous embarkation camp, its air teeming with flies and dung beetles in all shapes and sizes, and the ground punctuated by hastily constructed latrines, every last one of them filled precariously to the brim. The penetrating smell of sewage and the stinking sweat of the soldiery mixed with the whiff of burnt gunpowder to produce a rotten miasma, amplified by the heat of the stultifying Florida summer. Ashford pushed his way through the crowd of soldiers and laborers, noting the bustle of a thousand working men; tall, short, black, white, uniformed, and shirtless. Supplies for the expedition lay strewn in messy piles mostly consisting of countless cans, some labeled with their contents—*roast beef*, others *tomatoes* and yet others *baked beans*. Hundreds of containers of water and boxes of hardtack were getting loaded onto small rafts to be taken to the larger ships. Ashford walked toward what passed as the central office, swatting enormous black flies from his eyes and mouth.

The commanding general's post occupied an improvised shanty, built on sandy soil under the shade of a struggling live oak. The doctor entered the hut and saluted.

"Lieutenant Bailey Ashford begging to report, sir."

A gruff adjutant scrutinized the lieutenant from top to bottom. "Orders?"

Ashford stammered, "I…I have none at the moment, sir."

"You have none *at the moment*. Well, when will you have them?"

The red-faced lieutenant replied, "Never, sir. They are lost. Flew out the window of my train." His face a deep crimson from embarrassment, Ashford proceeded to explain who he was and why he was there.

The adjutant grunted. "Not a particularly auspicious way to start your mission, is it?" With a dismissive look at the doctor, he turned to his chief.

"General, here is a young man who claims he is a medical officer."

The commander kept writing at his desk without taking his eyes off his official papers. "And so?"

"General, sir, if you believe his story, please send him away and get him out of my way."

The general looked up, evaluated the officer standing at attention, and giving a contemptuous snort, hastily scratched out new orders. "Take these to General Schwan, who at this very moment is embarking with the Provisional Brigade of regulars for Puerto Rico."

Ashford stood at attention. "Thank you, sir. And where may I find General Schwan?"

The general gave Ashford a curious look. "Hell if we know, lieutenant. Probably on the pier somewhere, that's for you to find out." In an ominous whisper, he added, "Better you should hurry, if you want to catch him."

Utterly lost and unsure where to go among the myriad of men and ships, Ashford careened from wharf to wharf like a billiard ball unable to find its pocket. Most of the workers were Spanish-speaking Cubans, and when questioned, they stared blankly at the young officer and invariably pointed him in different directions. He finally encountered a burly sergeant busily barking orders and hurried to him. "Sarge, I've been running all over hell's half-acre trying to find General Schwan."

The sergeant looked up from his clipboard. "T'nant, ya may be out of luck, our fleet sails in fifteen minutes, and I bet the ginral's already aboard. But what the hay, come along anyways." The sergeant motioned for Ashford to follow and led him at a run, huffing and sweating profusely, to the point of embarkation.

Ashford arrived too late. General Schwan, the last officer to embark for the transport ship, had already left. The lieutenant gazed in complete disbelief at the gradually shrinking figure of his assigned commander, sitting nonchalantly in a wooden launch while six scrawny, bare-chested sailors rowed him out to the troop ship. As the commander gradually faded into the distance, so did young Ashford's hopes.

He swore in frustration. "Dang me, he's *gone!*"

The next moment, he resolved to signal for the return of the general's boat and began to run along the shore like a madman, yelling for the boat to return.

By now about 200 yards from the shore, Provisional Brigade Commander General Theodore Schwan could not help noticing that on the slowly receding pier, an officer in full dress uniform waved and jumped emphatically as he ran along the waterfront. The man was unquestionably demented, judging by his outrageous antics.

Schwan turned to his chief of staff. "Why the deuce is that soldier making such a spectacle of himself? He must very much want to leave Tampa behind. I guess I could see why, with all the stink, and man-eating flies and other pests."

"Not sure, sir, but judging by the way he is carrying on,

he may have some last-minute communication from General Miles in Cuba."

With that remark, back to the pier went the boat, and into the boat went the embarrassed lieutenant. He confessed that, no, he did not have any communications from General Miles. With this admission, a streak of the most profane curses descended upon Ashford, as each one of Schwan's aides took turns shouting ever-worsening obscenities. Schwan said nothing and simply stood immobile, glaring at the lieutenant.

That the unfortunate doctor was not bodily thrown off the boat was the first miracle of his campaign, but it would certainly not be his last.

Chapter Three

THE VOYAGE

L ife aboard the military transports was never easy, and Ashford participated fully in the general misery. He shared quarters with Lieutenant Patrick McAndrew, a thirty-year-old civilian physician from Pennsylvania, recipient of an expedited surgeon's commission because of the acute shortage of medical personnel. Not long after departing Florida, the two doctors sat together at the officer's mess, whining about the sea-crossing.

Ashford put down his spoon and spoke through a mouthful of stale bread. "This gets my goat, McAndrew. Not two days have passed and the men are already famished thanks to inadequate rations. They are only allowed canned tomatoes and beans!"

McAndrew gave a lopsided grin. "Colonel O'Reilly says that starting today, the beef rations will finally be distributed. For some reason, less than a quarter of the ration cans in Tampa made it onto the ships. The rest were apparently stolen by the stevedores, most likely to sell in the city."

Ashford grimaced, "Well, I am not surprised. What's worse, I have tried the water onboard—it's brown as mud and tastes like rusted pipes. We really should be boiling the entire supply."

McAndrew smirked, pointing his knife across the room. "The only good water aboard belongs to the general and his staff. You know, Bailey, the head waiter will happily sell you a glass for half a dollar."

Ashford was stunned. "What outrageous claptrap! Without good water, we'll all be sick by tomorrow!"

An orderly finally came by and placed two cans before

them, which the two lieutenants regarded with curiosity. Ashford had seen the endless piles of canned roast beef stacked at the dock in Port Tampa, and hungry as he was, he was impatient to try them.

The two lieutenants exchanged mischievous glances and excitedly rushed to procure four tall candles from neighboring tables. With mounting excitement, they broke into a bizarre ceremony, chanting and waving their hands over the unopened rations before bursting out laughing. They opened the first can with undiluted anticipation—and recoiled in disbelief at the contents. The so-called roast beef was little more than a filthy gelatinous sop, covered in a slime that gave off a nauseating smell.

Ashford dry-heaved. "Roast beef, my a—! This is more like roast *corpse*!"

A peculiar smell overwhelmed the mess hall as other officers opened their cans. All the beef rations had the same repulsive characteristics, caused by flawed canning procedures and subsequent exposure to the hellacious heat on the Tampa piers. And yet, the braver men tried their best to eat them. Ashford managed to swallow three mouthfuls before becoming wretchedly sick, a scene repeated countless times around him. The dinner was cut short as the men rushed belowdecks to deal with waves of uncontrollable nausea.

The following day, Ashford and McAndrew, to their great astonishment, again received a can of meat, supposed to last them for twenty-four hours. Ashford had planned to keep his own can as a souvenir, but a sudden pitch from a wave dislodged the unopened container from his hands. The can fell on the floor, where it immediately exploded with the sound of a pistol shot. The young doctor jumped back to find his trousers covered in gooey debris. The other soldiers didn't even bother to open their rations and immediately threw their cans out of the mess hall's windows into the sea. A disgusted Ashford grumbled at McAndrew, "I hereby abandon all further attempts at consuming the roast corpse and resign myself to hardtack and canned tomatoes!" He was true to his word for the rest of the voyage.

*****

"Lieutenant Ashford! Wake up!"

The young doctor reflexively sat up in his bunk. Through a thick haze, Ashford stretched and rubbed his eyes, trying to force the sleep out of his system. He looked at his clock, which read 3 a.m. He had been asleep for less than two hours.

A young enlisted man was yelling in his ear. *"Lieutenant!* Dr. McAndrew needs urgent assistance in the infirmary. All hell is breaking loose down there."

Yawning, Ashford asked, "What did you say, Corporal?"

"I said, *all hell is breaking loose*—the place is overflowing with patients!"

Ashford pushed his messenger away. "Corporal, what *are* you talking about? I finished my shift at midnight and everything was perfectly quiet."

The corporal handed Ashford his uniform. "You picked a bad time to leave, sir. In the last hour, twenty soldiers have come down, all at once. McAndrew and his medic are overwhelmed, and the men look sicker than a dying dog's puke."

In an instant, Ashford was up. He splashed water in his face, and dressed hastily while hurrying to the infirmary two decks below, at the aft of the ship.

The narrow corridor leading to the cramped infirmary was lined on both sides with men in various stages of undress, all sweating profusely and retching uncontrollably as they searched everywhere for any container in which to vomit. Their pasty green faces left no doubt as to how they felt.

Ashford raced through the narrow doorway to find McAndrew bending over a delirious man. The doctor's only assistant was a wide-eyed medic, looking all of sixteen years old, frantically waving smelling salts under the patient's nose as the sick man gesticulated wildly.

Ashford had to yell to be heard above the racket from the adjacent engine room. "Lieutenant McAndrew, what is happening? I was here not two hours ago!"

McAndrew shot back, "Ashford, this is insane! Shortly after the midnight bell, the first patient arrived. He'd been feeling unwell since before we left Tampa—one week of fatigue, worsening headaches, and severe chills. He reported to the hospital tent at the port and was told he had eaten too much for lunch. He was ordered back to work loading the boats!"

"What idiot told him that? Unbelievable! This man is clearly very ill!"

The sick soldier rolled over and vomited blood on the floor, missing Ashford's boots by an inch, and mumbled something unintelligible.

Ashford turned to the infirmary's medic. "Bring in the first two men from the line outside. This patient is in no shape to explain anything about his illness." The medic rushed out and returned immediately with two of the men seeking care.

Ashford addressed them, "What in *tarnation* is happening?"

The soldier stumbled through an explanation: many of them had felt miserable the last few days, dog-tired, and with a splitting headache and chills despite the terrible heat. "Back in Tampa, the man at the hospital tent told me I had port fever and that it would resolve as soon as we got underway. He swore sea air was exactly the remedy I needed."

"*Port fever*? What the hell is port fever?"

The other soldier spoke up, "We don't know sir, but it sure sounded impressive. The same man said I had eaten too many canned beans and sent me back to work—" The man paused, waiting for a wave of nausea to pass. "He…he…*ahhh*-- said not to worry, it would all improve as soon as we got some good meat rations onboard."

The delirious man jerked his head backwards, reacting to the pungent smelling salts, and the medic offered him water. A sudden, horrifying thought crossed Ashford's mind. Over the engine noise, he shouted, "Put the water down! And bring me a rectal thermometer!"

A bulb thermometer was quickly procured, which McAndrew inserted into his patient. He read the temperature—104 degrees. The man vomited again and held his abdomen in both arms, wailing. Above the racket Ashford could still hear the retching and vomiting from the corridor outside.

The two physicians exchanged looks of concern. Ashford raised the man's undershirt to look at his chest. Dozens of rose-colored spots about a quarter of an inch in diameter clustered into groups of four or five, covering different areas on the man's chest and upper abdomen. A sudden realization struck both doctors like a punch to the stomach.

McAndrew leaned toward Ashford and spoke directly into his ear, "There is no question…?"

Ashford replied ominously, "Yes, Patrick, this here… is typhoid fever."

To make matters worse, the two-dozen waiting outside likely represented only the tip of the iceberg. The gravity of the situation quickly dawned on the two young doctors. They faced a potentially devastating epidemic.

McAndrew recoiled, saying to his assistant, "Johnson, go find the colonel, on the double."

A bleary-eyed O'Reilly arrived shortly, irritated at being disturbed so early over what sounded like a straightforward outbreak of food poisoning. Only as he passed the growing number of men outside the infirmary did he realize that something entirely different was happening, something serious. The colonel found his two junior physicians finishing their exam of the stricken soldier.

The colonel burst out, "Gentlemen! Kindly explain what is going on!"

Ashford stood and addressed him in a voice barely above a whisper. "Colonel, we are facing an outbreak of typhoid, there is no question. All the cardinal signs are present in this patient, and the men lined up outside report similar complaints: fatigue, belly pain, and headaches. More than half of them already have the telltale rose spots on their chest."

O'Reilly was dumbfounded. The colonel was a veteran army doctor and no stranger to typhoid in army camps, but an outbreak aboard a transport ship promised to be a different thing entirely. He turned toward the two lieutenants. "What do you propose?"

McAndrew spoke up. "Colonel, the drinking water is going foul. We must boil all the water we give the men. Next, we should designate several of the crew's quarters as sick bays before we are completely overwhelmed, and then sanitize those rooms and the infirmary with carbolic acid."

O'Reilly nodded. "Very well, Lieutenant, see that it is done."

Ashford held up a hand. "Boiling the water will help contain the outbreak, but it is not going to bolster the strength the men need to overcome an infection. Sick soldiers require calories and nutrients." He then gave the colonel a pointed look, adding, "But the officer's mess has a large supply of condensed milk."

"Yes it does, Ashford. Requisition the supply of milk immediately. Go take it yourself if necessary."

"All of it, sir?"

O'Reilly struck his fist into his open hand. "To the last ounce! And wake up every physician, orderly, and medic on this ship. Have them report here without delay. I will alert General Schwan as to our outbreak, and the likelihood that every ship in the fleet may have one as well. If this illness continues to spread unchecked, we will not have an invasion force left to land in Puerto Rico."

Within an hour, the medical personnel converging on the infirmary had tripled. Men were moved from their bunks to allow for the creation of two large sick bays, each capable of holding up to fifty men. Ashford and Johnson commandeered the officers' milk over the angry objections of a diminutive major, whom Ashford threatened to flatten if he didn't "get his ragged ass" out of the way. When the superior officer replied that he was going to report Ashford for rank insubordination, the lieutenant told him to go ahead, and to please carry down some of the boxes of milk while he was at it.

Under the sliver of a waxing crescent moon, the small convoy harboring its deadly cargo of typhoid continued slowly south along Florida's Gulf Coast. If the physicians could successfully arrest the outbreak, the ships would sail around the western edge of Cuba to avoid the Spanish battle fleet under Admiral Cervera. Unknown to the American fleet, the outdated and outclassed enemy squadron had been obliterated two weeks earlier, when they attempted to escape from the harbor at Santiago de Cuba. In less than an hour, Rear Admiral William Sampson sank or disabled all of Cervera's ships and then, for good measure, managed to capture the admiral. For the Spanish, Sampson's action represented one more in a string of weighty defeats the Americans had been inflicting since the war had begun. But none of this would matter if the U.S. Navy were decimated by typhoid fever.

After eighteen hectic hours in the infirmary, an exhausted Ashford went up on deck, wanting desperately to exchange the stuffy atmosphere below for a breath of marine air. The night was fresh and clear, the air slightly heavy with a humidity that was pleasantly dispersed by the north breeze. Lovingly tucked under his right arm he carried an old, dull-looking violin purchased by his mother for five dollars and given to him on his tenth birthday. From the semi-decrepit instrument, the young student could coax the most exquisitely rich tones with an ease that had astonished his conservatory teachers in Washington. He found that music granted him a clarity that he relied on in moments such as these. *En plein air*, the lieutenant began to play a melancholy sonata, the dark notes disappearing into the rush of wind generated by the forward movement of the ship.

Some distance away, on the port bow railing, stood a somber Colonel O'Reilly. Spotting his superior, the lieutenant ceased playing, approached the colonel and saluted.

O'Reilly returned the salute and offered Ashford a cigarette. "Welcome to another beautiful evening on the Caribbean Sea, Lieutenant. Enjoy them while you can because within a week, you could easily find yourself in the thick of some very vicious fighting. You won't have any more time to devote to your virtuosity."

Ashford suppressed an embarrassed cough. He took a deep drag, and said, "Colonel, the situation below decks is finally coming under a measure of control. We have quarantined all the men with symptoms, and we are preparing to treat and isolate any others as they present. A detail from the kitchen is boiling our water supply and distributing milk to the sick. We have also set up all the Lister devices to spray carbolic acid in the patient wards without interruption." The Lister atomizer Ashford alluded to produced a thick, sweet-smelling cloud of antiseptic with which to sanitize rooms holding patients with infections.

The colonel smiled wanly, his troubled expression betraying his concern that their difficulties were only getting started. "You are well aware, Ashford, that these first forty-eight hours are critical. If the illness continues to spread, we will have to return to Florida and postpone our mission to Puerto Rico." O'Reilly looked up casually at the star-filled sky. "Not that either place is particularly conducive to the health of our troops."

Ashford's curiosity was aroused. "What do you mean, sir?" he said, leaning further on the veranda. Ashford had left Louisiana in such a rush he'd had little time to learn about the military objective.

"Our spies tell us that Puerto Rico is some goddamned backwater. One heaping platter of malaria, with a generous helping of yellow and dengue fevers on the side. The Spanish have largely neglected Puerto Rico in favor of Cuba. From all I have learned, conditions outside the few larger towns are unspeakable; misery runs far, wide, and very, very deep."

Ashford discarded his burnt cigarette overboard and immediately put another one to his lips. "Didn't McKinley offer to buy Cuba and Puerto Rico for almost $120 million? Maybe we won't be there very long."

The colonel obligingly lit up the lieutenant's smoke. "The Spanish will never sell, and now they stand to lose the whole lot, the Philippines included."

"It seems unthinkable to pass up such an offer. Maybe the Spanish think they may still win this war?"

O'Reilly shook his head, his expression dubious. "If in fact they ever did, I am convinced that they don't anymore." He signaled for Ashford to walk alongside him toward the rear of the ship.

"With so many lopsided defeats in Cuba, the enemy must suspect that the game is nearing an end. And yet, if they can hold us off in Puerto Rico for long enough, Spain may be able to hang on to the island permanently, or alternatively, use it as a token in peace negotiations. But McKinley and the Republicans plan to add the island to their war spoils, so it is up to Miles, Schwan, and this expedition to see that it is done."

Ashford responded, "I am sure they shall, assuming we can surmount this typhoid outbreak that is whipping our asses. The sooner we can get to Puerto Rico, the better. Frankly, the outbreak comes as no great surprise to me, given the conditions in Tampa with the general filth, garbage, overflowing latrines, and flies and mosquitoes by the millions."

O'Reilly nodded in agreement; his countenance grim. The two doctors knew that typhoid fever was caused by an aggressive and invasive intestinal bacteria spread by food and water that had been contaminated by infected human waste. The disorder thrived in densely packed areas, commonly wreaking havoc in congested military camps and overcrowded cities with poor sanitation. It could kill one-fifth of those who contracted the infection and deplete a fighting force within a short period of time. Those who did not succumb would be rendered useless as soldiers for weeks.

Two enlisted men walked by and acknowledged their superiors with crisp salutes. O'Reilly turned to Ashford. "I have seen hundreds, perhaps thousands, of typhoid cases in my day. That condensed milk you are providing is good but supplement it with beef tea. As nasty as these alleged beef rations are, do not allow the men to discard them." He detailed instructions to the lieutenant to boil the cans for thirty minutes and filter the broth. The resulting beef tea would be nutritious and cleared of toxins, and the meat itself free of bacteria, if equally foul in taste. In desperate cases, O'Reilly directed Ashford to administer the carbolic acid both in the aerosols and by mouth, five to ten grains[1], twice daily.

Ashford looked incredulous. Taking a deep drag from his cigarette, he stared squarely at O'Reilly. "Colonel, do you really mean to administer the carbolic acid orally? The same disinfecting phenol compound we put in the Lister sprayers?"

O'Reilly nodded. "Yes, Lieutenant, that is precisely what I mean. And make sure you measure that phenol very carefully—it is not the gentlest of compounds."

The two men stared into the distance for two or three minutes, smoking in silence, recharging their spirits in the fresh sea air.

As the transport ship signaled midnight with the appropriate number of bells, O'Reilly turned toward Ashford and

---

1   15 grains equals 1 gram, or about 1/4 teaspoon.

pinned him with a sharp gaze. "All of us will have to watch these native Puerto Ricans very closely. They are poor as dirt, uneducated, and generally lazy. Word is that they spend the days swinging from hammocks as they say a rosary or strum some wretched, beat-up guitar, all while smoking the vilest home-grown tobacco. When called to work, they say they have to soldier; if called to fight, they say they have to work."

"Well, if nothing else, the locals will be well-rested," Ashford replied with an ironic grin.

*****

The next two days on the transports brought a frenzy of activity for the medical officers. The typhoid outbreak worsened, with about thirty new cases discovered every day. Cooks prepared beef broths and reconstituted milk to the specifications set forth by O'Reilly. The sickest soldiers raved and hallucinated within a delirium brought on by their high fevers. The only remedy involved immersing them for half an hour at a time in tubs of cool seawater, which had to be hauled on board and replenished constantly.

The prevailing smell on the transports was of the vilest sewage. Diarrhea and vomiting took turns affecting the men in alternating waves of torment, and the sheer volume of infectious excrement approached the unmanageable. O'Reilly assigned Ashford to supervise a detail of fifty healthy soldiers to sterilize all the used bedpans with bleaching powder and then dump the material overboard by means of improvised bucket brigades. The pitching ships caused the slop to spill onto the decks, covering them in a treacherous, slippery film. Flies frolicked over the chamber pots with abandon, multiplying as if by magic into thick humming black clouds. The medical personnel fought back by ceaselessly replenishing their Lister sprayers. Ashford worked frantically, largely without sleeping, in a Herculean effort to keep his typhoid victims alive. If the patients could only hold on for two more days, perhaps they could improve on land. They would not have long to wait.

Chapter Four

UTUADO, 1897

Twelve months before the American Army embarked for Puerto Rico, Simón Báez and his lifelong companion, Josefa, prepared themselves to spend one last night with their son Rafael—or rather, with his corpse.

After a prolonged fight, Rafael had lost his battle against chronic anemia which was the principal manifestation of the *mal de la montaña*[2]. This would be the fourth child they had lost to the sickness of the mountains, a mysterious malady which had relentlessly decimated the inhabitants of the island for the last 300 years. Little Rafael had just turned five years old. Simón and Josefa's three other children had all died before the age of ten, wasting away slowly under their parents' tortured gaze, growing paler and thinner in agonizing and unrelenting increments. Simón and Josefa now had five living children remaining.

As with their other dead children, the parents had done what they could for their beloved boy. For a promise of a dozen bananas and a chicken, the only doctor around those parts had been summoned from the town of Utuado, three miles away over high mountain trails usually rendered impassable by the puniest afternoon shower. The poorly trained and overworked physician had diagnosed severe anemia and recommended an herbal concoction consisting of no fewer than two dozen rarely seen plants. For this special preparation, the worried couple had consulted Marta, a highly respected, fifth-generation folk healer, or *curandera,* who touted with remarkable conviction the herbal cures of the mountain coun-

---

2   Illness of the mountains

34

try. The ancient Marta had skin like dried barnacles and hair reminiscent of beached seaweed, and she walked with a pronounced stoop which belied her mental agility. She generally charged very fair prices for her remedies, some of which were truly remarkable and others perfectly useless. In the case of Rafael Báez, a successful concoction proved elusive, and the boy had not survived.

Come sunset, the traditional wake, or *velorio,* was supposed to begin and numerous preparations awaited the family before the sun sank below the horizon. The *jíbaros*[3] considered the wake to be more important than Communion or Baptism because, in a very palpable way, it provisioned the departed for their mystical journey after death and thus directly reaffirmed the existence of an afterlife. Moreover, and in a far more practical sense, the wake allowed Marta to watch the dead person for a period of at least twelve hours, ensuring that *el muerto* was truly dead and not at risk for live burial, as had almost happened on more than one occasion. The event would take place in an open-air *bohío,* somewhat larger than the common dwelling huts and specially constructed for important events such as meetings, dances, and the occasional wedding.

One hour before the wake, Simón and Josefa were staring down at Rafael's small body, lying inside a rusty metal tub just outside the door to the *bohío.* Marta gently coaxed them out of the way and proceeded to carefully wash the body in water specially cured with herbs considered both magical and holy. She passed the tiny corpse to Josefa, who dressed her son in a pure white shroud. Once the body was dressed, Simón carried Rafael to the center of the room and placed him upon a plain wooden table covered in reusable lace sheets. Colorful flowers freshly picked from the mountainside covered his gown, and a crown of aromatic jasmine encircled his head. Even though Simón had done hard physical labor at different haciendas for the last thirty years, carrying his son left him short of breath because he was suffering from the same disease that had taken Rafael's life. Now that everything was prepared, they sat

3 The ubiquitous Puerto Rican peasant, usually an agricultural laborer of the mountains, although the term was commonly applied also to workers in the coastal sugar cane fields.

on the floor of the hut and waited out the few hours that were left in the slowly creeping afternoon.

The recently departed Rafael Báez had come from a union which had never been consecrated. In those times and places, certain understandings were reached to save the money needed to pay the priest for the honor of his blessing or procure the pen and paper with which a marriage was inscribed in the town church. But in no way did the lack of formality diminish Simón and Josefa's commitment and devotion to one another.

Simón, the *pater familias,* was not quite forty, short in stature and small in build. Had he been a fighter, he might have made bantamweight with a good soaking. Behind his premature wrinkles shone the clear blue eyes of Spanish forefathers who had arrived in Puerto Rico sometime in the seventeenth century looking for economic opportunities. These ancestors soon found an escape from the unbearable heat of the coastal summers in the island's mountains, which offered a cooler climate reminiscent of their home in Asturias.

More than thirty years of working the coffee plantations had wrecked Simón, and now he plodded around slowly with a shuffled gait, forced to pause repeatedly to recover his breath. His chronic illness announced itself primarily in the one feature that proved so arresting to an observer not of those parts—a profound, ghostly pallor. Already of light complexion by virtue of genetics, Simón, like so many of his fellow *jíbaros* affected by *el mal de la montaña,* had acquired such a marked paleness that his skin resembled the whitest alabaster, and the sclera of his eyes, the purest unveined marble.

His companion in life was Josefa—Pepa, to their friends— with whom Simón had been living for twenty years. Not that they counted the years, because in Utuado time was measured by events, not by calendars. They began living together the year after the earthquake in Ponce had brought down the church roof and the subsequent giant wave had swept old Paco Ramírez and four others out to sea. Pepa was about thirty-five, somewhat taller than Simón but just as meager in build. Her family had settled in Puerto Rico from the Canary Islands, and this origin gave her skin a richer, darker tone than most. Her black hair was just beginning to show strands of silver, and the skin of her face was marked by the occasional blemish from smallpox she had contracted at the age of six. Somehow she survived, all while watching the disease take two sisters and her father over the course of a week.

A bad fall at eight had broken Pepa's right ankle, a fracture the local *curandera* had stabilized with splints of guava wood bound by strands of medicinal vines, which she changed daily as they dried and broke. Her fracture had healed about as well as could be expected, but having cut into the girl's growth plate, the break had caused her right leg to grow permanently shorter than her left. To compensate, Pepa's mother, at the cost of a month's wages, procured an item most decidedly rare in the mountains: a pair of shoes. These were fashioned from cheap leather set over wooden soles and fit rather poorly. But through deft handiwork, a clever neighbor had augmented the sole of the right shoe, thereby correcting the girl's uneven gait. So successful was the adjustment that, since her accident, Pepa rarely went anywhere without her shoes, and her distinctive, plodding approach warned mischievous children to stop their nonsense and oblivious lovers to break off their kisses. Unlike Pepa, few people owned shoes and fewer still cared to use them. Instead, the endless miles that were walked barefoot hardened the skin of their soles into giant calluses that served as permanent footwear. If going to a dance, church, or some other event, the *campesinos* hand-carried their one pair of shoes, regardless of distance, to their destination. The travelers then paused at the venue entrance to put on their shoes before proceeding inside. At the end of the gathering, the process was reversed, and the shoes were carried home and put away for weeks.

Together, the devoted partners had seen nine births over the course of two decades. Their eldest, Juan, had started working in the *cafetal* (coffee grove) when he turned eight. During the harvest time, he picked coffee daily alongside his parents, and during the off-season, he attended the one-room schoolhouse, located one hour on foot on the trail to Jayuya. Juan had already left the hard life of the coffee groves for the promise of better things in Ponce, twenty miles south. The second child, Caridad, sixteen, lived higher up the mountain with her forty-year-old husband. The last three surviving children were Carlos, Ana, and Rosa, who were twelve, seven, and two years old, respectively. The other four had died in infancy, slowly surrendering to a progressive anemia refractory to any treatment the overmatched doctors and folk healers could offer. Their children withered away while Simón and Pepa looked on, consumed with sorrow and powerless to help them.

The Báez dwelling was a miserable, rustic *bohío*, a small one-roomed hut of ill-fitting wooden planks, with walls roughly fifteen feet square and an earthen floor covered in palm fronds. The entire structure was lifted from the ground by short wooden stilts, barely high enough to keep the floor dry above floodwaters generated by the all-too frequent rainstorms of the hot summer afternoons, when the heavy air finally unloaded its oppressive humidity. More palm fronds mixed with mud gave form to a fragile and permeable roof, so that whenever a heavy shower passed, sheeting water filtered through the thatch as if percolating through a giant sieve. A few yards outside the hut was a pit lined with small stones, about three feet across, where the occasional hot meal was cooked over an open fire. There Josefa Báez prepared red beans in a prized iron *caldero*, passed down from her female line for four or five generations. Charcoal made weekly from the heavy wood of surrounding tropical trees fueled these smoky fires, and a rusty metal grate supported old utensils as they heated slowly from below.

The day of Rafael's passing had begun like any other typical day for the Báez family and thousands of other homesteads throughout the mountains. At sunrise, black unsweetened *puya* coffee was made, bread or cornmeal was prepared, and the children were awakened. The family dressed simply in long-sleeved cotton tops and long cotton pants, almost always in plain white and usually the same pants, shirts, or dresses worn the day before, and the day before that. Straw hats were common; footwear, absent.

Once the family was fed and clothed, each member proceeded by turns outside the hut, walked several yards downwind of the prevailing easterlies, and there, on the humid soil without so much as a hole, let alone a latrine, relieved bladders and bowels. None of them gave a second thought to these functions and much less to where they took place. In this they were like their neighbors: everybody's piss and crap were largely the same, a bond between all humanity, and like sex and gas, a source of endless humor and merriment. When one location grew foul, another one would be immediately procured not far away. The large tropical leaves did well enough for a quick wipe, and back to their shacks they went before starting the trek to the coffee groves.

Every morning, Simón walked about a mile uphill to the coffee plantation at Hacienda Las Alturas. He plodded slowly up the dirt path, forced to pause repeatedly to rest. Some days, especially during the harvest, Pepa would join him, and when money was especially tight, the children came along. Young Carlos also picked coffee while his younger sisters played below the coffee trees. At midday, Simón and the other workers took a break for water and a quick lunch of fruit and beans. Sometimes nature called and then, in a ritual similar to that of the early morning, a laborer would very considerately walk a few yards downwind from his cohorts, where the necessary excretory functions took place as usual and generally only semi-privately.

At the end of the day, the pickers trudged back to their respective huts to cook the one real meal of the day, usually some combination of rice, red beans, bananas, and some of the diverse starchy roots grown in the garden—*yuca, ñame, batata* (cassava, yam, sweet potato). Twice a week, perhaps, their dinner was augmented by a piece of dried cod, or *bacalao,* purchased from one of several local *chinchorros* (kiosks) in the immediate vicinity. The occasional chicken would be a rare luxury. Pepa hauled their water from a creek half a mile distant, carrying her jug up the slope on her head back to the hut, where it was used equally to drink, clean, and bathe. The creek was also the place where Pepa laundered their clothes and where she could share gossip with other women regarding the latest liaisons, births, accidents, causes and cures of illnesses, who had left, and who had returned.

But this particular day, which had started like so many others, had been marked by the death of Rafael in the early afternoon. Word spread quickly through the Utuado mountains that Juan and Pepa's boy had finally died, and that the *velorio* was to be celebrated that very night. Friends and relatives began arriving one hour before sunset, all of them carrying gifts for the dead boy's journey. Since Rafael had died before the age of seven, he was technically free of all sin and therefore guaranteed an expedited entrance into heaven and the presence of God. Since a dead child was as sure an intercessor as anybody could have, his successful and happy crossing had to be assured at all costs. As such, everybody attending the *velorio* was acutely aware that this would be their last chance to curry favor with Rafael.

The first guests carried clusters of bananas and plantains, avocados, mangoes, guavas, papayas, and similar fruits. The next mourners to arrive brought increasingly more precious foods, such as a recently killed chicken, a guinea fowl, or a piglet. Some people brought more flowers, others simple toys. The gifts were meticulously arranged on the table around its center, where the small corpse lay with his hands carefully arranged on his chest as if in prayer. Two stray dogs patrolled the wooden floor, attentive to any scraps that inadvertently fell from the table. To one side, an inconsolable Pepa sat weeping in the arms of the *curandera*, whereas through an opposite door Simón and two guests headed outside to roast the gifted animals which would feed the company. In a darkened corner, young Carlos and Ana played distractedly, largely oblivious to their mother's grief. On the floor of the bohío sat the youngest child, Rosa, a two-year-old toddler who earlier had helped gather flowers for her dead brother but now busied herself tossing petals she had torn into the air to watch them rain down. Rafael was her next older sibling and they had been inseparable; rarely could one be seen without the other toddling just behind them, until now. Rosa was a child of exceptional beauty with large blue eyes framed by a head of unruly chestnut hair, the only detraction being the abnormally pale skin and precariously thin limbs which hinted that everything was not quite right. As the sky darkened, the somber mood changed with the arrival of large quantities of moonshine *ron cañita* contributed by the last arriving guests, so that by midnight the scene was one of riotous carousing around the table bearing Rafael. In a dark corner, the bereaved parents cried and comforted one another by themselves, as there was no one left sober enough to console them.

The rising sun signaled the end of the event. Simón meticulously wrapped the corpse in a white cotton blanket. Some *jíbaros* could afford a makeshift coffin, but the Báez family could not. Rather, Rafael was to be buried in his blanket, near the family *bohío* and close to his predeceased siblings, where the family could pay their respects every *día de los muertos*. Buried along with him were food items left over from the previous night, as well as toys and rum. Pepa and Simón derived some solace in that Rafael was to be buried near their hut. Not everyone was this fortunate, and some families had to carry their loved ones several miles to Utuado's municipal cemetery. From time to time, these bearers would tire along the way and unceremoniously dump the body by the side of the trail, or worse, in a creek or river, and no one would be the wiser.

And so, with the burial of Rafael completed, the family went back to their unvarying routine of hardship and monotony. The next day, Simón headed up the path to Las Alturas as usual, worrying if the dreaded disease would surface again to cut down another one of his children. Pepa, back in the hut with Carlos, Ana, and Rosa, looked from one to the next, wondering, just like her companion walking up the mountain, if one of them would be next.

Chapter Five

LOS YANQUIS ARE HERE! JULY, 1898

On the 25th of July, 1898, the southwestern coast of Puerto Rico came into view off the port bow of the invasion fleet. Guánica Bay was a small harbor served by a narrow entrance no more than 500 yards across. This neck gave way to a bay of the deepest blue about two miles long by a half mile wide, ringed by a line of calciferous bluffs overgrown with tropical brush. The sleepy village of Guánica, home to a few hundred souls, lay at the northeast corner of the harbor.

The 800-ton gunboat *U.S.S. Gloucester* led the way into the tiny bay. Landing rafts were lowered, and three dozen Marines armed with Winchester rifles descended on the beach. The troops set up a machine gun nest, erected a cordon of barbed wire and rapidly secured a beachhead. The eight other transports waited at anchor while the remaining 1,300 soldiers prepared to land on rafts. The American force met only token opposition, exchanging a few rounds as they entered the village with the retreating local militia, but otherwise found little resistance. By nightfall, the Stars and Stripes flew over Guánica and the American Army was securely ensconced in the town, never to leave the island again.

Ashford was about to climb aboard his landing launch when O'Reilly called him back to the main deck. "Lieutenant, you will not be disembarking here. The two hundred men with typhoid still need looking after, and every medical officer must stay behind. Schwan has commanded that three transport ships be designated as hospital vessels, including this one. You will remain aboard as head medical officer here. Lieutenant Camp and Lieutenant McAndrew will take the other two."

Ashford glanced up at the transport's deck three stories above him. "Very well, Colonel. How long will it be before we can rejoin the invasion force?"

"I cannot say for sure. The transports will remain anchored outside Guánica for about forty-eight hours, by which time the hospital ship *Relief* will have arrived in Ponce. The medical staff will then accompany the patients to Ponce and see that they are safely transferred to the hospital ship. After that, you may rejoin the attack force."

The disappointed lieutenant climbed back aboard his ship. "Colonel, won't the physicians be needed among the invading troops?"

"Yes, but my guess is that we won't be moving against the Spanish for at least ten days. You should have enough time to meet the *Relief*, go ashore in Ponce, and find your command before we move out."

Ashford spent the next two days outside the entrance to Guánica Bay battling the remnants of the outbreak, which had finally begun to abate. On July 28th, the transports sailed twenty miles east to Ponce, where the fully-staffed hospital ship received the stricken soldiers. Ashford finally felt he could breathe easier. Through sheer determination, the medical personnel had managed to bring the typhoid under a modicum of control with minimum casualties, albeit with some costs. Repeated eighteen-hour work days had left Ashford exhausted, and he was more than ready to leave the transport ship behind.

Looking out from the deck of the *Relief*, Ashford was taken aback by the beautiful sight of the gleaming harbor surrounded by gradually receding verdant hills. *What a beautiful place this is— so different from Virginia, or even Louisiana*, he thought. He couldn't wait to get ashore. The expansive beach of yellow sand gave rise to hundreds of tall, slender coconut palms packed with fruit. The port was surrounded by a colorful village named La Playa, which extended four blocks northward from the sand with irregular and asymmetrical dirt paths riddled with potholes and horse dung. All around, the rich smell of the salt air mixed with those of the daily catch, stray dogs, and sweating oxen. Two miles to the north, elegant Ponce occupied a low elevation at the very end of a straight gravel road called Calle de la Marina. From its venerable old center, the city extended further up a gently rising hill, its neat rows of colonial houses painted in off-whites and pastels.

Ashford looked on as the harbor gradually filled with boats ferrying troops ashore. On land, the American cavalry was already galloping furiously, while batteries of light artillery raised thick clouds of dust when turning sharply around narrow street corners. That afternoon, accompanied by a company of sixty infantrymen, Ashford came ashore at the long wooden pier marking the southern end of La Playa. Hundreds of locals lined the entrance to the port and the road leading toward the center of town, crowding the byways, and watching the encroaching Americans with fixed gazes. Americans and Puerto Ricans knew little about what to expect from each other, and even less about how to overcome their language barrier.

Desperate poverty was everywhere. The crowd included people of all ages and both sexes, dressed almost exclusively in white cotton clothes which invariably had seen better days. Many wore homemade hats of straw or woven palm fronds, and very few had shoes. And yet, Ashford was struck by a sense of quiet dignity hidden behind the simple clothes and silent demeanors of those filling the streets. *They must be waiting for something better,* he thought. He did not know what that was and, worse still, he had no idea whether the Americans could provide it for them.

Ashford's orders were to rejoin the attack force to the west at Yauco, a mid-sized town and rail center serving as the rendezvous point for the land campaign. He took out the rough map O'Reilly had provided—hardly more than a bare schematic with a few named streets and a crude star marking the approximate location of the Ponce train station. By a happy coincidence, the road from La Playa to the city ended precisely at the terminal. Ashford and his company began their march under a broiling sun, and before long the soldiers were wiping away the salty sweat that stung the corners of their eyes. They tried hard not to stare at the crowds, who, in turn, regarded them with a curious fascination. Some seemed welcoming; others kept silent. Neither Ashford nor anyone in his unit could make out a word of what their spectators were saying. Even the few soldiers who prided themselves in their knowledge of Spanish could not work out the intonations and vocabulary of the local dialect.

Marching quickly, the two orderly columns of thirty soldiers reached the station in half an hour, their uniforms soaked through with sweat. A dinky old train was waiting to take them to Yauco, where presumably they would find their command. Ashford gave silent thanks that the Spanish, in their haste to retreat, had neglected to destroy both the station and tracks, saving him a full day on horseback.

In slightly over an hour, the train covered the twenty miles between the two towns. Arriving at the minuscule Yauco depot, Ashford and two other lieutenants procured mounts and headed out in search of their unit. The ride took them through rich tropical lowlands overhung with the high walls of towering green mountains. Surrounded by the lovely, lush vegetation, the sounds of raucous tropical birds, and the scents of sweet exotic flowers, the officers could hardly keep their eyes on the road. Ashford could never have imagined the beauty of this landscape, one so very different from anything he had seen before, a veritable paradise.

After a long traverse on horseback over hills and across streams, the officers came upon their camp just as the soldiers were in the process of bivouacking. The night was beautiful and cloudless, and it carried a delicious coolness that descended slowly from the slopes, bearing the scents of jasmine and plumeria. From all around the camp, loud choruses of tree frogs and crickets serenaded their new guests. A transfixed Ashford set his blanket down on a grassy berm to gaze at the boundless sky, pricked by the light of untold stars. Hypnotized, he soon fell asleep.

The next morning, the young doctor joined his detachment on their westward march. Schwan and the three thousand men of his brigade had been ordered to capture Mayagüez, a large port city on the coast about twenty-five miles away, where 1,500 enemy troops waited for the Americans. By the middle of the day, the invading force had covered ten miles to reach the stately old town of San Germán. It was a beautiful place, dating back to the sixteenth century, organized around a venerable old plaza, and surrounded by low hills on all sides. In San Germán, Ashford found an excellent Red Cross hospital, recently erected and well-stocked, and here he left some men who had been stricken by the ubiquitous typhoid.

Now less than a day's journey from Mayagüez, Ashford suddenly realized that this war was very near. He nervously secured his sidearm and obsessively reviewed his medical tools. He was well aware that war wounds were altogether different from peacetime injuries and expected to encounter a high volume of penetrating wounds, many of which might require amputations. In only a few hours, he might be called upon to perform critical operations while pressed for time and likely under fire. Self-doubt clouded his mind. *How would he respond under attack? What if he were wounded?* Ashford shook his head, pushing against his doubts with that abundance of self-confidence born of youth and inexperience. He had passed dozens of medical courses and completed rigorous training. *Surely,* he thought, *there was nothing he could not do.*

The following morning found both officers and men tense with the anticipation of an approaching battle. To add to the nervous strain, sympathizing locals were reporting that enemy forces had already left Mayagüez, marching south, and could be expected to materialize within a few hours. The enemy had the advantages of knowing the terrain intimately and, most importantly, of being well-rested and provisioned by short supply lines. Ashford knew that the Spanish would fight ferociously to rehabilitate their tarnished reputation. The island was mountainous and largely devoid of roads, lending itself perfectly to guerrilla operations if the main army were not defeated decisively. This possibility had to be avoided at all costs. Spanish irregulars with unorthodox tactics practically paralyzed Napoleon's *Grande Armée* for over three years, wearing it down with surprise attacks.

Shortly after 9 a.m., Ashford mounted his horse with sweaty palms, a dry mouth, and a pounding heart. Giving a final glance at his equipment, he spurred his animal forward towards the main line. Four hours later, the column abruptly came to a stop. As one of the few men on horseback, Ashford rode ahead to investigate, well aware that a stationary force in this terrain could quickly find itself on the wrong side of a shooting gallery. He found their lead units blocked by the Rosario River, running below the Silva Heights ridge overlooking the valley. American maps showed the Rosario to be a miserable little run, a mere trickle in the dry season. But now, swollen with the rains of summer, that same stream carried a very respectable current. Surprised that nobody had yet probed the stream, the confident Ashford spurred his mount forward and only narrowly avoided being swept downstream. Clearly, this creek could no longer be forded.

Ashford returned to his company and breathlessly addressed his commander, "Captain Travis, the river ahead will not allow us to cross. My horse was submerged nearly to the shoulder and only barely managed to maintain a footing."

Looking concerned, Travis tried to rein in his nervous charger. "This is truly awful ground, Ashford. We are sitting ducks."

Ashford pointed toward the rear. "Schwan is headed back toward the bridge. It is the only way to cross, sir."

Travis freed his rifle from the saddle. "Here, take my Winchester and ride over to ask for instructions from General Schwan. He may be considering a move from behind that high ground up ahead. Go! *Now!*"

The lieutenant saluted, whirled his horse in the opposite direction and spurred it toward the main body of troops. Reaching the general, Ashford found that Schwan, lacking adequate maps of the terrain ahead, had opted to forego the flanking move on the Silva Heights. Instead, Schwan ordered his tired troops to backtrack and prepare to cross the river at a narrow iron bridge below the Heights.

From farther back in the line, Captain Travis looked on anxiously as a bottleneck began to form in front of the bridge. Soldiers and horses crammed together shoulder to shoulder, and neatly organized companies soon began to dissolve into a crowd fit for a circus. Confusion and disorder intensified as men and animals shuffled across the bridge. The neighing of the frightened animals jumbled with the panicked shouts from soldiers growing increasingly aware of their exposed position. The bridge creaked and swayed as the men quickened their pace in a desperate attempt to cross and find cover.

Unbeknownst to the Americans, the Spanish forces advancing from Mayagüez had left earlier than reported and were already entrenched advantageously upon a ridge near the village of Hormigueros. The troops under Schwan blindly pressed northward, unaware of the enemy's presence.

Without warning, the Spanish opened the hostilities. Well-concealed in the hefty underbrush, the enemy delivered a withering fire from four hundred yards away. Soldiers fired using smokeless white powder, which gave no visual clues as to their positions. Bullets slammed into the branches above Ashford's head and whistled past his ears. His panicked horse reared on two legs and he barely avoided falling by grabbing the animal's mane. Within minutes, pandemonium ruled the field. The American troops in the vanguard received heavy fire while they searched for the hidden enemy without success. Disregarding the shots slamming into the ground with sickening thuds, Ashford pressed toward the hottest sector of the fighting.

The Spanish proved to be remarkably poor shots, or otherwise American losses would have been enormous. As it was, the sheer volume of bullets guaranteed American casualties. Ashford was fighting alongside Schwan when, not ten feet to his left, a major violently threw up his arms and toppled backwards from his horse. Within seconds, Ashford dismounted beside the stricken man. A bullet had struck the major's jaw, severing his facial artery, and sending blood gushing from the hideous wound like a fountain. Half-blinded by the sticky fluid spraying fully in his face, Ashford struggled to control the heavy bleeding as best he could. He had nothing to work with except for a pair of suspenders with crude metal grips used to hold up the major's drawers. Ashford cut the grip off and managed to improvise a clamp, which stopped the profuse bleeding just as the major lost consciousness. Next to him, his fellow lieutenant Charlie Camp worked frantically on a soldier shot through the liver. He yelled above the fray for stretchers to carry the wounded men to the rear, helping to heave their prone forms from the ground before turning back to the chaos.

The action around them proved relentless. Ashford wiped his face on his sleeve, spit out the blood that had settled between his lips and ran back into the fight with his revolver high in hand. Right behind him, Schwan's assistant fell from his horse, shot through the lower leg. Ashford ripped the sleeve from the man's uniform to apply as a tourniquet. Horrifying noises continued to fill the air: panicking horses, whizzing bullets, groans, and screams. The smell of spent powder, animals, sweat, and blood blended into a sickening stench that was impossible to escape.

Amidst the din and confusion, Ashford came upon Chief Surgeon O'Reilly. He was caked in dust and without a horse.

"Are you alright, Colonel?"

"Horse panicked and bucked me, Ashford. I guess I'll continue the fight on foot!"

"Take my horse, sir. I am spending most of my time on the ground treating wounds," Ashford answered.

"Keep your horse, lieutenant. I want you to ride to the sugar mill we passed about a mile back. Secure the main building and establish a treatment area. Take any supplies and personnel you may need."

"Right away, sir!" Ashford wheeled his horse around and left the fighting to comply with his orders.

By late afternoon, the American infantry at last gained the upper hand and made a series of decisive rushes toward the Spanish lines. Around 6 p.m., the increasingly outnumbered and outgunned Spanish forces broke the engagement and retreated toward Mayagüez.

Meanwhile, at the sugar mill, Central Eureka, Ashford had brought the makeshift hospital into line. The injured trickled in, most suffering from superficial wounds. In addition, a few curious civilians watching the fighting had also suffered injuries. Lieutenant Camp treated one elderly Puerto Rican man who, unable to get away from the fight, had been fatally shot through the stomach. Ashford examined a Spanish lieutenant carried in on a stretcher and attended by four Spanish hospital corpsmen. Apparently happy to be in the hands of an American physician, the Spanish officer pointed to a large wound in his right leg through which the femur was visible. While the wound was cleaned and treated, everyone in his entourage were offered cigars.

******

At 11 a.m. the next day, with General Schwan riding in front, their colors flying and their military band blaring, the American brigade marched unopposed into Mayagüez to the roaring approval of masses of residents. The enemy had fled north under the cover of darkness. No carnival or circus entering an expectant town had ever received such a riotous welcome.

Mayagüez was a charming, compact city of lattices, balconies, and walled gardens ablaze with tropical flowers. Behind it lay a semicircle of fertile green hills and before it the endless sea. Nature had provided the city with a beautiful harbor, a wide stretch of calm water protected by two projecting juts of land. The harbor allowed Mayagüez to enjoy the fruits of a considerable commerce exporting large quantities of sugar, coffee, oranges, pineapples, and coconuts, mostly to the United States. The city was connected to the neighboring town of Aguadilla by a tramway on one side and by a modest railroad to Hormigueros on the other. Mayagüez contained separate civil and military hospitals, an asylum, a public library, three modern bridges, and a handsome market constructed entirely in iron and stone, widely acknowledged as the best on the island. The narrow Yagüez River divided the town into north and south sections connected by two dainty iron bridges. Word had it that the sands of this river had formerly yielded much gold, and that there was still gold to be found if one had the energy to seek it.

The morning of the American occupation, the sidewalks, balconies, windows, and rooftops overflowed with wide-eyed citizenry of all ages and levels of wealth, colors, sexes, and sizes. In every street corner and from every square, great crowds of poorer folk split the air with shouts of "!*Que vivan los norteamericanos!,*" the degree of their enthusiasm seemingly determined by the size of the guns that paraded past them. In reply, the band erupted into a lively march. The crowd turned to look at the upper balcony of a stately house, where a beautiful young girl of sixteen leaned far over the iron rail and waved a crudely-fashioned American flag over the ragged ranks below. Every hat came off, and for the first time that day the soldiers exploded with a long cheer. The outbreak was infectious, and from every side the clamor swelled until it seemed as if the whole universe had vaulted into madness. The city's entire corps of firemen, dressed in the regalia of their full-dress uniforms, turned out with grave dignity to salute the soldiers passing below the large statue of Columbus in the center of the town.

The soldiers themselves presented a curious spectacle: gaunt, sunburnt, disheveled, unshaven, dirty, and dressed in tattered uniforms, with toes protruding from shoes and trousers hardly recognizable as such. They paraded in a hybrid step, somewhere between a march and a limp, which they had acquired during the arduous treks of the last week. Rumors had circulated among the islanders that every American was a full-fledged millionaire, but the military parade that morning permanently laid those whispers to rest.

In the early afternoon, the soldiers left Mayagüez to camp approximately two miles outside the city. The campground proved to be a poor choice, however, lying as it did within a slight depression formed by a circle of low hills. The ground was soaked and spongy to a degree approaching that of the worst Louisiana swamp. Since the common infantrymen were not allowed to reenter the city, they grudgingly resigned themselves to this miserable location, surrounded by an unwelcoming wilderness that harbored armies of mosquitoes bearing the gift of malaria.

Ashford missed the enthusiastic reception in Mayagüez, to his everlasting disappointment. His brigade had pushed onward into town, leaving him at Central Eureka without instructions. Left to his own devices, Ashford finally arrived in Mayagüez early that evening with his patients, handing them into the care of Red Cross volunteers who had improvised a hospital inside the municipal theater. Then, he walked the two miles to camp in a stifling heat, arriving well after dark only to be greeted by gunfire from a green picket, who had confused him with a stray cow.

The following morning, Schwan received credible reports that the Spanish had taken defensive positions near the hill town of Las Marías, some ten miles away. A force of three thousand soldiers moved out under the command of Lieutenant Colonel Daniel Burke, with Ashford attached as its principal medical officer. The brigade began their pursuit through rugged territory swarming with guerrillas, deserters, and bandits. There was no accurate intelligence on either the strength or the location of the enemy. Exhausting marches, heavy outpost duty, and the daily, drenching rains gradually wore the troops down. The roads soon became impassable for wheeled vehicles, and the troops made frustratingly slow progress. The next day the force finally caught up to two thousand men of the Spanish force occupying strong defensive positions a mile past the town of Las Marías. The two armies began firing at long range across the narrow valley of the Río Prieto until the exchange stalled late in the evening.

That night, Ashford camped in the open, where a relentlessly driving rain gave him a thorough soaking. It was the most miserable night of his life. Large puddles turned the ground into a crater field, and the few tarpaulins that had been erected either leaked profusely or blew down in the gale. Thousands of leeches patrolled the mud, while swarms of mosquitoes attacked the men with untamed ferocity.

The 13th of August dawned foggy and windless. The army faced another day of dogged pursuit when, toward midmorning, a lone rider appeared on the uphill trail from the south approaching at breakneck speed. He carried astonishing news. General Nelson Miles, the overall commander of the expedition, had ordered a cease to all hostilities. Coinciding with Schwan's attacks in the southwest, Miles had spearheaded additional fronts near the coastal town of Guayama to the east. From this new sector, the Spanish had been pushed north over the mountains toward their hub in San Juan, effectively abandoning the southwestern third of the island to the United States.

Across an ill-defined line, the two belligerents began an edgy coexistence, alternating between amicable and testy, which lasted for the many months it took to settle the terms of the peace. But for all intents and purposes, the United States had procured the island of Puerto Rico. The victory had taken a mere three weeks, at a cost of five dead and forty-three wounded.

Chapter Six

HACIENDA LAS ALTURAS

C offee was everything in the mountains of Puerto Rico. The island's rugged interior was highly favorable to growing the coffee trees, which preferred wetter soils, cooler temperatures, and dappled shade. The moderate elevations and volcanic soils resulted in a curiously sweet and non-acidic product with a penetrating aroma and high caffeine content, arguably the best coffee in the world.

This perfect combination of soil, elevation, shade, and rainfall, along with quality control and jealously guarded trade secrets, ensured that the coffee produced at Hacienda Las Alturas was of a supreme quality and always in vigorous demand. Las Alturas was unquestionably the pride of the coffee industry in Puerto Rico. It had a long and storied history dating back almost eighty years to when don Salvador Roig arrived penniless in Ponce, fleeing unrest in colonial Venezuela. What Salvador lacked in cash he made up for in grit and grind, and soon the teenager ran a modest business hauling light cargo up and down the coast in a single-masted cutter, which he leased at extortionist rates from a fellow *venezolano*. When the leaser's body was found face-down in the Río Bucaná, Salvador appropriated the boat by paying the necessary bribes to the pertinent authorities in Ponce.

Arturo Roig, the eldest grandson of Salvador, oversaw an enormous expansion of operations during the great coffee-growing boom of the 1870's. On the same morning that Lieutenant Ashford climbed aboard the flatboat bound for New Orleans, Arturo was proudly contemplating the mountains and fields that comprised his estate. He stood on the second-floor porch of his plantation house, a beautiful structure he had designed himself and ordered built from the finest tropical hardwoods surrounding the plantation. It was one of those beautiful mornings of the Puerto Rican highland summer, with an intensely blue sky and wisps of fair-weather clouds thinly interspersed within an otherworldly blue. To the east, over the high peaks in Jayuya, the sun had just risen in a flood of crimson and orange.

The Roig family home was built in a subdued but elegant colonial style. The lower level was made of bricks overlaid with stucco, painted in an off-white. A double-tiered staircase led to the spacious upper story, which was constructed entirely of native woods and brightened by numerous large windows with dark green shutters opening to the outside. Overall, it was an airy, welcoming home, worthy of the coffee aristocracy of the colony.

Roig enjoyed a cup of Las Alturas coffee as he began to organize his plans for the day. This one would start, like all others, with the *ronda*—a horseback tour around the 600 *cuerdas*[4] of his plantation, accompanied by his son, Sebastián, and his manager Luis Colón. Together, they would survey the fields, perhaps later pausing at the *Casona* building, and then moving to other points of interest such as the drying and packing bins. The inspection rounds always concluded with a visit to workers in the fields. In this way, Arturo constantly took the pulse of his plantation with an eye toward improvements and looking out for workers who had fallen upon particularly bad times and might need help.

Finishing his coffee, he placed the cup on a small breakfast table and headed to the stables, where Sebastián and Colón were already waiting for him. They had prepared the proprietor's beautiful, dappled Arabian, which had been specially imported from Spain. The three men cordially greeted each other with firm handshakes, and Arturo regarded his son proudly. Sebastián, just twenty-five, was a tall, strapping youth with fair hair and blue eyes who, in Arturo's mind, personified his fatherly dreams and the continuation of the Roig dynasty. Sebastián had just returned from Barcelona,

---

4   . 1 *cuerda* equals 0.97 acres.

where he had graduated near the top of his engineering class.

Don Arturo greeted his companions. *"Buenos días, Sebastián. Buenos días, Luis."*

"Buenos días. Today those words don't quite go together. Luis and I were up most of the night delivering your prize heifer."

"A difficult breech, but a successful outcome," added Luis.

Sebastián stretched, giving a loud groan. "What doesn't help are those new *gringo* roosters you had sent from Rhode Island. They crow a full hour before the native ones."

"Well don't wring their necks yet. Think of what we paid for them," countered his father.

"For the price of one of those roosters," Sebastián pointed out, "we can buy ten island *gallos.*"

"Maybe twenty," added Luis

"I am sure that in time you will come to appreciate this new breed, Sebastián. And remember that we are the first ones in Puerto Rico to get them. But let's get down to business. What's in store for today, gentlemen?"

Sebastián replied, "We need to examine the waterwheel and its dependent machinery, *Papá.* Luis tells me there have been troubles."

The slender, middle-aged Luis Colón concurred that the wheels were not moving the gears as they should.

Don Arturo took the Arabian's reins from Colón. "Well then, let's go have a look. Do you have the slaughtered piglet, Luis?"

"It's on my horse, *patrón,*" came the answer.

"Anything else before we start?"

Sebastián answered as his father swung up onto his saddle. "More of the usual—after we inspect the machinery, we will check on the workers and get their thoughts on the harvest." The coffee harvest Sebastián was referring to was scheduled to begin the following month.

"Very well," said Arturo. "We should also take some time to visit the Báez *bohío.* Luis heard their girl has taken a turn for the worse."

Colón nodded somberly—the family had been through hell the last few years. "Four children lost to *el mal.* It's incomprehensible, worse than awful."

Arturo agreed as he expertly mounted his horse and led his companions out of the stables and up the path that led to the *Río Jauco*. The trio of horsemen followed the narrow, mud-covered path through the dense tropical forest until they emerged in a large clearing, through which ran the burbling waters of the river. The *Jauco*, a short river no more than fifteen miles long, followed a precipitous downhill course that created tremendous hydromechanical power.

Thirty years ago, Arturo's father had introduced the most innovative farm machinery on the island, setting up a water wheel to harness power from the river's two waterfalls. The wheel drove machinery that saved countless hours of labor by separating the coffee bean from its fleshy pulp. Such mechanization, along with the high price commanded by the coffee crop, had brought ridiculous profits, especially after the San Narciso hurricane of 1867 wiped out the more marginal producers. By the time the third-generation Arturo took over Las Alturas, it employed half a dozen foremen and upwards of one hundred pickers at the peak of the harvest. Arguably, the plantation had become the most successful agricultural enterprise on the island. But recently, the good times had ground to a halt. Profits were suffering due to competition from vast plantings of lower-grade Brazilian coffee. These developments hung over Arturo Roig like a storm cloud.

The old wooden wheel had been recently replaced by two new steel ones, ingeniously engineered to maximize the river's power. Not far from the churning metal wheels stood *La Casona*, a large processing shed next to the riverbank that housed the pride of the hacienda: massive multi-purpose machines for depulping coffee cherries and grinding the dried beans. All the machinery was in turn connected to the wheels propelled by the *Jauco*.

Arturo turned to his son, Sebastián. "Here's where you prove the value of your education."

Sebastián broke into a wide grin. "*Papá,* I assure you the money you spent on my engineering degree was not wasted." He then turned to the manager. "Luis, what problems have you noticed?"

"The wheels are not running the gears as well as we hoped, and we have had to do some of the work by hand."

Sebastián dismounted and made his way into *La Casona* with Arturo and Colón following not far behind. Their inspection of the building and the new equipment took a little over an hour. Sebastián noted several problems related to the recent installation of the machinery and said he could have everything running normally in three days. Some of the metal pieces would have to be forged anew, but it was nothing he couldn't handle with the help of a few specialized laborers.

"Good news," said Arturo.

"Yes, but unfortunately there is also news that is not nearly as good."

Arturo and Luis looked expectantly at the young engineer, who now looked serious. "Considering the money and effort we invested in modernizing, I am surprised that *La Casona* has not been reinforced. The building was built reasonably well, but it's all wood and will never resist a major storm. We should consider upgrading to steel construction."

Colón looked dubious. "This is how we've always enclosed our machinery."

Arturo looked at his son with some concern. "I know what you are saying, Sebastián, but money is tighter now. I was hoping we could get by for a while, without having to take out a loan at exorbitant rates."

Sebastián pointed out that upgrading the machinery of the hacienda had increased their investment ten-fold. "Now we run the risk of losing a huge piece of our capital investment if we don't modernize La Casona's construction. We haven't had a big hurricane in thirty years—the law of averages will eventually catch up with us."

Arturo and Luis looked at one another other. The proprietor finally said, "I suppose you are right, son. No need to be careless now. Get me a plan for changing the building to steel after this year's harvest."

The men remounted and proceeded up the mountainside toward a large section of gently sloping land, where the coffee trees flourished. The trees themselves grew on gentle slopes, shaded by other valuable fruit trees, such as guava and avocado, which were known as the nurse trees. Five long years were required before a seedling could bear its first smooth-skinned fruits, called berries or cherries, which appeared after the many thousands of tiny white flowers dropped following pollination. In six months, the light green berries ripened to a deep red, and this signaled the start of the picking season, generally from September through December.

As the riders reached the first of the coffee trees they were greeted by the familiar sounds of a busy plantation: shouts and orders from the supervisors, prompt responses from the laborers, working songs interspersed with all the back-and-forth, people on break eating and chatting, and the occasional laugh.

Arturo hailed the closest foreman. "How was roll-call this morning?"

"About fifty percent, don Arturo."

Arturo frowned. Absenteeism this month had been on the rise, and he made a mental note to review this with Colón. Roig was not blind to the struggles of his workers, crushed as they were under abject poverty accentuated by chronic disease. He followed the latest recommendations in agricultural bulletins, promoted healthy conditions to increase productivity, and often paid wages whether or not a worker showed up on any given day. He believed that when they felt able, the *jíbaros* worked hard to earn the few coins they received. Almost to the last one, those who hadn't come to work that day were likely lying on the floor of their huts, feeling too sick to make the trek to the coffee fields and perhaps hoping that a day or two of rest would allow them to return. When money was scarce, Arturo sent the families fruits, chickens, or, like today, a piglet for special situations.

Don Arturo asked the foreman, "Have you seen Simón Báez today?"

The man answered that he had not seen Simón that morning, but pointed toward the next group of workers, about fifty yards away. "Check with his friends, *patrón*."

Arturo led his companions to the spot, where he saw Simón's closest friend, Gaspar Reyes, halfway up a coffee tree, balancing himself upon a homemade ladder which looked like it could collapse at any moment.

"*Cómo te va, Gaspar?*"

Gaspar paused for a few seconds to regain his breath. "*Buenos días, patrón. Todo bien.*" The *jíbaro* climbed down from the ladder to greet the proprietor.

Arturo looked into the sweaty face of the peasant. Gaspar had never been a picture of health, but over the last few months, it seemed that he was growing thinner, weaker, and shockingly pale. His words were punctuated by occasional gasps for air as he struggled to regain his strength.

But all the same, Gaspar smiled at his boss. "This is shaping up to be a bumper year, *patrón*."

Arturo could hardly disguise his excitement. "What are you seeing?"

"The rains this year came at exactly the right moment. The trees flowered like crazy, and then held on to their fruit. The number of berries the trees are holding is incredible."

Luis Colón interposed, "We may have to hire additional workers this year."

Arturo asked, "And the ripening fruit?"

Gaspar reached for a branch from the nearest tree. "Right on target, don Arturo. You can see the first berries turning from green to red. Soon they will soften, and we will be ready to fill our baskets."

When the harvest began, everybody would work together from sunup to sundown, earning wages determined solely by the volume of coffee they picked. As it was harvested, the coffee went into large baskets strapped around the waist of every man, woman, and child. A healthy man might fill two baskets in one day, and for this earned fifty cents. One of the many ten-year-olds working the plantation might make ten cents. But illness and malnutrition severely hindered productivity, which meant that earnings seldom approached those numbers. Arturo knew that a healthy, robust, and energetic coffee worker was a rare sight indeed.

Arturo asked bluntly, "How are you feeling, Gaspar?"

"It's nothing, *patrón*. Just a part of life. If work were easy, it would be called something else."

"What do you hear from Simón? Word is that his girl, Rosa,

is ill. We have a freshly-killed piglet to take to his *bohío*."

"Of course, *patrón*, they would be grateful, I know. Simón has not been able to come to work this week. Rosa has been struggling, and Pepa is at the end of her rope."

The proprietor rubbed his chin and stared at the ground. "Do they know what's wrong?"

"Simón said it was a bad case of the *mal de la montaña*. Marta has seen the girl every day this week, but nothing she does is helping."

Arturo frowned, looking distracted. Letting out a deep sigh, he turned again to Gaspar, saying, "You know, you can take some days off here and there. I would see that you are still paid something."

"Thank you, *patrón*. We are all right for now."

Arturo, Sebastián, and Luis resumed their trip over a steep ridge and down the trail that led to the workers' *bohíos*. The huts started about a mile past the last of the coffee trees, where the steep slope eased off into a flatter section. As they neared the huts, a slight wind brought to their nostrils the unmistakable smell of human excrement, growing stronger as they drew closer to the first dwelling. In Arturo's opinion, hygiene among the workers was worse than deplorable, but then, the *jíbaros* seemed hopelessly set in their ways. No amount of urging on his part had convinced them to build latrines. *But other than the nauseating smell, surely there is no other harmful effect*, he thought.

The riders pulled up to the Báez hut. Sebastián and Luis remained on their horses, while Arturo dismounted and tied his horse to a nearby *guayacán* tree. The two children, Carlos and Ana, looked up at Arturo as he approached the makeshift door of palm fronds. When he inquired about their father, Carlos pointed lazily to the hut and went inside to get him.

Simón Báez emerged from the hut, followed closely by Pepa with a listless girl of about three in her arms.

Simón spoke first. "Don Arturo, welcome to our home. To what do we owe this special visit?"

Arturo looked from Simón to Pepa, and finally to the child. "Luis Colón informed me that your daughter has taken a turn for the worse. We came to check on you and bring a fresh piglet for your family."

Simón managed a feeble smile. "Yes, don Arturo. Rosa has gotten much worse this week. We have tried everything, including taking some of the other children's food to give her." Smiling bashfully, he then added, "We even tried scaring her, telling her that El Águila Blanca would come and take her if she refused to eat. It was all foolish…"

Pepa interrupted Simón. "Don Arturo, he wants to send again for the *curandera*, but I am sure she cannot offer us anything else. I don't know what do anymore. What happened to Rafael last year is now happening to Rosa."

The tiny figure moved little and breathed with difficulty. She seemed like a small marble statue cradled in her mother's arms.

"Simón, Pepa, I have a friend who is the most respected physician in Ponce. Would you be willing to see him? If there is not much Marta can do for your daughter, then why not give Dr. Zeno a chance?"

Simón replied, "I don't know, *patrón*. With Rafael, we had no better luck with the doctor than with Marta. And the money…"

Arturo motioned for Luis to hand the piglet to Carlos. "As to the doctor's fees, we will work something out. But you don't have much time to decide."

Simón and Pepa looked at one another, then nodded silently.

"I will write Dr. Zeno this afternoon, to tell him you are coming."

Chapter Seven

A NEW LIFE IN PONCE

J uan, the oldest of the Báez children, had worked picking coffee seasonally since the age of eight, and other year-round chores at the hacienda since the age of ten. Clearly gift-ed with brains and not lacking in ambition, he had made the most of the informal off-season schooling available to him, and his plans did not include picking coffee for the rest of his life. He could read and write reasonably well and knew the basic arithmetic needed to get by in everyday affairs. By contrast, his life in the Báez *bohío* was a filthy and cramped experience which only promised to get worse because in another month his mother Pepa was expecting her ninth child. She had been pregnant probably twice as many times, but this was the ninth child that promised to be born alive.

The young Báez disliked the daily trek to the hacienda, over trails covered with thick mud into which his bare feet sank with each plodding step. Every day, he walked a mile uphill to arrive at another monotonous day of mindless berry picking, ignoring the hard green berries while searching for the soft crimson ones, a task which became progressively more diffi-cult as the season advanced and ripe berries became harder to find. He was repulsed by the hygienic practices of his fellow workers, who could hardly be bothered to urinate or stool in a predetermined location. For Juan, moving from one coffee tree to the next required a constant use of the art of the zigzag and the sidestep to negotiate the many turds that littered the ground. The tedium and disgust Juan found in his every-day life might have been bearable, had he not also been afflicted with the same wasting illness as his father. Standing together, Simón and Juan resembled a pair of pale, gaunt wraiths more at home in a graveyard than among the coffee trees.

But each offseason brought a drier, cooler climate and more diverse tasks, and this proved more agreeable to the boy. The ground dried out, the stench from his coworkers' leavings dissipated, and the non-harvest work was in general less tedious. And in the offseason, he simply felt better. With each month that passed after the harvest was completed, he noticed an uptick in his energy, an improvement in his breathing, and, unknown to him but noticeable to any casual observer, a gradual return of the healthier pink hue that slowly displaced the ghostly white of his skin. By mid-summer, he actually felt pretty well and could enjoy life in true teenaged fashion for a few weeks before August and September returned, bringing once again the dismal routine of the harvest.

Juan turned sixteen during the picking season of 1894, which was a particularly rainy one. Not one month after the harvest began, Juan felt himself slowly sickening once more. This time, however, his fatigue was worse than ever before. Juan could hardly catch his breath, and his head pounded to the beat of his racing heart. By the time harvest ended in early January, neither Juan nor Simón could have managed to work another day. Juan finally concluded that to stay in the *cafetal* could only mean death, and that while his parents and younger siblings might be stuck among the coffee plants, he certainly was not. He promised himself that if the coming offseason restored some of his energy, he would leave for Ponce at the first opportunity. Like clockwork, not a month passed since he picked his last coffee berry than he once again began to feel stronger. The month after that brought further improvement in his health, and at the end of May, he decided to leave.

Simón and Pepa were not surprised, and although the family was going to miss Juan's wages, as doting parents they felt some relief, if not joy, at his announcement. Like his son, Simón was also convinced that something in the hacienda slowly killed its workers, something more than the difficult and monotonous labor, or the lack of nutritious food. Whatever it was, it was so inscrutable that the doctors could not explain it. It was something that spared a few random workers like Pepa, and bypassed don Arturo and his family, but turned the vast majority into ambulating ghosts. To Simón, it all seemed little better than a curse, and the sooner his son fled from it, the better.

The next day at sunrise, Juan packed some fruit in a bundle of burlap, threw it over his shoulder, and headed down the mountain. He had ten Puerto Rican *pesos* in silver coins which his father had given him, the clothes on his back, and the fruits in his sack. When he left Utuado, Juan was barely five feet tall and well under one hundred pounds, his handsome features hidden by the ravages of disease. His skin tone was the sickly, creamy yellow of the anemic Spanish-descended Puerto Ricans of the mountains, and the extreme thinness of his face allowed its bony framework to show plainly. The same could be said of Juan's body in which his ribs could easily be counted at a glance.

His journey mostly followed the long and gently sloping ravines that led south in the direction of the coast, and once he had turned off the mountain trails and onto the main road to Ponce, the going became easier. The boy saved what was in his bundle and picked fruits from the side of the road at every opportunity. He drank from the mountain creeks that once again ran full with the return of the rainy season, and spent the night by the side of the road, covering himself with fronds which had fallen from the immense royal palms lining the road.

By the following morning, the youngster had arrived at the top of *El Vigía* hill just outside the city. He stared at the vast expanse of commercial and residential buildings that stretched toward the vast blue of the Caribbean Sea and wondered if the city would deliver on the opportunities he so desperately sought.

Into this frenzy of activity, Juan stumbled dusty and tired from his journey.

*****

Friday and Saturday nights in Ponce were magical, when it seemed that everybody was out mingling in the plaza. In the vibrant evening air, multitudes strolled around the square, vendors loudly peddled their wares, musicians played to an open hat and colorfully dressed young women paraded alongside their mothers.

Even before Juan left his family three years before to seek a better life in Ponce, he had been known as *el ruiseñor del monte*, the mountain nightingale, because he was gifted with an unusually beautiful and pure tenor voice. On occasion, he employed his talents at *velorios* and other gatherings for fifty cents a night, twice what he made in a full day at the coffee fields. He performed throughout Utuado and even in the neighboring municipalities of Adjuntas and Ciales.

"Mira Juanito, qué está pasando?"

Juan turned toward the voice and saw his friend Miguel coming toward him. Miguel was the bongo player of the Pleneros, the Afro-Caribbean band he had joined shortly after arriving in Ponce. Juan was now their lead singer.

"Miguelito, cómo estás? That was quite a crowd in front of the Guadalupe today, wasn't it?"

Miguel gave the singer a slap on the back. "You really were extraordinary today, *mi hermano*. With a voice like yours, I'm surprised you don't have more skirts following you."

"There are a few out there. I am—you know—evaluating."

Miguel burst out laughing. "If you have extras, please send one my way."

Juan's performances were legendary. Pedestrian traffic on the plaza would come to a standstill as large crowds stopped to listen to the new singer. Young women swooned and threw flowers at his feet. These evening concerts gave Juan a strong sense of belonging—to a new community, to new friends, and to his music, as well as a way to push away grief and restlessness. For the first time in his life, Juan felt that he could look to the future without dread.

The friends parted until the next evening's concert, and Juan continued alone across the plaza. When he first came to Ponce at the age of sixteen, he had found the large square overwhelming because of its size and grandeur. Plaza Las Delicias abounded in tall shade trees, and was oddly divided into two parts by the imposing Church of Our Lady of Guadalupe, built awkwardly in the middle of the plaza, instead of across the street as was customary. Behind the church stood a striking building built in an eclectic mixture of Moorish and neo-Gothic styles, which served as the city's fire station.

Juan crossed the main street, Calle Comercio, and walked by the elegant mid-century town hall, as well as stores, pharmacies, a large hotel, and countless two-storied colonial houses, easily the equals of the best in San Juan. Perhaps he would never live in one of those houses, but since coming to Ponce, he sometimes felt he was living a different life. The stately homes stretched along the streets for several blocks, side by side with multiple banks, the large *La Perla* theater, two hospitals, and numerous open markets. Ponce served as a second capital to the island, and in terms of finance, industry, and culture, it far exceeded the official political center in San Juan, ninety miles away over treacherous mountain roads.

"*Por favor, señor…*" A ragged beggar called out to Juan, and the young man handed him a twenty-cent *peseta*.

The man reminded Juan of his first days in the city, when he was homeless and destitute. He had earned his first few cents in the corner of the plaza, his straw hat upside-down on the ground, singing in the evenings for those passing by in the haunting, clear tenor which had made him famous in Utuado. These pleasant evenings were followed by difficult mornings. Juan would wander around the town, asking to work in whatever menial job was available. His money had evaporated, when, after a particularly difficult week scrubbing floors for twenty cents a day, a store owner suggested that he might try to find employment at the port.

"Never mind that you're short and thin," the man said. "Right now, commerce in Ponce is so good that more hands are always needed to load and unload the ships. You'll get something." Taking this advice, Juan made inquiries at the port, which was located three miles south of the city just past the village of La Playa.

His willingness to work for half wages ensured that he was hired every day. All openings involved some degree of physical labor and for Juan, who was underdeveloped and anemic, it was backbreaking work. He persevered because it was by far the best work available. After he returned faithfully to the docks every day for eight weeks, the scraggly boy began to garner the attention of the foremen, who noticed that he had memorized the names of the ships, their tonnage, cargo, ports of origin, and destinations.

The deputy collector quickly figured out that this short, bony youth was special, quite simply because he could read. One day, he called Juan into the business office at the end of his shift.

"Juan, the foremen have noticed that you have some organizational skills that could serve you well here at the port. You are not much of a longshoreman, but you might do better in an office. Can you read and write?"

Juan answered that he could, and before he knew it, he had his first promotion as an assistant clerk, earning ninety cents per day. This was three times what he had made at the hacienda, for far less labor and under incomparably better conditions. The young man trained in the basics of port management: keeping track of the cargo manifests, the comings and goings of the ships, the value of the goods, the payment of duties, and the wages of the men. He worked twelve-hour days, six days a week, and within a year, he was clerking at the customs house for two *pesos* a day. He could now afford to rent a small, one-room house near the port and for the first time in his life, he dressed decently and owned several pairs of comfortable shoes. The only recurring reminder of his life in the Utuado mountains was the periodic arrival in the port of his old boss's son, Sebastian Roig, who came every month to supervise the loading of the hacienda's crops.

Juan now underwent a complete metamorphosis. Far from the mysterious poisons of the *cafetal*, Juan turned into a strapping young man, gaining a good amount of muscle. His body, once freed from the constraints of the monotonous and poorly-balanced mountain food, shot up in height. Best yet, his lifelong anemia slowly and steadily resolved. Color returned to his pale cheeks, the sickly yellow of his arms and legs changed to a healthy tan, and his mind felt sharp and alert. He met other young people and began to explore his new home, which seemed to acquire a whole new life at sunset.

In his first three years in Ponce, Juan returned to Utuado

only twice. He stayed for three or four days, helping his father with repairs, helping his mother with the young children, and wandering about the forests, pondering what would have become of him had he remained in the mountains. He never stayed long. He found he could not bear to relive the misery of his childhood for more than a few days, nor the ever-present, nagging fear that the mountain would again make him sick if he stayed too long.

Now, as Juan followed Calle Comercio on his way home with his mind occupied by memories of tougher times, he became aware that he was being followed. A rider on horseback seemed to be gaining on him rapidly. Nighttime robberies were not unknown in the streets south of the town center, and Juan picked up his pace. He was about to break into a run when he heard a voice from behind, "Juan—*Juan Báez?*"

He wheeled around to face a man who looked vaguely familiar. He was dressed in typical *jíbaro* clothes and rode bareback on a scraggy horse.

"Yes, I am Juan Báez."

The rider replied, "It's a miracle I have found you. I have ridden around the town for the last two hours. I must have failed to recognize you."

"Do I know you?" asked Juan

"It's been nearly three years since we saw one another, and we have both changed. You for the better."

The singer suddenly recognized the rider. "Domingo Reyes! You are Gaspar's son, my father's *compadre*."

"Yes, Juan. Simón asked me to ride down from Utuado with an urgent message."

Juan swallowed hard, and his mouth went dry. The year before, a similar encounter had given him the news of his brother's death. "What—*who*—has something happened?" Juan leaned back against a wall for support. "Is it my father—?"

Domingo replied, "Something is wrong with your sister, Rosa. She has become very ill in the last few days."

"*Rosita!*"

"Yes, Marta the *curandera* has been with her every day. Nothing's working. Simón and Pepa are bringing her to Ponce; they must have left Utuado by now."

Juan felt the knot in his throat tighten and his eyes starting to moisten. "Then, they will be here tomorrow."

"Yes. They will meet you in front of the Guadalupe at noon."

Juan sat on the sidewalk, disconsolate, lost in fearful thoughts. *What would happen to Rosa? She was only three years old!*

Juan held his head between his hands for a minute. Slowly, he looked up at Domingo. "Very well, I will be there to meet them. There is nothing more to do until then."

An awkward silence followed before Domingo spoke. "Juan, I have had a hard ride down from the mountains, made worse by carrying this bad news..."

Juan shook the fog from his mind. "Of course, Domingo, please stay with me until you are ready to go back."

And so, the two old acquaintances resumed their trek, one on foot, the other following on horseback, both completely silent for the twenty minutes it took to reach Juan's small home.

Chapter Eight

SUMMER DIFFICULTIES, 1898

For Simón and Pepa Báez, their children were the source of their greatest joy. Although they missed the absent Juan, and mourned the children they had lost, they saw Caridad every few weeks and they still had Carlos, Ana, and baby Rosa with them. All were handsome children, but the beauty of the lot was three-year-old Rosa, sometimes affectionately known as the little rose, Rosita. She had arrived one week after Juan had left for Ponce and being the most recent of Pepa's many births, she was out and on the ground before the *curandera* could make it to the hut. The wizened folk-healer finally tottered in, leaning on her *guayaba* cane and carrying the indispensable bundle of herbs and vines necessary for the postpartum cure: leaves of thyme, taro, and lime to prevent infection, and roots of *yerba clavo* to slow the bleeding. She crushed this plant material in her mortar, applying the dark green paste to the umbilical cord after dividing it with the specially sharpened knife which Pepa had placed in boiling water shortly after going into labor.

Rosa arrived alert and ready to meet the world with wide-open, big blue eyes, a trait not unusual among the pure-bred Europeans of the mountains of Puerto Rico. Despite her puny size, she was a vigorous pink baby, born to a relatively healthy mother who was seemingly immune to the widespread anemia affecting her husband and her other offspring. The first six months of Rosa's life were her best time, her most vigorous time, her time to enjoy and be enjoyed. Before long, she began to crawl, which she did with a big smile and yelps of delight on the floor of the hovel. But shortly after this milestone, as so often happened with the infants in the coffee country, Rosa's growth began to slow, her vitality to ebb, and her skin ever so slightly to pale. The arrival of the harvest season meant that the entire family headed daily to the coffee fields, where Simón, Pepa, and Carlos worked the trees while young Ana looked up at them from her mud pies, and baby Rosa sat bare-bottomed on the ground, waiting to be fed.

When Pepa weaned the baby at two, the toddler's health entered a new phase of deterioration, which no dietary adjustment or plant teas from Marta the *curandera* could arrest. The child stopped growing and gaining weight, and her parents went from being concerned to desperate. They had seen this pattern many times before with their other children, and now they watched their daughter with growing anxiety. They finally resolved to seek help when the child started eating dirt by the handful. Pepa had heard it said that seriously ill people at times ingested soil or sand, as if trying to obtain some unknown nutrient missing from their diet, and she remembered vividly having caught Rafael with dirt-stained palms numerous times as he sickened. This time, they did not summon the local doctor from Utuado, but at don Arturo's suggestion, immediately started planning to take their daughter to Ponce.

Thirteen-year-old Carlos was left in charge of the hut and his sister Ana. Simón hired a mule at the cost of two weeks' wages, packed some meager provisions in a rickety basket and with Pepa beside him, began the trip down the mountain trails to find Juan and consult the renowned physician, Manuel Zeno Gandía.

A journey of a day and a half brought them to the outskirts of the city. From the tall hills above Ponce, Simón and Pepa glanced down at the large expanse of buildings extending toward the sea and wondered if there they would find whatever it was their daughter needed to get well. They made their way through the town and then to the plaza, just as the midday bell began to chime. As agreed, they met Juan in front of the Guadalupe Church at noon. Juan beamed at the sight of his family while Simón and Josefa stared joyfully at the son they had rarely seen in three years. Juan was now a well-proportioned man who towered a full eight inches over his father, with a handsome face and bright hazel eyes under a mane of straight, dark-brown hair. He was dressed in inexpensive but immaculate clothing—a fitted shirt, long pants, socks, and leather shoes. Gone was the sickly, pale, thin teenager who had left his home in the *cordillera* with dirty clothes and bare feet.

As pleasantly surprised as his parents were by his robust appearance, so, too, was Juan dismayed by the pitiful sight of his youngest sister. All his old fears rushed back with the knowledge that the mountain was killing her. The girl was languid, shockingly pale, and appeared to have barely grown since Juan's last visit. Her beautiful sky-blue eyes were dull and sunken and her once luscious hair was now thin and stringy about her narrow face. Juan began to worry that his family's journey had not come soon enough.

Juan led his family to the southern edge of the town and closer to the port, to his small home off the main street, Calle Marina. He arranged cots and prepared food for the travelers as they sank into their seats to plan their visit to Dr. Zeno. Rosa breathed with difficulty, ate scantily, and said nothing.

The next morning, they carried Rosa to the office of Dr. Zeno, three blocks north of the center of the city by the stately Tricoche Hospital. He was a man of forty-five years or so, short, and slightly paunchy, with large whiskers, thick glasses, and a kindly manner born out of an intense compassion for the *jíbaro* poor of Puerto Rico. His reputation was unsurpassed, for he had studied in Barcelona at one of the leading medical schools in Europe. He was not only a physician, but also a novelist, poet, journalist, and politician. He never talked down to his patients, always addressing himself to their native intelligence and practical minds, so they could readily understand complex medical concepts when explained patiently and succinctly. Zeno welcomed the family to his office near the center of Ponce, offering them food and black coffee.

Simón and Pepa hoped that they had not waited too long with their baby girl, and that the wise physician still had time to work a miracle. Zeno looked at the family with some sadness, for he could sense that a very familiar and predictable scene was about to unfold yet again in his examination room.

Rosita's evaluation was as meticulous as it was anticlimactic, for there were no surprises. Zeno's assessment revealed the classic signs of advanced pediatric anemia: markedly pale skin the color of ivory; sunken eyes, bloodless lips, an emaciated frame, a racing pulse, and a loud heart murmur. One month prior, the forward-thinking Zeno had acquired a microscope and a blood counter with which to measure the severity of anemia in his patients. He had been aware for some time that virtually all barefoot patients who came to see him from the mountains suffered from anemia to some degree, whereas those that walked from inside the city limits almost invariably did not. With his new instruments, he could now quantify aspects of the disease and keep detailed notes on the history, examinations, and laboratory values of each person.

This he now did for the Báez's daughter, first by drawing a few drops of blood from Rosa's finger, and then expertly making a thin smear on a glass slide. Next, he stained the smear with a special dye and examined it under the microscope, carefully counting all the red cells present in one small section of the slide. Their number was very diminished, and those that were present were small and abnormally colored. Zeno estimated that the girl's blood was operating at less than one-third of its normal capacity.

Grimly, he turned to the parents. "Your Rosita's case is grave; there is no question that she suffers from severe anemia. Her blood is very depleted, and she needs immediate and aggressive care. I recommend that we improve her diet, specifically by increasing her animal proteins. If we can get her to eat more meat, the anemia may well improve. I am also aware that deep in the mountains of Utuado where you live, it is next to impossible to procure appropriate quantities of meat and other iron-rich foods she needs to get well."

The diagnosis came as no surprise, since the couple had lost other children to anemia. But Zeno's confirmation of Rosa's severe condition devastated her parents. They resolved that they would do their best to follow the doctor's recommendations with their meager resources. Choking with emotion, Pepa asked, "What can we do? We just lost our precious Rafael last year, and maybe now we will lose Rosita… and to the same sickness!"

Dr. Zeno met the grieving mother's eyes with a steady gaze. "At all costs, we must avoid repeating the errors made with her siblings. No *curandera* will save this girl, and I can assure you that if Rosita returns to the mountains, she will not outlive the month. The best and, in my opinion, only course left to us is to admit her to a hospital where she can be fed and cared for properly. I also plan to start her on iron supplements to help replenish her blood. I will prepare and personally deliver those to the religious Sisters that run the hospital on behalf of the Ladies' Association of Ponce. They are remarkable nurses, and in their hands, Rosa has the best chance of survival."

Simón threw up his arms and raked his hands through his thick gray hair. "Doctor, that is all well and good, but Pepa and I—*we*..." Simón's voice cracked, and he swallowed thickly, bowing his head before finally admitting, "We cannot afford a hospital. And I cannot be gone from work longer than the time we have here, unless we want to lose our *bohío* as well."

Juan spoke up. "I can cover the costs and you can go back to Utuado. *Mamá* can remain with me in Ponce while Rosa improves."

Dr. Zeno interrupted. "There will be no costs of any kind. The Ladies' Association raises all the funds needed to run the hospital. There are ample funds contributed by banks, sugar mills, and coffee planters to help families like yours."

They were in no position to refuse the aid needed to help Rosa recover, though Simón's pride balked at the thought. Nonetheless, Dr. Zeno quickly wrote out a letter with instructions and nursing orders which he gave to Simón to present at the hospital, and then gave them each a warm handshake, promising to see Rosa early the next day. The family left the office, their spirits kindled by the hope that with better food and clean water, and the care of the Sisters and the doctor, their daughter would get well.

The family left the office and walked the quarter mile to El Santo Asilo de Damas, a small hospital staffed by the religious order of the Servants of Mary. It was a one-story structure with about two dozen rooms, built around a small courtyard planted with fruit trees. One of the rooms housed only pediatric cases, with six tiny cots neatly arranged in a row, six feet apart. Only one other bed was occupied at the time of their arrival, upon which sat a boy of about five or six, looking at a picture book. It appeared to the Báez family that he had no parents or any other adults staying with him, but every few minutes a sprightly novice bounced in, pinched his cheek, or tickled his toes, and after giving him a quick looking over, left to continue with her other chores.

As she passed her daughter over to the Sisters to examine, Pepa learned that the boy was from *barrio* Jayuya in Utuado, not far from where the Báez family lived. His mother had died of "apoplexy" and the father, having five other children to look after in addition to his own responsibilities as foreman at Hacienda Gripiñas, had sent the child to Ponce to be cared for by the Servants of Mary, rewarding them with a generous monthly donation. Accompanied there by an indifferent uncle, the boy had arrived underweight, anemic, and withdrawn. He had been there six months, and the sisters had grown extremely fond of him, for it soon turned out that he was bright, somewhat mischievous, and unusually kind-hearted. Best of all, he had thrived under the assiduous care of the Servants. For Pepa, this young boy was living proof that severe deterioration could be arrested and reversed when addressed in the proper environment.

The boy's name was Carlos Juan, and upon hearing the names of her two older brothers together in one name, Rosa opened her eyes wide and managed a feeble smile. For his part, Carlos Juan was captivated by the pretty girl with the big blue eyes that followed him wherever he went. Pepa's heart swelled with joy at the discovery of the other child, whose story offered the promise that her daughter might recover after all. Simón headed back to the mountains the next day and Juan returned to his labors at the port, while Pepa remained in the pediatric ward. There, she slept diagonally on a child's cot with her feet hanging off the bed and her ankles supported by the frame as she huddled under a blanket provided by Rosa's nurse, Sister Mary Elizabeth.

Mary Elizabeth Oates belonged to the order of the Sisters of Mercy. She had arrived in Puerto Rico two years previously to learn Spanish and assist with patients at the Santo Asilo de Damas. She was a young nurse of remarkable ability, plain-spoken, and prone to the occasional swear-word or two. Sister Mary Elizabeth's sympathy was quickly piqued by the sickly girl and her stalwart mother, for she could plainly see that Josefa Báez had endured unimaginable hardships. As such, Sister Mary Elizabeth determined to throw herself, body and soul, day and night, into the care of little Rosa.

Within a week, it became clear that the right decision had been made. The spotless and sanitary surroundings, improved diet and loving care of Sister Mary Elizabeth began to breathe life back into the child. At the Damas hospital there were three meals a day, unlimited clean water and fresh juice from oranges and guavas. Patients and nurses alike adhered to a meticulous standard of hygiene set forth by Dr. Zeno as medical director of the institution.

Mostly non-verbal up to then, Rosa soon began to speak again, encouraged by entreaties from her new friend, Carlos Juan. Dr. Zeno visited frequently at first, then less often as his dietary orders and iron pills began to work a miracle. Carlos Juan frequently sauntered over from his cot to sit on Rosa's, where he chatted endlessly without a reply from the girl who simply smiled during the long harangues. Pepa could see that her daughter appeared to be improving, and she was willing to wait as long as necessary for a complete cure. Despite the dire circumstances that had brought her to Ponce, Pepa felt strangely content. Juan visited daily, and if only her husband and her other children could have been there, her happiness might have been complete. If truth be told, Pepa spent the long hours in the ward having serious thoughts about whether to return to their miserable existence in Utuado.

A week passed in this manner when one bright morning, Dr. Zeno came to see his two young patients. One was completely well, the other making unmistakable progress. Pepa Báez approached the doctor smiling gratefully. "Rosa looks so much better. The food and the iron pills have helped her very much. Thank you, doctor."

Zeno beamed proudly. "She still has a way to go, but things are definitely looking better for her."

"But, Doctor Zeno..." Pepa hesitated, strong emotions wrestling across her face before she finally confessed, "I am so afraid to take her back to Utuado. There is something in the mountains and the coffee fields that makes the children sick!"

Zeno turned serious. "Children and adults, both. The children have fewer reserves and tend to succumb more quickly. Some unknown factor in the rural areas is causing widespread anemia; the medical profession quite simply doesn't know what it is."

"Maybe it *would* be better if Rosa could remain in Ponce. She could possibly remain with her oldest brother, Juan, but he is so busy with his life and his work. We cannot all move here; our whole life is tied to the mountains. I am at a loss," Pepa muttered and began to weep softly.

Dr. Zeno took her hand. "Josefa, do not despair, we will not worry about those things for now. Rosa will be here for several more weeks, and that will give us time to think of an arrangement. I agree with you that we should have her remain in Ponce, somehow."

Rosa's recovery began in July, and as the fruit ripened on the attractive guava trees in the courtyard, word began to spread throughout Ponce that one million *americanos* had landed, either in Yauco, or Guánica, or maybe it was Guayama. Even in El Santo Asilo de Damas, stories spread of how they had whipped the Spanish army in a day and now owned everything and everybody on the island. Variously, the invaders were gentlemen, cads, friends, bandits, saints, atheists, dupes, rapists, sages, or idiots. What they didn't already own, they could easily buy because all *norteamericanos* were millionaires. And to boot, as of the day before, the Spanish language had been outlawed and all communication thenceforth was to be by means of hand gestures and winks, except for the few lucky rich who spoke some French, which was apparently still allowed.

But as they had not yet seen a single American soldier with their own eyes, the people of Ponce mostly ignored the rumors and continued with life as usual. This included the Servants of Mary, whose joy in the two *jíbaro* children continued as they kept up their remarkable progress. The sisters loved Rosa as much as Carlos Juan, and they enjoyed watching the two pint-sized humans interact in their refreshingly innocent fashion, caring so deeply and so unconditionally for one another in the way particular to children. More than anything, the nuns enjoyed watching Rosa's improvement over the course of three weeks, as her angular frame filled out, life returned to her captivating eyes and the abnormal, sickly whiteness began to melt away.

So, it came as a total surprise when one day in late July, amidst the disturbing news that the Americans had indeed landed a dozen or so miles to the west, the girl began having recurrent, periodic fevers, vomiting, and headaches. None of Sister Mary Elizabeth's heroic efforts bore fruit, and the girl started to sink. After two days of worsening symptoms, her skin suddenly turned a bright yellow color, and Dr. Zeno was urgently summoned shortly before midnight. He rushed to the hospital under a raging downpour, random flashes of lightning intermittently illuminating his way through the inky night.

He entered the room to find Josefa Báez distraught, leaning over her daughter, who was curled in her cot next to Carlos Juan's. When the lethargic girl caught sight of her doctor, soaked to the very skeleton, his thinning hair plastered to his pate, she giggled feebly and her eyes lit up. "Hello Dr. Zeno. I am sorry I got worse again, but I promise to get better soon."

Zeno beheld the little patient, her shoulders shivering as she fought through a shaking chill, her skin and eyes colored a sickly pumpkin yellow. He took Rosa's delicate hand in his, and replied, "Of course, *mi querida niña*, I am here to make you well. By morning everything will be fine."

Pepa could hardly suppress her distress. She beheld the scene through eyes brimming with tears: the kindly doctor holding Rosa's hand, the worried nuns looking in from the doorway, and Carlos Juan bending over her daughter in silence with apprehension and fear painted on his handsome face. His exam completed, Zeno turned toward Pepa and led her away from the child. "The sudden worsening is due to malaria," he said gravely. "She must have contracted the illness either shortly before you left Utuado, or on the journey to Ponce. It is only now manifesting itself, almost three weeks later. The malaria is attacking many of the red cells that have only just begun to recover from the ravages of anemia. Her yellow color tells me that these new cells are once again being destroyed. We should send for her brother. I am sorry, but there is not much more that can be done for her now."

Pepa could contain herself no longer and rushed from the room to hide her grief. The nuns put their hands over their mouths, Sister Mary Elizabeth shaking her head in disbelief. Only Carlos Juan continued to look at Rosa, tenderly holding those beautiful eyes with his for the last time as he climbed onto the cot by her feet.

The malaria soon finished what *la anemia* had started. Two severe shocks to Rosa's blood proved to be too much, and by six in the morning, the child was dead. When her breathing became labored, Sister Mary Elizabeth administered morphine to ease Rosita's struggle, and in the end, she passed peacefully in the arms of her mother. Pepa, who would now bury her fifth child, was beside herself with grief. The hospital staff was inconsolable, and Carlos Juan sat, stunned, in abject silence. Dr. Zeno could not recall a death affecting him so much. The feeling of helplessness and the anguish at seeing yet another tiny corpse distressed him to the point of despondency.

Juan had been awoken late in the night by what he thought to be the booming of thunder. Only after several minutes of pounding had he realized there was someone at his door, and upon opening it, had received the grim news. He rushed to the *Santo Asilo* and entered the quiet room, his hair dripping with rain and his feet splattered with mud. With one glance, he understood what had just happened and sank to the floor, a chill deeper than rain sinking into his soul.

A fog of gloom fell over the hospital that morning. The appearance of the ghostlike Rosa, her sudden death after her initial improvement, and seeing the suffering of his mother changed Juan forever. He cursed the coffee fields, wishing fervently that some cataclysm would arise to destroy them and deliver new life to the mountain.

Meanwhile, on the same afternoon of Rosa's death, the first Americans rode into Ponce and their medical transports anchored in the bay.

Juan took one week away from work to bring his sister's body back to Utuado and help his father organize the *velorio* to provision Rosa's spirit for its supernatural journey. When he returned to Ponce after the burial, he found the American army in complete control of the city and preparing to move on the enemy.

The end of Spanish rule in Ponce meant some minor shake-ups at the port, which Juan easily survived. The Army proved scrupulously respectful of the locals and their traditions, and other than the appearance of some English signage and currency, nothing else changed in Juan's day-to-day existence. Save for the knowledge that, once again, the mountain had stolen something from him that could never be returned.

Chapter Nine

RAFI MOORE

For Ashford, the cease fire of August 13th meant that he could finally return to the comforts of Mayagüez. Sick soldiers could now be treated out of the city's tidy, compact military hospital, which even boasted a relatively well-equipped operating room. To clear space at the barracks, the doctors lodged at the Hotel Paris near the main plaza. Evenings were free for the officers to socialize with the residents, and Ashford found the upper classes of the small city to be sophisticated and refined. Young women of the aristocracy had no problems kindling the interest of the young American officers. Few of the locals spoke even a modicum of English, which made the getting-to-know-you formalities rather amusing. Needless to say, hand signals and smiles served as the common language.

Two weeks after his return to Mayagüez, Ashford was called to see post commander Colonel Daniel Burke in his office. Entering Burke's office, Ashford noticed a young man standing next to the colonel's desk. He was tall, thin, of fair complexion and held a confident air about him. He had black hair and hazel eyes, a refined nose, and a soft mouth.

Burke motioned to the young man beside him. "Lieutenant, I want to introduce your interpreter, Mr. Rafael Moore. He is a civilian working for the Army, and I hope you find his services helpful. From now on, he will accompany you on your hospital visits and travel with you about the town. You should also employ Mr. Moore to further your study of the Spanish language and local customs."

The two men perfunctorily shook hands, exchanged a few pleasantries, and left the office together. Ashford cast a discreet eye over his new companion. Rafael Moore could not have been more than twenty. Ashford suspected that his new acquaintance had no trouble befriending members of the fairer sex, and he certainly dressed the part. He wore a coat and tie under the bowler hat that was *de rigueur* among upper-class gentlemen. Overall, he made a favorable first impression, one which was enhanced as soon as their conversation started.

Rafael Moore smiled enthusiastically. "Doctor Ashford, I am delighted to serve as your interpreter. I look forward to teaching you Spanish in our spare time as well." Moore spoke in perfect English marked by the telltale quirks of a New England accent, which brought a smile to Ashford's face.

The two passed by several outdoor cafés which dotted the streets around the *Plaza Principal*. The square vibrated with people hurrying about, generating a loud hum of background noise. Ashford and Moore sought relief from the midday sun under the red and yellow awning of the Café del Yagüez.

"It is very good to make your acquaintance, *Señor* Moore." Ashford motioned for his companion to sit at an empty table and offered him tobacco with which to roll a cigarette.

"Please, from now on, call me Rafi, as do all my friends."

Ashford nodded and ordered coffee and a lunch for two.

"So, what brings you to Mayagüez?" Ashford asked, thinking the answer might help to explain the young man's interesting accent.

Rafi frowned. "That is a long and complicated story," he said. "I am not sure where to start. Could I presume to ask you first, sir?"

"Very well, Rafi. Let's see… I was born and raised in the District of Columbia. My family are originally from Northern Virginia, proud Southerners to the last one."

Rafi grinned broadly. "My father's a dyed-in-the wool Yankee, sir, from New London, Connecticut."

"Well, the war's been over for thirty-three years, so that shouldn't come between us. Even though my father was a proud Confederate, a colonel, to be exact."

Rafi took the coffee from the waiter's tray and offered some to Ashford. "My uncle served in the war, a surgeon with the 22nd Connecticut. Killed at Chickamauga—mortar shell."

Ashford tasted the coffee and took a drag from his cigarette.

"Tough break. My father was also a surgeon. He survived the war and later became Dean of Georgetown's Medical School. He even treated President Garfield—told them not to probe for that danged bullet, but they didn't listen."

Rafi leaned forward, intrigued. "Your father—he continues at Georgetown?"

"No, he passed away, only forty-one years old. Quite unexpected. I was only eight at the time, with four brothers and sisters left to look after. We had to move in with my grandparents in Washington. They were old Virginia aristocracy, and like many others, had gotten crushed by the Jay Cooke railroad scandal of 1873. They managed to keep their house, but not much more."

The waiter came by with their lunch of creole chicken fricassee. Ashford extinguished his cigarette and inhaled the aromas of garlic, onion, and pepper wafting up from his dish. Ashford found his lunch overflowing with flavors. When he was growing up, his mother would have thrown some salt in a pot, boiled a chicken thigh, and called it good.

Ashford resumed their conversation. "My father always was my idol. I dreamed of being a physician and working with him, which sadly never came to pass. My mother would have preferred for me to become an Episcopalian minister, but I had other plans."

Through a mouth full of chicken Rafi mumbled, "My mother wanted me to become a professional pianist, the new Liszt of the Caribbean. My father wouldn't hear of it."

"A *pianist*, that's something," he replied between bites. "I play a bit on the violin myself. We must play together sometime."

Rafi next recounted the story of his American father, who had come to Puerto Rico as a young man and succeeded as a merchant. "He began with one brig of two-hundred tons, which he named the *Charles A. Moore* after himself, and sailed between New London, New York, and Puerto Rico carrying dry goods and agricultural products. My mother bore him two sons—my brother José, followed five years to the day by your humble servant."

Rafi told Ashford that by the time he was born, his father

was nearing fifty and had prospered to the point where he owned three ships, the command of which he delegated, giving him ample time at home. The senior Moore much preferred the climate of Puerto Rico to that of his native state and made the island his permanent home. He took a house in the heart of the Old City, a stately Spanish residence from the early eighteenth century barely a stone's throw from the governor's palace of La Fortaleza.

The plates were cleared and more coffee set before them as Rafi continued, "At home, my mother spoke to us in Spanish until precisely one in the afternoon, not one minute more and not one minute less. After that, we were required to speak in English the rest of the day. This rule was absolute and no compromise was ever allowed. Communicating with our mother, who spoke only halting English, made the afternoons and evenings a challenge, to say the least."

Ashford grinned broadly; he was beginning to enjoy this tale. "Imagine that—a proverbial Tower of Babel right in your home!"

"It was something like that, truly, because we also acquired a healthy dose of *Français* from the priests at the parish school. Through this schizoid formula, José and I became fluent and literate in two languages and could get by reasonably well in a third."

Ashford lit another cigarette. Rafi drank his coffee, and continued, "Going back to the music discussion, one could say that my best friend growing up was our Pleyel piano. I remember clearly the day that the *Moore* returned from France with the instrument on board. It was the most beautiful thing I had ever seen. With my mother as my teacher, I progressed rapidly, and on my thirteenth birthday, I played the entire *The Well Tempered Clavier* to a packed audience at the Tapia Theater."

The significance of this precocious achievement was not lost upon Ashford. "I would like to hear to you play at the first opportunity."

Rafi leaned back and stretched in his chair. "At times, being the local prodigy could be tiresome, though. My mother committed me to playing every Friday night at the Carmelite convent on Cristo Street. Imagine an impressionable young-ster entering an immense, gloomy, three-hundred-year-old building inhabited by short, veiled creatures with barely their eyes showing."

Ashford began to titter, taking out another cigarette as Rafi continued. "The nuns were desperately poor, and I remember how they surreptitiously welcomed a paying audience by a small side door facing the terraced alley, *La Escalinata de las Monjas.*"

At this, Rafi burst fully into an infectious laugh, until tears came to his eyes. "Luckily for them the bishop never found out, or he would have asked for a cut. You see, the nuns charged two *pesos* for the privilege of listening to me. But they also expected me to play for free, telling me that my efforts were an Offering to the Glory of Our Lord. Imagine Moth-er Superior's face when..." Rafi paused, fighting for breath around his guffaws, "—when I asked for *half the total take*. She practically came out of her habits!"

Ashford doubled over laughing. "And they let you return?"

"Oh yes, I was one of their very few profit centers."

Rafi explained how he always played for exactly one hour and thirty minutes and not a minute longer, at which point he would give a curt bow and exit boldly by the main entrance. Freed from the stuffy atmosphere of the convent, Rafi would then proceed up Cristo Street to Calle de la Luna, there to per-form at some of the seedier establishments of the capital city. These were largely all the same. A few brick steps led up from the street and through a narrow doorway into a hazy room filled with the noise of raucous human beings enjoying drinks and the preambles to love-making. In the main taproom, where the thick fog of burning tobacco blended with the faint-est tinges of urine, a beat-up bar backed by a long mirror ex-tended the entire length of the room. Cheap art covered the pock-marked walls stained with tobacco juice and splattered bugs, and invariably featured a likeness of El Águila Blanca, a romanticized mountain outlaw and folk champion venerated by the iconoclastic patrons.

Rafi leaned closer to Ashford to allow his voice to be heard over the buzz of the plaza. "I played for tips, which were always very generous given the brisk business of those venues in a port city like San Juan. The girls would bring me cigars and madeira, and with a broad smile place them atop the piano. Some of them occasionally invited me upstairs. They would lean close to my ear and whisper hoarsely—here Rafi pitched his voice up into a light falsetto—"*Oh Rafaelito,* we have a new instrument we want you to play," or another time, when they had given up on musical innuendos and said, 'Our mackerel tabby recently had kittens, and they are *so very* adorable." Rafi then burst out laughing. "They were so disappointed when I told them that the piano was plenty hard already and that cats give me a rash."

Ashford beamed. "Their cats gave you a rash? *Really!* So, I take it you don't have any love interests?"

"Certainly not there. Never mix business with pleasure. Yourself?"

Ashford gave a half-grin. "Not at present. My fiancée left me for a banker when I joined the Medical Corps. Didn't want to be dragged all over the world chasing wars, she said. Probably a good thing considering the abundance of womanly beauty in this place. Quite the thing, really."

Rafi nodded enthusiastically. *"No hay nada como la belleza de las puertorriqueñas.* You will not find prettier women anywhere in the world."

Ashford changed gears, "What happened with your family, now that the war is over and the island has a new government?"

"My brother José was sent to Cuba to study pharmacy, but I wanted to see my father's native country, the 'Colossus of the North,' *Los Estados Unidos.* My father sent me to New Haven to the laboratory of John Robert Smith at Yale. I had just turned seventeen years old. It was a revelation, and my love became the science of hematology. Preparing blood smears, counting red cells, and distinguishing among the half-dozen subtypes of white blood cells: I love it all. In less than a year, I learned more microscopy than any of the graduates of the medical school. I had always thought about becoming a man of science and studying mysterious things which can only be seen through a microscope."

Ashford nodded in agreement. "The microscope is the instrument of the future. Every day, it seems, we can link more microbes to diseases. Take malaria, for example."

"I am no stranger to malaria and quinine," Rafi responded. "I have had it twice—even rich people get the disease."

Suddenly, Rafi then lowered his voice and looked around uncomfortably. "I would have gladly joined the medical class when I was invited, had it not been for my visceral and overwhelming dislike for *coprogenous material*!"

Ashford stared at Rafi with a blank expression. "For *what*?"

Rafi leaned forward, cleared his throat, and stammered somewhat louder, "Co-pro-ge-nous material!"

"Rafi, what on Earth is that?"

Distressed, Rafi practically shouted, *"Feces! Poop! Doo-doo!"*

Ashford's mouth fell open.

Rafi looked down at his feet. "Yes, Dr. Ashford. I sweat, my legs wobble, my head spins, I start to black out and I get a wave of uncontrollable nausea. I have experienced this from as early as I can remember. I have secretly tried some rather unorthodox ways to overcome my aversion, but with no luck. If anything, it's gotten worse, and I fear I may never be a clinician."

Ashford was having difficulty not laughing in his companion's face. "Nonsense! A minor impediment, that's all," the lieutenant said loudly, hardly believing that this accomplished person could harbor such a trivial phobia.

Recovering his composure, a red-faced Rafi continued. "I was still in New Haven when the *Maine* exploded in Havana in February. Anti-war protests tore through the university while the United States made increasingly outrageous demands from Spain."

"You must have made it back just in time!"

"I arrived in Puerto Rico the week after war was declared to find my father confined at *La Princesa* in Old San Juan, a prison where inmates routinely disappear without a trace. The governor had ordered my father arrested on trumped-up charges. As a rich and well-connected American he was a risk to the interests of the Spanish."

Ashford's forehead furrowed. "Is he still there?"

Rafi shook his head. "He was finally released after a month of abuse and exiled for the duration of the conflict. I once considered myself a loyal Spanish subject, but I could no longer close my eyes to their cruel and incompetent regime. Their treatment of my father was the last straw. It convinced me to support the invasion."

Ashford drew his brows together. "How did you come to be here in Mayagüez? Your interests lie mostly in the capital, do they not?

"Soon after, I learned that my own arrest was only a matter of time. Staying in San Juan was no longer possible." Rafi related how friends arranged his escape from the city in a leaky yawl under cover of darkness. He had made his way across the mountains and finally slipped into the town of Guánica, seemingly one of many street vendors selling mangoes.

Ashford drew briskly from his cigarette. "Rafi, *I'll be…!*"

"I waited there for most of June and July until the American army arrived. I invited myself to Army headquarters, and to their great surprise introduced myself in perfect English. Schwan attached me to the invasion force, and with them, I marched through Yauco, San Germán, the Silva Heights, and Mayagüez. When the hostilities ended, Colonel Burke asked me to serve with the Medical Corps."

Rafi sat back in his chair. "And that, my friend, is how I find myself in this outdoor café in Mayagüez, drinking the local coffee and tasting a savory *fricasé de pollo* in your delightful company."

Ashford smiled broadly as he signaled for the check. "Rafi, your story has bowled me over six ways from Sunday." If this man was half as good a medical assistant as a revolutionary, they should get along famously. Their meeting had taken up only about an hour, and since it was only the early afternoon, Ashford decided to put the new relationship to the test right away in the wards of Mayagüez's municipal hospital.

Chapter Ten

EL HOSPITAL DE SAN ANTONIO

When they reached the hospital, Rafi stopped at the doors to admire the impressive façade. The *Hospital de San Antonio* in Mayagüez was a solid, two-story structure from 1865, built in the style typical of Spanish civil architecture of the mid-nineteenth century. It was constructed mainly of stone and brick, and a light-yellow color covered the outside walls, interrupted only by an off-white for the frames around the windows and dark green for the wooden shutters. The doors stood wide open, as they did year-round, from one hour before sunrise to one hour after sunset, to receive all who had use of the institution, from doctors, nurses, and chaplains to orderlies and patients of all classes and races.

Entering through the main double doors into the courtyard never failed to fill Ashford with boundless energy, as if he had downed ten cups of the local black coffee in one gulp. He had never seen a hospital quite like this one, with its airy architecture of repeating arches and spacious wards, which allowed fresh Caribbean breezes to constantly replenish the poisoned air of illness. He was immeasurably happy to be working here.

Ashford ushered his new colleague into the courtyard to admire the small fountain in the center, decorated with bronze cherubim that spouted water from sundry places into a multi-tiered stone basin. From this central patio, they could see the series of spacious, high-ceilinged rooms surrounding it that served as the patient wards. A white stone staircase led up to the second floor, which housed the kitchen, storage, library, and offices, along with a smallish but well-equipped operating room.

Everywhere, the odors of alcohol and ether fused into a

pungent but invisible cloud which escaped through the open windows into the streets.

Rafi crinkled his nose. "If there is something you can count on, it is the unmistakable smell of a hospital. You know, from five blocks away a blind man can easily follow the vapors to the entrance."

Ashford smiled. "I rather like it. It may seem strange, but it gives me a charge, really gets me ready to work."

Rafi shook his head. "Well, for what it's worth, it was the same in New Haven."

"The hospital boils every drop of water they use in large iron pots over open fires behind the building." Ashford then broke into a wide grin. "I don't know how they keep the ether from getting back there and blowing us up to heaven!"

Rafi responded with laughter. "I sure hope that doesn't happen. In any event, it is an impressive hospital. The city must take great pride in it."

Rafi followed Ashford into one of the wards. It was lined with three rows of five cots each. The ward they had entered was for patients who did not fit into the other three wards, which were devoted to infectious diseases, cancer victims, and surgical cases. They surveyed the room. Some of the patients in this mixed ward suffered from mild mental illness, not deemed severe enough for the asylum. These souls were kept in this decidedly happier place through the intercession of its compassionate chief of staff, José García Rodríguez, who had been superbly trained in medicine and surgery at Columbia University.

Other patients here were American soldiers, transferred from the Army tent hospital in the swampy bowl outside the city to this markedly healthier environment. While here, the soldiers were under Ashford's care, and he began his rounds with Rafi in tow. The military patients that morning were for the most part stable, with several suffering from old gunshot wounds from the battles at Silva Heights and Las Marías. A month had passed since the fighting had ended, and the much-improved men were nearing their discharge from the hospital. At most, they required a dressing change or the occasional wound check for signs of delayed infection. Two soldiers still suffered from the lingering effects of typhoid, but in all of the others the prolonged high fevers were either resolving or had already resolved. All that they required now was supportive care with pasteurized milk and juices along with an improved rendition of the ever-present beef broth.

Dr. García Rodríguez entered the room. The head of the medical staff was short and burly with abundant curly black hair and thick glasses which gave him a professorial air. The two physicians greeted one another warmly.

"Good morning, Dr. García. I would like you to meet my new assistant and interpreter, Mr. Rafael Moore."

Rafi acknowledged the introduction in Spanish, and shook García's hand firmly. The latter began by saying, "Dr. Ashford, I am always honored when you ask me to consult on your patients, but I am afraid this time, it is I who must ask for your help."

"Most certainly, how can I help you?"

"If you would follow me to the surgical ward, there is a child I would like you to examine with me."

Ashford eyes lit up. "Of course, Dr. García, it would be a pleasure."

As the three men headed down the balustraded corridor, the Puerto Rican physician explained the case. "The patient in question is a sixteen-year-old boy who arrived last night because of bloody vomiting. His parents have observed a gradual deterioration of his appearance over the last six weeks. But when he began to vomit dark red clots, they were frightened and brought him in from their home in Lares, twenty miles away."

The trio entered the room which had been designated as the surgical ward, a large square room topped by a tall, flat ceiling crisscrossed by exposed supports of thick wooden beams. The cots were arranged into three neat rows of five beds each, with roughly five feet between patients. Every bed, whether occupied or not, was meticulously made up with immaculate white sheets. In one of the cots in the middle row was a pale, thin boy, with large black eyes that darted around the room with alarm. Next to him were his parents, looking equally concerned. It struck Ashford that if this was the patient in question, he looked more like seven or eight years old rather than the reported sixteen. Rafi translated for Ashford while the two physicians listened to the boy's parents tell their story. The couple revealed that over the last six weeks he had become increasingly lethargic and withdrawn. His occasional abdominal pains had become more persistent and pronounced, his bowels had started to manifest some light bleeding, and most concerning of all, his abdomen had begun to grow alarmingly as his limbs and face became progressively thinner. The concerned parents had turned increasingly desperate after seeing their son vomit large quantities of dark blood following a soft dinner of boiled plantains and rice.

First, García and Ashford took turns performing the physical examination. The boy's abdomen had expanded so frightfully that the unfortunate child could hardly breathe against the pressure it exerted on his chest. Large, distended veins were visible under his translucent skin, running up the length of the abdomen and onto his breastbone and ribs. Examining the liver, the two physicians agreed that it was mildly enlarged, particularly toward the breastbone. Next, they searched for the nature of the swelling that was making the abdomen as tight as a drum. First García and then Ashford tapped their patient's swollen belly with staccato raps of their fingers and then, between their two hands, each took turns grasping the abdomen and firmly guiding it in alternating movements, first to the left and then to the right, repeating this motion several times.

The two colleagues looked knowingly at one another. There was no question in their minds that the increased size of the abdomen was due to fluid, and lots of it, probably somewhere in the range of six to eight quarts. Lastly, the physicians examined the spleen. The organ was massively enlarged, so much so that its forward edge, which normally was hidden under the ribcage, was clearly visible as a ridge under the skin of the boy's left flank.

García rose from the bedside and said glumly, "For my money, I have to say that this is a very severe case of liver failure."

Ashford nodded. "Agreed, but what is underneath it all

and how to treat him? That is the problem."

"He looks anemic as well," added Rafi, picking up the patient's clammy right hand.

García looked down at the languid figure on the bed. "There is no question that this patient suffers from anemia—his skin tone is unmistakable. In fact, it would be unheard of for a patient from the Lares mountains not to have some degree of anemia."

With his fingers, Ashford gently raised the boy's upper eyelids. "He's clearly low on hemoglobin, but the question is whether that is the reason he has deteriorated so quickly. I doubt that it is."

García shook his head. "His anemia is chronic and making his recovery more difficult, but my impression is that there is another process at work here. Some unidentified factor is operating on a different system and at a different level. It is this undetermined element that must have caused this sudden decline."

Ashford passed his fingers through his hair, puzzled. "I agree that the main problem here is liver failure, and that anemia in this case is a red herring. The degree of enlargement of the spleen is worrisome, exceeding what is normal by a factor of three or four. I propose that whatever is causing the liver failure is also leading to the enlargement of the spleen."

"The spleen size is indeed disquieting," García agreed. "But the true danger here comes from the amount of fluid in his belly, unheard of in someone so young. It is asphyxiating him."

Rafi kept translating the discussion for the parents as it occurred, artfully sanitizing its more graphic and distressing points.

García and Ashford agreed that to provide some much-needed relief, a significant volume of the fluid should be extracted as soon as possible. Curtains were brought in to shield the other patients from the spectacle. Next, the skin over the mid-portion of the boy's abdomen was scrubbed repeatedly with alcohol.

García smiled at his patient and looked directly into his nervous eyes. With a soothing voice, he said in Spanish, "This may look scary, but it will help ease your pain and improve your breathing. You will feel a slight pinch, and then all that bad water inside you will begin to come out into this basin. If you have pain, please let me know. Do you have any questions before I start?"

The delicate figure looked at García leaning over him, and weakly asked, "*¿Doctor, me voy a morir aquí?*"[5]

The doctor put a hand on his patient's bony shoulder. "No, my friend, you are not going to die. Just the opposite, we are going to make you feel much better."

With a long needle and rubber tube, both sterilized in boiling salt water, García expertly inserted the needle two centimeters above the boy's belly button, and aspirating carefully, allowed several pints of straw-colored fluid to drain into a large basin over the course of thirty minutes. The patient's breathing rapidly eased, and a look of relief spread across the boy's face. The doctors shook hands with their brave patient, who, as they learned only then, was named Cirilo. The physicians approached their next patient while excitedly analyzing the case, which they agreed required clarification through further tests. Meanwhile, looks of concern and uncertainty had started to spread through the other patients of the ward as the doctors discussed Cirilo's condition in strange and incomprehensible English.

Because the causes of Cirilo's illness could be many, and the truly effective treatments were very few, his physicians harbored scant hope that his fluid would not return soon, requiring repeated drainage procedures until his liver either recovered, or gave out entirely. All they could do in the meantime, was ensure he received the best care possible. This consisted of restricting his salt, and replacing the fluid drained from his abdomen with water and pasteurized juices, supplemented by remedies of fenugreek, juiced gourds, boiled *garbanzos* and other strange nostrums which to Ashford approached the magical. The plain truth was that Cirilo's underlying illness was very advanced, and his survival was very much in doubt.

Back in his comfortable hotel room, with a belly full of steak

---

5 "Am I going to die here?"

and potatoes instead of the straw- colored fluid of illness that filled Cirilo's, Bailey Ashford poured his worries into his violin. Puerto Rico had begun to captivate him, and he was beginning to feel very much at home in this proud land with so many strange traditions. His heart ached for its people, so blessed with the beauties of nature, and yet so cursed by the ravages of poverty and disease. This sharp dichotomy left him with a sense of profound impotence. He let out a long sigh, and shaking his head began to pass his bow gently back and forth over the strings so that his instrument filled the night with a dark and gloomy melody.

Chapter Eleven

AGUADILLA! OCTOBER 1898

With the end of the fighting, an aura of generalized confusion descended upon the large mountain estates, mostly coffee and tobacco plantations owned by wealthy Creoles. A few overzealous peasants, thinking that their new American masters appreciated some show of military devotion, attacked defenseless *élites,* killing many of them and burning their farms. The Army was kept busy restoring order among the *jíbaros,* a task complicated by a lack of competent interpreters and the inaccessible terrain. In the developing chaos, increasingly reckless bandits patrolling the countryside shot indiscriminately at anybody who happened to come along.

The worst of these were led by José Maldonado, El Águila Blanca, a ruthless mountain outlaw who in the vacuum of the Spanish retreat had set up what was practically his own independent country. Maldonado defended his turf using heavily armed thugs, whom he ruled despotically. The bandits specialized in kidnapping wealthy landowners whom they ransomed for hefty sums, assuming they managed to survive weeks of ill treatment and starvation. After the Americans' arrival, El Águila expanded his targets to include vulnerable soldiers he could pick off from picket or patrol duty, reasoning that the Army could be made to part with funds faster than the planters. To encourage the Army to pay, Maldonado's victims were required to write to headquarters daily, including in their letters the finger or toe lost in their most recent torture session. Nerves were frayed among the soldiers and nobody dared to leave their encampments except in large groups of well-armed men, for to travel alone might easily mean ambush and death.

This open lawlessness plagued the country surrounding Mayagüez when, a few weeks after the military occupation of the city, Colonel Burke sent for Ashford.

The colonel paced his office as he gave Ashford his orders.

"Lieutenant," he barked, "you are to ride over the northwest mountains to Aguadilla and prepare a report on the conditions of the countryside and the physical state of the local people you encounter. To get to Aguadilla, you will be crossing the territory of this man Maldonado and his followers, who, as you know, have developed a taste for abducting and ransoming American soldiers. If you encounter this Águila bastard, treat him and his followers as you would any enemy force within sovereign U.S. territory. You will depart tomorrow. Be ready to submit your findings within two weeks."

The doctor acknowledged the order with a crisp salute and went to look for his interpreter.

"Rafi, Colonel Burke is sending us on a fact-finding mission to Aguadilla. One week, possibly as long as two."

Next, Ashford went in search of the one man he most needed to help organize the expedition. He found Sergeant First Class John Moretti collecting his winnings from the latest hand in an anarchic game of poker. He was about thirty years old, with a large head topped by unruly black hair and built like an oversized icebox, with the energy to match his size.

"We must cover twenty-five miles of country roads over remote terrain controlled by Águila and his thugs, Ashford explained. "We will need no less than two dozen men on horseback armed well, but with economy and intelligence. On the way to Aguadilla, we will gather information on the health, diet, and living conditions of the inhabitants."

The sergeant grinned broadly. "No worries, Lieutenant. If this outlaw Eagle fellow happens to cross our path, we'll make him wish he'd never met us."

Moretti assembled a platoon of volunteers. From the surrounding farms, the soldiers procured what to the islanders passed for horses, but to the Americans represented an equine version of the Puerto Rican peasant: impossibly small and scrawny, more like oversized rats with ribs protruding through meager flanks and hip bones pointing awkwardly in opposite directions. How such animals could carry anything on their backs, let alone a fully provisioned soldier, was never satisfactorily explained to the American soldiers, accustomed as they were to the fine Morgans of the U.S. armed forces.

With some trepidation, the troops mounted and headed north to Aguadilla, a midsized town on the Western coast where local lore held that Columbus had anchored 400 years earlier. Given the relative importance of Mayagüez and Aguadilla, Ashford expected the way to be decent, with well-kept trails and the occasional paved stretch of road. As soon as they left behind the colonial houses and wide streets of Mayagüez, the force entered the steep hills leading to the town of Añasco, half a dozen miles to the north.

The roads were mostly deserted, but occasionally the platoon overtook a barefoot pedestrian or two trekking between towns. The locals regarded the soldiers with a mixture of awe and suspicion, feelings that were reciprocated fully. Ashford, for his part, judged these encounters more often with a medical eye. The people they passed were universally short, almost without exception far below the average height of the soldiers, and impossibly slim, perhaps more accurately described as gaunt.

But what struck the young doctor most were the skin tones of the native Puerto Ricans. If white, their faces exhibited an odd, unusually severe pallor, truly spectral in character, and most striking in its universality and uniformity. In the few people of color, dark skin tones were drained of their richness, substituted by a certain peculiar beige in which usually beautiful browns gave way to the ashen grays of illness. The locals on the road became more numerous as the soldiers approached Añasco, and with the increasing encounters, the small force began seeing children afflicted with the distended abdomens of severe malnutrition and protein deficiency.

The dusty column of silent soldiers was deeply shocked by this introduction to the *jíbaros*—the agricultural laborers of the island, almost all of them white, with only the occasional person of mixed race. Regardless of skin color, however, they were all universally destitute. In Añasco the troopers procured new mounts, these horses seemingly even more precarious than the ones in the first group, and the journey continued toward the next town. As they rode, they continued to encounter others who are equally ill and impoverished, and by nightfall, they drifted into Aguada, to rest for the night.

The next morning, Ashford and his party arrived at their destination. Aguadilla was a prosperous port town of about five thousand people, rich with commerce and surrounded by vast fields of sugar cane, which, from shore to piedmont, extended in one uniform expanse of slender, light green stalks. The city center itself was compact and elegant, organized around a small plaza which served as the nerve center of the population. Across the narrow streets on each side of the square, Ashford could see the predominant pattern he would soon recognize in all the towns of the island: the small white church in a subdued baroque, the ever-important pharmacy specializing in bizarre concoctions of little or no medical value, the *alcaldía* (town hall) with its arched entrance, and on the remaining side, the attractive houses of well-to-do planters of coffee, tobacco, or sugar.

The town stretched for one mile along its long axis, from north to south along the sea, while only tentatively venturing inland. The beautiful, green-crested Monte Jaicoa rose behind it with slopes completely covered by orange, lemon, and palm trees. Only one, thin city block separated the plaza from the sea, accessible by walking westward past a minor Spanish fort of eleven guns known as the Fortín de la Concepción. Sunset beachgoers often enjoyed spectacular color displays, with flares of pink and orange shot across the sky as if the Fortín's cannons had cheerfully opened fire on the bay.

Aguadilla marked the northernmost point of the island under United States administration, having peacefully welcomed the American army the third week of September. By the time Ashford's small expedition arrived, the transfer of buildings and weaponry was complete and the town was under the command of a United States colonel. It was thus a strictly routine matter for the arriving platoon to settle comfortably in the town and for Ashford to continue his observations unmolested.

Waiting for their arrival at the small, improvised headquarters was a letter, which the desk sergeant handed to Ashford. The envelope, written in a most beautiful hand, was addressed to "The Principal Medical Officer or Science Officer."

Sir,
I will be much obliged if you could meet me in front of the church of San Carlos tomorrow at 3 p.m. With your permission, I will show you around my native town and engage you in a discussion of the state of affairs as it pertains to the general health and illnesses of the common man of these parts.
I am respectfully yours,
A. Stahl

Ashford pondered it for a minute before tucking it away. The sergeant knew nothing of the origin of the letter. After reporting to their commander, Ashford took Rafi and headed to the town hall to inquire into Mr. Stahl and the reasons he could possibly have to contact an American military physician.

In contrast to the desk sergeant, the town hall secretary had no difficulty answering questions about the letter's author. "Don Agustín is a medical doctor, very well-known across the island. He lived here in Aguadilla as a youth but moved to the capital years ago. I recall that he was rather unusual—clearly very gifted, but somewhat eccentric. I think his parents were German or Dutch, something along those lines. Now, he mostly studies plants."

With his interest piqued, Ashford resolved to attend the proposed meeting. At the appointed time, Rafi and Ashford sat waiting on a wooden bench facing the San Carlos church. The lieutenant's uniform easily marked him as an American soldier, and before long his counterpart had located him. A tall, thin man about fifty years old approached and extended his hand, saying in perfect English colored by a distinct Germanic accent, "Good afternoon, I am Agustín Stahl, doctor of medicine. Welcome to Puerto Rico."

Ashford firmly shook the proffered hand. "Dr. Stahl, it is a great pleasure to meet you. I am Lieutenant Bailey Ashford, medical officer of the Provisional Division under General Schwan. This is Mr. Rafael Moore, my interpreter, although it appears we will not be needing him."

"No, Dr. Ashford, I don't believe we will. I speak fluent English as well as German, French, and of course, Spanish. Pay no mind to my accent. The locals suppress a smile when I speak their tongue with my *doichismos*, the result of a German father and a Dutch mother."

The lieutenant thought that he himself compared rather unfavorably with Dr. Stahl, knowing as he did a total of one-and-a-quarter languages, if he counted the medical Latin he had learned at Georgetown. Ashford regarded his new acquaintance with interest. His height, fair complexion, piercing blue eyes, and formal European deportment singled him out like a white egret among some short reeds. Beyond this, Dr. Stahl appeared weary, as if he carried some mighty burdens deep within him.

"Lieutenant," Stahl continued, "I am fortunate to have found you, as I am fortunate the United States Army has finally arrived. Yesterday morning, I returned to Aguadilla from Santo Domingo, where I have been exiled for my views regarding Puerto Rican independence. For several months, I was without a country, hopelessly lost away from my island. When I heard that the Spanish army had been beaten and expelled from southwestern Puerto Rico, I made arrangements to cross over from Hispaniola without delay. There is an expectation among our many patriots that the United States will grant us self-rule, as they have promised Cuba."

Ashford sidestepped the implied question. "As a military man, I cannot comment on any political matter. What I can say, I will say to you as a colleague. We have all been most profoundly affected by our first glimpse of the inhabitants of these parts. Surely there is a way to help your unfortunate countrymen; they appear to be severely undernourished, frightfully thin, and markedly pale, to the very last one. I found myself staring at them indiscreetly as I passed them on the way from Mayagüez."

Stahl sighed. "Therein lies my desire to meet with you today, Lieutenant. Will you please come with me? I wish to show you around, if you can spare the time."

Rafi excused himself, and the two physicians began their stroll toward the bay. Walking at a leisurely pace, they arrived at the narrow road fronting the ocean within a few minutes. A man and a young boy about ten years old sat on the sand beside the road, slicing the tops off from some coconuts with a *machete* to sell for three cents apiece. The pair broke into wide smiles and rose from their work when they saw Stahl.

"*¡Buenas tardes, doctor!*"

"*Buenas tardes a ustedes,*" replied the doctor.

Both father and son showed clear signs of the malady that so baffled Ashford. He studied the pair closely: they were clearly Caucasians of a very pale-white hue, with green eyes sunk into their sockets, skin hanging in folds from their forearms and clavicles that were too easily traced. The father had swollen ankles, the son, a swollen abdomen. Ashford, the father, and Stahl conversed as the old doctor translated for all. Unnoticed at first, the child squatted once again. Ashford watched, appalled, as the boy scooped up a fist full of sand from the ground, let some of it filter through his thin fingers, and shoved the rest into his mouth without so much as a blink. Suddenly realizing what the boy was doing, the father grabbed his hands and forced them open, shaking the remaining sand onto the beach.

Clearly embarrassed, the man muttered, "Excuse me, *querido doctor* Stahl, but Toñito has gotten into this habit of eating *tierra*. He prefers the dark soil of our garden, but when he finds himself here, he will eat sand just the same."

Ashford stared incredulously. He had read of the practice of geophagia, the eating of earth and sand, in medical books, but never imagined he would see it.

Stahl responded nonchalantly. "Very well Mario, bring him by the house tomorrow, and I will see what can be done for him."

The father beamed. "*Gracias doctor,* I will bring you a hen and some plantains, or, if you prefer, maybe a dozen or so *aguacates.*"

Agreeing with a smile and a wave, the two physicians continued their walk.

Stahl turned toward his younger colleague and asked, "Dr. Ashford, what are your thoughts on the young man, if you please?"

The question caught Ashford unprepared. "Ah... I was struck by the young boy's eating of mineral matter, particularly when there are wonderful fruits all around and juicy coconuts right in front of him."

"That young boy, as you call him, is seventeen years old."

Ashford stared at Stahl. "Surely not!"

"Oh yes, quite so," the German doctor nodded, marking Ashford's shock. "He looks nine or ten, but he is at least seven years older, severely undernourished, underdeveloped in body and intelligence, and completely dependent on his father. As you know, the distended abdomen is a sign of his severe protein deficiency, and, as you will also recall, the eating of soil and sand can frequently be seen in patients with severely depleted blood."

Over the next four hours, the men encountered and bantered with a dozen locals, passing many others with a friendly wave. Clearly, Agustín Stahl was a man who was deeply loved and respected here, and many of those they spoke with bore a close resemblance to the man and boy on the beach. Night came slowly, the sun setting in vibrant tones of peach, amber-gold, and blood red which glinted across the Bay of Aguadilla. Gradually, they made their way back to the deserted plaza immersed in the deepening shadows.

Dr. Stahl turned to his companion, looking weary. "Well, Dr. Ashford, you have gotten to meet our malady in person, the omnipresent condition we call *la anemia*. Severe anemia is the rule in Puerto Rico. If you think it common here in Aguadilla, outside the larger towns it is even more so. Chronic anemia is so widespread that death certificates commonly report a person's demise as due to '*natural causes, la anemia.*'"

"Most people suffer from an advanced case," Stahl continued. The total volume of the blood in their circulation is normal, but the number of red cells it carries is precariously diminished. Instead of healthy blood, a strange, straw-colored liquid runs through the veins of those most severely affected. *La anemia* does not discriminate between man, woman, child, or infant—and it is darkly mysterious and selfish about its or-igins. At times, the disease improves when people move to the city, but soon resurfaces if they return to the *campo*. In some, eating beef and pork will bring improvement, in others, diar-rhea and death. The coffee pickers in the mountains are gener-ally more commonly and more severely afflicted than the cane cutters of the coast, and across all groups, darker-skinned people seem to fare better."

"Puzzling group of facts, no doubt," Ashford responded. "What do you see by way of symptoms?"

"First and foremost, pervasive exhaustion, a universal lack of energy. Imagine going to harvest coffee or cut sugar cane with your hemoglobin hovering at half of what it should be. For me, an even greater puzzle than the origin of this disease is that those afflicted can do *any* work at all, however occasion-ally. By the greatest good fortune, the warm climate allows for year-round food gardens and provides fruits which can be foraged close to home. Otherwise, nobody but the wealthy could live here.

"And the patients' blood smears—?"

"Yes, well… for that information, I will refer you to my col-league in Ponce, Dr. Manuel Zeno Gandía. He reports nothing unusual in the blood smears except the paucity of red cells. I expect that after the peace treaty is signed, the Army will likely assign you to the hospital in Ponce, which is by far the largest and best equipped on the south coast. Anticipating this possibility, I will write to Zeno at once introducing you."

Ashford gave a slight bow. "I am most grateful for your offer."

Stahl extended his hand in farewell. "Dr. Ashford," he said, "forgive my silly pun, but what we desperately need here, medically and scientifically, is some *new blood*—a new group of physicians, a new look at the clinical picture, some novel scientific insights. Here, the same scientists search aimlessly for answers while the disease strangles the nation." Ashford shook the proffered hand, and the two physicians parted with a warm farewell.

Stahl's revelations left Ashford at a loss for words. The pub-lic health conditions on this island war-prize were starting to appear to be far worse than he had imagined. By every indication, Puerto Rico was suffering a crisis of calamitous proportions. It began to dawn on him that the American government had been unaware of this before deciding to invade. Worse yet, in just a few weeks Spain would hand over complete political control to the United States and, along with it, full responsibility for a catastrophe in the making.

The rest of the week Ashford spent with Rafi gathering impressions, interviewing locals and condensing his observations into a succinct report for the chief medical officer in San Juan. Ashford wrote his report the afternoon before returning to Mayagüez and included a summary of his impressions of the *jíbaros*. On the only official stationery to be had, grimy with the mud of the passage through the hills, the young physician concluded his report: "To the very last person, the local peasants appear as a pale, dropsical, unhealthy-looking class, evidently suffering from lack of meat, although there must be something else, not yet understood..."

His work complete, Ashford, Rafi, and their detachment began their return journey to Mayagüez. Ashford turned the cases he'd seen over and over in his mind, revisiting them so often that he soon wondered if he weren't sickening as well. As it turned out, it was not simply his imagination playing tricks on him. While on the long ride back to Mayagüez, Ashford developed a nagging headache, followed by nausea and finally, bouts of semi-projectile vomiting to which he surrendered awkwardly from the back of his horse. A few miles outside the city, he worsened further, becoming delirious and desperately cold despite the oppressive heat. He collapsed into his bunk immediately upon arriving, shaking the bed uncontrollably with recurring chills. When his urine turned a most peculiar amber color, he decided to seek help. Ashford staggered into the infirmary where he practically collapsed into the arms of his old coworker from the typhoid outbreak, Lieutenant McAndrew.

McAndrew performed a full evaluation and rendered his verdict. "Bailey, I suspect that like so many others, you are coming down with tertian fever from contracting malaria. You have almost all of the early signs, and I can already see the color of jaundice creeping into your eyes. You can expect a high fever every third day like clockwork until the quinine begins to take effect. Few things taste worse, but if you mix it with carbonated sugar water, it's not half bad. Can you believe that in India, the Brits add gin? They swear the concoction is the best-known malarial remedy."

Ashford did not share his colleague's enthusiasm, rasping, "Right now I couldn't give a rat's ass about the stupid Brits and India. I have never felt so lousy in my life. I would ask you to shoot me, but you'd be wasting a perfectly good bullet."

McAndrew smiled back. "You feel awful now, but quinine is a proven remedy. Get it down, and you will surely improve in a matter of days."

Ashford gave a violent shake, accidentally biting his tongue. "In a matter of days, there may not be anything left of me to treat…"

With this new diagnosis, the lieutenant was sent by horse-drawn ambulance thirty miles to Ponce. Once there, he was added to the roster of soldiers convalescing inside his old haunt, the hospital ship *Relief,* anchored half a mile offshore. Amidst recurring spells of delirium and fever that returned with uncanny precision every third day to the hour, the physician-patient passed ten days onboard. He subsisted on liquids and bland foods washed down with repugnantly bitter quinine water for breakfast, lunch, and dinner.

The only saving grace to the malaria strain in Puerto Rico was that young, healthy soldiers seldom died from it. The parasites wreaked havoc on the body for several weeks, and then, knocked down by the combination of quinine and the immune system, they retreated to renew their attacks at some other time, usually in a few months, or occasionally, years.

By early November, Lieutenant Ashford found himself much improved and ready to return to Mayagüez. He was anxious not only to resume his medical duties there, but also to learn more about some of the local ladies. It was no secret that strong bonds had developed between several American officers and some of the wealthy young women in Mayagüez. Ashford, for his part, admitted that he found most Puerto Ri-

can women ravishing. He had felt deprived of female attention since arriving on the island and was ready to win their
admiration. This he planned to do with stories of combat her-
oism, as well as ill-advised, graphic tales of his surgical ex-
ploits. Soon he would have to change his approach; the *señoritas* were finding his war stories exceedingly distasteful.

Chapter Twelve

A REQUEST FOR HELP, NOVEMBER 1898

Ashford resumed working at both the military and *San Antonio* hospitals in Mayagüez as soon as he recovered from malaria. Cirilo, the young man with liver failure, lingered in the ward, following an up-and-down clinical course in which he progressively got better, but never completely well, and then worsened, but never seriously enough to die. This pattern went on for over a month, a testament to the superb care he was receiving, without which he would have already succumbed to his illness.

Cirilo was known in his village of Pezuela as *el enjuto,* "the thin one," because even among his scrawny companions he stood out as particularly angular. He lived with his parents and two brothers on the road to Las Marías, near Lares, where they had seen the invading Americans pass in front of their home as they pursued the Spanish.

Before the conflict reached their shores, Cirilo and his family had for many years lived a peaceful life, measured in personal successes and heartaches shared among the community. About two hundred yards away from their small house, Cirilo's parents and some neighbors had partially dammed a good-sized creek that emptied into the *Río Prieto.* This created a rather large *charca,* a freshwater pond of about half an acre in surface area and up to eight feet in depth, in which people could bathe, wash, do laundry, fish for shrimp, or just fool around. The incomplete obstruction of the dam allowed for some lazy circulation within the *charca,* assuring that its water was deceptively clear, somewhere between translucent and barely murky. The hot season from May until October never failed to find people either in or around the water.

Occasionally, there was an outbreak of stomach illness, or coughing, or some other brief malady, which a few malcontents blamed on the pond. They argued that the dam was not God's work, and that altering the natural order of things was sure to bring them bad luck. Nobody denied the strange fact that after enjoying that beautiful and soothing body of water, not infrequently the most hellish irritation of the legs and feet followed. This *piquiña* itch could be relieved with poultices of onion, garlic, ginger, and *cúrcuma,* the turmeric that had recently become the latest medicinal rage. Cirilo, who was a huge fan of the *charca* and therefore no stranger to the itch, had become a truly gifted herbalist by experimenting with ingenious remedies.

Life might have continued in this way for Cirillo until, over the course of a few weeks late in the summer, his energy began to wane and his belly began to swell, alarming his parents. He lost the desire to feed himself and had been slowly wasting away for over a month, when the appearance of the bloody vomitus sent the family rushing down the mountain trails toward Mayagüez.

Cirilo went into the hospital, met García Rodríguez and "*el doctor americano*," underwent the ritual minor indignities of the "complete" physical examination, and settled happily into his new surroundings. For the boy, the place was pure heaven: a private cot elevated off the floor, a dry roof, clean sheets, regular meals, pretty nurses and other unimaginable luxuries. If he hadn't felt so lousy, he would have wished it could go on forever.

And yet, end it did for Cirilo. After an initial period of stabilization that lasted five weeks, his ups and downs settled into a worrisome trend including more downs than ups. The fluid in his abdomen would stubbornly return only days after each uncomfortable draining. Nights were punctuated by fearsome episodes of dark vomiting, and even drinking inordinate amounts of fluid could not keep up with his insatiable thirst. On the tenth day of his final downturn, Cirilo's belly pain suddenly became unbearable.

Now, the most cursory examination of his abdomen elicited groans of pain from the boy, and a mere accidental bumping of the cot resulted in agonizing screams. Through tears of fright and frustration, Cirilo bravely endured what he could. The sad irony in the lengthy course of this illness was not lost on his doctors: now completely certain of their new diagnosis, they were equally certain that nothing more could be done for their patient. Cirilo had developed what the doctors told his parents was spontaneous peritonitis, a generalized infection of the miserable fluid trapped in his belly. Within a few hours, he would die.

With the end rapidly approaching, the doctors were free to make a liberal use of one of the few drugs that was as available as it was effective— morphine. With morphine injections, Cirilo was made somewhat comfortable. He passed away in a strange delirium of opioids and sickness while his parents looked on helplessly.

Nothing can prepare a physician for the death of a young patient, especially a death so horrid and brutal, and even more so when feeling completely powerless to stop it. If any benefit to society could be gained from the death of this young man, it was now up to the doctors to find it. But to gain even the smallest hint of a silver lining within this dark cloud would require a post-mortem.

Autopsies at the *San Antonio* had been uncommon. But just in the last year, due to an explosion in medical knowledge and new techniques, the number of procedures had multiplied exponentially. Well-trained physicians like García and Ashford could perform a good autopsy, recognizing that this was the only way to solve the mystery of a patient's death. It was another matter altogether to convince Cirilo's family to allow it. Cirilo's parents, like many *jíbaros*, held the pragmatic view that autopsies were bizarre rituals celebrated behind closed doors, in which strangers peered at parts meant to be hidden within the holy vessels of their loved ones, vessels made in the Image of the Creator. For the *jíbaro*, they were ghastly and blasphemous interventions which did too little and came too late. What the family desired above all else was to get the corpse home for the *velorio*, so that Cirilo's spirit could find its way to purgatory and beyond.

García's entreaties were to no avail. He did, however, win

a small concession from the boy's parents. They allowed the doctors to obtain minuscule samples of the boy's liver and spleen, provided that no cuts or deformities remained visible on the body. The extreme enlargement of these two organs made it possible to obtain samples through a minute opening in the skin, which Rafi then expertly closed, while the two doctors procured the next sample. He buried and inverted the white cotton sutures under the cadaver's skin to hide the filaments, and when he finished, only the barest hint of an incision remained visible upon the waxy skin.

Ashford then covered the small cuts lightly with a paste made of zinc, ochre, and vermillion, all suspended in lard. This was a prized formula a certain *Madám* Dufresne had secretly given to García as partial payment for care she received during a bout of what she called an "occupational illness." Ashford and García proved superior in treating the patient's cadaver than they did in treating the patient, and the task was soon completed to the satisfaction of all parties, if not to their complete happiness. Cirilo was carried off for burial; the samples were taken for study.

The samples needed to be kept for two weeks in a solution of potassium dichromate and sodium sulfate in order to harden before embedding them in molten paraffin. Once solidified, the resulting block was brought to one of the most prized possessions of the hospital: a Cambridge Scientific rocking microtome, acquired in Boston at great cost thanks to a kind donation from don Ramón Belisario López, the publisher of the newspaper *La Correspondencia*. With uncanny precision, the treasured microtome sliced the embedded tissues into wafer-thin sections that could then be stained appropriately.

The doctors then examined the colorful slides using their two excellent German microscopes, which had, in turn, been generously donated by the directors of the coffee trust. The whole process, from autopsy to microscope, proceeded at a slow pace, and it was not until a month after Cirilo's passing that the highly anticipated slides could finally be reviewed. Ashford, García, and Rafi took turns examining the slides under different magnifications and varying intensities of light. The three took obsessively detailed notes and sketched their observations with colored pencils; they ended up equally befuddled by what they saw. The structures and patterns were unfamiliar to them, and they could not piece together the story the microscope was trying to tell them. They showed the slides to other members of the staff, eliciting many varying opinions and many discussions, but in the end no consensus on the diagnosis could be reached.

It was already mid-November before the slides could be examined. By then, Ashford and Rafi Moore had settled into a pleasant routine consisting of morning rounds, a leisurely outdoor meal in one of the cafes, the occasional afternoon *siesta*, evening rounds, nighttime drinks with fellow officers and doctors, and home. The cases at both hospitals presented mostly the mundane with a smattering of the esoteric, and ranged from scarlet fever, rheumatism, and diphtheria, to diabetic and post-traumatic amputations, and the rare appendectomy.

Then a curious pattern emerged that began to shed light on Cirilo's untimely death. On occasion, a person presented to the *San Antonio* with a clinical picture very similar to that of Cirilo, but not nearly as advanced. Unlike Cirilo, these patients managed to recover fully following a brief hospitalization. After the fourth such case in the space of three weeks, Rafi went to Ashford.

"Dr. Ashford," he said, "I have talked to all of these patients presenting with abdominal fluid and two out of the three live within half a mile of Cirilo, whereas the third recently visited family in the area."

The story intrigued Ashford. It sounded very much as if the accounts depicted an outbreak of an infectious process. But the great question was: an infection of what nature and due to what organism? He had never seen liver failure associated with recreational swimming. But something about the whole situation bothered him. Somewhere in the far recesses of his mind, an irksome little bell was ringing...something, somewhere...*if he could only recall what it was.*

In the small, tidy hospital in Mayagüez, the doctors desperately needed ideas. Ashford decided to turn to his former professors at Georgetown. He wrote letters seeking opinions from his teachers of general medicine, as well as specialists of the liver, the spleen, the lymphatic system, and finally, to his professor of transmittable diseases and parasitology. These letters went by army post, the only reliable way to get them to Washington, D.C.

One of Ashford's letters arrived in the middle of November, 1898 at the office of Dr. Charles Wardell Stiles of the Department of Parasitology at Georgetown University.

Dear Professor Stiles,

Referring you back to my time as a student of your course in 1894, when you so graciously offered your kind assistance as the need might arise during our battles against transmittable disease, I have taken the liberty of holding you to your promise. I share the story of an unfortunate sixteen-year-old male from here who recently died of liver failure. You'll find his medical record and a summary of all pertinent medical and social history enclosed with this letter. Tissue samples from the patient's liver were examined microscopically and revealed a most peculiar and pronounced pattern of thick and parallel scarring and occasionally in between these, very prominent curious ovoid structures of about 100 microns, tapered toward the ends and encased in a thick band of integument. Many of these show a large spike reminiscent of that found on Prussian army helmets, somewhat offset from the long axis, and everywhere a most intense inflammation with an abundance of eosin-staining white cells. I beg you to please examine the slides at your convenience, and share any thoughts that might be of assistance to us.

I remain,

Bailey K. Ashford
U.S. Army Medical Corps
Mayagüez, Puerto Rico

One month later, an official-looking letter arrived via the army post in Mayagüez, addressed to Lieutenant Bailey Kelly Ashford. It was his long-awaited reply from Professor Stiles at Georgetown. But it did not reach Ashford, who, much to his distress, had recently left the city, transferred to the General Hospital in San Juan.

Chapter Thirteen

SAN JUAN, DECEMBER 1898

Several weeks after the death of Cirilo Pérez, Lieutenant Ashford received official word that he was to be transferred from Mayagüez to San Juan. The Department of War was centralizing its presence, and this required an expansion of the medical facilities in the capital. In his new post, Ashford would assume command of his own company.

He was extremely disappointed to leave Mayagüez, a city that he had come to know and like. He had developed a strong camaraderie with Dr. García and enjoyed consulting on the civilian cases. These were usually far more interesting and varied than those at the military hospital, which had become largely prosaic since the cease-fire. The civilians, moreover, were appreciative and grateful almost to a fault and invariably wanted to pay him in fruits and chickens. These Ashford respectfully refused, explaining that he was already being compensated adequately by his *Tío* Sam, an awkward attempt at humor that drew blank stares from the locals.

Rafi was not transferred with Ashford—another disappointment—and for the time being, would remain in Mayagüez. The day of Ashford's departure, they bid farewell to one another at the lone pier in the city's small port. Ashford grasped his friend's hand warmly. "Rafi, hold down the fort in my absence. I sincerely hope that we can work together again soon."

Rafi nodded and handed an envelope to the lieutenant. "Dr. Ashford," he said, "here are some of my contacts in San Juan, including my father's address; I have written him already asking him to look out for you. He has many friends in the government now that it is run by his fellow countrymen, and he should be able to assist you, if need be."

Ashford took the envelope and put it in his coat pocket. "Thank you, my friend. I will be in contact with your father as soon as I arrive."

Rafi began walking with Ashford toward the gangplank. "You might also consider getting in touch with Ramón Belisario López, the publisher of the daily newspaper, *La Correspondencia*. He is a good friend of the family and knows everybody who is worth knowing in Puerto Rican society, both in San Juan and here in Mayagüez."

"That would prove valuable, without question."

Rafi grinned. "You may enjoy meeting his young daughters as well."

Ashford's eyes lit up. "Well, that is even better! We won't let a slight language incompatibility get in the way now, surely?"

"María Asunción, his eldest daughter, and I have been friends since the age of ten. If I know her at all, I would say that she is already speaking half-decent English. My father teases her, which makes her angry, so she is always trying to learn words and phrases with which to put him in his place."

Ashford grinned. "Your friend María Asunción must be something." Then he added with a sly look, "Maybe I can teach her some useful American phrases. But in the most proper fashion, of course!"

Rafi winked knowingly. "She might enjoy that, Dr. Ashford."

Ashford turned serious. "Rafi, what do you plan to do now?"

"I will work for Colonel Burke until the end of the year. I suspect that after that, I will most likely be assigned to Ponce. As much as I have enjoyed my time in this beautiful city, the real action around here will be in Ponce, since the army plans to administer this section of the island from there."

"Well then," Ashford smiled wistfully, "With luck, I may see you in Ponce someday."

The steamer announced its imminent departure with a series of horn blasts. The two friends shook hands one last time and Ashford jogged up the gangplank, disappearing into the ship for the quick overnight trip into the harbor at San Juan.

The next morning, the steamer docked in San Juan before 8 a.m. Ashford walked the few blocks up the incline of Cristo Street to the Nuevo Hospital de la Concepción, which occupied an entire city block at the extreme western end of the Old City. It was an impressive building, looking to Ashford like a much larger version of the Hospital de San Antonio in Mayagüez: two stories high, and designed in an elegant classical revival style, with arched corridors organized around a large interior courtyard.

The building dated to 1780, when the Archbishop of San Juan had it built to care for the many indigents of the city. In former days, it had welcomed up to five hundred patients. As Ashford walked closer, he could see the small bridge that was being constructed to link the hospital to the immense Ballajá barracks across the street, not only to expand the capacity of the hospital, but also to allow the soldiers and staff easier access to their living quarters. Rather than calling it the Hospital de la Concepción, English speakers often referred to it simply as the San Juan General Hospital.

The hospital was under the command of Colonel John van Rensselaer Hoff, a distinguished-looking man who was the scion of one of New York's oldest Dutch families. Ashford found his office just past the hospital's large entrance on San Sebastián Street, next to one of the arched corridors on the first floor. He entered the stark office and saluted, "Lieutenant Bailey Ashford reporting, sir!"

Colonel Hoff rose from behind his desk to return the salute. He was a curious looking man of about fifty, slightly below medium height and somewhat corpulent. He had a round face with smooth, pale skin overlain in reddish tones, a full head of unruly auburn hair and a large, bushy mustache in the style of his friend and governor-elect of New York, Teddy Roosevelt. Although it was barely midmorning, he was dressed in the full ceremonial regalia of a colonel on parade, complete with white gloves, plumed hat, and dress saber.

Hoff shook Ashford's hand with a chipper grin. "Lieutenant, welcome to the San Juan General Hospital. You have had the great fortune of arriving in time to attend the daily inspection of the troops!"

Ashford tried not to show his surprise. "The inspection of the troops, sir?"

The colonel nodded; his face lit with enthusiasm. "Yes, Ashford, I review the medical personnel every morning in the courtyard. Everybody is required to attend: nurses, doctors, orderlies, janitors—it helps keep the staff sharp, if you know what I mean."

For a moment, Ashford stared blankly at his commander. Then, he realized that the colonel was absolutely serious. "Of course, sir, I think I understand," replied the befuddled lieutenant.

The medical personnel were duly inspected at full attention in the large central patio, courtesy of their ridiculously-attired commander, who paraded ceremoniously in front of the ranks, intently looking everyone up and down with an almost liturgical expression. The sun beat down mercilessly on the impatient staff while they submitted to the ritual. When the inspection was completed, Colonel Hoff led Ashford and two other lieutenant physicians into his office. There, he took off his white gloves and his saber, and beaming, announced enthusiastically, "And now, let us go to the wards and visit the sick!"

Thus was Ashford's first introduction to Colonel Hoff, whose military yearnings seemed to far outweigh his regard for the calling of Hippocrates. In Hoff's eyes, the ritual of the drill was as sacred as the Eucharist. Conventional wisdom held that the colonel couldn't care less if his young underlings thought a patient's heart was found on the right side and the liver on the left, as long as they could effectively drill a squad of four men. He could often be seen standing in the middle of the parade ground with his splendid uniform in the manner of the Kaiser, ceaselessly barking instructions at four gawky hospital corpsmen until they could handle litters with military precision.

At the Hospital de la Concepción, Hoff placed Ashford in command of all the Medical Department troops, to be reorganized into a single large company for the sole purpose of training them in the soldierly arts. These troops were treated like any other regular company in the Army, and during his first day of command, Ashford looked on in amusement as its membership of doctors, nurses, janitors, orderlies, and stretcher-bearers drilled awkwardly, about as well as rag dolls with sawdust for brains. Ashford malevolently imagined that if it had been possible to perform a rectal examination by the book and in impressive military style, Hoff would have included the procedure in his magnum opus, *The Drill Manual for the Medical Department.*

But despite his bitterness, Ashford could not pretend not to understand the Colonel's motives. Over the last year, Ashford had grown painfully aware of a lamentable incongruity of perception that was widespread in the military: medical officers were viewed in a different light from other army officers. Fighting disease was not exactly on par with fighting enemy soldiers, and Ashford soon realized that Colonel Hoff felt that he was an officer by courtesy only. Hoff compensated by making it his own personal mission to see that he and his medical staff were the most soldierly of all the soldiers. Unfortunately, he had allowed his private campaign to cross into the absurd, thereby becoming the butt of countless jokes, both inside and outside the General Hospital.

Adding to the misery were Colonel Hoff's regular flashes of inspiration. One week following his arrival, Ashford was asked to see the colonel in his office. The commander welcomed him with wide grin and a firm slap on the back.

"Lieutenant I have had the most wonderful idea. Starting today, there will be an Officer of the Day on duty at the San Juan General Hospital!" Ashford stiffened and leaned imperceptibly forward, waiting for the *coup de grace.* Hoff continued on, delivering his next sentence in one breath. "Officer of the Day duties will alternate between the lieutenant physicians who will perform various functions of the greatest importance while on duty and will at all times be in full dress uniform including his saber and will respond to all medical as well as military calls during the night while spending said night on duty at the hospital for which purpose I have ordered that a cot be prepared in the orderlies' room." Having successfully delivered his thought in one continuous stream, it seemed to Ashford as if Hoff were going to pass out from lack of air, but he did not.

The three physician lieutenants soon found out that the grandiloquent title meant nothing like it implied. In addition to wearing his saber all day and being constantly on duty, the Officer of the Day was not allowed to leave the hospital building for twenty-four hours, a miserable restriction for those that had romantic interests in the capital. Given all this, Ashford rejoiced when all this paralyzing silliness was interrupted by a letter that had been forwarded to him from Mayagüez. The letter showed a return address from his medical school. It arrived a full six weeks after he had written to Stiles.

Department of Parasitology,
Georgetown School of Medicine, Washington, D.C.
December 1, 1898

My Dear Ashford,
....Thank you for providing the wonderfully prepared slides on the case of the unfortunate Porto Rican man recently dead of "liver failure." Your detailed clinical history I found most interesting and relevant. The transcript of the final consultation will read, in part:

"...liver sections showing extensive reticuloendothelial cell hyperplasia and marked granulomatous changes. Many intrahepatic venules are totally replaced by granulomas that occlude the lumen. There is an acute endophlebitis of numerous intrahepatic vessels. Extensive inflammation and destruction of blood vessels with thrombosis is also seen. There are multiple light brown, elongated ovoid structures lodged in small vessels of the portal system, some apparently embryonated. These light brown ova measure approximately 110 by 60 micrometers and are marked by an offset thorny spike, which is diagnostic."

CONCLUSION: SUBACUTE AND CHRONIC GRANULOMATOUS HEPATITIS SECONDARY TO BILHARZ'S DISEASE (BILHARZIASIS), AT TIMES KNOWN AS SCHISTOSOMIASIS.

Thank you for your consultation, I will forward a note with in-

voice and fees etc. to the War Department, and wishing you very
well,
   I remain,
   Charles Wardell Stiles, PhD

A flying microscope could not have hit Ashford's head with a force greater than those few lines. He and his colleagues had all missed the correct diagnosis of bilharziasis, one that they should have gotten right, even if it ultimately made no difference to poor Cirilo. Reviewing the letter, once again, Ashford concluded that the boy was probably doomed long before arriving at the hospital. But the lack of any known cure for bilharziasis provided Ashford no consolation. He clearly remembered studying it under Stiles: a chronic disease caused by parasitic flatworms which had been first reported in Egypt some forty years prior, but that had since been found on all of the Caribbean islands. The life cycle of the diminutive flatworm, or schistosome, which was barely one quarter of an inch in length, was not yet completely understood, but strong evidence suggested that slow-moving bodies of fresh water played a critical role in enabling the parasites to spread the disease. Ashford suddenly recalled what they had learned about Cirilo's community up in Lares, where people washed, played, caroused, courted, and made love by the dammed creek and its enticing pond. There, within the soothing waters of the *charca*, the nefarious flatworms must have made their den.

Once recovered from his initial shock and after reading and re-reading the report, Ashford immediately composed a telegraph to Rafi in Mayagüez with instructions. First, he was to find García and relay the news of Cirilo's diagnosis. Second, Rafi was to travel the twenty rugged miles to the affected community; there he should explain to its leaders the importance of removing the obstruction to the creek so that the current would flush the worms and their illness down to the killing saltwater of the ocean.

Ashford also sent a separate letter to García including a handwritten copy of Stiles' report, to doubly ensure that this critical information got to Mayagüez. Then he went in search of Colonel Hoff, whom he found by the latrines, drilling the stretcher-bearers on the most proper and military way of emptying a bedpan. Colonel Hoff listened patiently and most agreeably to the story of the dead boy in Mayagüez, and then, smiling kindly, reminded Ashford that he was the Officer of the Day and to please not forget to drill the janitors, who seemed to be slacking.

Chapter Fourteen

THE SWIMMING HOLE

Rafi had been deeply disappointed to see Dr. Ashford transferred to San Juan, and to be unable to follow, since the Army had asked him to remain in Mayagüez through the end of the year. He continued lodging at the Hotel Paris, where early one evening he received a telegram from the doctor. Once he got over his initial apprehension, he eagerly opened the envelope.

> *Cirilo death due to Bilharzia/Notify García/Confirm with Army you can proceed to Lares/Drain pond in all haste.*
> *Ashford*

All at once, everything made sense. Stuffing the paper in his pocket, Rafi ran down the narrow wooden staircase to the lobby and out the hotel, arriving at the San Antonio Hospital in minutes. Dr. García had already left for the day. Rafi proceeded to the center of town, passed the old square with its large statue of Columbus, and turned toward the doctor's house. He bounded up the few steps to the porch, where García and his wife were enjoying their after-dinner coffee, and, handing the doctor the telegram, sat breathless on the floor.

García read the telegram twice, his face betraying deep concern. He handed the cable to his wife to read and turned to Rafi, saying, "Tomorrow we will go see Colonel Burke and obtain permission for you to go to Lares and explain to the Pérez family what is happening. They must be persuaded to remove the dam and restore the normal flow of the creek. Bring back with you any person you suspect of having bilharziasis who is willing to travel to Mayagüez. We will treat them at the *San*

Antonio as best we can."

The next day, Colonel Burke received García and Rafi in his office at the *alcaldía*. He was a perceptive man, a good soldier, and, above all, a devoted humanitarian who had grown to like the island and its people. He readily granted Rafi leave to travel to Lares, accompanied by two privates and a corporal, all of whom looked about fifteen years old. They selected some of the better horses of the local stock, which in the care of the Army had almost doubled in weight.

On their trip to Lares, the group used the same roads that the Army had taken to their last encounter with the Spanish at Las Marías. Two miles past the site of the battle, the group left the road and entered the rustic mountain trails that followed the Añasco River toward the interior. The way proved challenging, leading mostly uphill and following a long ravine hemmed in by steep slopes on either side with the fast-flowing river at its base. The growing darkness added to their difficulties, and they made camp for the night by the south side of the river. Rafi and his three companions cooked their rations over a blazing fire, trading stories of successes in battle and defeats at the hands of the local women. The night was clear and the mountain air clean and cool, and Rafi slept soundly. The next day, they resumed their travel at sunrise, and by late morning they were nearing the Pezuela *barrio* of Lares. Another half-mile brought them to Cirilo´s village.

Puerto Rico was divided officially into seven large departments, and unofficially into seventy smaller entities, the *municipios,* each of these named after its principal city or town. In turn, the municipalities were subdivided into smaller wards or *barrios* which were named after their main settlement. The municipal district of Lares extended over approximately sixty square miles and was ruled by a semi-autocratic mayor, the *alcalde* Eugenio Pérez, who held court in the town of Lares proper. Don Eugenio was Cirilo's uncle, the elder brother of Cirilo's father, Ernesto, who served with Eugenio's blessing as the unofficial chief of the *barrio* of Pezuela.

The arrival of the four horsemen, three of them in the sharp khaki uniforms of the United States Army, brought the curious out from their shacks. A scrawny youngster ran to find chief Ernesto, while Rafi and the soldiers headed toward the creek. They had no difficulty finding it. From the tall mountain slopes to the south, a perfectly clear stream about twenty feet across flowed over granite boulders polished to a glistening smoothness by the relentless action of the waters. The stream descended rapidly from above, following the slopes that eventually led it to empty into the Río Prieto near Las Marías. In places, the creek was up to three feet deep, but for the most part, it ran far more shallow, so that the water bubbled vigorously over and around the rocks with hypnotizing resonance. In Pezuela, the stream was diverted into a man-made pool of sixty by thirty yards. Rafi found this pool, known colloquially as El Hoyo, "the hole," about two hundred yards outside the village.

A small crowd gathered behind Ernesto when he met the soldiers by El Hoyo. Here, the clean transparency of the stream succumbed gradually to an increasing opacity as the swiftly flowing water approached the impoundment. The dam, a source of endless pride and a magnet of the community, had been built twenty years before under Ernesto's supervision. The entire village shared in the labor, entertainment, and fellowship of the project.

Men, women, and children had worked for four months, erecting a solid base of branches and logs driven into the bed of the stream. They built upon that with bark, rocks, mud, grasses, leaves, and masses of plants, forming a superstructure roughly six feet high and ten feet thick. The crude dam obstructed about 90 percent of the stream's flow, which had backed up to form a large pond. A rough spillway atop the dam regulated the discharge of water according to seasonal variations in rainfall.

It was a modest but effective structure, and almost everyone enthusiastically agreed that it greatly improved the lives of locals and visitors. During the hottest months, people from as far away as Las Marías and San Sebastián thought nothing of hiking five miles to swim in El Hoyo. Upon arriving, they paid the designated fee collector twenty cents per family, a not insignificant sum which greatly contributed to the health of the community coffers. The pool was the center of social life for miles around, and not a few human beings had had their start there, acquiring life either alongside or inside the waters of the precious lake.

Rafi Moore and the small company dismounted and approached Ernesto Pérez, who shook their hands with an air of self-confidence born from his status as town leader. Ernesto stood taller than his companions, and made a distinguished impression. He was dressed in a white linen shirt and pants, both immaculately clean, ankle-high leather boots, and a brand-new fedora hat. By and large, his companions adhered to the usual wardrobe and demeanor of the *jíbaro*—they were small and scraggly people, sickly pale if white, waxy amber if black, all of them dressed in worn cotton clothes, and to the very last one, barefoot.

Ernesto readily recognized Rafi from his care of his dear departed Cirilo. Rather than feeling embittered by the futility of the treatments, he was profoundly grateful for all of his efforts. The doctors had done their best, communicated frequently and effectively with the family, and demonstrated great concern and compassion throughout the sad ordeal. Ernesto wasted no energy second-guessing whether his boy's treatment had been the correct one, or if something more should have been done, or any other such questions. In Ernesto's practical mind, some things were meant to be, and God had given him sixteen years with Cirilo, *Amén*.

"Don Ernesto," Rafi said to the *barrio* leader, "it is good to see you again. Once more, I offer you my deepest sympathies for the loss of Cirilo. We think of him often at our hospital in Mayagüez."

Ernesto looked down. "My son was a good young man, respectful, gentle, and very well liked. He showed promise as a healer. He wanted to become a real physician, but it was not meant to be."

"A noble dream," Rafi said softly. "Don Ernesto, to honor the memory of Cirilo is why we have come. By allowing us to remove the small organ samples from your son after his death, you helped us to garner certain clues about his illness." Rafi cleared his throat. "We asked for help from an expert doctor in the United States to determine the cause of Cirilo's death.

We sent him the small samples of tissue to study under a microscope."

This revelation caused every onlooker to look at their neighbor and nod their approval with a collective *"Aaah!"*

Rafi waited for his audience to settle, then continued.

"There is no question that the boy died of a severe case of *la bilharzia.*"

Some leaned closer toward Rafi so as to not miss one word while others looked around quizzically, hoping for further clarification. Most of the people in the crowd had heard of the *bilharzia* disease in passing, but nobody really knew what it was—some said it was a heart thing, others swore the condition affected the lungs, or maybe it was a form of diarrhea. Two or three of them knew for sure that bilharzia caused your manhood to turn purple and fall off in three equal pieces. Most Puerto Ricans were fascinated by the mysteries of illness and cure, the more enigmatic the better, especially if they involved a living adversary such as a microbe, an insect or, best yet, a *worm.*

Rafi continued, "The bilharzia is a tiny, invisible worm that lives in the water and crawls into you through your skin, then it lives in your body until it kills you."

His audience stared at Rafi without so much as a blink or a scratch. Nobody said a word, but they were all thinking the same thing: All the worms they were familiar with were wiggly creatures that crawled about on the ground. But now this youngster was talking about a worm that lived *underwater,* and not only that, but an *invisible* worm that lived underwater. This was all so outlandish that it must be true.

Doña Inés, the local *curandera,* feeling somewhat threatened by all this fabulous science, gave voice to everyone's thoughts. "What you are saying here, if we are to understand you correctly, is that there is an evil killer worm that nobody can see but that you *know* lives in the water and can pass through your skin like a ghost passes through walls? Who has heard of such a thing?"

"Yes, it sounds incredible," Rafi answered. "But with a microscope these worms can be seen inside different parts of the body, including the liver and the intestines. Moreover, the worm isn't in all waters, but only some bodies of freshwater. Specifically, *your* freshwater. We know that people who do not go into freshwater lakes and streams cannot contract *la bilharzia*. This has been shown again and again. It is a scientific truth."

Noticing several heads nodding around her, doña Inés pressed Rafi. "An invisible water worm that also lives in the body, you say?"

At this point, Sancho Jiménez, a man gifted with a knack for the most inopportune and colorful commentary, loudly volunteered that he had a nephew who had once contracted tiny white worms that crawled out of his *culo* hole at night to "get busy." He had been completely cured with enemas of garlic and honey, administered three times daily and held tightly for periods of an hour or more.

Many of those present noisily confirmed that they knew of a very similar case, but that *those* worms were green, or maybe purple, and yes, many of them were two or maybe three-headed and crawled out once a day, every day except on Sundays.

Waving to quiet the villagers, Rafi thanked the crowd for their comments. Ernesto then interjected, "What do you recommend we do?"

The pivotal moment had finally come. Rafi took a deep breath and spoke as calmly and deliberately as possible. "Don Ernesto, *El Hoyo* has to go. The dam must be dismantled. The creek must be allowed to flow freely and carry those dangerous worms far away to the ocean."

A general bustle of protest erupted as if on cue. Don Ernesto waited for five minutes before he signaled for silence and was again granted the floor.

"Rafael, I don't have to point out the gravity of what you are saying. This pool is part of our life, it defines our *barrio* around Lares, Las Marías, and San Sebastián. I am not sure we can agree to your wishes. After all, you are barely older than Cirilo. Where do you get your authority?"

Rafi tried to sooth the anxious crowd. "I understand and sympathize with your dilemma. I also admit that this disease is not yet completely understood. But I can tell you that communities in other parts of the world that have changed their habits concerning standing freshwater have reduced the illness to a great extent. It may allow your sick villagers to improve, while preventing healthy ones and visitors from becoming infected."

"Without the pond, there won't be any visitors," mumbled Ernesto glumly.

Undeterred, Rafi continued to address the crowd, "Most of you are already suffering from serious anemia due to poor nutrition. The *bilharzia* makes you feel that much worse and in cases like that of poor Cirilo, it will kill you."

The discussion continued for the better part of an hour, after which a truce was called. Don Ernesto promised to consider Rafi's proposal and consult with his brother, the *alcalde* in Lares, while the crowd noisily continued to argue over invisible, double-headed, sex-crazed worms that must be very smart, for they knew how to keep the Sabbath.

Throughout the entire debate, the soldiers had stood at rest, listening with amusement as the animated dialogue took place at lightning speed in unintelligible Spanish. The discussion over at last, they mounted their horses shortly before noon and headed down the slopes toward Mayagüez, where they arrived, exhausted, early the following morning.

That afternoon Rafi recounted his trip for Colonel Burke, who did not seem particularly surprised at the lack of commitment from Ernesto Pérez and his neighbors. He decided to give matters a week to settle down before sending Rafi back to *barrio* Pezuela. This time, Rafi would travel with three army engineers, with orders to talk to Mayor Eugenio directly, if necessary. Not that this would have mattered. Burke had already decided that Rafi would not leave Lares until the pond had been drained. Burke privately hoped that the community would voluntarily remove the dam without the Army having to take direct action. If the locals agreed to dismantle it, then the engineers would conveniently be on hand to assist them.

In any event, the colonel's contingency plan proved unnecessary. During the short week that separated Rafi's two trips to Lares, don Ernesto had met with his brother the *alcalde* and other town leaders. In their customary way, they shared numerous anecdotes and ideas over meals finished with black coffee spiked with moonshine rum, slowly finding their way to the matter at hand through memory and shared experience. The distilled wisdom in these meetings held that the *gringo* scientists might possibly be right in blaming some bizarre invisible creature for the mysterious malady. But regardless of the true cause, the village leaders believed that if they did not remove the dam, the Americans would do it for them, adding humiliation to the loss of their precious *Hoyo*. And so, when Rafi crested the final hill on his return to Pezuela, he was surprised to see the dam already dismantled and the *barrio's* precious pond surrendering slowly to an unsightly mud hole while the perfectly clear waters of the mountain stream flowed unhindered downstream, burbling indifferently over the polished boulders.

Chapter Fifteen

MARÍA ASUNCIÓN, DECEMBER 1898

The transfer to San Juan might have hindered Ashford's scientific endeavors, but it did much to enhance his amorous ones. A growing number of his fellow army officers had been falling for local beauties, and the gallant lieutenant was no exception. Some engagements had been celebrated already, starting surprisingly soon after the soldiers entered Mayagüez. Catalina Palmer, the young woman who had welcomed the American Army from her balcony waving a homemade flag, had already married an American officer. Others soon followed their example.

The height of polite society in the capital was the semi-monthly *fête* held on the first and third Friday of every month. It was hosted in rotating fashion by the brighter lights of San Juan society and organized by local civic leaders. The purpose of such activities was ostensibly to make the officers feel welcome in a strange country, but in reality to improve the marriage prospects of the wealthy single women of the island, who in the blink of an eye, had found their Spanish connections rendered worthless. The resulting "Panic of '98" meant that the more affluent local *señoritas* of marriageable age had to start investing their love anew.

On the first Friday in December, Lieutenant Ashford arrived for the dance in the spacious Old City home of don Ramón Belisario López, publisher of the island's first daily newspaper, *La Correspondencia de Puerto Rico*. Ashford had been invited by don Ramón, one of the people that Rafi Moore had recommended as a contact. The lieutenant wore his finest uniform, *sans* saber, and looked forward to meeting the prominent newspaperman. Walking into the spacious marble-floored salon of the López home, Ashford found don Ramón conversing with a raven-haired beauty of about twenty. She immediately captured his attention. Swallowing his nervousness, the lieutenant approached them.

"Good evening, sir," he said to don Ramon. "My compliments on this most beautiful home that you have opened for us tonight." He introduced himself, adding, "My associate, Mr. Rafael Moore, sends his regards."

The ravishing woman immediately replied, without waiting for her older companion to speak. What she lacked in fluency of the English language, she made up in confidence.

"How…is…*Meester* Moore, my dear friend, Rafi?"

The lieutenant was not sure whether to answer in English or try his hand at broken Spanish, but he was quite certain that he wanted to answer this angelic creature any way he could. He decided to show his mettle and went with Spanish. "*Oh sí, sí, Rafi…is…*ahem…*muy bueno, bien*, ahh…*bueno?*" With this babbling, Ashford felt his cheeks begin to prickle and, with an inward groan, realized that his face was turning a bright shade of crimson.

The young lady smiled broadly, "Yes, *Teniente* Ashford, that was…aah…*un buen esfuerzo*[6], but one says *que* Rafi *está bien*. But please, no worry, my English is about so bad like your *español*."

Don Ramón finally edged into the conversation, "Doctor Ashford, may I introduce to you my daughter María Asunción?" The older man's English was much more passable.

Ashford awkwardly extended his hand—the customary greeting of a dashing American man meeting a lady. She grasped his hand, and then, quickly leaning in toward the lieutenant, proceeded to plant a kiss upon his right cheek, in the customary greeting of a Puerto Rican woman meeting a man. If Ashford had been blushing before, he could now feel his entire blood reserve abruptly rush to his face which suffused with the most intense heat. Beads of sweat appeared on his brow, and his mouth went dry. A new concern streaked rapid-fire through his head—how could this beauty with such observant and captivating coal-black eyes fail to notice that he was about to pass out? This must be love at first sight—*More precious than rubies is she, and all the things you canst desire are not to be compared unto her.* Absolutely sure that he was sunk, he realized that, to make matters worse, there were no smelling salts to revive him. If he fainted, he was never going to live it down with his brother officers.

Gathering himself, he simply muttered, "Thank you, Miss María."

She replied quizzically, "Thanks you me for what, *Meester* Ashford?"

Ashford had meant to thank her for the kiss on the cheek, but suddenly realized that this was probably even worse than not thanking her for a harmless kiss. Then came the sudden, horrible thought of a rapidly vanishing opportunity: Maybe she expected a kiss back? He bent down to kiss her soft, white cheek, but he had waited too long. In the kissy-cheeks custom of Latin Americans, the affectionate exchange should have taken place simultaneously, and Ashford had missed his chance. He ended up kissing air as the María Asunción turned to her father and smiling, whispered something in Spanish much too difficult for the doctor to decipher. Feeling that he had bungled the introduction far beyond any hope of recovery, Ashford prepared to make his exit when María Asunción reassuringly asked him where he was working.

"Oh! I am at the San Juan General Hospital four blocks up the street," Ashford replied cautiously before pulling himself to attention and adding, "I am in charge of all the Medical Department troops. And where do you work?...*ahem*... Do you work, or not? Or maybe you are in school?"

Gradually, the two fell into a more comfortable conversation, and don Ramón, with a twinkle in his eye, kissed his daughter's cheek and excused himself. María Asunción waved away her father and turned back to her erstwhile suitor with a smile that would have flipped Ashford's heart, had it not been whirling already. Once María Asunción had given him that kiss, no matter how innocent or how small, the lieutenant was beyond all help.

The two spent much of the evening together, communicating with creative phrases and comical hybrids of their two languages, punctuated by vigorous hand gestures and hilarious facial expressions. Ashford's dancing was passable; María Asunción's was stupendous. He showed her the mazurka, she showed him *la danza*. She kept her left hand gently upon his shoulder and her right firmly clasped in his, while he gently hugged her waist. Ashford wished the night would never end. By the time the party finally drew to a close toward three in the morning, they had agreed to meet without waiting the two weeks for the next dance. Ashford returned to the barracks whistling a jaunty tune from *The Mikado,* and that night he did not sleep a wink.

For their next encounter, María Asunción suggested attending a performance at the municipal theater, *El Teatro Tapia,* located in front of the San Cristóbal castle at the entrance into the Old City. Her youngest sister Mila had been bribed to serve as their chaperone. The show was one of those popular, light Spanish operettas known as the *zarzuela.* María Asunción calculated correctly that the stock characters and predictable plot needed no explanation for her Spanish-impaired friend and that the music, in any event, served as a universal language.

She did not guess that her companion enjoyed the unintelligible *zarzuela* about as much as an unabridged rendition of *Hamlet* in Spanish. But so long as María Asunción was with him, Ashford would have sat through one hundred *zarzuelas* and all of Shakespeare's historical pieces. After the performance concluded, he invited the López sisters for a leisurely stroll in the cool evening air to explore the Old City, starting with the half mile down Fortaleza Street to the governor's mansion. Both sides of the street were lined by old Spanish homes, built of brick covered in stucco and painted in delicate pastels of yellow, pink, green, and orange. All the homes had stone or wrought iron balconies extending out from the second story, where their residents sat drinking coffee or wine in the vibrant orange of the setting sun.

They turned left onto Cristo Street to look at the small chapel at its very end. The two sisters took turns sharing its story with Ashford.

"In the eighteenth century," María Asunción began, "this

street served as a race course. The horses ran down the steep incline from the General Hospital, to where we are now. Here, the riders took a sharp left turn and continued downhill on Calle Tetuán towards the waterfront."

"During one race, a teenaged rider failed to stop his horse in time to avoid the precipice immediately past the finish line. Together, man and horse flew over the lip of the ravine, much to the horror of the onlookers. At that moment one of these observers called out for divine providence to save the rider…"

"Then, a few minutes later," Mila interrupted, "just as he had been given up for dead, the rider reappeared unscathed at the edge of the precipice. As one, the crowd cried, 'Miracle!' and declared the spot hallowed ground."

María Asunción shot her sister an annoyed glance. "The bishop soon gave permission for the construction of a small memorial chapel by the cliff's edge, to protect future riders from a similar catastrophe. And here it is, La Capilla del Santo Cristo de la Salud, from 1770."

"From 1780," Mila corrected.

The story fascinated the doctor, but not nearly as much as the young woman who told it. Ashford soon understood that María Asunción was a brilliant woman of many talents, academic, musical, and linguistic. She spoke fluent French, as well as semi-passable English, all with a charming accent that brought a smile to Ashford's face and a glimmer to his eye. María Asunción showed more than a passing interest in Ashford's medical work, too, asking questions and commenting intelligently on current treatments. Theirs was truly a whirlwind romance, one of dozens of relationships arising between American soldiers and Puerto Rican women. So quickly did Ashford tumble head over heels that after the next dance in December, Ashford walked María Asunción back to the López home, and, taking her hands in his, asked her to marry him.

María Asunción refused the offer. Ashford was crushed. He was positive that his feelings were reciprocated, and he had already rehearsed his pitch to his presumptive father-in-law. But that would not be necessary now. Scraping together what he could of his dignity, he rose off the street and bid María Asunción a hasty good night. Ashford strode across the cobblestones, reviewing the events of the last few weeks, turning over and over in his mind every word, glance or gesture that had passed between María Asunción and himself, trying to glean new meaning from past conversations. But he could not come up with anything to indicate that he had been wrong to propose.

He arrived at the General Hospital deeply dejected. Walking into the patient ward, he found Captain Andrew Thompson, an officer recovering from complications of a ruptured appendix. Ashford had successfully operated on him ten days earlier. Thompson was the personal physician to the recently named governor, Major General Guy Henry. The captain had claimed the ward entirely for himself and was now lounging comfortably in his bed, paging through a book. Ashford found his emotions bubbling over.

"Captain Thompson," he exclaimed, "Today I proposed to María Asunción, and was summarily rejected!"

Thompson startled at the sudden interruption, but after registering Ashford's words, passed his hand under his chin. "Goodness gracious, aren't you in high dudgeon," he muttered, marking his place and setting the novel aside. Looking up at the anxiously pacing doctor, Thompson continued, "When you were about to open me up, you gave me some excellent advice which I am going to repeat to you now: *'Don't think too hard about this.'* You might have rushed things a little, that's all."

Ashford grabbed his head with his hands, continuing to feverishly pace the captain's bedside. "You're right... Perhaps I was a little fast with the question. Maybe it's impossible... she's too young... or maybe there are too many differences between us..."

The captain sighed, shaking his head with a rueful smile. "Nonsense, Ashford. I proposed to my Puerto Rican girl every week for three weeks in a row before she accepted me."

Ashford halted his rapid movement, floored. "You proposed for three consecutive weeks?"

"Yes, I did! And once she finally conceded, Ana Isabel revealed that women here accept serious proposals only on a propitious day. Supposedly, this brings the couple good luck after they marry. How was I—or you—to know such a thing?"

"A propitious day? What in hell is *that*, Captain?"

Thompson began to laugh heartily. "Apparently Church holidays. By pure luck my third proposal fell on the feast of the Immaculate Conception. It was immediately accepted, although I had been rejected only six days previously."

Ashford's mind began turning like the flywheel on a steam engine. "Captain, today is December 20th. What would you say the next lucky date is?"

"Isn't it obvious?"

Ashford's eyes lit up. "Of course! December 25th, Christmas!"

Thompson sat up and reached for a book on the shelf beside his bed. "And this might come in handy."

Ashford took the volume from his patient's hands. The cover was reddish brown with bent corners and yellowing pages. The title page read: Velázquez *Spanish-English Dictionary—1870.*

Thompson smiled devilishly. "Even includes a pronunciation guide. Try it, lieutenant. I know it helped me with my courting."

Starting that evening, an anxious Ashford began memorizing words and trying to piece them into phrases that might impress María Asunción. Each of the next few nights, Ashford spent hour after hour at his desk bent over the dictionary by the light of an oil lamp. *Amor, querida, permiso, anillo, boda...* The requisite words went on and on, without any rhyme, reason, or discernible pattern. Studying for his Georgetown finals had been far easier; *this might all be hopeless,* he thought.

To make matters more difficult, now that he had settled on a particular date for his newest proposal, the whole ridiculous ordeal of serving as Officer of the Day really began to grate on Ashford. These duties made it impossible to see his paramour whenever he wished, and, moreover, María Asunción's friends began to tease him about failing to serenade his beloved from under her balcony as was the local custom. An exasperated Ashford replied that he was prohibited from leaving the hospital by order of Colonel Hoff, and immediately received a good-natured rebuke—his commander could not possibly be more important than his beloved. This said, María Asunción's friends all burst out laughing, which only added to his discomfiture.

The last straw came when his next Officer of the Day turn fell precisely on Christmas Day. Fed up with this charade, Ashford decided to take matters into his own hands. That evening, the hospital was quiet; the patients were doing well and no urgent military communiqués had been received (not that they ever were). The lieutenant determined he could make a brief appearance at the Lopez's holiday party, located a mere four blocks away. The trick was to pull it off without incurring Hoff's wrath.

It was a few minutes after 7 p.m. when Ashford put the finishing touch on his scheme. Captain Thompson was almost completely recovered from his emergency operation and planned to return to *La Fortaleza* within the week. Ashford hoped that, in Thompson, he had a ready ally. He found the captain semi-reclined on his hospital cot, staring blankly at the walls. His book lay forgotten on his lap and he seemed bored, impatient, and annoyed.

"Captain," Ashford began, as politely as he could muster. "I am stuck on this blasted Officer duty tonight and María Asunción is having a Christmas party. This is one of those very few propitious dates, as you called them. I will be eternally grateful if you could fill in for me, just for an hour or so. Everything is deathly quiet, and all you have to do is sit at the desk in case there's an emergency or an urgent communication. If that happens, simply send an orderly to fetch me. In any case, I will be back no later than nine."

Captain Thompson turned his glazed eyes toward the lieutenant. "You mean to be completely gone then, Ashford?"

"Yes, if you are willing to stand watch for a couple of hours, at the most."

The bedridden man shifted under the blankets, considering. Finally, a slow, creeping grin spread across his face as he said, "Very well, that will be fine. Go enjoy your party, and best of luck proposing to your girl."

A delighted Ashford walked the four blocks down to the López residence on San Francisco Street, where he was met with an uproarious greeting. It was a grand party, Puerto Rican-style; tables overflowed with food and drink, and a small orchestra played ballroom music in the background. As the American officer mingled with the crowd, don Ramón walked up to Ashford and said quietly, "You know Lieutenant, this is the very first time that this house has held a party on Christmas. Instead, in Puerto Rico, we celebrate the feast of The Three Kings on January the sixth. I think that we are being assimilated after all!"

"Quite so, quite so," Ashford replied distractedly, mustering his nerve. Before don Ramón could walk away, he seized the occasion. "Señor López, you know by now how I feel about your daughter, María Asunción. She has already refused my proposal of marriage, but I am not ready to give up on her. Do I have your permission to try again?"

Don Ramón smiled benevolently. "*Mi estimado teniente,* maybe you shouldn't worry so much. Regarding important decisions such as marriage, *how* and *when* something is said is every bit as important as *what* is said."

"With all due respect, don Ramón, you just said that Christmas is not widely celebrated here. Should I wait until the January feast day?"

"Is Christmas important to you?"

"Yes it is, sir."

"Then that is what matters." Don Ramón laughed heartily and waved to María Asunción to join her beau. "Good luck," he said with a smile and a wink before taking his leave.

Ashford again summoned all his courage.

Sitting alone with María Asunción on a large sofa in the side parlor, Ashford gently grasped her hand. He knew that after deploying the three opening phrases he had perfected with the help of the Puerto Rican hospital janitors, he was on his own.

The opening lines went well, since Ashford had memorized them phonetically after much drilling by an amused cleaning crew. María Asunción listened with rapt attention, her eyes wide with surprise as she listened to Ashford make sense in Spanish for the first time. She broke into a pleased smile as the words flowed forth in a funny *jíbaro* accent that pointed to the likely teachers.

And then Ashford stopped. His face turned a deep shade of red, just as he had done the night they first met. He mumbled and fumbled for words which did not come. Growing increasingly agitated, and with sweat beginning to mark his forehead despite the cool December air, Ashford reached into his pocket for some handwritten notes. With unsteady hands he struggled to unfold the crumpled sheet of paper. María Asunción looked from his face to his hand and back again, and then put a hand to her mouth. A worried look covered her features.

"Mi que...que...querida María Asunción," Ashford continued, looking up from his notes.

"Por favor, continúa," she encouraged him, noticing that his color had changed from red to pale gray.

"Ah..ah...matrimonio...ahh...tú y yo?" He pointed at her and then at himself, and then at her left ring finger. She stared at him in fascinated attention.

"Por favor, continúa," she said once again.

An uncomfortable silence followed.

"Damn it all, this is not going well." Ashford said. "Here it goes in English, come what may!"

In a slow, deliberate voice he said, "I am not an easy man to deter. Only a few days ago, you did not take me as your future husband. However, I have hope that tonight might be different. Once again, I ask you to be my wife."

María Asunción had a feeling all day of what was coming, and now she made an effort to hear and understand every word that came from Ashford's lips. When he had finished, she smiled and looked deeply into his blue eyes, which she considered the most beautiful she had ever seen. She replied with a simple *"¡Sí!"* and a gentle kiss sealed the deal. The couple returned to the main salon to announce their engagement to María Asunción's parents, and then the company as a whole.

For two hours, Ashford thoroughly enjoyed himself, stealing an occasional glance at an elaborate grandfather clock to make sure he did not overly inconvenience Captain Thompson with too late a return. After all, his poor friend was back at the hospital covering his watch, and while still recovering from a delicate and painful operation. He owed Thompson an enormous favor.

When the clock struck nine, Ashford decided to return to the hospital. He said his goodbyes, kissed his darling María Asunción on the cheek, and headed up Cristo Street toward the hospital. A few minutes later he entered the courtyard, where everything seemed as eerily quiet as when he had left. Grinning broadly, he proceeded to the main desk to thank Captain Thompson for covering his watch. He had even brought him some roast pork and *pasteles* to break the monotony of the tasteless hospital fare.

Ashford walked into the office and swept the food from behind his back like a magician revealing a rabbit. "Thompson, I hope you are ready for roast pork, because—" Ashford trailed off, surprised not to see the captain occupying the desk. He went to the patient ward the captain had to himself, but Thompson was not there either. Growing alarmed, Ashford began a systematic search for his patient, starting with the first ward by the hospital entrance and going into each successive room along the corridors. He searched upstairs as well, with no better luck. Most of the patients were sleeping soundly, oblivious to his growing distress. He inquired from the few nurses on duty if they had come across the missing Thompson recently. They all reported having last seen him in his room, but surely that had been at least a few hours previously.

Ashford wrestled with wild thoughts: either the captain was passed out in a bar on Calle Luna or was lying dead in a gutter by the piers. Increasingly frantic, he continued to search the kitchen, the library, the operating room, the orthopedic room, and even the latrines. Ashford broke into a cold sweat. He had no idea how he was going to explain to Colonel Hoff that he had lost his patient—not lost him metaphorically by way of *death*, but actually, physically lost him. He had visions of a court martial and a summary dismissal from the Army. He conscripted the small group of nurses and orderlies working at that late hour to expand the search. For the next three hours, everybody looked for Captain Thompson in all the most unlikely places, but he was nowhere to be found.

Sometime after midnight, the defeated and desperate lieutenant had just finished lighting a cigarette by the hospital's main entrance on Calle San Sebastián, when the dim lights of the street revealed a vaguely familiar figure approaching casually about two blocks away. The man slowly came into focus, and in another instant Ashford recognized the long-lost Thompson approaching nonchalantly, nursing a slight limp from his recent abdominal surgery. Ashford's initial sigh of relief turned into raging indignation as the lost patient saluted tipsily and stumbled past him into the courtyard. The lieutenant could feel his blood collecting in his brain and his fists tightening at his sides. Ashford extinguished his cigarette against the wall of the building and followed the captain inside, bursting with profanity. "Where in holy hell have you been, Captain Thompson? The entire hospital has been turned inside and out looking for your ass these past three hours!"

Thompson swung around and clumsily patted Ashford on the shoulder. "My dear Lieutenant, please don't get too worked up. Rejoice with me, I was attending a wedding."

"*What in tarnation!* A wedding? Whose wedding?"

"Why, but my own of course! I am, as of tonight, a newly and happily married man!"

Ashford could not believe what he was hearing. Surely the story was still a part of the sick joke of his disappearance. "Captain, don't piss on me and tell me it's raining. You've been to Luna Street, getting drunk and chasing tail."

"No, Ashford, I am telling you God's very own truth. Tonight, I married Miss Ana Isabel Rivera, daughter of one of the cabinet ministers. We had barely set the date before I came down with my bad appendix. She wanted to postpone the ceremony, but I assured her that it could still happen and that I was not going to miss my own wedding."

"Captain, you are aware that you are not due to be discharged for another week."

"Yes, highly inconvenient that was, my dear friend," Captain Thompson nodded, his expression grave, before letting out a huge belch, "I was hoping to come up with some scheme to leave for a few hours. Imagine my delight when you told me this afternoon that you, the Officer of the Day, were planning on being absent yourself! It was, quite simply, the most incredible stroke of luck. When you so obligingly departed, I proceeded to Ana Isabel's house, and there we were joyously united as planned. It was a most capital affair, and I long debated whether or not to return here at all. By the way, she sends her warmest regards. We planned to invite you and María Asunción as well, had it not been for the obvious difficulties."

Ashford did not know whether to be angry or relieved. In the end, Captain Thompson's conviviality loosened him up, and he accepted the humor of the situation, which, after all, he had brought entirely upon himself. He smiled at the newlywed, and with a slap on the back said, "Well, Thompson, since you have once again graced us with your presence, I suppose congratulations are in order. It is only midnight, let's celebrate with the roast pork from my party and tickle our livers with wine from the stores. I toast to you and to your Puerto Rican bride. *Salud!*"

"Yes sir, and I will toast to your own black-eyed beauty!"

Their peculiar party lasted until sunrise. It remained to be seen whether Colonel Hoff would be all the wiser. The big joke, of course, was that the entire hospital knew of Thompson's Christmas Escapade, while the colonel appeared to remain blissfully unaware of the entire event. One week later, Captain Thompson was discharged from the hospital, and with a knowing look and a mischievous smile, firmly shook Ashford's hand.

"Lieutenant, I will miss you and your daily visits to my bedside. If you need anything, I am at your service at Governor Henry's office. Good luck to you."

"Good luck, Captain Thompson, give my best to your bride!" With that warm handshake, the two new friends parted.

Eight weeks later, the marriage ceremony between Bailey Kelly Ashford and María Asunción López took place at her home in Old San Juan. Both the groom and his best man, Captain Thompson, were in full dress uniform, including white gloves, plumes, and sabers. As a token of the high esteem in which his new family held the lieutenant, don Ramón graciously asked the Episcopalian chaplain to officiate the ceremony in deference to the Protestant Ashford, although the López family were all devout Catholics. With his marriage, Ashford now considered himself a full-fledged islander. His wife and most of his close friends were all Puerto Rican, and his progress with the language and culture had been expeditious. From then on, Ashford never felt fully at home unless he was somewhere on the island.

The next five months passed routinely. There were many Officer of the Day tours during which the couple had to be apart, a difficult proposition for the newlyweds. Nevertheless, Ashford had learned his lesson and dared not leave his post, even if the commander himself offered to cover his watch. One afternoon toward the middle of May, just as the oppressive heat of the summer was beginning, Colonel Hoff sent for Ashford. He saluted his superior and waited to hear the reason for the summons. "Lieutenant Ashford," Colonel Hoff began, "This morning I received orders that you are to be transferred to Ponce as of July the fifteenth. There, you will be in charge of the former Spanish military hospital, El Hospital Militar de Ponce. It is not nearly as large as this one, but it will be all yours to command. You should consider this move to be tantamount to a promotion, and a corresponding advancement in rank can be expected within six months."

Ashford tried to recover from his shock. "Thank you for the very good news," he managed. "I am pleased, sir. I have always wanted to run my own hospital." He then added, with a half-suppressed smile, "I hope that I might lead the troops in Ponce half as well as you do here, Colonel."

Hoff ignored the comment and continued, "It appears that your old patient, Captain Thompson, has said some very positive things on your behalf when he returned to Washington with General Henry. He refers to you," and here Hoff read from a letter, "as an excellent clinician and surgeon whose consummate skills are second only to his devotion to duty, as manifested by his exemplary performance as Officer of the Day, in this endeavor easily surpassing any and all other such Officers I have elsewhere encountered."

Ashford could hardly keep from bursting out laughing and coughed loudly instead, his face going a deep crimson red.

The only three such ridiculous Officers in all of the Army were right there in San Juan.

"Yes, sir, that is quite...*ahem*... the compliment, Colonel Hoff. It is more of a testament to your leadership than my conduct."

"Indubitably," Hoff replied, his tone remarkably cool as he looked at Ashford with a raised eyebrow. "He also wrote to thank me for the gift I sent him 'on the occasion of my marriage last December 24th.' I had not realized that Thompson had gotten married during his stay at this hospital. I must have somehow missed the ceremony," remarked the colonel, boring a hole in Ashford's face with his gaze.

Ashford almost choked. "Was that the date? I was quite unaware. I must have missed the party as well. I must ask McAndrew if he was invited, or was on ... *ahem*... duty, sir!"

"Well, that won't be necessary now. In any event, I am happy for Thompson and you, having both found the most beautiful and accomplished local ladies to marry. Next time, I will be delighted to cover you as Officer of the Day, should you curry an invitation. Dismissed!"

"Yes, sir and thank you very much, sir!" Ashford saluted, and without turning around, backed out of the office, his eyes on Hoff's glowing countenance. It seemed that nothing could escape the old fox, after all.

Early in the afternoon of June 29th, Bailey and Mariá Ashford repeated their marriage ceremony in order to comply with the new laws regarding civil versus religious marriage celebrations. Their union was thereby made not only official but legal. The next day, the happy couple departed on the train for Ponce by way of Mayagüez, the city of María Asunción's birth. It was a fateful move, not only for the newlyweds, but for the entire island of Puerto Rico as well.

Chapter Sixteen

EL HOSPITAL MILITAR, JULY 1899

While Ashford courted María Asunción in the capital, Juan Báez, still in Ponce, made the acquaintance of a young man his age working for the Army. The two had initially met one Friday evening in the plaza, after Juan's new companion saw him perform with the *pleneros*. He had walked up to Juan, and, after congratulating him on his fine voice, had introduced himself as Rafael Moore, from the capital city. Juan soon found out that this young man could make the piano come to life with an ability he had not seen anywhere else. He spoke Spanish and English with equal proficiency, and seemed well-poised to advance his fortunes with the change in regimes. Before long, Juan Báez and Rafi Moore became good friends. They were both ambitious young men, brimming with intelligence and purpose, and together they enjoyed the vibrant nightlife of Ponce. They met after work to see what was going on in the plaza. On more than one occasion, they had walked into an open-air bar and taken it over, Juan with his fine voice and Rafi on the piano.

The differences in their upbringing, which seemed so alien and incomprehensible, yet so fascinating to one another, somehow fostered the growing mutual respect. Juan shared his story of growing up the oldest of nine children in abject poverty, picking coffee from the age of eight to make ends meet and watching his family slowly dwindle from chronic illness. Rafi, in turn, told Juan about growing up in the capital city, his late-night escape from San Juan, the overland campaign against the Spanish, and the brilliant young doctor he had worked with until recently. Rather than feel intimidated by Rafi's privileged upbringing, Juan was captivated by his new friend's adventures.

They engaged in lively conversations, sharing their dreams for the future. Rafi told Juan about his plans to become a microbiologist. He described his time in Connecticut, and his desire to return there someday, but not while so much was happening on the island. Juan confessed that his hard upbringing had interested him in public service, and that he had attended some meetings of the fledging pro-statehood party. Juan had quickly realized that to nurture these ambitions, he had to become proficient in English. He had enrolled in an English course offered through the Army liaison office, but his progress was slower than he wished.

"The best way to learn the new language," Rafi advised, "is to live in the United States for at least a year, maybe two. You will quickly learn to speak, read, and write English well. When you return to the island, you will be someone to be reckoned with."

While Rafi and Juan became acquainted, Ashford and María Asunción finally arrived in Ponce toward the middle of July in 1899. They settled into comfortable quarters at El Castillo, a stark two-level rectangular edifice built as the Spanish barracks shortly before the American invasion. It now housed American army personnel in rather cramped quarters, with the one attraction that married officers were permitted to reside there with their wives. María Asunción soon befriended the other three women in the barracks, all of whom were from the mainland. María Asunción used her impeccable island pedigree to get them all admitted to the Asociación de Señoras Damas de Ponce, a women's civic group responsible for running many critical charities in the city, including the Asilo de Damas.

The Hospital Militar de Ponce under Ashford's charge had been constructed by the Spanish Royal Corps of Engineers as their army's hospital. The attractive building followed the usual neoclassical style typical of nineteenth-century Spanish military architecture. It was a well-proportioned, single-story building of brick, rubble work, and stone, all covered in stucco painted a pale yellow on the outside. Like the hospital in San Juan, this building was organized around a rectangular courtyard, with open galleries on all sides leading to the patient rooms located on its periphery. Three arches ornamented with Tuscan pilasters welcomed visitors to the main entrance. Only a seventy-foot water tower erected in the courtyard intruded on the aesthetics of the building. Ugly and intrusive in the lovely tropical setting, the steel tower's four metal feet were cemented to the ground, and heavy rope cables secured it to the four corner pillars of the courtyard.

The *Hospital Militar* stood on the brow of a modest hill and was cooled by breezes that never reached the lower part of the town. From that enviable location, one could admire Ponce as it sprawled out below to finally meet an unending expanse of enormous sugar cane fields, with the sparkling Caribbean Sea as its backdrop. The Spanish had built the hospital at the northern edge of the city, where it was surrounded by large grassy fields untouched till now by development. Surveying the hospital placed under his charge, Ashford was filled with a sense of pride and responsibility. Still merely a lieutenant, he had been trusted with a great deal of authority.

Ashford's first order of business was to establish a working relationship with the local physicians, who regarded the military hospital up the hill with unease. Ashford hoped to reassure the local medical establishment that he wished to cooperate, not to antagonize. Dr. Stahl had kept the promise made in Aguadilla, graciously writing a letter of introduction to Manuel Zeno Gandía on behalf of the lieutenant, in the hopes that the elder doctor could prove a dependable advocate for the young man. Dr. Zeno was perhaps the most respected and sought-after clinician in Ponce. Almost as soon as he and María Asunción were settled, Ashford sent a message to Dr. Zeno requesting an interview at his convenience. The Puerto Rican replied with an invitation to come to his house that Friday at eight that evening.

Ashford arrived and was admitted into the grand hall of the residence. It was an elegant setting, paneled in mahogany with Spanish tile flooring. Just beyond the arched doorway, the lieutenant stepped into an attractive courtyard. This central patio was hemmed in by eggshell-blue walls, with archways on each side leading to the rooms. Here he found the venerable, bewhiskered physician and author, who cordially extended his hand in greeting.

"Dr. Ashford, welcome to Ponce and welcome to my home. It is my most sincere hope that the presence of your illustrious and democratic people will be of benefit to this miserably poor island." Ashford worded his reply with care.

"Dr. Zeno, I am honored to be your guest tonight. The kindness of your fellow islanders has been most deeply felt. As you are aware, I am the commanding officer at the former Spanish military hospital north of the city. I hope to be able to cooperate with you and your colleagues on the problems we have inherited from your old Spanish rulers."

Dr. Zeno glanced wearily at his young guest. "That has been, and will continue to be, no easy task. It is no secret that for years, I pressed the Spanish for a greater voice in our own affairs, believing that greater freedom would bring improved social conditions. Until the last few months of their rule, the Spanish governor in San Juan was an imported military autocrat with instructions to keep the natives in line. No dissent was tolerated. We watched helplessly as our Latin American brothers left us behind politically, economically, and socially. Now, I fear the damage may be difficult to reverse."

Ashford replied, "Didn't the Spanish grant political concessions shortly before the fighting started?"

"Yes they did, Lieutenant." Dr. Zeno nodded, and beckoned his guest over to a small table already laid with a pot of steaming coffee and a tray of *gateau*. "But the Autonomy Charter of 1897 arrived too late to fulfill the promise of integration. Although it was a sincere and generous arrangement, the new government was barely a week old when your forces landed in Guánica. The invasion put an end to that chapter on self-government."

As they sat and poured coffee into their delicate demitasses, Dr. Zeno explained that he now focused on medical concerns, specifically the deplorable condition of the hundreds of thousands of landless, malnourished rural peasants. He enumerated the endless panoply of illnesses that bread in the tropical climate: smallpox, malaria, and rampant typhoid fever.

"Even the flatworms described by Dr. Bilharz," the doctor

continued, "were found to be common as soon as he published his report. And social ills brought about by the general lack of work are everywhere: alcoholism, illiteracy, and depression hang over the land like a cloud, seemingly with no chance of lifting."

"Well then," Ashford replied, "something will need to be done. I offer my service to that end. I have travelled throughout the country, from Ponce to Aguadilla. I am particularly concerned by the striking appearance of so many of the inhabitants. All the locals seem so…well, *so very small*. Short and underweight, faces drawn in, with sunken eyes and darkened circles underneath. It is all heart-wrenching, really."

Zeno responded, "Malnutrition is a big problem, no question."

Ashford continued, "But what I find even more striking and enigmatic is that in this tropical setting, with the bright sun beating down on the inhabitants mercilessly…Even in the face of this beautiful and intense sunshine…"

Zeno interrupted. "Yes, Dr. Ashford, you are most observant. I believe you refer to the ghostly pallor that envelops nearly every man, woman, and child you see."

"It is the most remarkable and shocking thing," Ashford made as if to throw his hands in the air, forgetting that one held his coffee and nearly splattering it onto the tiles. Recovering himself, he continued, "All faces are devoid of any tinge of color, they are of the most absurd and pronounced ghastly shade of white one could ever imagine. Moreover, these sickly skin hues are impossible to miss, for they are evident everywhere. It reminds me of how some unfortunate patient would look if they were slowly exsanguinating from an intestinal tumor, or a stab or bullet wound, and the gradually creeping waxiness that signals death is approaching as blood is uncontrollably lost."

"You are right again, Dr. Ashford. Virtually every person living outside the larger cities is anemic. And they are not simply anemic, but severely and almost incomprehensibly so." Dr. Zeno shook his head, his shoulders slumping in weary defeat. "Most of my patients are anemic, as were those of my mentor and those of his professor before him. I was taught that the poor, unvarying diet and some mysterious unhealthy air were responsible for this misery. If Spain could have somehow improved conditions so that the *jíbaros* could have had more than the occasional slice of cod, then maybe the anemia problem would have resolved. I grew tired of waiting for the Spanish to come around to our way of thinking. Then you *americanos* arrived."

Ashford raised his eyebrows, surveying his host thoughtfully. "Can you tell me about the blood studies in the anemic patients?"

Zeno replied, "We are somewhat limited in our clinical resources here, but I can say with some confidence that their red cell counts regularly run at about half the values of those expected in healthy people, and the cells that are present are small and pale. It resembles mostly an anemia of the so-called chlorotic type. Personally, I have seen several children with red cell counts below thirty percent of normal."

Ashford recoiled in horror. "How can that be? How can they walk, play, indeed, how can they do anything?"

"They don't." Zeno regarded Ashford with a long and steady gaze over his cup. "They lie on the thatch floor of their hut, utterly helpless. Their mothers care for them as if they are still infants although many of them are adolescents. I know one family in Utuado who has lost five of their nine children to *la anemia*, and may soon lose the father as well. For their dying children, there was no hope of a recovery. At the end they were breathing corpses, pure and simple."

"And the adults?"

Dr. Zeno replied that the adults all had to work even while they were deathly ill, whether they had the energy or not. The loss in productivity was incalculable, through no fault of either the laborers or their employers.

Ashford frowned as he carefully picked some cake crumbs off his shirt and laid them on his dish.

"I have become very interested in exploring the science behind this illness," he said. "We have a good laboratory at the military hospital, with quality microscopes and numerous dyes to mix into different stains. I have already requested that two hemoglobinometers for evaluating red cells be sent from

San Juan. And best of all, I have an assistant coming to join me who is an excellent microscopist and a knowledgeable student of the blood. Maybe we could make some progress in our spare time."

Dr. Zeno drained the last of his coffee. "Dr. Ashford, the medical community here welcomes any effort, although it is rather attached to the idea that this anemia is nutritional and will persist until dietary trends are improved."

"For now, at least, that seems to make the most sense," Ashford replied diplomatically.

Ashford rose to leave soon after, thanking the older physician for his hospitality. The two men exchanged cordial expressions and shook hands in parting.

As Ashford walked home to María Asunción and El Castillo, passing tidy shopfronts and distracted pedestrians, he reviewed what he had learned about the anemia problem. If the atrocious diet of the *jíbaros* was truly the cause of the disease, then perhaps the Department of War, which was now responsible for governing the island, could devise a way to improve the quantity and quality of the available food. Yet he had become increasingly skeptical of the dominant role being ascribed to nutrition. In his mind, the anemia was simply too severe and too widespread to be due exclusively to an inadequate diet. The words he had used in his earlier report echoed in his mind: *"there must be something else, not yet understood…"*

Chapter Seventeen

THE HURRICANE, AUGUST 1899

On July 31, 1899, Her Majesty's Ship *Hortense* steamed lazily in beautiful weather three hundred miles southwest of the African coast. The summer sun was high and hot, the sea inauspiciously calm and the winds light. Leaning against the port rail, Captain McWay and his mate examined the far eastern horizon through binoculars. Away in the distance they could barely make out towering clouds building to colossal heights, cotton billows darkening. The steady breeze, which for days had blown persistently from the east, had started shifting ever-so-gradually toward the north within the last half-hour. The ship's position, time of year, changing wind, and unnatural calm all signaled trouble.

McWay ordered barometric reports every thirty minutes. To no one's surprise, the readings began to fall steadily. As the breeze freshened, the skipper ordered full steam and an immediate change of course to the south. There was no doubt that they faced a developing tropical storm, and the wisest course was to give it the widest berth possible. In his many years crossing the Atlantic, McWay could not recall ever seeing a cyclone so far to the east.

Nine days later, the morning of the eighth of August brought the feast of St. Cyriac to nearly 300 million Catholics around the globe. Not many people besides the clergy and the overly pious cared about this largely forgotten martyr of late antiquity, and Lieutenant Ashford most certainly was not among them. In his outpatient clinic at the Hospital Militar de Ponce, he was preparing to tackle yet another steady line of patients. Rafi Moore as usual served as Ashford's assistant and translator. Since they had reunited in Ponce, a strong bond had developed between the two young men. Ashford's deepening love and respect for his friend's country and culture nourished their friendship. Since landing in Ponce almost exactly one year earlier, Ashford had married a Puerto Rican woman, identified the best taverns and cafés in Ponce, and made inroads into the intricacies of the Spanish language, with its gendered nouns and interminable bizarre conjugations. In short, he was becoming more assimilated.

Sick call generally started very early, while the city still slept undisturbed by the first tentative rays of sun. The morning of August 8th began like so many others—warm, humid, and enriched by the sweet aromas of jasmine and mint. But in spite of this beautiful start, those in the know were on edge. The U. S. Weather Bureau in San Juan had issued a hurricane watch owing to a gradual wind shift to the north: a worrisome trend when accompanied by a rapidly falling barometer.

For Ashford, news of a potential storm was hardly a footnote in what promised to be another routine day. The clinical problems that day appeared straightforward, as no new outbreaks or serious health issues had arisen since the cease-fire. Occasionally, he still came across a case of typhoid, but most patients' issues were mundane: minor fractures or maybe a case of appendicitis. His life had settled into a rather pleasant routine, which the lieutenant took at an unhurried pace surrounded by grateful patients, a few good friends, and a beautiful wife to welcome him home in the evenings.

At precisely seven in the morning, Ashford and Rafi took their seats in a small examination room and the lieutenant imperiously called out, "Sergeant, bring in the first patient!" An elderly man promptly came in, was interviewed, and examined. It proved to be a straightforward case of constipation. The man received a course of cathartics strong enough to cure an elephant and was duly dismissed. Next came a civilian whom they had agreed to see because of possible heart failure. With this case, the team took more time. "Rales in the lung, enlarged heart with a loud murmur and a low apex point... Rafi, please tell Mr. Díaz that we will start him on some tincture of digitalis and ask him to stop putting salt in his food." Ashford turned to the patient and said, "We will see you back in ten days, my friend," and the man left thanking Ashford profusely in Spanish.

Next, a young soldier made his appearance, looking exceptionally nervous and avoiding all eye contact. Ashford suddenly had a strong hunch as to the direction the conversation would take. The young man stared at his boots and recounted his afternoon of leave the previous week, which he spent in town "making friends," as he called his activities. These new friends turned out to be some very sociable females, from whom he had caught a very social kind of disease. The soldier was as pale as a ghost, and Ashford had no doubt that he had heard the widely circulating horror stories concerning the standard treatment for his condition. After completing his story, the private stood at attention, shaking in his shoes.

Ashford finally broke the ice, "Well soldier, let's have a look."

The private pleaded, "Couldn't you just go ahead and prescribe me something, doc? I think it is getting better all by itself."

"Nonsense! This problem is not going to just get up and walk away—Private, drop those drawers on the double!"

The order was obeyed, and the private's private areas examined.

"No surprises here soldier, you have a fine case of what you fellows call the clap," said Ashford, struggling to look completely serious, and managing only with the greatest difficulty. "We must treat at once!"

The private went pale, then green, and suddenly swayed on the verge of fainting. Rafi reached for smelling salts of ammonia and alcohol, which he waved repeatedly under the soldier's nostrils. Giving a sharp backwards jerk, the man was partially restored.

Ashford addressed him again, "I assure you, soldier, that the treatment is very effective and strictly routine."

The smelling salts had to be administered once again.

Ashford whispered, "Mr. Moore, if our brave private looks to faint once more, let's leave him be, he might prefer to be unconscious for a few minutes."

The soldier stared in wide-eyed terror as the doctor reached for a most unique contraption, which was especially reserved for these cases. It was a type of syringe, but instead of being tipped by a needle, it held a very small but rather stiff rubber tube, apparently to insert into the narrow confines that provided the body its plumbing. Four assistants arrived to help the man, in reality, to save him from any indignities should he come unglued and attempt to flee naked past amused onlookers.

When all was ready, the doctor carefully inserted the narrow tube into the inflamed orifice and with the utmost care filled the urinary system in retrograde fashion with colloidal silver, a more humane preparation than the silver nitrate which until recently had been employed for this purpose. The soldier's consolation in his hour of trial was that colloidal silver was every bit as effective as it was uncomfortable, and he could expect to be cured with reasonable certainty after only one treatment. The whole ordeal took only fifteen minutes, but that was enough time for the private to learn his lesson. In Ashford's experience, they almost always did.

Before he could begin to examine the next patient, Ashford had to request a portable lamp. In just the few minutes that it had taken the team to treat the patient with gonorrhea, dark clouds had completely surrounded the area. Through the lone window in the exam room, Rafi and Ashford watched, transfixed, as a deathly, oppressive calm surrendered to the initial gusts of the wind which suddenly exploded into an otherworldly fury. In rapid succession, the lights went out, their alarmed patient hid under the table, and the study lamps shattered against the paved floor, driven by the gale rushing through the open window. The full wrath of a Caribbean hurricane descended upon them and everything soon became enveloped in a ghostly gray of sheeted water and deafening screams from the wind.

At regular intervals amid the howling gusts, Ashford could hear the sound of a distant peasant shack slamming against the hospital's walls, splintering like so many toothpicks. Ramshackle huts like these were mostly built of scavenged materials—old boxes and scrap wood—with roofs of corrugated tin sheets or flattened kerosene cans. Such structures provided little defense against wind and rain of such magnitude. Ashford's thoughts immediately turned to María Asunción, who was attending a meeting of the *Asociación de señoras* in Ponce. He had no way to communicate with her and did not know when he would be able to do so.

Meanwhile, the storm had only just begun to bare its teeth.

*****

In the mountains of Utuado, Tuesday, August 8th, had also dawned bright and clear. Earlier that morning, high up in the central mountains at Hacienda Las Alturas, administrator Luis Colón became concerned when he was summoned to the big house one hour before daybreak for an urgent meeting with don Arturo Roig. Several other foremen were already present when don Arturo began to speak. "The word in San Juan is that we have a *temporal,* a major hurricane, on the way to the island. Some of my friends at *La Fortaleza* say that there is no doubt. Already, there are reports of hundreds of dead on the islands of Monserrate and Santa Cruz. Unless there is some last-minute miracle, we face a catastrophe."

Colón asked his boss whether they should prepare for the worst.

"Without a doubt," don Arturo nodded, his face etched in grim lines. Nothing could be done for the coffee trees, although a few might be saved that were protected by the lee of a slope or by one of the larger guava or avocado trees. In the San Narciso hurricane back in '67, he explained, they had lost nine out of every ten trees, and it had taken five years for coffee production to recover.

Someone spoke up: "And what about the workers?"

Looking around at the group of concerned faces, don Arturo replied, "I will ask three of you to help me secure the plantation house with boards and battens, for which you will receive a generous bonus pay. The rest of you, go to the fields and warn the workers back to their homes, to save what they can and to look after their families. Then, all of you should do the same. By midmorning, all employees should be seeking shelter with their loved ones. Now go! There is no time to waste. God be with you all."

For the occupants of the Báez hut, the precise day of the week, or the date, or the month made no real difference and were only imprecisely known. The foreman at the coffee hacienda marked Saturdays with an early dismissal, followed by a day of rest on Sunday. Beyond this, the days of the week blurred and flowed seamlessly until the next Saturday arrived to reorient the families. On that particular Tuesday in August, the priest in Utuado town might have reminded the peasants that it was the feast day of San Ciriaco, but only a small number of them would have seen him. Instead, the day was a day of work like so many others. The morning coffee was made, the children were fed, the worn garments put on, and the multitudes of men and women began to make their way to the coffee fields.

Simón quietly pulled apart the palm fronds that served as the front door to their hut and walked barefoot to the forest edge to pull down his pants and defecate in the soil. He was followed by young Carlos, dressed in holed cotton skivvies and leading his sister Ana by the hand. She was dressed in nothing at all. Together, they performed the morning drill of evacuation, the older child there to assist the younger without embarrassment or concern for anything except the task at hand. Finally, it was the mother Josefa's turn. As usual, the woman wore her shoes to allow her to walk without the pain caused by her deformed lower leg.

With all such business accomplished, the couple headed to the hacienda to pick the very first of the ripening coffee berries.

"This day is starting out so very warm," Simón remarked as they began their hike up the steep, muddy path. "Especially for so far up the *monte.*"

"Be quiet old man, complaining will only make the day longer. It will cool off soon enough," Pepa gently scolded from behind her partner.

Simón fell silent. But it really was quite uncomfortably warm, the result of higher temperatures and a lack of breeze, an unusual combination in the higher elevations of the central mountains. Simón could not shake a feeling of foreboding, arising from faint memories going back to when he was a child.

"Pepa," he tried again, "you can't remember it like I do, because you were so young, but I was about seven or eight years old and living in Cayey when the day started exactly like this—hot, heavy, and quiet. One could *smell* something coming on."

"And it was—?"

"El huracán de San Narciso."

Simón and Pepa made it to the coffee plantation in the usual half hour it took to walk the uphill trail. By then, the wind had picked up, and ominous clouds were building to the east. They found the grove abuzz in frantic conversation. Luis Colón stood on the stump of a large mahogany tree, trying to impart some calm among the arriving pickers.

"Everybody, *todo el mundo*, listen here, please! We have been warned that there is an approaching hurricane that will hit us later today. The storm will be fierce, and has already caused deaths on neighboring islands. You are all released from further work arrangements, pending developments. Hurry back and see to your families. Everybody is in danger! We will get word to you when the hacienda reopens for the harvest."

The Báez couple turned around to descend the trail back to their *bohío*. The drizzle that had followed them up the mountain was now strengthening into a generous tropical downpour. The earthen path, uneven and pocked in the best of times, soon resembled an obstacle course as the mud deepened underneath their feet. Every few steps, Simón had to grab at tree limbs by the path's edge to keep from falling. Pepa, because of her awkward shoes, found the going even trickier, relying on Simón to hold her by the waist and prevent an unwelcome meeting of rear end and mire. Already, rapidly flowing rivulets of clear mountain water streamed down the slopes, crossing their path every few minutes and adding to their peril. Despite the downhill trek, it took them an hour to return to the hut. Through the sheets of water blowing all around them, the couple could barely make out their home. The palm frond door was gone, and the wooden walls groaned and creaked ominously to the rhythm of the gale. Inside, the children could not be seen.

Simón and Pepa swallowed their fears and began to search. Their calls were drowned by the awful din of the storm, and with the visibility so poor, their quest consisted of enlarging spirals around the hut in the shape of an ever-growing snail's shell. The parents happened upon their two children, protected behind the trunks of several large and sturdy royal palms, soaked through but safe.

The family struggled back to the *bohío* as the wispy structure began to disintegrate. The old planks of the tiny hut were no match for the wind, and with humanlike malice the storm groped under the stilts and blew the hovel up and over, the structure coming apart as it tumbled along the ground and collided with the giant trees. Nothing was saved. They were left only with their ragged attire, saturated and translucent, the cotton clinging immodestly to their drenched skin.

Simón gathered everyone around him and shouted above the wind. "This is only the beginning! The foreman told us that this storm will be a bad one. We should head back to the big house, and try to seek shelter there. It may be the only thing able to withstand this wind."

Pepa yelled back, agreeing they must go at once. She scooped up little Ana and they set off.

For the second time that morning, the family began the mile-long trek uphill, slipping and sliding barefoot on the slick red clay of the mountain, Pepa struggling to clear her wooden soles from the muck. They knew their way intimately, so many times had they traversed the paths in sheeting rain. The powerful wind was another obstacle altogether, but with plenty of trees everywhere to provide support and liana vines to grip, the four made their way up to the hacienda.

By the time Simón, Pepa, and the children arrived, the hurricane was in full force. The elegant plantation house had acquired the air of a fort under attack. The shutters were bolted closed and the bricks were stained with streaks of mud, while the upper story groaned increasingly under the push of the storm.

The Báez family were not the only ones who thought to seek shelter with don Arturo. To his credit, the hacienda's owner welcomed all he could into his house. Those that he couldn't fit, he sent to the sturdier outbuildings of the plantation. The family made their way up the double-tiered staircase to the second floor, where don Arturo greeted them each by name, passing out candles and blankets and other supplies kept in storage for such emergencies, which, though rare, had recurred unpredictably from time immemorial. As the family crowded in among their neighbors, Simón looked up at the darkened ceiling and saw that despite the house's solid construction, water was coming through the roof and around the windows. The wooden upper story swayed unnervingly, battling the cyclone on unequal terms. Rich and poor alike stared silently at each other, sharing knowing looks of dread.

The wind and rain built steadily throughout the morning. Whenever it seemed that there was a climax in the spectacle, the storm went on to new heights of ferocity, bringing a corresponding uptick in fear among the huddled *jíbaros*. Around noon, concerned by the ominous jarring of the upper story, don Arturo came upstairs and invited them to crowd in with the others on the first floor. They silently filed down the stairs to join those huddled within the sturdier masonry walls of the first story. More candles were lit, additional prayers said, and some food passed around while the peasant children held ever more tightly to their parents. The elements furiously pounded the house for what seemed an eternity. Over the screaming wind and driving rain, Simon remembered the San Narciso hurricane he had lived through as a boy. This cyclone, he feared, was much worse.

*****

In Ponce and nearby, the brutal storm evicted everyone from the hundreds of ramshackle huts by degrees. Newly homeless people dragged children, parents and grandparents with them, everyone groping blindly through the murky half-darkness. They dodged an endless wave of projectiles—tree limbs, earthenware and metalware, and most dangerous of all, the sheets of razor-sharp zinc roofing rotating through the air like giant scythes. These rain-drenched souls finally converged at the gates of Ponce's hospitals and public buildings, all of which had been opened to shelter victims.

Within the thick walls and heavy wooden doors of the military hospital, the refugees were safe. Its flat brick roof proved indestructible, though other structures were not as lucky. With the first fury of the hurricane, the unsightly water tower cemented to the courtyard began to sway rhythmically, and in the blink of an eye, with loud reports from snapping cables, it was gone. The steel skeleton catapulted over the roof of the building, somersaulting downwind to be found the next day a quarter of a mile away.

With the climax of the hurricane, Ashford witnessed the saddest procession he had ever seen: a single-file line of the injured, stains of blood punctuating tattered cotton rags, marching with their heads bowed forward in quiet resignation. Many bore cuts; others suffered from fractures of legs, arms, or skulls. From time to time, a group of three or four men appeared at the hospital, struggling with a makeshift hammock bearing an unlucky person suffering from fearful wounds caused by the airborne zinc sheets cutting into their chest, abdomen, or thigh. Before long, the hospital wards were overflowing with the injured and the homeless. Victims squatted in silence, gazing blankly into space as the wind roared beyond the walls. They were hungry, thirsty, and wet, but nobody complained. For them, the hurricane was simply an act of God.

Ashford and his assistants spent the worst of the hurricane working on the injured, improvising procedures while they attempted to block images of uprooted trees, tangled wires, fallen poles, and demolished houses from their minds. In the early afternoon, the eye of the hurricane passed over Ponce, and the winds suddenly shifted from northeast to southwest. In the momentary quiet, the hospital continued to fill with the injured and sick. Just before the sky darkened once again, a woman brought a child whose arm had been severed above the elbow by a flying metal plate. Ashford rushed to stem the bleeding. The boy's shirt, already soaked with rain, was too saturated to hold all of the lost blood which streamed relentlessly onto the floor. But as the hospital fell back into a stormy night, the doctor's heroic efforts could not save him, and the young doctor's grief was soon lost in the renewed howling of the storm.

*****

In the main house of the coffee plantation, after five long hours of unabated assault, the wind miraculously died down to a moderate breeze. The upper story still remained above them, and the downstairs shelter had endured the ordeal fairly well and remained reasonably dry. Outside, the sky rapidly cleared, and the sun peeked through the dissipating clouds, revealing a most beautiful day to those who looked timidly from the windows. The house was submerged in an eerie quiet, in part thanks to the stupefied silence of its occupants, but mostly because outside, all the insects and songbirds had been blown away or killed.

In a land used to tropical cyclones, most people knew about the phenomenon of the *ojo del huracán*, the passing of the eye of the hurricane. On the one hand, the eye provided a much-needed relief, but on the other, those who found themselves in the eye knew that worse destruction would come, and soon. It was anybody's guess, but they might have anywhere from twenty to thirty minutes to regroup and hunker down for the rest of the storm. They used the time to replenish water, food, and candles.

Several of the refugees wandered outside to relieve themselves or check on their friends and family in the outbuildings. Don Arturo, his son and some of the foremen went upstairs and, from the splendid porch, looked out at the coffee bushes that had once stood in neat rows, stretching away endlessly under umbrellas of shade trees. Now they lay toppled across the ground like a fallen brigade after a lost campaign. The occasional tree stood out in lonely defiance, but otherwise the desolation was quite complete. A sudden, deep despondency settled over the planter. As the winds began to return from the opposite direction, he led the way back downstairs with his head bowed in defeat.

The second part of the hurricane of *San Ciriaco* did not disappoint. With the return of the eye wall, the wind rapidly ramped up to full power, and within fifteen minutes, the upper story of the plantation house was ripped away, along with part of the lower ceiling protecting the refugees. Water poured in, the candles blew out, and horror and confusion ruled. The next three hours brought a living hell, combining the fear and cold of the huddled masses with the deafening roar of the hurricane. The occasional tree flew overhead, spinning within a mass of flying debris hard to comprehend, as though some giant invisible hand was scooping away handfuls of the mountain side to hurl over the huddled *jíbaros*.

Not until nightfall did the worst finally pass. Except for the persistent rain, a complete stillness descended upon the scene. Simón, Pepa, and the other workers sat on the stone floor to await the dawn, knowing they had no homes to return to and unsure of where to turn.

With the break of day, the victims of the hurricane ventured outdoors. The scene struck them all like a kick to the stomach. The wooden outbuildings had all collapsed, leaving survivors to shelter behind whatever trees they could find, and a handful of corpses strewn about the mud. The machinery in the *casona* lay scattered in pieces. The waterwheels had disappeared. Many larger trees and palms were stripped bare, and everywhere the coffee plants lay uprooted and upended.

Inside what remained of the plantation house, all eyes turned to the proprietor like a congregation turning to its priest as he elevates the host. Don Arturo spoke in a heavy voice, looking as though he had aged years since that morning. "After today, nothing will ever be the same for any of us. I regret to inform you that there is no hacienda and no coming harvest. My family and I will start rebuilding right away, and I will need a few skilled laborers to assist us. But I can no longer provide employment for the rest of you. Here on the mountain, there is scarcely any food, no shelter and no work for you. I urge all of you to leave this place and head toward the cities. Ponce is only twenty miles away, and the United States military likely has facilities there to feed and shelter you. They also have a hospital and excellent Army doctors to treat those who are wounded or sick. In my dealings with the new government, I have found the *norteamericanos* to be a fair and responsible people, and you should seek their aid. There is nothing good here for you now, so please, go, I beg you."

With this last entreaty to his former workers, don Arturo turned to survey the ruin of his home, feeling the eyes of the peasants burning into his back while his own eyes prickled uncomfortably. Eventually, soft murmurs began to rise behind him, and the sounds of a hundred feet shifting in the mud could be heard over the rain, fading slowly as the workers left the plantation where many had toiled their entire lives.

Finally, after twelve hours of blowing at hurricane strength, the winds died away late that night. The torrential rains, however, continued unabated into the next morning, pounding the backs of the *jíbaros* leaving Las Alturas behind them.

Chapter Eighteen

THE CARAVAN OF SPECTERS

A strange caravan of the dispossessed, its members even poorer than they had been the day before, began a two-day journey down the steep southern slopes toward Ponce. As they headed down the gradually widening trails leading away from coffee country, more and more people joined the silent procession. Progress was slow for all but the few who owned a donkey or mule, or maybe stumbled upon a stray pony on the way. To the refugees, the scenes on the road mirrored the destruction on the hacienda. Trees were stripped, the road was interrupted by mudslides, and a few mangled corpses could be seen by the wayside, killed by an airborne tree limb or other debris.

The survivors foraged for fallen mangoes, avocados, bananas, and the occasional orange. They drank from muddy, overflowing streams flowing downhill toward the coast. As the caravan continued through the countryside, the full impact of the hurricane began to reveal itself. Whole coffee plantations had simply slipped down the slopes and into the rivers. The bananas, plantains, guavas, and mangoes which made up over half of their food, and most importantly, the half that was free, were practically all destroyed as well. The wide path of the cyclone had destroyed two-thirds of the agriculture of the island, striking the delicate coffee trees particularly hard. The hurricane could not have come at a worse time, hitting the island one month before the peak of the coffee harvest. If the *jíbaros* had been able to ask don Arturo about the future, he would likely have said that the industry would take five years to recover, if, it ever did. Now hungry and homeless, their clothes hanging from their pale emaciated frames, droves of displaced and desperate agricultural laborers now set their sights on Ponce and its promise of food and shelter.

Simón, Pepa, and their two children formed part of that caravan of specters—people with nothing of value, ghostly white from chronic anemia, exhausted by their disease, and searching for help they did not know where to find. They numbered in the thousands.

Upon reaching Ponce, the crowd began to disperse randomly throughout the city. Like Simón, some had family with whom to shelter, while others knew a priest, or had a friend who worked for the mayor. Others planned to continue on to the neighboring coastal towns, to find out whether any sugar mills had survived and could offer them employment. Many had no plans at all.

The Báez family walked down from the Vigía Hill into Ponce with only the clothes on their backs and the few mangoes and bananas they had gathered along the way. For Simón, the walk had been more exhausting because of his debilitating disease, whereas for Pepa, traveling was made more difficult because of her limp and uncomfortable shoes. Their two children followed behind them with that enthusiasm born of innocence that can ease the suffering of hardships.

The family headed toward the port to find Juan. As they began walking through Juan's neighborhood, their fear intensified. Most of the houses, being built of wood, now lay strewn about like so many matches spilled from a box. The awful weather they had lived through had given way to the most sparkling days, and in the clear air, the devastation was revealed at its worst. The August sun and an oppressive humidity frayed any nerves not already stretched to their breaking point by the hurricane. Everywhere Simón and people looked, ghost-like refugees sat on the sidewalk with looks of numb disbelief, while others combed through the ruins for possessions or food, or maybe for missing loved ones. People drank from the ditches as stray animals roamed through the streets and sniffed around the leveled dwellings, disputing over scraps of raw garbage.

Juan's family was relieved to discover that his house, constructed solidly of cement blocks, was still standing. The roof, however, was missing, and all the windows had been blown out. They knocked, then walked inside. Everything down to the walls had been ruined by the wind and rain. Worst, there was no sign of Juan. His parents tried not to reveal their mounting fear, and they put themselves and the children to work cleaning out debris from the storm.

After several hours of this, Simón and his family gave into the exhaustion and turmoil of the past several days. They sat on the floor, dazed and inert, unable even to eat. Ana went to play outside.

It was Ana who spotted her big brother as he walked back toward the house. She ran to him, arms wide. Smiling broadly, Juan bent down so that she could jump into his outstretched arms. Carlos was not far behind, and Juan embraced his brother with one arm while clutching Ana to him with the other.

"Where were you?" they cried.

"I went to the docks to look at the damage where I work," he said. "But I kept coming back here to see if you had arrived. And you did!"

Juan hugged them close. His worst fear since the hurricane was that little Ana, or Carlos, or, God forbid, his whole family, had not survived and that he was waiting in vain. Everywhere, he heard speculation regarding the massive loss of life, and the destruction scattered across the city made such claims more believable. No rumor seemed like an exaggeration, and this only fed his mounting dread. His parents, hearing voices, came out of the house and ran toward him. His mother sobbed as she embraced him. She looked much older, her grief at the death of Rosita still heavy on her shoulders. One year had passed since that last visit to Ponce, when a ray of hope had been cruelly extinguished by acute malaria just as the child was beginning to conquer anemia.

Juan then regarded his father with astonishment. Simón had always been a small, sickly man, but still being in his late thirties, he had been able to push through his frailties thanks to pure determination and the love he felt for his family. Now, the trek from Utuado seemed to have finished him, and he looked more than twice his age. He appeared abstracted and apathetic, and his white skin, always so pale, had taken on a new hue of a sickly straw yellow. His father was dying, and Juan knew he had nothing to offer him. Fighting back tears through a forced smile, Juan passed off his siblings to his mother and took his father in his arms, holding him for a moment. Simón was light as a feather, and Juan could easily feel his father's skeleton through his wasted muscles.

Juan swallowed the lump in his throat and said, "*Papi*, it is good to see you again. This *temporal* has reunited us once more, and where there is family there is always love and hope. We will figure out a way to get you strong again."

Simón looked up at his handsome son, standing a full head taller than his own. He smiled wanly and patted his son's cheek with fingers that were little more than bone. "My dear Juan, I am so proud of you. I regret that I didn't have the courage and the foresight to take the family out of the hacienda when you left. Maybe our dear Rosa would still be alive."

Juan replied with a trembling voice, "Don't say that, *Papi*. You did the best you could."

Simón broke down in tears. "But now we have nothing, and my time is short. I have no energy left to fight for my family."

Ana interrupted to announce that she was hungry. Juan took stock of the meager supplies his family had brought with them from the mountains. There was nothing left to eat but the fruits they had collected on the way, and even those were running out. The trees in Ponce had been stripped bare of their leaves and fruit, except for the occasional sprig that had somehow kept avocados or mangoes on its limbs after toppling over. These few were of supreme interest to all the victims, as anything remotely edible was rapidly consumed, often after violent altercations.

Juan realized he could not stay in the remnants of the house with his starving family for even a day. His father was terminally ill; his siblings were malnourished and ailing. Without food and fresh water, he stood to lose most of what remained of his family. He had been thinking as they ate, and finally he spoke.

"*Mami, Papi*, there may be a way for us to get some help. I know a young man about my age, a remarkable musician and a good scientist. He works for the Army Medical Corps out of the *Hospital Militar*. We are good friends, and through him, I have met some of the American officers who come to listen to us play music on Fridays and Saturdays. The *americanos* are friendly and courteous. My friend, Rafi, says that the doctors he works with are superb and are concerned with the sickness and the poverty in the city. If we go up to the hospital, the army doctors may be able to aid us. I don't know if they will have enough food or water for all of the people but we have nothing to lose. Maybe they will be willing to help *Papi* get well, even though he is not an American soldier."

They did not argue with Juan's suggestion. The family rested for an hour, finished the fresh water that Juan had stored, and headed to the military hospital. As they made the hour-long journey to the northern edge of the city, they were joined by others with the same thought. The United States had entered the country barely one year before, and the locals weren't entirely sure how to regard their new masters. But many of them, like the Báez family, were out of options and hoped that the Americans might be willing to help them. The procession of *jíbaros* that had descended on Ponce, having found nothing to eat and fleeing the many looters and thieves, congregated once more—this time to head up the hill toward the hospital. After a few days in the city, it would number close to one thousand.

Three days after the hurricane, the Báez family entered the hospital building through the main portico and walked into the large central courtyard. Several hundred refugees already sat at the edges of the raised arched corridors, speaking softly among themselves. Juan left his parents and went to inquire after Rafi. Glancing around for any signs of his friend, he walked into the first room off the east corridor, which served as a combination reception area and office. A fidgeting corporal sat facing him behind a desk. Juan thought the young soldier looked very worried, undoubtedly about the massive influx of locals continuing to trickle in through the open gates and doors.

Juan approached the desk, and, in halting English asked whether *Señor* Rafael Moore was in.

The harried corporal sent an assistant to notify Rafi about

his visitor, and ten minutes later, Rafi came in and greeted his friend. Juan brought him to the courtyard to meet the family about whom Rafi had heard so much over the last six months. Despite what Juan had told him about life in Utuado, Rafi had to suppress a groan of horror at the appearance of the Baez family. Simón, in particular, was obviously very ill, and the entire family urgently needed food, water, and a place to stay.

Rafi hurried to find Ashford in the clinic, who was in the middle of daily sick call for the first time since the hurricane. The doctor was evaluating a soldier with the chipmunk cheeks characteristic of mumps when Rafi interrupted the examination. "Doctor Ashford, the courtyard is beginning to fill with refugees seeking help."

Raising a hand to signal patience, Ashford finished the examination, before leaving his patient with a nurse. Noting the concerned look in Rafi's eyes, Ashford followed him and looked over the central courtyard, where civilians kept arriving in ever-increasing numbers. Ashford gasped and covered his mouth with his hand, his eyes watering. The words to the Psalm overtook his racing mind: *I would hasten my escape to the place of refuge; from the windy storm, and tempest.*

"Rafi, I was hoping to finish clinic this morning, but I see that those plans will have to wait indefinitely," Ashford said at last, his eyes fixed on the teeming mass of people below. "This is only the beginning. We need to plan for a massive influx of refugees, and from the looks of it, some of them are very ill already."

"We have dozens of tents left from the land campaign," Rafi responded. "We could raise them on the ground surrounding the building, to house these displaced civilians."

Ashford nodded. "Please find Sergeant Moretti and ask him to get that organized. Meanwhile, I will cable Colonel O'Reilly in San Juan." Ashford immediately wrote the Surgeon in Chief requesting provisions, staff, and funds to turn the hospital into a camp capable of supporting up to three hundred of the homeless. Even as he made this preparation, Ashford knew that this must be just a fraction of the thousands aimlessly wandering the narrow streets of Ponce. They would have to seek shelter at the other hospitals and charitable institutions of the city.

Later that afternoon, Ashford finally managed to take the mule ambulance into the center of Ponce in search of María Asunción. She was safe at the home of the consul—she and a few neighbors had sheltered under heavy beams after the structure had been destroyed. Together, the couple started back toward the barracks at El Castillo. The sight of the devastated city left them stunned. The venerable old town of 25,000 inhabitants was crushed. Its beautiful old trees lay prostrate, and climbing roses and jasmine hung like wet strings from shattered balconies, the walls they once clung to little more than flooded rubble. They passed the ride in stunned silence, barely able to grasp the destruction around them.

Ashford bore silent witness as the days after the hurricane unfolded. They were the most terrible the city had ever experienced. Ponce was isolated by the raging torrents of nearby rivers and wreckage strewn about the roads. In the course of twelve hours, the Portugués and Bucaná Rivers, usually shallow, narrow creeks coursing near the center of the city, received the entire outflow of the nearby mountain range, bursting their banks to fill the streets. After the initial storm passed, torrents of water came raging down the slopes with hardly a warning, swamping the city in one prodigious flood of brown.

Ashford and Rafi watched helplessly from the protection of the hospital up on the hill, while blocks of houses down below were inundated higher than their balconies, and the central plaza and the cathedral were covered in muck two feet deep. Muddy slime washed over the floors of the exquisitely appointed homes of the wealthy and would remain for days.

The battered city's population kept increasing as droves of desperate peasants arrived looking for food and shelter. A severe shortage of food developed, and widespread hunger added to the general misery. Three days after the hurricane hit, milk, bread, and eggs sold for twenty times their usual price, if they could be found at all. Difficult days were followed by worse nights, with shots, screams, and wanton violence consuming the city.

The Army took control of the volatile situation and immediately issued one million dollars' worth of food rations. The military governor, Major General George Whitefield Davis, launched a rescue effort based in San Juan that spared no expense or efforts. On his part, Colonel Hoff in San Juan declared that not one more person was to perish from lack of food. Colonel O'Reilly granted all of Ashford's requests for supplies and medical personnel. Within days of Ashford's request, the rations were delivered, refugees were parceled among the tents, and the hard work of putting lives back together began.

The parade of sallow figures that had stumbled wearily down the mountains now streamed into the tents. In the overflowing camp on the hospital grounds, dozens of people sat in the mud and rain, waiting for the soldiers to finish erecting the field hospital. Luckily, not all of the refugees were sick. Like Juan Báez, those who could work were housed in tents and given food in exchange for their labors. Pepa, Juan, and his siblings shared their tent with another family from Utuado. Simón, who was in serious condition, was housed close to the main building and provided with the most aggressive care available. The treatments were unfortunately extremely limited, and expected to perhaps delay, but not change, his grim outcome.

As the field hospital took shape, hosts of volunteers arrived to lend their assistance. They included nuns from the Servants of Mary and the Sisters of Mercy, as well as some of the wives of prominent city leaders. María Asunción also came with the other military wives, who rode from El Castillo to the *Hospital Militar* in mule-drawn ambulances sent by Ashford. María Asunción, as the wife of the hospital's commander, took charge of coordinating the civilian volunteers at the hospital, organizing supplies and helping hands with the same tenacity with which she had tackled the English language before marrying Ashford.

The men, women, and children who packed the hospital were almost all affected by varying degrees of anemia. Everywhere, the striking pallor of these ghosts from the mountains stood out in comparison to the healthy volunteers and workers.

Ashford barely had a moment's rest. When he wasn't treating infected wounds or giving wellness checks to the new arrivals, he walked constantly among the refugees, looking at their starved, diseased bodies and thinking about their plight. He reasoned that if malnutrition, specifically a lack of animal protein, was causing their anemia, he could probably solve the problem relatively easily. If anything was still to be found with some abundance in the commissary, it was meat—primarily beef and pork.

One week after the hurricane, the crisis was only worsening. María Asunción sat in her husband's office, helping to coordinate efforts for the day. Exhausted from many sleepless nights, a gruff Ashford called the sergeant in charge of the commissary into the office. He was a rugged Irish man and, as a member of the "old soldier" school of thought, harbored very strong opinions. Knowing he needed to present a strong front, Ashford spoke in his best authoritative voice. "Sergeant Major Ryan, practically all the refugees are deathly ill from low blood counts brought on by their terrible food. While they are here as our guests, we have a perfect opportunity help them. As commanding officer of this hospital, I order that beginning tomorrow, each adult will consume at least one pound of meat and the children an appropriately smaller amount which will be proportional to their weight."

Ryan stared back incredulously. "Of course, Lieutenant. You are wasting our time, but I will see to it right away, sir."

Ashford's face began turning a light shade of crimson. "What do you mean, Sergeant?"

María Asunción interrupted quickly. "My love, what Sergeant Ryan means is that these people won't eat Army beef, pork, or whatever. They are creatures of habit. They want their rice and beans. They want comforting foods that they are accustomed to eating." Sergeant Ryan nodded, punctuating María Asunción's words.

The lieutenant rose from behind his desk and waved dismissively. "Well, see to it anyway!"

"Yes sir, right away, sir." The sergeant saluted and departed on his mission.

María Asunción turned to Ashford with a raised eyebrow. Ashford said impatiently, "Well? Say it, *darling*!"

María Asunción smiled softly. "The sergeant is right, Bailey.

The *jíbaros* won't eat our beef, pork, or chicken no matter how much or how emphatically it is put into their mouths. It is not their way."

Ashford shook his head. "But it has to be, my dear. Out of the three hundred or so people living in tents, we lose at least ten *every single day* to malnutrition and anemia, ailments we can likely cure if we can just get some protein into their diet. Adults, children, infants—they are slowly dying, and on our watch. And this represents only what we can see right here, under our very nose. It does not take a deep thinker to deduce that the situation must be much worse outside the hospital."

María Asunción held up a hand. "You are doing all you can."

Ashford stood and paced around the room. "Are we? One year exactly the United States has been on this island, and the people are every bit as sick and as poor as when we landed in Guánica. The hurricane simply made all the simmering poverty and chronic illness boil up to the surface. It is up to us to put a stop to it, and by Jove, we will!" Knowing her husband's moods as well as her own, María Asunción put her attention back to assigning volunteers for the day, and the Lieutenant poured his pent-up frustration back into the hospital.

Three days later, Sergeant Ryan returned to Ashford's office. He started to speak, halted, stammered, and finally slumped in a chair in an uncomfortable and prolonged silence. A stern Ashford stared directly at him, until the sergeant could no longer stand his icy gaze. Finally, he blurted out, "Lieutenant if you insist on stuffing all these peasants with meat, I'll be damned if we don't kill them all! Every one of them has the runs from hell, and they all say the only way they can be cured is with their rice and beans, and *bacalao*."

Ashford took Rafi to the tents to investigate, muttering curses under his breath and making a mental note to research the punishment prescribed for an insolent sergeant who thought himself smarter than a Georgetown medical graduate. The field hospital was overrun with refugees. The *jíbaros* lay in their tents sheltering from the sun, many covered with bandages and all of them in rags.

Ashford soon discovered the situation to be exactly as Ryan

had described. Most of the *jíbaros* emphatically refused to co-operate with his grand plan. The few that tried to eat meat were stricken by severe diarrhea, caused by their inability to adapt to the richer food. Over and over, they let Rafi know this was not what they ate in the mountains and that they wanted their rice, beans, roots, and dried cod.

Back in his office, Ashford called again for the sergeant major. Hiding his intense chagrin behind an impassive face, Ashford issued a new order. "I want you to quadruple yesterday's order of rice and beans, as well as the codfish." The sergeant saluted, turned on his heels and hurriedly walked away. As he exited, the rest of Ashford's directive reached his ears, "And order only one quarter of the amount of meat!"

As soon as the sacred rice, beans, and codfish arrived, morale improved. The refugees still supplemented their usual fare with a modicum of meat rations, which increased gradually as their systems acclimated to the larger quantities of protein and fat. Weeks passed with the *jíbaros* eating the improved food, but not the faintest tinge of healthy pink surfaced in their pale faces, and many continued to deteriorate and die.

The political implications were disturbing. Having thrown the Spaniards from the island, and with them the new law granting Puerto Rico self-government, the United States also faced the question of whether their unsolicited presence was a net positive for the islanders. Puerto Rico had been forced to exchange a familiar master going back centuries for a new one of just fifty weeks, one that spoke a different language, worshipped in a different church, governed with new doctrines, and dragged along a past carrying a troubling racist tradition. Worse yet, the government had not yet realized that the medical men were running out of ideas about as fast as they were running out of time. Back in the United States, anti-expansionist, opposition newspapers looking to embarrass the McKinley administration could exploit reports of the atrocious conditions on the island to hurt Republicans in the election of 1900, barely one year away.

In early October, after a particularly disheartening and grueling day, Ashford called Rafi to his office. They sat in the small, stuffy room facing one another with blank expressions, until Ashford broke the silence. "Rafi, we are losing our war against this crazy illness. The anemia cannot be due only to malnutrition. Although the patients are now eating good food, the majority aren't any better."

Rafi nodded in agreement. "And it has even less to do with a mysterious foul air of the mountains or any such other ridiculous things. There must be something very basic that we are missing here."

Ashford stood up and began to pace. "The anemia is so severe and so very widespread that it is no longer merely an epidemic disease. We must recognize it as a pandemic."

"A pandemic, yes, but of what?"

"That is the question."

Rafi ran his fingers through his hair. "The numbers of the sick are so great that we are drowning in clinical work. We must organize ourselves better. While the rest of the Medical Corps continues with supportive treatments, why don't we select a subset, say one hundred patients, to study scientifically?"

Ashford paused, thinking for a moment. "Rafi, you are right. Simple clinical impressions are no longer sufficient. We need data. Consider this: we select patients along the entire spectrum of the disease and conduct detailed examinations of all systems—circulatory, respiratory, intestinal, urinary, skin, eyes, nose, throat—*every system*. Each observation, however irrelevant it may seem at first, will be recorded in tables to allow for ready comparisons. It is time that we got out the microscopes, stains, and those hemoglobin counters O'Reilly sent us."

Rafi rose from his chair. "Dr. Ashford, I would like nothing better. Test and investigate. Let's go to work."

The 25-year-old army lieutenant and his assistant had just assigned themselves a daunting task. The work promised to be difficult, fraught with doubters, petty jealousies, and possibly even interference from local doctors. But Ashford hoped that this work might start his adopted land on a new path, a path very different and far superior to the old one.

Chapter Nineteen

TEST AND INVESTIGATE, SEPTEMBER 1899

Ashford now faced the formidable task of organizing the flood of sick refugees so that he could approach the pandemic scientifically. In his mind, the problem boiled down to two questions: why were some people more severely affected than others, and why did some survive for years, while others rapidly worsened and died? Answering these was tantamount to discovering the causes of the illness. He went without sleep for the better part of two nights planning his attack on the pandemic. Finally satisfied, he headed home for the first time in a week.

When Ashford met Rafi the following morning in the courtyard, his utter exhaustion showed in the bags under his eyes, and he looked like he needed a good shave. He downed two cups of the strongest local coffee before presenting his plan.

"Rafi, I propose that we begin by separating the patients into mild, moderate, and profound anemics. Then we will take their clinical history, examination, and blood draws for laboratory studies."

Rafi frowned. In their field hospital, there were hundreds of patients to sort through as Ashford proposed. "Very well, Doctor Ashford, but how will we determine the degree of severity?"

"The appearance of the skin and mucous membranes should suffice, I believe. At least, at first. I intend to divide patients simply by how pale they appear and begin our study with those who appear less afflicted, then gradually progress to sicker patients. We will record all their vital statistics, then work through the first group with examinations and laboratory studies. If there is a causal agent to be found in the blood studies, it may become more apparent as their anemia worsens. When we conclude with one group, we will proceed to the next, and so on, until we have a satisfactory number, no fewer than one hundred patients."

"Until we have a satisfactory number, or until they fire us," Rafi muttered under his breath.

Ashford tightened his jaw in frustration. "Do you have any better ideas? I admit, my dear Rafi, I'm at a loss. It makes some sense that the awful diet of the *jíbaros* is behind it all, but it simply can't be the whole explanation. It might not even be the most important part. A few of the milder cases have improved since we began feeding them better, but most have not. And they continue to die at the same rate."

Rafi scratched his head. "Maybe it has something to do with the malarial parasite—it's so common throughout the island."

"There is no question that having malaria, or bilharzia, or any another parasite can accelerate the deterioration, but by itself, it doesn't explain why these people have lost so much blood that they have become anemic." Ashford steepled his fingers in front of him, staring absentmindedly into the middle distance. "Most of our sickest patients have no risk factors for bilharziasis and no history of the periodic fevers of malaria. Something else is destroying their blood, something that can outpace the bone marrow's ability to replace the losses. The marrow falls behind in the race, and as the blood progressively gets poorer, the patients become paler, more fatigued, and so on, and so down the slippery slope they go."

"And," Rafi added, "I can't recall another disease process that is so pervasive. Nine of every ten coffee laborers having anemia is hard to believe."

"That number may be trying to tell us something, Rafi. Dr. Stahl and Dr. Zeno say that coffee workers are virtually all affected, but sugar cane workers on the coasts are much less so, about half of them, perhaps."

"You know, there's also a difference," Rafi said, "between the *jíbaros* and the workers of African descent in the coastal areas east of San Juan. Those people do not suffer from severe anemia. Somehow, they are able to retain their blood better."

Ashford nodded. "Their diet is about the same, and yet darker-skinned people are not as sick, that much is true. All those points make for interesting observations, but we need to make sense of it all. I am now completely convinced that we have to look closely at their blood for more clues. I'd bet the farm that the answer will be found in the blood smears."

"Please hold off on wagers, you don't have a farm to lose," replied Rafi, grinning broadly.

The two began to organize the tasks that lay ahead and divide the work. They began the first task, gathering subjects to study by walking around the camp separately to screen potential patients. Rafi explained their plan in Spanish while Ashford did the best he could, communicating in infinitives animated by vigorous hand gestures. His attempts at communicating were met with a combination of amusement and appreciation. Ashford had helped them greatly by opening his hospital to feed and shelter hundreds of displaced poor. If the *americano* doctor wanted to listen to them and their endless complaints, look in their mouths, poke fingers in sundry places and draw a little blood at no charge, they would happily go along. If nothing else, it relieved the crushing boredom. In a few hours, the duo selected thirty patients who showed, if white, the slightest tinge of yellow in their skin, or pastiness if their skin was dark.

Their investigation began early the following morning. Wanting to push forward as quickly as possible, the two men worked independently and María Asunción assisted with record keeping. First, Rafi interviewed each person regarding their history and symptoms while María Asunción took down the copious amounts of information the patients shared. Rafi's list surpassed one hundred questions, covering every body system and aspect of a patient's medical history with no detail too small to consider. Meanwhile, in an adjoining room, Ashford and a nurse performed physical examinations and drew blood from every subject.

The first patient was a young, white woman of about twenty, short and thin, her skin pale, but not exceedingly so. Rafi thought he could detect the faintest hint of yellow hue in her skin.

Rafi greeted his patient warmly. Her name was Luisa, and she lived in the village of La Playa. María Asunción recorded her name in the logbook, and under *"Skin color"* wrote *"Sallow."*

Luisa replied with no hesitation or embarrassment. Pointing to her upper abdomen, she said, *"Señor doctor* Rafi, *me da mucho dolor aquí después de comer."*

Rafi noted her abdominal pain after eating, and looked up to encourage her to continue.

Luisa blushed slightly, looked at María Asunción and said, "The pain also goes with heartburn, gas, and fullness in my stomach. Sometimes, I am very hungry, but then, if I eat too much, the stomach pains come with nausea and then I vomit." After more questions about her digestive organs, Rafi went on to ask about her sleep, concentration, and energy.

Luisa answered, "I feel tired many times. It is hard to wake up every morning and go work in our store, but I have to go, you know? *Papi* needs help. Sometimes, I forget what day it is. If the store is slow, I put my head on the counter and fall asleep."

María Asunción looked at Rafi, who nodded back discreetly. She wrote down, *"Patient reports some loss of mental acuity and energy. Also mentions a tendency to fall asleep at odd moments."*

Having their full attention seemed to invigorate Luisa. She continued, "I often have headaches, and feel *mareada,* I am so dizzy I can hardly walk straight."

Finally, the interview was complete. Rafi rose and thanked Luisa and sent her in to see Dr. Ashford. She found the young doctor in the adjoining room, accompanied by a matronly nurse who served as interpreter.

Over the next hour, Ashford completed his assessment. Luisa measured exactly five feet tall and weighed ninety pounds. Ashford noted a slight yellowish discoloration to her skin, which was otherwise normal. Her heart and lungs were unremarkable, except for Luisa's pulse, which was elevated. Examining the woman's abdomen, he noted mild discomfort just below the ribs, but no abnormal enlargement of any organs. Through his interpreter, Ashford asked Luisa to perform some cognitive tasks, testing her memory and reasoning skills. He then asked for permission to draw Luisa's blood later in the week, when they would begin to gather samples.

After the young woman left, Ashford and Rafi began again with the next person, repeating the process many times throughout the entire day. By the end of the day, they had evaluated sixteen patients. The next day, they planned to tackle the remainder.

Once they had completed the interviews and examinations for the first group, the team dedicated the next two days to drawing blood and preparing smears. Rafi would first place a drop of blood on a microscope slide and, before it could clot, rapidly spread it out with a coverglass. This created a thin blood smear, which they allowed to dry before examining it. Viewing the smear at this point was impossible because of the lack of color and contrast between different blood cells. He solved this by employing dye mixtures to stain the smears. Different cells absorbed different colors in varying amounts thereby giving distinct patterns to the slides. Once any excess dye had been removed with distilled water or alcohol, these stains left behind the most vividly colored specimens, which easily allowed for the accurate counting and classification of different blood elements.

Ashford and Rafi were particularly well suited for the examination and quantification of blood samples. Both were superb microscopists, well-versed in the nuances involved in operating their instruments, as well as the different stains used to enhance the blood smears. They had at their disposal four of the Army's standard portable microscopes, which Ashford considered to be of excellent quality and well suited to their needs. Moreover, Ashford and Rafi were expert phlebotomists, an important skill given that drawing blood from the very ill or the very young could be difficult. Finally, the two were excellent diagnosticians, extremely capable of piecing clues together to coax answers from the little slides that began to fill their lab.

After examining a smear under the microscope, they used the hemoglobinometer to measure the amount of hemoglobin, the oxygen-carrying red pigment of the blood. To do so, Rafi treated each sample with acid to change its red color to brown, then added distilled water until the color of the specimen matched a color standard. The less water required to match the sample to the standard, the more anemic the patient. The result was then reported as a percentage value. A result of "50 percent hemoglobin" meant that the patient had only half of the hemoglobin expected in a normal person.

In the late afternoon, María Asunción returned to the barracks. Ashford and Rafi completed the laboratory studies of the first group of patients and met to discuss their first impressions over fine brandy, at the Army's expense. Ashford admitted to being disappointed in their findings.

"The first group doesn't show many abnormalities," he complained. "From my review of your notes, it appears that most of their problems have to do with fatigue, headaches, and dizziness."

Rafi looked down at his notes. "I agree completely, Dr. Ashford. The patients are thin and look pale, but other than those symptoms, and some belly pains, they report not much else. They all seemed somewhat lethargic, notwithstanding. Many of them told me about memory problems."

Ashford closed his eyes, thinking. "It strikes me, Rafi, that prospective employers could misinterpret this as laziness or apathy, when in reality they are among the earliest and most common symptoms of the illness."

"Yes," Rafi answered. "But the laboratory studies may be more telling, especially while comparing these first samples with later test groups. It appears that these mild anemics maintain a relatively good proportion of their red blood cells, and furthermore, that these cells retain their normal size and shape. But the hemoglobin measurements show a reduction to between sixty and ninety percent of normal."

Ashford mused that the evidence so far suggested the anemia manifested as a loss of hemoglobin rather than a loss of red cells: the same pattern seen in iron deficiency cases. Yet, if this were a matter of low iron stores, he reflected sourly, their protein plan would have done the trick.

So far, their findings had not been very helpful and their labors had been exhausting. They finished the brandy and stood as the light weaned from the sky.

Ashford suggested they play duets to unwind. As they went to retrieve the doctor's violin, Rafi spoke. "I'm afraid this job is too great for the two of us. If we are to make reasonable progress and help these poor souls, we all need help, particularly with the laboratory studies. There is just too much data to catalog."

Ashford agreed to request funds for a technician the next day. With the prospect of another pair of hands lightening their labor, their mood improved and together they tackled the Bach sonatas for violin and piano. But the exhausted and distracted musicians could not do the music justice, and after a half hour or so, they stopped rehearsing and parted for the night, nursing their hopes for the following day.

Their request for a laboratory assistant was cabled to San Juan and swiftly granted; solving the anemia mystery was a top priority for the Army. Ashford expected this new person to be another civilian, probably from outside the hospital staff, and, with any luck, a native Spanish speaker. He had to be able to draw blood and prepare samples; it remained to be seen if the position could be filled.

That afternoon, Ashford and Rafi were deep into planning the next phase of their investigation when into their cramped laboratory room walked an unexpected form—a diminutive woman clad all in white, in an unusual garb: a heavy serge robe pleated at the neck and draping to the ground. Her cap and wimple, both white as well, and the large rosary hanging from her belt, all marked her as a Catholic sister. She had pulled up her white veil, revealing a pleasant face.

As one, Ashford and Rafi stood and stared at the small figure in amazement. They could have been called rude, except they were powerless to look elsewhere. The amused woman walked up to them, extended her hand, and said in perfect English, "I am Sister Mary Elizabeth of the order of the Sisters of Mercy. I come from Baltimore, but I have lived in Ponce for the last two years. My order helps the Servants of Mary run a small clinic and hospital named the Asilo de Damas. We received word that the doctors here needed assistance caring for the hurricane victims, and I have come to help."

The men exchanged glances.

Ashford cleared his throat. "Thank you, ah, Sister Mary....?"

"Sister Mary Elizabeth."

"Yes, Sister Mary Elizabeth, we were rather hoping for a Spanish-speaking lab assistant to help draw blood and prepare slides. For nursing duties, I can refer you to Sergeant Moretti, who's in charge of assigning shifts."

Sister Mary Elizabeth's gaze bored into Ashford. "My Spanish is excellent, I am perfectly able to draw blood from any patient, and if you care to show me the laboratory procedures, I do not doubt that I will learn those very well. I come from a medical family, and none of this is new to me. Also, I can start right now."

Ashford and Rafi could hardly hide their surprise. They had expected a male Puerto Rican civilian assistant, and instead had been sent an American nun.

"Sister Mary Elizabeth, is this really the place for you?" Ashford protested. "We work from dawn until well after dark on the sickest of patients, many of them near death. Even after a long day of interviews and examinations, we have to continue in the laboratory for hours, studying blood samples. That hardly seems the proper place for a person with your—inclinations."

Sister Mary Elizabeth pressed her offensive against the doctor's preconceptions. "*My inclinations?* Let's see—Dr. Ashford, I am curious, what microscopes do you utilize?"

"I don't see what difference that makes," he sputtered. "But we have four portable Bausch and Lomb Army models, all in excellent condition."

Sister Mary Elizabeth gave an appreciative nod, grinning broadly. "I trained on Zeiss instruments at Hopkins, but Bausch is a close second. I assume you will be staining the samples according to the method of Wright?"

Ashford raised his eyebrows. If the nun knew of James H. Wright and his hematological techniques, then she was no lightweight. He countered, "After weighing the relative benefits of several different stains, I actually settled on Ehrlich's triacid method."

Sister Mary Elizabeth replied, "I am very familiar with Dr. Ehrlich's stain. It gives beautiful colors to the smears and can easily distinguish between the seven types of blood cells. The problem, as you must know, is that Ehrlich's stain spoils rapidly in the heat and humidity of the tropics."

Rafi's head swiveled back and forth between the two contenders. He could not help staring at the small figure in white, nor squirming a bit in discomfort. He was acutely aware of the one glaring drawback of their stain. "Right you are, Sister Mary Elizabeth. Combining the Orange G, acid fuchsin, and Methyl Green dyes is tricky and highly labor-intensive, and must be repeated often. That was one of our reasons in asking for help."

"Hmm, I see." Sister Mary Elizabeth frowned thoughtfully. "The timing of the blood draws, processing of the smears, and mixing of the dyes must all be carefully orchestrated. Have you considered adding an acetone stabilizer to your stain? It could prolong its shelf life considerably."

"Sister," Ashford intruded, his face threatening. "I assure you that our protocols are working very well. What we need is help putting our chosen methods into practice!"

Sister Mary Elizabeth looked straight into Ashford's face, a full head above hers, clearly unfazed by his Southern-bred chauvinism.

"Dr. Ashford, I am not afraid of hard work. I have seen many patients as badly affected as yours. If you object to my sex or my vocation, then you should say as much, but don't object to my abilities, which are easily the equal of anyone's here!"

"I have no problems with either your sex or your religion. I am simply looking for a quality laboratory assistant."

The nun lifted her chin and declared, "Then, I believe you have found one."

After a few more half-hearted objections, Ashford surrendered. "Very well, Sister Mary Elizabeth. For now, you may join us. My assistant here is Mr. Rafael Moore, a very accomplished microscopist."

Sister Mary Elizabeth broke into a smile of triumph. "Thank you. I am tired of watching so many people die little by little—such a waste."

"We are in complete agreement there, Sister Mary Elizabeth," Ashford replied. "But I am convinced that, given the chance, these people's true spirit will come alive. You may join us in our clinic later today, and afterwards, we will begin showing you our laboratory protocols. We are grateful for your help."

The next day, the team started seeing sicker patients, those whom they had classified as suffering from moderate anemia. Rafi took each patient's history, then passed them to Ashford for examination, who, in turn, led the patient to Sister Mary Elizabeth for the blood draw. This modified assembly-line approach allowed the investigation to move much faster, since thirty or more patients could now be seen each day. The team then spent evenings studying slides and remixing bottles of stains that had spoiled in the heat.

Moderate anemia was very common in the field hospital. Rafi found the patient complaints and specific symptoms similar in kind to those of the mild cases, but much more pronounced. Almost all patients reported nausea, vomiting, and diarrhea, as well as a voracious, insatiable appetite. So pronounced was this craving for food, that when prodded, one in five admitted to eating dirt.

When examining these patients' circulatory system, he was surprised to find such serious issues. Whereas in the first group patients had few cardiac complaints, heart palpitations in these patients were almost universal, and seemingly independent of exertion. All the patients had shortness of breath, usually accompanied by sharp pains in the chest. There was also a marked susceptibility to cold and tingling in the feet. Many of these patients complained of noises in their ears and frequent headaches. There were frequent mentions of sexual dysfunction, too, manifested as partial impotence in the men and loss of periods in the women.

For his part, Ashford noted the pallor of these subjects had become striking and readily apparent not only on their skin, but also in the mucous membrane of the mouth and nose. When he examined these patients' circulation, Ashford found abnormally enlarged hearts to varying degrees—some of them as large as cantaloupes, which he attributed to the increased workload required to pump the depleted blood.

These enlarged hearts were inefficient, giving rise to the rapid and thready pulse so common in these sicker patients. Not infrequently, machine-like murmurs could be heard without a stethoscope and dilated neck veins commonly stood out like oil pipes. These ominous findings, when taken together, pointed to advanced cases of heart failure.

Cognitively and psychologically, these patients in the second group appeared depressed, passive, and generally confused. Their short-term memory was compromised, as was their ability to solve the most simple problems. Any exertion required supreme effort. It struck Ashford that these patients behaved as if they had received large doses of some powerful narcotic. Their hemoglobin levels ranged 30 to 60 percent of normal. Examined under the microscope, the total number of red blood cells was also noticeably low. But for the first time, the team also noticed a very specific change in the kinds of cells in the smears. Mingling among the normal blood cells were certain white cells that went by the tongue-twisting name of eosinophils. Their function remained unknown, but they were easy to see on the stained slides thanks to a striking, even pretty, pattern of tiny red specks, known as granules. Generally, in a smear from a normal person, only one out of every thirty or forty white blood cells were eosinophils. But the team noticed that in these patients with moderate anemia, the number of eosinophils was increased, and often remarkably so, routinely appearing at ten times the frequency of a healthy individual.

That night, the three scientists met again in the courtyard to review their findings of the day.

"With these more afflicted patients," Ashford began, "we are starting to see some patterns emerging. Now, an increasing pallor corresponds closely to worsening laboratory values."

Rafi chimed in. "Anywhere else, those we are calling moderate cases are considered moribund. A hemoglobin level of thirty percent to me is almost incomprehensible. I can't imagine what we are going to see when we get to the severe patients."

"*Sanguis Christi!*" Sister Mary Elizabeth exclaimed. "Those are incredible values! And the eosinophils! Dr. Ashford, what do you make of the overabundance we're seeing?"

Ashford smiled at the nun's enthusiasm and threw his hands up in the air. "Sister Mary Elizabeth, this may point to our first real discovery. It *has* to be a clue. I am not surprised to find the red cells disappearing, but to find these eosinophil numbers so very high... and we find them increasing exactly when the red blood cells are decreasing. Now, whether this is a cause, or an effect, of the disease remains to be seen."

"Why does the bone marrow bother to make all those eosinophils instead?" Rafi added. "In these patients, the marrow should be making new red cells as fast as it can. We know the eosinophils don't help with what is most needed, carrying oxygen to tissues. What are they doing there? Are they fighting something?"

"What are they doing, indeed." Ashford shook his head. "But I still think these cells may hold the key to the illness."

Ashford did not say so, but somewhere in the back of his mind, a faint memory was stirring. He had heard, or perhaps read, something somewhere, maybe in one of those brief esoteric reports from a far-away corner of the medical world, so common and so commonly discarded after one reading. Something about these eosinophil cells, he pondered. *Something*...what a nagging thought it was. Finding it just beyond his reach, Ashford remained silent, turning instead to listen to Rafi and Sister Mary Elizabeth.

With their day concluded, Rafi walked Sister Mary Elizabeth back to the Damas hospital before heading to his hotel room. Utterly exhausted, he collapsed on his bed and dreamt about diminutive cells filled with pretty red granules.

The next day, the team proceeded to evaluate the sickest patients, those they regarded as suffering from profound anemia. These patients were easy to find, not only because they were numerous here, but also because they sorted themselves out by remaining in their cots all day long. Weakness prevented them from leaving their beds for any activity, whether eating, washing, evacuating, or going to see the doctors. The team therefore went to them instead.

The first patient of many was an old mulatto worker named Damián. Approaching slowly, Ashford introduced himself and his team to the decrepit man. Damián's skin color was a waxy dark amber. His feet and hands were swollen, and his face puffy and partially paralyzed. His eyes were sunken and lifeless, and he could only turn his head with difficulty.

The duty nurse walked into the tent just then, and reviewed his medical history for the team. "Damián reached the camp after the hurricane, already in a pitiable condition. He was doubled up, very weak, and could only crawl from place to place on his hands and knees. Since then, he has continued to deteriorate, and now, he is completely bedridden."

Ashford replied to the nurse in a low voice. "This patient is clearly terminal. Even with the best of care, he has only a few days to live. You and your team of nurses have done an admirable job making him comfortable."

The nurse's face remained impassive at the compliment, but her throat bobbed as she swallowed hard. "Thank you, doctor," she replied in the same voice. "You—You make his death somewhat easier on all of us, do you understand?" Ashford nodded and turned back to the older man as Rafi knelt to begin his interview.

Ashford was well aware that the patients in this last group had reached the stage in which death could come at any moment. Like the unfortunate Damián, there were many others whose pallor had become so extreme that the pink color of their lips blended fully with the skin of their face, and the lips seemed to disappear. All the patients suffered from swelling of their ankles and feet, together with a very noticeable puffiness of their faces. Their skin was dry, harsh, and wrinkled. Nausea and vomiting were frequent, and profuse diarrhea was a serious problem.

In Damián and others like him, Ashford found severe enlargement of the heart and abnormal murmurs so pronounced that they could be heard from across the room. Their lungs were filled with fluid, and everyone suffered from a pronounced shortness of breath worsened by the slightest movement. All the patients complained of dizziness and roaring noises in their heads. In addition to delirium, many suffered from manic depression, catatonia, and schizophrenia.

The advanced weakness in these patients meant that the investigation progressed slowly. The medical instruments and blood drawing equipment had to be carried from patient to patient, delaying the completion of their work. Yet they could not afford these delays—with so many cases very near death, the work was too urgent. Some patients had stopped eating altogether, others had to be examined while unconscious. The grueling effort affected the three team members physically and mentally. When the evaluations were at last completed late one afternoon, Ashford sent his companions home to rest without bothering with the evening discussion.

"Let's meet here in the office tomorrow. Try not to think of the patients at all; we will do better if we can clear our heads tonight."

Rafi and Sister Mary Elizabeth gladly left. Ashford remained at the hospital, ruminating over the data and pondering their next steps. A thousand little cells containing bright red circles kept popping into his brain, and when he finally lay down to sleep, they whirled before him in the darkness repeatedly jarring him awake. After struggling for two hours, Ashford gave up any hope of rest and chained-smoked the night away just outside the hospital's entrance.

Chapter Twenty

THE NEW WAR, OCTOBER 1899

One week after the hurricane, Simón had finally settled into life at the field hospital. Separated from his family, he shared a tent with seven other men, all of them, like him, suffering from severe cases of anemia. Around the camp, the sickest patients continued to succumb daily in spite of the hospital's very best efforts. Dr. Ashford and Rafi checked on Simón and his tent mates several times a day.

After a few days in the field hospital, he began to receive meat with each meal, including breakfast. There was meat stew, boiled beef, thinly sliced *bistec,* minced pork, and shredded chicken—just about any meat available and cooked in just about every imaginable fashion, yet always distinguished by what the patients perceived as the American preference for plain, bland flavors. Like the other *jíbaros,* Simón was grateful but simply could not abide the thought of eating this food, even if the doctors swore it cured all ills. Gone were his rice and beans, boiled roots, bananas, plantains, and his precious salted cod, all of which Simón missed sorely after his first day on the new diet.

As he struggled through the change in food, Simón noticed that the sicker his friends and neighbors were, the less they could tolerate the new diet. Some of them tried it and worsened, while others simply refused to eat altogether. Those who worsened, died. Simón finally complained to the staff, who complained to Ashford, who came to see for himself. He quickly understood that his approach was a failure, and within three days of its inception, this experiment and treating the anemia with meat had ended. Protein was still provided to the anemic patients, but more as a supplement than as the focus of their diet.

The hospital then settled into an uneasy routine, and Simón Báez along with it. The weeks passed quickly at the field hospital. Simón's family visited him frequently, and the Báez children began to look better with the improved fare and sanitary conditions of the tent hospital. Juan repaired his house to where he could take Pepa and his siblings with him. Meanwhile, Simón stabilized somewhat, but remained too weak to venture out from his tent.

One day in mid-November, Simón received a visit from Dr. Ashford, Rafi Moore, and a small nun dressed in the white nursing habits of the Sisters of Mercy.

Rafi walked up to his cot, shook his hand, and spoke to him in Spanish.

"Hola Señor Báez, y muy buenos días. I wanted to ask if you might allow us to obtain your medical history and conduct an examination to try to shed some light on the anemia that affects almost everybody in this camp. Dr. Ashford you already know, and this is Sister Mary Elizabeth, who helps us run the laboratory. If you allow us, we want to draw some of your blood and collect some urine to look for clues that might help us determine the nature of your illness."

Simón was flattered that such important, knowledgeable, and distinguished people were asking for his permission to do anything, particularly if it involved his poor, useless body. He liked the idea of being the center of attention and talking about his many complaints at length. Regarding the part where he was supposed to get poked with a needle by a nun who looked about twelve years old—of that, he wasn't so sure. But the deference he was getting was certainly worth a little pain.

Rafi began with a few open questions concerning Simón's background and his general well-being. They were looking for a patient's perspective on the illness: how long he had been sick, whether he could remember some event that had brought on his infirmity, who he knew that was sick, and who he knew that was relatively healthy.

Simón answered slowly, not only because he basked in all the attention, but also to pause and catch his breath and recover his memory, which the anemia had severely affected.

"I believe I am thirty-eight years old," he began, his breath wheezing through his chest with his words. "I am not completely sure of this because my parents soon forgot the year that I was born. I was never inscribed in any official register, but I was seven or eight when San Narciso struck the island."

Ashford interrupted, "San Narciso? What is that?"

Rafi translated the question.

Simón broke into a big smile, took a few deep breaths, and gestured with his hand as he told them of the well-known event. "¡El temporal de San Narciso! It was supposed to be the worst hurricane in the history of Puerto Rico. But it was nothing, I want you to know, compared to this one, San Ciriaco."

Ashford accepted this assessment and begged him to continue.

"I was born in a coffee-working family in the town of Cayey. Both my mother and father picked coffee for a living and died in their forties from anemia. I moved to Utuado at eighteen and soon met my companion, Josefa. Together we have had nine children, but only four are still alive."

Ashford suppressed a gasp of horror, sharing a long, pained look with Rafi. This man had lost more than half of his children. His sorrow had to be incomprehensible. Yet, Simón proceeded to talk haltingly about his deceased children, his grief evident in the short silences between words, particularly when recounting the recent death of his youngest, Rosa. At once, Sister Mary Elizabeth recognized the man before her: this was the same Simón who brought his family to Ponce last year, desperately seeking help for his three-year-old girl! She crossed herself, remembering; Rosa was a child Sister Mary could never forget. But the man himself was almost beyond recognition—he had aged ten years in one, and had wasted away to practically nothing.

Simón let out a long sigh and continued, "I do not remember the last time that I felt completely well. The way I feel today is what I consider 'normal.' Looking at my dear Pepa, who is much healthier than I, reminds me of how strong I used to be. I also look at Juan nowadays and see that his moving to the city has made him well. Three years ago, he was every bit as sick as I am today."

Here, Simón began to cough alarmingly. Rafi put a hand on his shoulder and asked, "Don Simón, perhaps you should rest now?"

The patient raised his hands and shook his head.

"Not yet. I walked twenty miles from Utuado just like this. I can answer a few questions if I can only get a minute to catch my breath."

Still frowning, Rafi resumed after a brief pause. "Do you recall what might have brought on your illness?"

"Frankly, I do not," Simón cawed, hoarse from his coughing fit. "But in the mountains, we know what we see. People that leave the coffee plantation for the cities often improve, like my son Juan. The overseers seem healthier than the workers, as do the owners of the plantations. Don Arturo Roig and his children never have, and never will, suffer from *la anemia.*"

Ashford prompted Rafi to ask the patient why he thought that was.

Simón shrugged. "It might be that the owners eat better. Certainly, the overseers eat better than us. They all have bigger and better houses that protect them from the bad air that everybody knows moves through the mountains. But rich people are so odd, it's anyone's guess as to what they really do."

At this, the trio of clinicians broke into subdued laughter. Simón good-naturedly joined in their merriment. "The fancy people may appear smart and cultured, but we do not think them very wise, or even practical. They seem to be overly concerned about trivial matters, such as whether to wear this suit or that, whether beef should be eaten with plantains or potatoes, and even the right place to go to the bathroom!"

Ashford's ears perked up when he heard his friend translate what Simón had said. "Rafi, ask what he means by that."

Simón went on.

"The fancy people seem to be obsessed with where they do their '*necessary business.*' They have a few small sheds covering a hole in the ground, and they will stubbornly walk half a mile uphill to use them when all around is perfectly fine ground, with plenty of trees to hide from oglers. We workers are not allowed to use those holy shrines, and neither do we want to."

Simón then looked warily at Sister Mary Elizabeth and, not wishing to offend her feminine sensibilities, leaned closer to the men and whispered: "For our particular bathroom needs, we have our own special code, a sort of evacuation etiquette. When somebody needs to go *cagar*, to take *the dump*, they walk downwind and hide behind the first tree they find. This works well and saves us a lot of time."

Rafi and Ashford's eyebrows went up. Sister Mary Elizabeth managed to hear the whole thing and was the only one who was not surprised. She had heard all these stories before from her patients at the Asilo de Damas. Ashford now decided to allow Simón a much-needed rest, while the three scientists headed to the plaza to have lunch at a small café.

They sat at a table under the shade of some large banyan trees. Rafi and Ashford looked blankly at each other, positively dumbfounded at the blitheness of Simón's admissions, while Sister Mary Elizabeth's expression said she had heard it all before.

Ashford broke the silence.

"All this time, we've been focused on nutritional factors—but sanitation, or lack thereof, could be equally important. And no one mentioned this during our numerous interviews. Whether they were too self-conscious, ashamed, forgetful, or just plain indifferent, we were lucky to hear from someone about it now."

"Actually," Sister Mary Elizabeth said, "I'm surprised you haven't heard more about these evacuation habits, so to speak. I can assure you that further questions will reveal that similar hygiene practices are followed by all members of the family. Even Pepa Baez, despite being relatively healthy, surely adheres to these unwritten guidelines. Moreover, Simón knows his neighbors in the hacienda do the same."

"But Simón's partner is not nearly as sick as he," Rafi put in. "Why is that?"

Ashford thought over this new information and made a mental note to consider it further. He looked at Rafi and shook his head. "I'm not sure why she is so much healthier, if they live in the same place and share the same habits. But it can't be mere coincidence that all who ignore the most basic rules of hygiene, including the rest of the Báez family, and their neighbors, are ill."

When they were finished, Ashford paid their bill, and the group left to return to Simón at the field hospital. Rafi resumed the interview by asking Simón about his clinical history, beginning with his digestive system.

The patient broke into a wry grin. "Oh, that part—*los intestinos*, they have never worked well for me. I always have had a pain in my stomach, *el dolor de barriga*—it hurts when you press here, and here, also." Simón pointed to his belly button and his ribs. "And *los intestinos* either don't move for ten days, or they move ten times a day. I rarely know which it's going to be, but I am always able to make it outside the hut, so everything's alright, I guess."

Ashford repressed a smile while Rafi somehow managed to congratulate Simón on his agility with a straight face.

"I do want to tell you," Simón went on, "that all that stupid *condená* meat you tried to stuff in us some weeks ago made the old intestines far worse. I couldn't keep my pants on, I kept *cagando* so much."

Ashford and Rafi broke into hysterical laughter, and Simón, with a weak laugh, joined in their mirth. Sister Mary Elizabeth regarded all of them sternly. "*Domine Deus*! What is it with men and bodily functions!"

When they had again settled down, Rafi asked about Simón's heart and his breathing.

"*El corazón lo tengo muy bien.* My heart is very good, I think. I can feel it pounding away crazy fast. Isn't that good? Look, you can see it right here." The older man gestured toward his chest, just below his seventh rib, where the rhythmic thumping of his heart was clearly visible under a paper-thin layer of skin and muscle. Ashford and Rafi exchanged glances as they watched the organ quiver like a bag of twisting worms. Simón had no idea how bad his heart really was.

Simón continued, "Unfortunately, the breathing *no está bien,* I am always having to catch my breath. It was somewhat better when I was younger, but now… not so good… *No está bien.*"

Mustering his courage, Ashford ventured into Spanish, stumbling through a question to Simón about his appetite.

Simón chuckled at the doctor's infinitive tenses and funny accent, which the locals in camp parodied to no end, provoking attacks of laughter rivaling those of the drinking binges at Christmas. Then he regained his composure. "There was a time when I ate everything in sight. I was always hungry and there was never enough. I was starving from sunup to sundown."

He muttered a quick aside to Rafi, "I confess, Rafael, that at times I was so hungry, I had to resort to The Vice, *El Vicio.*" He glanced warily at Sister Mary Elizabeth, who glanced back with a single raised eyebrow.

"*El Vicio?*" Rafi asked, completely lost.

"Yes, Rafael! The Vice! *I began to eat dirt!*" Simón covered his face in his hands. "I was so embarrassed; I always hid it from Pepa. But now, you know the truth."

Her face softening, Sister Mary Elizabeth looked away and pretended to scribble something in her notes, hoping to spare the sick man from shame during his momentous confession.

Simón added quickly, "But I haven't had that urge in well over a year. I am not as hungry as I used to be. Now, I must force myself to eat a little rice and beans for lunch."

Nodding, Rafi sat back and relayed this information to Ashford. While they were all aware that some patients suffered from an irresistible compulsion to eat dirt, none of them had known that the *jíbaros* had a special name for it.

They finished the history and proceeded to the physical examination. Ashford performed his examination while Sister Mary Elizabeth took dictation, writing down every finding no matter how trivial it seemed. Simón's findings were typical for those with severe cases: pale yellow skin, a bounding pulse, a massively enlarged heart, abdominal pain and fluid in the lungs. Nothing in his story or examination seemed to shed any new light on the problem.

Sister Mary Elizabeth proceeded to draw blood. She strapped a tourniquet on Simón's right arm and began to wipe his inside elbow area with alcohol. He squirmed at the chill touch of the cotton, sat up, and stared blankly at the tent ceiling, his face tight with concern. Taking notice, Sister Mary Elizabeth resolved to make this the quickest blood draw she had ever completed and expertly inserted the needle into the antecubital vein. With this, Simón fainted and fell back upon the cot. In a split second, Sister Mary Elizabeth dodged the falling man and secured the blood sample against her white habit, all without spilling a drop. Ashford hurriedly elevated the man's legs and vigorously massaged his thighs to coax some blood back into Simón's brain while Rafi reached into his pocket for the smelling salts.

After Simón recovered, the team made their way to the next patient on their long list. After many hours of conversation and examination, the dwindling daylight brought their survey to a close. Even then they were not done; they still had the last smears from that day to process and stain. Once this was completed, Ashford sent Rafi and Sister Mary Elizabeth home with instructions not to think about patients, anemia, or anything remotely relating to their work. They needed to rest their minds and be prepared to resume their investigations in the morning.

Meanwhile, Ashford retired to his call room at the hospital, where he would remain in case there were emergencies. Despite his request to his colleagues, he could not block thoughts of his patients, anemia, and death. Unable to quiet his thoughts, Ashford lifted his violin from its case, took some deep breaths, and applied the bow to the lowest string. He began to bring forth from his instrument the most wrenching laments and cries of despair, which rang from his room and into the halls—like the cries of his dying patients.

Chapter Twenty-One

DISCOVERY, NOVEMBER 1899

The next day dawned mercifully bright and clear. As was typical of most November days, the air was fresh, the humidity was tolerable, and not a cloud was to be seen in a sky of the deepest blue. In spite of his gloom from the night before, Ashford found his spirits improving. He looked forward to meeting his colleagues and sorting through the findings of the previous three days. Of all their subjects, it had taken the longest to gather the data for approximately their thirty or so most severely affected patients—time that had been thoroughly dismal and depressing. But now, bolstered by the fine morning, he felt a surge of energy to tackle the work.

Rafi, too, woke up much refreshed. He breakfasted heartily, and headed uphill toward the hospital with a bounce in his step. He arrived precisely as Sister Mary Elizabeth entered the building, and together, they went in search of their superior. Seated by a mahogany table in the middle of the old courtyard, Ashford waited for his team with fresh black coffee and hot bread from the hospital bakery.

He greeted them with a broad smile. "I hope this beautiful morning will clear our minds so we can make some real headway. By now, we are all very familiar with the signs and symptoms in our anemic patients." His assistants settled themselves, and Ashford distributed slices of steaming bread. "Our observations show that as the anemia process accelerates, there appears to be a gradual progression in the severity of symptoms related to the digestive, cardiovascular, nervous, and respiratory systems. And the laboratory studies also worsen as symptoms become more pronounced."

Rafi produced his notes and reviewed their blood analyses.

"The laboratory values in some of these people are so abnormal as to be practically unbelievable. At first, I thought our instruments were wrong, until the same ridiculous values kept recurring in patient after patient—hemoglobin values at twenty to thirty percent of normal. In all the time I spent in the clinical laboratories at Yale, I never saw a hemoglobin level that low."

"Neither have I," added Sister Mary Elizabeth.

Ashford nodded in agreement. "During my own service with the Army, I personally have never seen counts even approaching those values. I have seen reports of seriously wounded soldiers whose hemoglobin sometimes drop to those extreme levels, but very few of them survived their injury, even those who received clean water, nutritious food, and uninterrupted nursing care."

"So, most of them still died," Sister Mary Elizabeth noted.

"Most still died," Ashford repeated. "So, it's hardly surprising that these poor *jíbaros*, who live in appalling conditions, are also dying at a high rate. What is truly miraculous is that some of them have survived this long."

Rafi looked at his notes, passing his fingers over the numerous entries. "And what about the curious increase in the eosinophil cells so noticeable in the moderate cases? Yesterday, we had a few cases where these cells were up tenfold."

Ashford frowned. "Those eosinophils are interfering with my sleep."

Sister Mary Elizabeth smiled, fingering the rosary beads hanging from her habit. "Dr. Ashford, before you become a full-fledged insomniac, remember that the very worst patients, those that were practically unconscious during their examinations, do not show blood smears with high levels of eosinophils. In fact, in those patients, they're practically absent!"

Ashford stood up and began to pace around their table, his hands clasped behind his back. "I admit, it's a puzzle. Could it be possible that when those patients are close to death, the bone marrow is quite simply starting to fail? In other words, is the bone marrow so stressed that it can no longer make many cells of any kind? This would mean that for terminal patients, crashing eosinophil levels must mean that the end cannot be far."

There was a prolonged pause as the group considered this new, grim idea and attempted to regain their focus.

Sister Mary Elizabeth broke their daze, "If that's true, this certainly clarifies our timeline for any given patient. We might as well return to the laboratory. There are still those slides from yesterday's patients to examine."

Ashford took a deep breath. "Yes, right away. Maybe these slides can show us something we haven't seen before."

Back in the cramped, windowless laboratory, they proceeded to review the slides prepared the previous day, but these proved no different from ones they had examined before: the same low numbers of pale red blood cells, and on many smears, high numbers of eosinophils. Two patients even showed an incredible, fifteen-fold increase in the normal number of eosinophils.

As Ashford looked through his microscope at the curious excess of pretty cells with bright red granules, he once again felt a stirring far back in his mind, the niggling of some obscure fact encountered long ago, possibly in one of his many medical school classes. Straightening up from the instrument, he alternated restlessly between looking in the microscope and staring at the walls, trying to chase down the stray thought, while a voice in his head kept repeating David's Prayer: *Bow down thine ear, and hear the words of the wise, and apply thine heart unto knowledge; criest after knowledge, and liftest up thy voice for understanding.*

Suddenly a thought struck Ashford dumb. Out of nowhere, he remembered an article in some obscure journal by a certain Dr. White, or Dr. Green, or maybe it was a Dr. Brown—he could not quite recall the investigator's name, but he thought that he had saved their report. It was likely stuffed somewhere in his office among many other such seemingly forgettable papers. In that article by an otherwise obscure doctor named after a color, Ashford vaguely recalled that there had been a comment or observation that was now pertinent. He rose abruptly and, without saying a word, hastily exited the laboratory.

Sister Mary Elizabeth looked bewildered. "*Rex tremendae majestatis!* Where is he going in such a hurry?"

Rafi shook his head. "I guess to his office. He probably forgot something—it happens more often than you'd think."

But Ashford had not forgotten anything, quite the opposite. Arriving in his office, Ashford moved books to the floor, turned over the papers on his desk and indiscriminately opened files. He had a habit of never throwing away medical articles and now started rummaging through old reports that had once piqued his interest five or more years ago, rifling through papers with a building anxiety. After ten minutes of looking, he found what he wanted and hurried back to his companions in the laboratory.

Ashford came in with his eyes on fire, startling his companions as he slapped a thin, nondescript packet of papers on their table. "Here it is, a journal article by Dr. Paul Brown from Massachusetts, reporting on a dozen persons sickened after consuming undercooked pork meat, affected by the so-called pork measles." At Rafi and Sister Mary Elizabeth's confused expressions, Ashford explained that "pork measles" was a term used by meat packers to describe the prominent white pockmarks inside carcasses affected by cysts of juvenile pork tapeworms.

"People consuming the tainted meat without cooking it properly frequently developed adult tapeworms in their intestines. Brown noticed that a large number of patients showed huge increases in eosinophils. He had the foresight to comment on this curious observation, despite not knowing why it occurred or what it meant."

Ashford stopped to gather his thoughts. He knew that tapeworms did not cause anemia and only infrequently gave their hosts any problems, but he couldn't escape the feeling that there could be some correlation between the elevated eosinophils of Dr. Brown's tapeworm hosts and those of his patients at the field hospital. Ashford looked intently at his partners, who stared back in rapt attention.

"Can it be that this anemia pandemic in Puerto Rico is somehow related to an unknown parasite? Perhaps, even to a species of parasitic worm?"

Rafi closed his eyes, trying to grasp the implications of Ashford's question. "If this anemia is caused by some unknown parasite, it must be quite unlike the malaria organism that lives in the blood. If there *was* some microscopic animal infecting the blood, we've looked through enough smears that we should have come across it already."

"Well," Ashford prodded, "if it's not to be found in the blood, then where? The liver? The gut?"

Sister Mary Elizabeth slowly shook her head. "Many different kinds of intestinal worms have been observed in human beings. But can they lead to such severe anemia? Intestinal worms are generally harmless organisms, more an embarrassment to their host than anything else."

Then, by the slow increments, they began to read each other's minds—*an intestinal parasite was making more and more sense.* Each watched the same realization dawn on the others' faces, and after several minutes, Ashford finally gave voice to their thoughts.

"I think we are going to have to look at some feces under the microscope."

Rafi felt a wave of nausea. Collecting and studying the gooey, runny pale-yellow human waste that filled the camp with the most nauseating odors both day and night was going to take some fortitude.

Sister Mary Elizabeth's face betrayed her relief. "*Deo gratias!* Finally—a new way to attack our problem."

Ashford asked, "To which patient does that last set of slides belong? Maybe we should start there."

Rafi said, "Those blood smears come from my friend's father, Simón Báez."

Ashford nodded, his brow creasing thoughtfully. "Remind me, what did his tests show?"

Sister Mary Elizabeth reviewed her notes. "*Hmm…*His results pointed to very severe anemia: 1.5 million red blood cells per cubic millimeter, or approximately thirty percent of normal levels. Red blood cells … small and pale, and eosinophils markedly elevated at fifty percent of total white cells, more than ten times what's found in healthy individuals."

"Then I think Mr. Báez will be a good person with whom

to start." Ashford looked straight at Rafi, his face the picture of expectation.

Rafi had barely recovered from his last wave of nausea when a second struck him even more forcefully. If he understood correctly, he was supposed to casually walk up to his friend's father and ask him to evacuate his bowels into a small bowl, from which he was to scoop up some dark green goo and bring it back to the lab. He stared at Ashford, mouth agape.

"Your Spanish is by far the best among the three of us," Ashford pressed. "I think this will come in handy when trying to describe to Mr. Báez the particulars of providing a stool sample. It will also help when you have to explain why we need to look at his material under the microscope."

Rafi went weak in the legs and broke into a cold sweat. He had once told Ashford about his excretory phobias, and now these had been brushed aside with the cold indifference of clinical necessity.

Seeing Rafi's shoulders slumping, Ashford patted him on the back. "This may be bad for the stomach, but it is good for the soul. Be brave, and let's not waste a minute." So, Rafi steeled himself and resolved to go to his friend's father and in the most professional manner, ask for a small part of his evacuations.

Rafi got up from the table and headed to the field hospital. He did not need to hurry, for Simón Báez was exactly where they had left him the day before, sitting on his cot, struggling to finish his bowl of rice and beans. When he saw Rafi walk into the tent, Simón broke into a broad smile. Rafi desperately wanted to ask the other patients in the tent if they could step outside, but this was not possible, as most were too feeble to move far and one was sleeping soundly.

"Hi Rafael," Simón said. "You are back so soon. What can I do for you?"

Rafi was not sure how to start. "*Señor* Báez, I returned because I have to ask you a question."

Simón smiled benevolently. "Of course, *hijo mío*, what is it?"

"Well… as you know, we have been trying to discover the cause of this severe anemia that nobody knows too much about, except that it kills thousands every year."

"Yes, I understand. I hope you have great success. Did the blood you took from me yesterday help you?"

"That's what I came to talk to you about."

Simón broke into a broad grin. "Then it did help! I am so happy to have been of use to *el gran doctor* Ashford."

"It was somewhat helpful," Rafi amended.

"*Oh?*"

"I think... Dr Ashford thinks...well, we all believe that we should take a look at your *excrement*."

At this, the other tent residents turned toward them as one.

"*Ooooh?*"

"Yes, the team of scientists thinks... that it would be valuable to look at your... aah...*caca* under the microscope."

Simón considered this for a moment. "Oh, *ya veo*, I see... The little nun thinks so too? Does *she* want to look at that as well? And you want to use a *microscope* to look at it? Can't you see it perfectly well without one?"

"Yes, she wants to look at it... I mean we *all* want to look at it..." Rafi sighed in despair; he was surely making a mess of things.

Simón finally put him out of his misery with another easy smile. "If that is what you want to do, then go ahead. It so happens that I have just finished my lunch of rice and beans and I feel the sudden urge to go *cagar* right now."

And without further ceremony, the patient reached for a chamber pot and, pulling down his pants, proceeded to his business without giving it a second thought. The vilest smell immediately permeated the entire tent, which seemed to amuse the other patients immensely.

Holding back a strong desire to vomit, Rafi grabbed the chamber pot, muttered a hasty farewell, and, holding it at arm's length, left the tent in the direction of the main hospital. Rafi re-entered the laboratory, his head turned fully away from his cargo, his face the color of a ripe olive.

"Well Mr. Moore, did you meet with success?" asked Ashford with a devilish smile.

Rafi answered him with an unenthusiastic half-grin and placed the chamber pot at the doctor's feet.

Ashford looked at the glob, his nose wrinkling. "Rafi, that stuff would make a maggot gag. Take it over yonder, *please.*"

The nun stepped up, rolling her eyes and muttering *Josephs and Marys* under her breath, set the loaded chamber pot outside the room, where it was sure to stay until they decided how to process the material.

Although he accepted the necessity of expanding the investigations beyond the patients' blood to examine their bodily functions, Ashford felt a fierce jab to his pride at this development. This was not only because of the foul nature of the specimens. A part of him considered this exercise to be, in plain terms, *unscientific.* If blood was royalty among tissues in the body, then excrement was pointedly the exact opposite. Studying the gut and its products reminded Ashford of the countless charlatans who made a living traveling the countryside, professing to treat intestinal worms in animals and human beings alike. They were known as the "worm doctors," itinerant medical losers pandering concoctions to patients suffering, at most, from the symptom of embarrassment. To Ashford, the worm doctors represented the lowest of the low, the bottom feeders among physicians, and he had no desire to be associated with them—or worse yet, remembered for all posterity as the "Worm Doctor of Puerto Rico."

At first, the whole notion that this frightful epidemic might be caused by a common and lowly parasitic worm seemed preposterous, if only for the fact that something so small could cause such devastation. But this was where their science was leading them. The three team members were aware that parasitic worms lived in the intestines of millions of people, and not only in poor nations. Pinworms in American children were quite commonplace, regardless of socioeconomic status. Yet, none of those patients had anemia, and usually all they complained about was an itchy rear end. And so, they went to work on the fecal sample.

Sister Mary Elizabeth relieved Rafi's worries when she offered to process the specimen. Ashford, on his part, settled on a common and straightforward protocol for their analysis. A macroscopic inspection came first—simply looking over the material with the naked eye. As expected, they learned nothing from this. There was no visible blood, only a few streaks of mucus mixed with fiber. Then, Sister Mary Elizabeth put on gloves and proceeded to do a wet mount of the specimen for examination with the microscope. A bit of material the size of a match head was removed with a toothpick and placed on a glass slide. Upon this, she then placed a thick cover glass and compressed it, so as to give a thin, clear center to the specimen. When at last all was ready, the wet mount was placed under the microscope. In order to examine the slide, Ashford chose a combination of the one-third objective lens and the number 4 ocular viewer. This combination of lenses gave a decent but not overpowering magnification, which, in turn, allowed a rapid and accurate examination of the entire slide.

Ashford sat down, took a deep breath and set his eye to the ocular. He peered intently through the lens, but saw nothing of importance. There were occasional strands of thin fibers, but mostly only an opaque mess with no cells to classify. Without an adequate stain to use on this material, everything was of the same dull color and impossible to differentiate. Ashford reached for the diaphragm on the microscope. By closing it, he could reduce the light going through the specimen and increase contrasts within the specimen itself. He slowly moved the slide across the stage, back and forth and up and down, beginning to feel increasingly demoralized. What could he expect to find? It was like searching for a white weevil in a bushel of rice…

And then he saw it—an insignificant nothing of a structure that at first glance seemed not to belong in the specimen. And yet, there it was, clear as day, as if holding court right in the middle of the slide and defying Ashford to identify it. The object was a minuscule oval body, just under one-tenth of a millimeter in diameter, with a distinct outer coat and four fluffy gray balls inside.

Ashford exhaled sharply. *"Well, I'll be…"* he thought, relief and excitement and curiosity spinning inside him like a growing summer squall.

Aloud, he asked himself, "What is this crazy thing doing here?" Suddenly a flash of recollection came back to him from Dr. Stiles' parasitology class. "Is this an egg? *Yes! It is most undoubtedly an egg!"* The structure bore a strong resemblance to the schistosome eggs they had observed last year from Cirilo's liver. It had the same oval form, and the same prominent outer coat, but this one had no thorn, and was only about half the size. It was, therefore, definitely not a schistosome egg. So then, to what creature did it belong?

Ashford jumped out of his chair. "Rafi, Sister Mary Elizabeth, look at this!" He left the slide exactly where it was on the microscope stage, with the encapsulated oval body at the very center, haughtily looking back at any examiner like the eye of a cyclops.

First Rafi, then Sister Mary Elizabeth took their turn looking. Both had studied parasites many times before, and right in front of them, on this slide containing the feces of a poor man dying from anemia, they saw what was clearly an egg, and very likely the egg of some kind of intestinal worm.

Trembling with excitement, Ashford reached for his copy of Manson's *Tropical Diseases*, and feverishly rifled through the pages. And suddenly, there it was. Hiding in an out-of-the-way corner of a page was the image of an egg exactly like the one in the slide. Under the illustration were the words: "*Ancylostoma duodenale*, ovum." Ashford was vaguely familiar with the *Ancylostoma*, a parasitic worm about the size of a comma in a large-type book, one with a highly distinctive shape that gave rise to its common name, the hookworm.

All at once, waves of long-forgotten information began flooding into Ashford's mind. In particular, he recalled the famous cases of dozens of Italian miners stricken by severe anemia while digging the Swiss Saint Gothard tunnel twenty years before. He searched through his files once again and found the report. The brief, two-page article had appeared in the *British Medical Journal* in 1881, written by the celebrated Dr. E. Bugnion in Geneva. The author recounted how the previous year, two Italian scientists had solved the problem of the European "mountain wasting disease," a type of chronic fatigue and lethargy that affected workers laboring under poor hygienic conditions in the dark, damp tunnels of the Alps. Although this wasting disease was originally attributed to bad diet, filthy water, and the "bad air of the mountains," the Italian scientists had found that this was, in fact, a severe anemia. And furthermore, after an exhaustive investigation, they had found eggs of this very same *Ancylostoma duodenale* in fecal specimens of those anemic workers.

The parallels between the Italian miners in the Alps and his patients in Puerto Rico were too remarkable to be the result of mere chance. To Ashford, everything suddenly made perfect sense. *The anemic disease of the miners in Switzerland was, quite simply, the same illness from which millions had suffered and died in Puerto Rico.* Another implication came to his mind as well. It was entirely possible, in fact probable, that the anemia pandemic was not limited to this one small island. In all likelihood, it also existed to some degree in other nations of the Western Hemisphere similar to Puerto Rico in climate and geography.

Ashford's thoughts turned to the voluminous quantity of influential academic literature, which whether through racism, intolerance, or simple misunderstanding, had repeatedly and most unscientifically chronicled the laziness of Mexicans, Central Americans, and other peoples of the old Spanish Main with total abandon. It was this supposed indolence of the Latin American workers which conveniently served to justify their unfair treatment at the hands of their white bosses—an indolence that it now increasingly appeared they owed not to their culture, but to disease. In the space of one morning, Bailey Ashford became convinced that the hookworm was to blame for the health and social crises rampaging not only through his hospital, but throughout all of Puerto Rico—so recently under the care of the United States, and so very, very sick.

Chapter Twenty-Two

TREATMENT

Rafi and Sister Mary Elizabeth could not stop admiring the tiny structure on the slide while Ashford feverishly paced around the laboratory, bouncing back-and-forth between the books and articles and the microscope, wanting to shout his discovery to the world. And yet, though he knew he had a valuable discovery here, that alone would be of no help to anyone. He was going to have to come up with a treatment, because, after all, their work was about making people well. The first order of business, however, was to communicate his discovery to his superiors. He sprinted down the hill to the town's telegraph office, where, arriving out of breath, he wrote:

Ponce, November 24, 1899
   Chief Surgeon, San Juan
   Have this day proven the cause of many pernicious, progressive anemias of the island to be due to Ancylostoma duodenale.

Ashford

His next stop was the home of Dr. Manuel Zeno Gandía, whom Ashford had met soon after arriving in Ponce. Ashford knew that Zeno was arguably the most respected physician in the city, and he wanted to gauge Zeno's reaction to his news. Ashford rang the bell, bouncing on the balls of his feet as he waited impatiently for the approach of shuffling footsteps from within. When the door was finally opened by a servant, he caught sight of the gray-haired physician writing in his back office. At this critical moment, no place was sacred to

Ashford. He sidestepped the startled doorman and strode in unannounced.

"Dr. Zeno," he proclaimed, "today I discovered the cause of anemia in our *jíbaros*! It is a worm! Not climate, nor bad food, nor bad hygiene, nor malaria, nor anything of that sort, but a worm, *an intestinal worm!*"

Silence filled the room in the wake of Ashford's announcement. Only the breathless heaving of Ashford's chest pierced the stillness of the office. The venerable doctor smiled and looked at the young man in his office, his face impassive. He laid aside his glasses, waiting for Ashford to catch his breath. With a benevolent expression, he remarked in a soft voice, "You know, Ashford, this can be a very trying climate for you northerners."

"What?" said Ashford between gasps, still breathless from his haste.

"The heat," Dr. Zeno continued pleasantly, his voice still quite kind. "It often times doesn't sit well with those accustomed to cooler temperatures. The brain warms and you become overexcited. I would never say hysterical, but most certainly a little manic. Why don't you drink some water, catch your breath, and take some time in the shade?"

"But I— You don't understand, we just found—" Ashford stammered out.

"I heard you," Dr. Zeno continued, his voice remaining unperturbed. "But my dear doctor, what an earth do you think you are going to do about it?"

That should have been Ashford's first clue that if he was expecting to be celebrated as a conquering hero, he might be sorely disappointed. Ashford was fully convinced that any self-respecting scientist, physician, or politician was surely going to embrace his hypothesis at once. After all, the science and methods behind the discovery were solid. Likewise, he never conceived that anybody might have the temerity to challenge what, in his view, was the unequivocally clear cause of the anemia disease, or worse yet, be indifferent about immediately applying their findings in the clinics. He had prematurely allowed himself visions of legions of doctors falling over each other in their eagerness to cure all these despairing people overnight. Instead, as described in the Holy Book, he was going to have to proceed the long, slow way to Jerusalem.

Returning to the field hospital, he took Rafi to see Simón. "*Señor* Báez, how would you like to leave your tent for a few minutes?"

"*A dónde vamos, doctor Ashford?*" asked a confused Simón.

"We are going into town to have your photograph taken, because thanks to you, today we made a great discovery."

"This will be a first for me. I have always wanted my picture done," replied the feeble man, struggling up on his toothpick arms.

"We will treat you like a newly-hatched chick on the way, and have you back before you know it," Ashford said, his voice jovial as he beckoned over some orderlies. Together, they carefully arranged Simón in the back of a mule ambulance among pillows and blankets. For the first time in his life, the *jíbaro* felt like a king.

Rafi was flummoxed. "Dr. Ashford, are you sure this is a good idea?"

"Some fresh air will do him some good," Ashford said in a voice that brooked no argument. "We will return him in half an hour. I will ride in back and watch him."

With his patient in tow, Ashford proceeded into the city, to the studio of the local photographer, where he had his patient immortalized for the ages. Then he went by El Castillo, picked up María Asunción and headed back to the military hospital. To the ailing *jíbaro*, this was the most fun he had had in years. At the hospital once again, Ashford gathered his team. "I have notified my superiors in San Juan about our recent discovery," he told them. "I also notified one of the leading local physicians, who, incidentally, did not seem impressed. But no matter, our next task will be to find the adult worms and link them to the egg we just found. For that to occur, we must kill the worms we believe are in his intestines, so they can release their hold and be passed. What do we have by way of anthelminthics, the medicines against worms?"

Rafi said, "There are several preparations available, almost all derivatives of the carbolic acid we use in our sprayers to sanitize the air."

Sister Mary Elizabeth raised her eyebrows, grasping his meaning. *"Genetricis Domine nostrum!* You say that instead of merely spraying the compound around sick people, now you have to give it to them to swallow!"

Ashford beamed. "That is all exactly right. All of these phenol derivatives are highly toxic to the enemy worms." Then he added in a more subdued tone, *"And highly toxic to people,* as well. The trick is to employ them at doses high enough to expel the worms, but low enough to spare the patients."

Rafi, María Asunción, and Sister Mary Elizabeth stared at the doctor, wide-eyed, suddenly seeing the thin knife blade they would have to walk on during the treatments. Ashford didn't have to admit that he was largely unfamiliar with the treatment of parasitic diseases; his colleagues were well aware that he had trained in the Army tradition of general medicine and battlefield trauma. Moreover, the derivatives of carbolic acid, or phenol, as it was also commonly called, were not drugs that Ashford employed regularly—he had mostly used them as aerosols in the Lister sanitizers. When taken internally, these drugs were known to be nasty, both for the patients to ingest, and for their immediate and unavoidable side effects.

All the same, Ashford reached for his copy of the *United States Pharmacopeia* and scanned through the pages.

"Here it is," he exclaimed, running a finger down the page. "The drug of choice for deworming appears to be thymol, administered in gelatin capsules." He summarized the text for the others. Thymol was a powerful chemical with strong antiseptic properties found in the oil of several herbs, particularly *Thymus vulgaris*, better known as common garden thyme. The chemical thymol gave the plant its characteristic smell and taste. When purified and concentrated, it turned into white crystals with a distinct aroma akin to mothballs. Ancient Egyptians employed the compound in the mummification of corpses, and a tisane of thyme leaves could also be used to treat dental caries and gingivitis. He set the book down opened to the page, lifting his head to look at his companions. Clearly, thymol was both useful and potent; Ashford simply hoped that it would work for them.

In his *Tropical Diseases,* Manson had not failed to include frightening stories of patients dying from inadvertent thymol poisoning. There was an account of the particularly horrid death of a patient in India and the extensive internal damage found at autopsy. After his demise, rumors soon started in that community that a highly respected doctor had essentially murdered his patient by giving him 60 grains, or 4 grams, of the drug.

Ashford was not at all sure what dose of thymol would be both effective and safe. The *Pharmacopeia* recommended a dose of only 2 grains. Ashford considered this a puny amount, and at those dosages the worms might never be expelled in time to help anyone. And yet, a dose of 60 grains was clearly not the answer either; the correct dose lay somewhere in between. Ashford pulled a number out of his head, and set the amount somewhat randomly at 15 grains, or exactly one gram of crystalline thymol. Ashford took a deep breath, hoping that with luck, this would be the right amount of drug to kill the worms but not his patients.

While the lieutenant went back to consult the Manson book, Rafi began to research antidotes for accidental overdoses of phenolic compounds, including thymol. None existed. But he did find a very practical suggestion—patients should avoid alcoholic beverages until the medicine had completely left their system. Re-reading the account of the doctor in India, he found that the well-meaning man had apparently administered the drug with a chaser of pure whiskey. The alcohol had rapidly dissolved the thymol, allowing the drug to be absorbed from the intestines into the bloodstream. As toxic as it was in the gut, thymol was far more harmful when absorbed into the blood, poisoning the patient instead of the hookworms.

With this in mind, Ashford formulated his first two challenges: to administer enough drug to kill the worms and to make the drug pass through the intestines as quickly as possible and with the least amount of absorption. This could be accomplished by chasing the thymol with a strong cathartic in order to quickly purge the bowels of any leftover poison.

While María Asunción feverishly wrote detailed notes, Ashford shared his ideas with the remainder of the group.

Rafi and Sister Mary Elizabeth readily agreed with the plan. They were still seeing anemia deaths daily, and if the hookworm discovery pointed to thymol as the required therapy, then they were in favor of using it as soon as possible, no matter the risk. Even if they hadn't agreed, within the confines of the military hospital, Ashford governed as an autocrat, and whatever he decided was law. So, 15 grains of thymol it would be.

First, Ashford obtained the medication from the hospital dispensary. It came in the form of tiny white crystals wrapped in paper and stored in a glass container. Then, standing over the laboratory bench, Sister Mary Elizabeth put on a pair of gloves and ever-so-carefully measured one-gram aliquots of the white crystals, which came out to about one-fifth of a teaspoon. Even from such diminutive samples, the strong, distinct smell of thymol filled the air of the small room. Using a small spatula, the nun then carefully put the crystals into a prefabricated gelatin capsule and closed it. Her task done, Sister Mary Elizabeth peeled off her gloves and rested her hands in her lap as they looked at each other with anticipation. At long last, the time had come to forge ahead and treat someone, come what may.

Their choice was Simón Báez. His anemia was severe enough that it required addressing as soon as possible. Without treatment, he was sure to die within weeks. In addition, he had been willing to cooperate with his doctors, and he clearly liked Rafi Moore. Late that afternoon, the team visited Simón in his tent. His eyes lit up when Rafi and Ashford walked in, but he gave an embarrassed cough when he saw the two women following close behind.

Rafi shook his hand and said, "Don Simón, we may have a medicine to help you fight your anemia."

"!*Qué bueno!*" Simón exclaimed. Leaning conspiratorially toward Rafi, he whispered, "Did the nun find something in my *caca*?"

"We have found some worms that could possibly be making you sick," the younger man conceded.

"*Oooh*, worms?" Simón proceeded to explain that he knew of the worms that came out your behind, he had some friends

216

who had them. One of them even claimed that his worms could tell the day of the week.

"Yes," Rafi agreed, "these worms are somewhat similar to the pinworms you describe, but in other ways are very different, and we think, much worse. Unlike those harmless pinworms, the ones we are looking for kill people."

Silence followed and Rafi grew somber. Looking directly into the eyes of the man struggling to breathe in front of him, he said: "We are worried these worms may have killed your children, and that now they are slowly killing *you*."

Simón at first could not fully understand what Rafi meant. Had he really just said that some nearly invisible and harmless-looking creature was responsible for killing his children?

Simón stared in disbelief at the young man for what seemed an eternity.

"We want permission to treat you with an immensely powerful medication," Rafi continued. "You should first know, however, that we have not used this medicine before, so you would be our first patient to receive it and there are some unknowns as to how your body will react."

Simón recovered from his initial shock and adjusted by dismissing Rafi's caution with a wave of his hand.

"I've tried weird remedies before. I remember when I was a youngster in Cayey, we had this old *curandera* who swore that chewing *orégano* leaves and twigs made your sickness go away. I used to chew a lot of *orégano*, but then I moved, and with this and that, I stopped. I wasn't sure how much it helped, anyway."

Rafi knew that *orégano* was one of the many local names for thyme, so the old remedy made perfect sense. The problem with the folk cure was that *orégano* twigs and leaves likely did not contain enough thymol to work efficaciously. Simón would have had to swallow thyme like a ruminant for the herb to work on his hookworms. Seizing on this, Rafi explained, "We have some crystals that work somewhat like that *orégano* cure. They are inside this capsule, which we want you to take."

Simón was enthusiastic. "*Muy bien*, let's see this thing. Up in Utuado, we chase our pills down with some moonshine *ron cañita*, to make it go down easier," he said with a grin.

Rafi paled. "This one we would prefer if you swallowed it with some water, and afterwards, we are going to give you a purgative, *un purgante.*"

Simón never really questioned the plan. These were his betters, these learned doctors, and they had already done a great good for the community. Moreover, doctors like these *always* knew what they were doing. He agreed to take the strange capsule as they asked, and they would all see what happened.

Ashford approached the bed. He picked the capsule from his coat pocket and offered it to Simón with a glass of water. The other patients sharing the tent followed the scene with gazes so focused that their eyes could have leaped from their sockets. Everyone held their breath. Their suspense, magnified by silence, was almost unbearable.

Simón looked curiously at the capsule, which appeared harmless enough. It was transparent, as if made of glass but somewhat softer. He turned it over with his fingers. *"What could possibly happen?"* he thought. He took the capsule, placed it in his mouth, and swallowed it with one gulp of water. He looked up, smiling proudly.

Then, everything changed. Simón felt a terrible burning in his throat and all the way down into his stomach, followed thirty seconds later by the most severe nausea he had ever experienced, his stomach twisting as if it were full of snakes. He was about to vomit violently when Rafi grabbed his face, forcibly closing his mouth to prevent him from losing the capsule. Down went the medicine again, followed by more burning, and then Simón doubled over in his cot with the most horrible abdominal pains.

The room began to spin around him as a cold sweat broke across his brow. All eyes in the room followed Simón's every move and expression with growing horror. A petrified Ashford stared at Simón while Rafi gamely stood by for more vomiting. Sister Mary Elizabeth jumped back a step, and the other patients screamed wildly for help, before realizing that the help they wanted was already present, and moreover, it was these helpers who had given their friend the strange object with unknown crystals. Poor Simón was sure that he was on his way out. His tent-mates screamed conflicting advice simultaneously at the top of their lungs, their cries drowning out the sound of Simón's groans. In the middle of his gut-churning anxiety, Ashford made a mental note to administer future doses in private, if, in fact, this first patient somehow managed to survive.

After a very animated half hour, the crisis began to abate, leaving Simón weak and trembling on his cot. It took a masterpiece of diplomacy and persuasion to convince him to take the purgative of sodium sulfate. Despite the burning still wracking his abdomen, Simón finally took the cathartic and, muttering some prayers to the Virgin, lay down in his cot, fully expecting to die before sunrise.

Leaving the tent, the members of the medical team felt utterly drained. Ashford ordered them to go home for the evening, while he volunteered to check on Simón at intervals throughout the night. Rafi took María Asunción and Sister Mary Elizabeth into town, and, finding himself too wound up to eat, headed to his favorite bar. There, he began to pound out scales on the piano while he considered how he was going to tell his friend Juan that his dear father had died during the night, and moreover, that he, Rafael Moore Campos, had killed him with a capsule of poison.

If Simón had worried about that night being his last, his fears were confirmed by the frequent returns of a worried Ashford, who showed up like clockwork every half hour to check his patient's pulse and count his respirations. Each visit woke the inhabitants of the tent, who struggled into semi-recumbent positions so as not to miss the newest development in the unfolding drama of their dying companion. A discreet betting pool was soon started based on whether or not Simón would last until sunrise. After Ashford's tenth visit, Simón, in his best broken English, ordered him not to return again until morning. If he was going to die, he wanted to do so in peace, preferably while asleep, and the interruptions were not helping him along. "Away, you no come here until *mañana*," he said to Ashford, who could only reply with, "*Sí*," and then left for good.

None of the team members slept that night. One hour before sunrise, Rafi and Sister Mary Elizabeth were back at the hospital looking for their chief. In their small laboratory room, Ashford paced restlessly back and forth, debating with himself as to when he should go check on his patient, who he was certain was sprawled out dead on his cot while the seven *amigos* prayed noisily over his corpse. Ashford decided to wait until 8 a.m. The last hour proved interminable, but finally the lieutenant steeled himself and breathing deeply, said, "And now, my friends, it is time."

The three left the hospital building through the main entrance, proceeding out of the gate and to the field hospital. They made their way through the many neat rows of tents to the one housing Simón and the choir of doomsayers. The team paused briefly for the last time outside the entrance, listening for the faintest sound. Then, with Ashford leading the way, they entered, their hearts pounding.

In the center of the tent, their faces illuminated by two oil lamps, the patients were gathered around Simón, who was very much still of this world. They were all staring in amazement at a large metal basin on the floor in the middle of the tent. Simón looked up proudly at the doctor and pointed to the pan. *"Ahí están, doctor Ashford."*

And there they were indeed. Pushing aside the cluster of onlookers to get a better look, Ashford, Rafi and Sister Mary Elizabeth could easily see floating aimlessly within the brownish froth, a small clan of about twenty tiny creatures, most definitely wormlike and most definitely dead. Simón reported that he had evacuated his intestines four times already that morning, but as he could not see well from the darkness, had simply given the basin over for the orderly to empty. But with the improving light of morning, his most recent excretory results had looked promising, and he had summoned the others to look at the tiny things mixed into the stink and foamy particles of his stool. The floating wisps really looked like tiny animals, they had all agreed, and when the doctor finally entered that morning, he was presented with this precious gift. The diminutive animals were fished out with forceps and placed in a glass dish to take back to the laboratory. The medical colleagues left the happy anemia sufferers waving and cheering. Not one of the patients could recall a grander night of entertainment in his life.

In the lab, the contents of the glass dish were carefully rinsed in saline solution, filtered and examined. With the naked eye, the tiny creatures were unmistakable as worms. They were about a quarter of an inch long, sleek and thin, like tiny pieces of white thread. They looked roughly cylindrical and sharply bent at one end. One of the worms was placed on a slide to be examined in a microscope, prepared at its lowest power.

With the added magnification, a more detailed picture emerged. Ashford recognized immediately that this creature was most definitely a nematode—a type of roundworm, this particular one with a distinct, sharp curve of the head that resembled a tiny hook. It had two dorsal and two ventral cutting plates around the anterior margin of its mouth, with a pair of small teeth located closer to the rear of the throat. Selecting a second worm and putting it to the microscope, Ashford saw that there were two distinct types of worms, slightly different in size, girth, and structure, most likely corresponding to males and females. Rafi opened Manson's book to the section on the hookworm. Staring back at them from the center of the page was their very own animal, clearly labelled: "*Ancylostoma duodenale*, adult."

The three scientists let out a simultaneous howl of delight. They had finally identified a parasitic worm, along with the corresponding egg of its same species, in a Puerto Rican patient with severe epidemic anemia. Moreover, this was the *exact* same worm, associated with the *exact* same anemia, *exactly* as it had been identified in Switzerland in 1880. And better yet, they had given their patient a known and effective deworming medication, thymol. After a quick round of shoulder slapping and hugs, their elation began to cool as they remembered—it still remained to be seen whether Simón would, in fact, get better.

"What will we do," Rafi said, "if he doesn't improve?"

Ashford returned to the Bugnion paper on the miners, but there was no help to be found there. "The Italians used a different anthelminthic to deworm their patients, a male fern extract dissolved in ether. I can't find any reference to thymol. If, in fact, he doesn't improve, I would be inclined to believe that maybe the dose of thymol was incorrect. Or, if the dose was correct, then subsequent dosages are needed to rid him of all the parasites. But just like we guessed on the initial amount, we will have to guess by how much to increase it, or how many more times to give it."

Sister Mary Elizabeth spoke up, "Dr. Bugnion points out that there were hundreds of worms per patient, as many as 1,200. This may be a hint that we should be looking for more than the twenty or so we got from Simón this morning."

Rafi added, shaking his head, "We may never know now how many hookworms he was harboring—he said that he had already relieved himself four or five times before keeping some material for us."

Ashford smiled devilishly. "Rafi, you know what that means, don't you?" He wished he could have photographed Rafi's horrified, incredulous look. "You don't mean that we are going to count all the hookworms that come out of future patients?"

"Yes, that is exactly what I mean. I propose to change our protocol, like this: First, we will administer the cathartic of sodium sulfate the night before the treatment to clear the gut. That way, there won't be any roughage left to protect the hookworms from the thymol. The next morning, we administer one gram of thymol at 8 a.m., and if it's tolerated, we repeat the dose two hours later. Then, we will repeat the cathartic at noon. The difficulty will be collecting all the excretions for a lengthy amount of time, say, three days. We can count all the hookworms in that seventy-two-hour sample, and if we get a number approaching a thousand parasites, as reported in the Italian miners, then we know that we have a viable treatment protocol."

"*Jesu pie!*" Sister Mary Elizabeth cried. "I think the patients will be too shocked not to go along. Collecting and then *saving* their evacuations for three days! They will think it so outrageous that they may very well cooperate, only so they can compare notes in conversation."

"That is exactly what I am counting on," concluded a smiling Ashford. For the first time in a week, he felt he could leave the hospital and go home to María Asunción.

The team waited expectantly to see if Simón responded well to the treatment. By the fifth day, they could not deny that he was making progress. Simón's color was improving, if ever so slightly, as was his appetite. When, on the seventh day, he greeted them standing straight, with the pink outline of his lips starting to show again and asking for more of the awful, yet miraculous medicine, there could no longer be any doubt. Not only that, but the other patients in the tent began to crowd around Rafi and demand similar treatment.

"*Cuanto antes, mejor,*" they said to him—the sooner, the better. Ashford was beginning to understand the language reasonably well after fifteen months on the island.

"*Muy bien*, we start right away." he replied

Chapter Twenty-Three

SUCCESS

To the dismay of many, Ashford chose only four patients, all from Simón's tent, to treat that day: Javier Benítez, Manuel Paz, Luis Quiñones, and Francisco Rodríguez. He wanted to get the protocol right and was still leery about Manson's reports of deaths following thymol treatments. Rafi explained the plan to those selected and warned them that any rum they may have smuggled into the tent, if taken with the thymol, would surely kill them. Two *jíbaros* looked guiltily away.

That very evening, the four men began their treatment with 30 grams of the sodium sulfate cathartic, which soon extracted a furious diarrhea from their fragile intestines. But by the next morning, all had recovered and wanted to continue the treatment. They were inspired by a much-improved Simón, who was at that very moment out for a casual stroll about camp. Ashford produced the thymol capsules, which were duly swallowed by the patients. Two hours later, after having recovered from the nausea and burning produced by the first dosage, they swallowed a second of *"las bolitas de cristal"* —the little balls of glass—the name now given to the capsules by the *jíbaro* patients.

Still semi-conscious after two hits with thymol, the four patients bravely took their last dose of sodium sulfate—which if anything, was worse than the *bolitas* —and then lay back down on their cots. At this point, like Simón, they were convinced that this would be their last day on the planet. The nurses were instructed to watch over their wards like hawks, and inform the doctor right away if any patient became distressed. Most importantly, they were not to forget that every last morsel exiting these patients from below had to be collected for *three whole days.* After that, the fun would begin for the worm counters.

The four patients, aided by the second cathartic, began producing results almost immediately. Everything was faithfully collected as planned, sorted carefully by name and reported to Dr. Ashford, who obsessively visited the tent almost every hour. The patients received plenty of fluids to keep up with the losses from their guts, and then the waiting game began. The next seventy-two hours passed uneventfully for the four patients. But by the end of those three days, they began to notice a strange feeling coming over them, a feeling they had not experienced in years—a tiny zest, a spark, a zing, a fire. It was the feeling of life, slowly returning to their ravaged bodies.

In the end, each patient contributed about half a gallon to the cause of science. The material was brought to the laboratory, where the tallying would soon begin. María Asunción set up a blackboard to keep track of the tabulations while a few orderlies arranged a long wooden trough nearby. The key to the worm-counting procedure lay in this shallow trough, which had been slightly raised at one end, then sanded and painted black to better showcase the whitish hookworms.

Ashford explained their process, gathering his companions around the chalkboard. "We will start by filtering larger particles with a gross colander. What filters out, we will pass once again through a finer sieve. Next, we dilute this fraction with saline, and then filter everything again through paper. The paper then goes into a jar filled with saline to suspend any hookworms present. Finally, María Asunción, will use a dropper to deliver portions of the material to the elevated end of the trough so it flows toward us. As worms drift by, the rest of us will count them, averaging our tabulations for the final result."

Thus agreed, the team began to work, aided by a game María Asunción, who hadn't exactly been told beforehand how extensively she would be helping with the smelly tasks. They went by alphabetical order beginning with the products of *Señor* Báez. They were processed and filtered, and then the suspension was sent toward the counters. The process took

90 minutes for each patient, from preparation to tabulation. A long day was spent in this work, but by the evening they had their results:

Benítez	969 hookworms
Paz	1,237 "
Quiñones	1,114 "
Rodríguez	1,345 "

The numbers of expelled parasites were very much what they had hoped for. It seemed likely that the two separate doses of one gram of thymol, when administered to a clean, purged gut, was sufficient to kill and expel virtually all the worms. With luck, this should set the patients on a clear path to recovery, much like that of Simón Báez, who now returned to his tent only for meals, so busy was he flirting with nurses and playing dominoes with the soldiers. On one of the occasions when Simón returned to his tent, his nurse passed on a request for him to go to the main building to see Ashford. When he entered the office, a beaming Ashford greeted him enthusiastically in broken Spanish. He wanted to conduct an examination post-treatment and obtain blood for more laboratory studies, to which Simón jovially agreed.

With just a casual glance as Simón clambered onto the exam table, Ashford could see that the man's color had markedly improved. He now showed a blush of pink on his cheeks, with no trace of that sickly yellow superimposed on ghostly white which had identified him as suffering from severe anemia only three weeks before. His pulse was normal, his lung fluid had cleared, the swelling in his legs had disappeared and his abdominal pain had resolved. He was more alert and positively giddy with energy. His appetite had returned, his bowels had stabilized, and he wanted to join the rest of his family at Juan's house. Only his heart remained abnormally enlarged. Although Ashford expected this to improve somewhat, he knew it would most likely never return to normal.

Simón's blood was drawn, the smears made and stained. The laboratory studies likewise reflected a marked improvement. His hemoglobin had recovered to 60 percent of normal while the red cell count had increased to over three million and the eosinophils were returning to expected levels. Ashford and his companions agreed to treat him once more with thymol to see if any hookworms remained, then discharge him the next morning without waiting three days for a full collection. The next day, with the protocol completed, Ashford discharged Simón from the hospital. The team then examined his sample and found it to contain only ten to twenty dead hookworms. Compared to the thousand or so he likely harbored before getting the thymol, this was a trivial number, and yet it indicated that for a complete cure, more than one treatment might be necessary. A fuller picture would gradually emerge as their efforts expanded to more and more people, allowing for Ashford to refine their methods as they went.

Simón walked the two miles to Juan's home without difficulty. He thoroughly enjoyed himself, sauntering through the paved streets like a teenager, people-watching and taking in the houses and the trees now slowly replenishing their leaves after the storm. He entered the house through its new front door, his shadow crossing the threshold just as Pepa was preparing lunch for the children. She had not seen him in over two weeks, and almost did not recognize him.

When she did, she dropped her plate of food, scattering red beans and rice all across the warped floor. Standing before Pepa was her partner of twenty years, restored to life and appearing like a new person. Gone was the ghost-like figure of a broken man. Their embrace was long and warm, the first true joy they had felt since *la anemia* had taken Rosa from them fifteen months ago. Tears streamed down Josefa's face as Simón held her, patting her shoulders in his embrace. Carlos and Ana joined them and held on to their father by his waist.

Juan arrived in the late afternoon from the port, which was again brimming with international commerce and shipments of aid from the capital. Ponce's infrastructure was being rebuilt, uprooted trees removed, telegraph wires repaired, and the train to Yauco would soon be running smoothly. After clapping his restored father on the back, Juan turned the conversation toward Carlos and Ana. The children's stay in Ponce had been extremely beneficial. There was no question that their health was improving quickly here in the city. Without a doubt, they had blossomed away from the coffee plantation where the hookworms supposedly thrived, hiding in trees or on the ground, or perhaps even suspended in the evil air, relentlessly stalking the unsuspecting *jíbaros*. The elimination of the parasites had transformed him—of this Simón had no doubt. However, although Carlos and Ana were looking better, he had very real concerns about a relapse.

Simón walked up to Pepa and gently put his hands on her shoulders. "I think we should take the children to the *Hospital Militar* and have Rafi and the *americano* doctor treat them with the magical *bolitas de cristal*."

Pepa recoiled slightly. "Do you think it is safe for the children, Simón?"

Simón reassured her. "I trust them. In a few weeks they have accomplished what years of treatment by our doctors and the *curanderas* could not. They will be honest in telling us what to do."

Unable to deny the truth of her own eyes, Pepa embraced her partner. "Very well then, that is what we will do."

The next day, the family headed up the hill to the hospital building. The place was abuzz with news of Simón's apparent cure and the rapid improvement of his former tent-mates. Hearing of their recent recovery, Simón went in search of his former tent-mates. He found his four friends cursing loudly at one of their own who had apparently been caught cheating at a game of cards. Like Simón, they, too, had been transformed by their treatment, and greeted him with noisy welcomes and a ready seat at the table, though he waved them off to return to his family.

The Báez clan met with Ashford and Rafi during their lunch hour. Simón began, "Doctor, we want to ask you to please treat Carlos and Ana. They have been ill with anemia since they were infants, and we don't want them to sicken again."

Putting down his fork and napkin, Ashford went over to the children and examined them.

"From what I remember a few weeks ago, they seem much improved already," he commented, bending over the children. "Ponce must be doing them good. However, if we adjust the dose of medicine to account for their size, we can treat them safely, and this may result in even further improvement. While you are here, we will have Sister Mary Elizabeth give them the medicines. We will observe the children for most of the afternoon, and if they do not show any evidence of complications, you can all return to Juan's home this evening. We will show you how to collect their waste, and then see you here again in three days."

The doses were cut to half a gram for Carlos, and to a quarter of a gram for Ana, who took the capsules without any fuss. As she watched the two children bear the inevitable stomach cramps and burning, Sister Mary Elizabeth noted that neither child complained nearly as much as the grown men. All the same, she rubbed their backs and offered them water as they bravely pushed through the medication together. Whether they truly felt less discomfort, or were simply inclined to less drama, she was not sure. Five hours elapsed, and once it was clear that the thymol had been tolerated, the family was allowed to return to Juan's house. Three days later, the children indeed showed improvement. Their samples were processed and the hookworms counted: both children expelled about 200 dead worms.

The mood at the evening's meeting was decidedly upbeat. Ashford invited comments from his assistants, and Sister Mary Elizabeth opened the discussion by saying, "It's interesting that the hookworm load in the children was relatively low. This corresponds to the relative mildness of their cases compared to their father, for example."

Rafi responded, "When Carlos and Ana arrived here in August, they looked far worse than they do now. I would have bet good money that if we had counted their worms then, we would have seen close to a thousand. Their brother Juan once told me that he arrived in Ponce half-dead from anemia. But staying away from that coffee plantation made him well, even without any treatment."

"It might be interesting," Ashford mused, "to find out if he has any hookworms left, after living in Ponce for three years. I wager he has none, or so few as to be insignificant."

María Asunción spoke up, "What will happen to your patients when they return to their homes in the mountains? A few will stay in Ponce, but there is not enough work for everybody here. On the other hand, proprietors will soon be rebuilding their haciendas in the mountains of Utuado and Adjuntas; there will be jobs and probably government aid for owners and workers alike."

"Mrs. Ashford, you make a valid point," Rafi said. "If the *jíbaros* lived there when they were sick, they will surely want to live there once they're healthy."

Ashford leaned back in his chair, passing his fingers through his hair. "The important thing is to prevent the people from becoming reinfected. There are still hundreds left to treat, so we have time to work out a prevention strategy. Then they can return to the coffee haciendas without danger of being overrun by hookworms."

"I wonder," Rafi said, "if there is some weakness in the life cycle of this parasite that would allow us to attack it?"

"I've been researching the *Ancylostoma,* in the hopes we could find a solution to that very problem. The central question is the route of infection. If we knew how the worms entered the body, we could take measures to break that cycle."

"Isn't it obvious?" Sister Mary Elizabeth put in. "The worms are swallowed by unknowing victims drinking muddy water, or eating with dirty hands, maybe even eating contaminated soil directly as we've seen a few times."

Ashford nodded. "That would seem the most obvious route. And that is Dr. Manson's theory. But I'm not convinced."

Rafi held up his hands. "How else would they become infected with an intestinal parasite if not by mouth?"

Ashford closed his eyes, concentrating. "What if—Rafi, do you remember what seemingly innocuous symptom almost all these victims report? A complaint so mundane, it could be ignored completely?"

His listeners looked at one another with blank stares.

Sister Mary Elizabeth blurted out, *"Confutatis maledictis!* That ubiquitous skin irritation, *la piquiña!"*

Ashford banged his fist on the table. "Exactly! Could it be possible, just consider this for a moment—could it be possible that the worms are entering *through the skin*?"

Sister Mary Elizabeth shook her head. "How could that possibly happen? Yes, the worms are tiny. But they seem much too large to enter through intact skin. And even if they *do* come through the skin, how do they find their way to the gut?"

"What if," Ashford countered, "the relatively large adult hookworms were not the attackers?"

Rafi nodded, finally understanding Ashford's thinking. "We know that adult hookworms arise from far smaller juvenile stages, and other parasite species are known to be especially adapted to enter via the skin."

"Yes," Ashford said. "It may be possible that these juvenile hookworms find a cut, or a dilated pore, probably in the victim's feet, where they can bore through the skin and into a blood vessel."

Rafi began to chuckle. "Back at Yale, I remember there was this fellow studying needle worms who actually saw this taking place. He infected himself with the larvae by putting them on his skin, and found out about six weeks later that he was, in fact, passing viable needle worm eggs!"

María Asunción gave a half-smile. "Well, at least no one can say he wasn't committed to his field."

Sister Mary Elizabeth's eyes lit up. "So, the eating of dirt we see in the severe cases is then not the cause, but a result of the infection with the *Ancylostoma*."

"Exactly right, Sister. I am starting to think that eating sand and dirt results from the urge to satisfy a ravenous appetite rather than serving as the source of infections. The patients probably become infected from walking barefoot over contaminated farm soils."

"But whether they are picking coffee bushes or cutting sugar cane," Sister Mary Elizabeth said, "the barefoot workers don't notice the skin invasion because the process is painless."

Rafi's eyes narrowed. "Painless, but nevertheless, it produces *la piquiña*, the frequent itch in their feet and ankles."

Ashford rose, and began pacing around their table, his eyes narrowed in thought. "Yes, *la piquiña* results from the larvae tunneling through the skin. If you recall, Rafi, the same thing was happening to the swimmers from Cirilo's village in Lares that were coming down with bilharziasis. The worms of the bilharzia also invade through the skin, producing a dreadful itch."

A sudden realization dawned on Rafi's face. "And Cirilo was popular because he had a remedy for the itch that actually worked. But unfortunately, his cures helped the people go back into the water, where they then acquired more of the bilharzia parasites."

María Asunción asked, "Are the bilharzia flatworms and the hookworms very similar?"

Ashford shook his head. "Not too much. The bilharzia organism is far more primitive—it lacks a mouth altogether. It's essentially an egg-laying machine. Those eggs become wedged in minuscule veins, leading to horrendous scarring that damages the organs."

Rafi's eyes lit up. "You see, Mrs. Ashford, the hookworms are more clever. In the small intestines, the youngsters mature into adults and live happily for a few years drinking blood and having a giant orgy —*ahem,* excuse me— where they mate and produce thousands of eggs daily. They keep recycling billions of eggs back to the soil in the waste of infected persons, who, without knowing they are infected, pollute the soil where it is most convenient…"

María Asunción finished the narration, "And so the number of parasites grows steadily with every new skin invasion. The hookworms kill their hosts by sucking them dry through sheer numbers."

Ashford looked down, frustration clouding his features. "Precisely. But few here have heard of latrines, and those who have regard using them as a huge inconvenience and the source of the 'bad air' on which every ailment around here seems to be blamed. Eggs and larvae have been passing from host to soil to host for centuries. The cycle can be broken only if people wear shoes, move to the cities, or change their hygiene practices."

Rafi added, "Juan used to tell me about the habits of his family up in Utuado. I simply could not believe it, but he assured me it was the norm, and that even he relieved himself on the ground and thought nothing of it. When he arrived in

Ponce, he started wearing shoes and walking on paved surfaces, his diet improved and, after fighting daily against constant fatigue, he slowly began to get well."

"It makes sense," Ashford agreed. "Once Juan broke the cycle of reinfection, his anemia improved as the parasites aged, died naturally, and were passed without being replaced. Eventually, the number falls to the point where a reasonable diet allows the bone marrow to replace lost red cells."

Sister Mary Elizabeth pulled the Manson book, which lay on the table open to the illustration of the *Ancylostoma*, close enough to examine the image. "Our hookworms appear virtually identical to these here, but I can't help but notice that their heads and teeth look different."

Ashford frowned. "That concerns me as well. The hookworm in Manson's book looks very similar to ours, except that his worms cut into tissues with four sharp, claw-like teeth, and ours do not. These Puerto Rican hookworms instead use razor-like cutting plates to attach themselves to the intestinal wall."

Rafi asked, "Could this mean we're somehow wrong in thinking that these worms are causing anemia?"

"We are most definitely *not* mistaken," Ashford replied. "The parasites are similar enough. I am not a parasitologist or a helminthologist, but I hope Dr. Stiles at Georgetown can confirm our findings, and perhaps advise us on the implications of the anatomical differences between the two worms. I have leave coming in a few weeks. María Asunción and I are going back to Washington. I can take advantage of our trip to show some of the preserved worms to Stiles. In the meantime, we will continue treating, and once we have collected enough data, we can present a paper explaining our findings, and maybe gain enough attention to launch a national initiative. We could truly change the island's situation for the better."

Sister Mary Elizabeth brightened. "We won't suffer from a lack of volunteers wanting treatment. Word is already spreading through the city that this hospital is in possession of a miraculous cure. Soon, we may see a tidal wave of people seeking treatment."

María Asunción spoke up. "We should draft guidelines on

how to prevent reinfection. Only one in thirty patients is literate, so this will have to be read to them one by one as they come in for treatment. With luck, the information will spread through more and more communities by word of mouth."

Rafi scrunched up his face as he calculated out loud, "If we assume that hookworm infections are nearly universal among poor agricultural workers, and if we conservatively estimate that these laborers represent two-third of the households on the island, then we are looking at…."

"Six hundred thousand patients," interrupted Ashford, his voice heavy. "If this fight against the hookworm is to continue, we are going to need more help, and lots of it."

Chapter Twenty-Four

DISAPPOINTMENTS, DECEMBER 1899

Sister Mary Elizabeth's prediction proved to be correct. Over the next month, word spread rapidly among the *jíbaros* that American doctors in Ponce were curing anemia victims. Simultaneously, the physicians of Ponce became aware that a young American lieutenant, barely twenty-six years old, claimed to have solved the mystery which had eluded them for well over two hundred years. According to him, a worm barely visible to the naked eye killed thousands of Puerto Rican peasants every year. These rumors were met with raised eyebrows.

Ashford tried holding open forums for his Ponce colleagues to discuss and explain his findings but was repeatedly rebuffed. In fact, his latest lunch seminar had attracted no attendees. Not only did the local physicians not listen to him, but it seemed they were not bothering to investigate on their own, either to prove or disprove the hookworm hypothesis. For the most part, these conservative, Spanish-trained physicians continued treating their anemia patients as they always had—recommending iron-rich meats the *jíbaros* could rarely find, much less afford.

Moreover, it seemed to Ashford that these doctors were falsely enamored with the diagnosis of malaria. Blaming malaria reflexively was part of the medical culture in Puerto Rico—most likely because it was one of the few infectious diseases they knew how to treat. So, when pressed to administer a medication to patients with end-stage anemia, many invariably chose quinine, a medicine Ashford knew to be efficacious against malaria, but of no value whatsoever against the hookworm. In fact, he remembered Dr. Zeno attributing his own good reputation to an uncanny ability to avoid misdiagnosing malaria, thereby sparing his patients unnecessary side effects from a worthless course of quinine. As such, the open skepticism and obvious errors of the Ponce physicians filled Ashford with frustration and anger.

After a particularly long day, Ashford and Rafi were practicing for a performance for the people of Ponce, to be given the following day in the hospital's courtyard. The city was returning to normal; people were being cared for and gradually beginning to find their own way back to some semblance of stability. The anemia treatments appeared so far to be working well, but that evening Rafi found his boss sullen and withdrawn.

Ashford put down his violin. "Rafi, these local practitioners are so damnably stubborn. They could start an argument in an empty house with their claims that the prevalence of anemia on this sad island is the result of bad food, bad air and malaria, and that the hookworm is an incidental finding, a red herring. And it *is* an empty house, because I can't even get them to meet with me, let alone debate me on the worst health crisis their nation has ever faced."

Rafi grinned and continued to play, swaying from side to side as his hands glided over the keys. "They seem to be very set in their ways. Or maybe they're just embarrassed that a foreign physician, still wet behind the ears, worked out in a few weeks what they could not in several hundred years."

Ashford rolled his eyes. "I would've hoped that they wouldn't sink to schoolyard jealousies. I described how well the first twenty patients had recovered after deworming, how their blood levels largely normalized within a month. Those doctors replied that it was due to the meat we were giving them."

Rafi stopped playing and turned to Ashford.

"Remember that they're used to worms in the gut being harmless: pinworms, roundworms, tapeworms," he counseled. "They have years of anecdotes to show that people can have worms without having anemia. Moreover, they have seen how patients who have these larger worms removed don't get better."

Ashford shook his head. "They're equating the size of the parasite to the severity of the disease. Those large worms they can see with the naked eye are more like alley cats rummaging in the garbage, harmlessly feeding on junk. But those tiny vampire hookworms, the kind you can barely see without a microscope—those are the real killers."

"And the Army's not much better," Rafi added.

"They have been somewhat supportive," Ashford replied glumly, "but they will not intervene with local health practices unless the War Department gets involved. I don't see that coming anytime soon."

"In the meantime," Rafi added with a smirk, "we are providing the material for one tremendous joke, and the name Ashford is becoming the punchline. The press is spreading disparagements all over the island."

Ashford's blood rose to his face. "Don't tell me—they're comparing me to those worm quacks peddling medications around the countryside. Have you glanced at a newspaper lately? Even my own father-in-law's paper, *La Correspondencia*, is literally choked by ridiculous advertisements, whether for Dr. Van Ness' *Lacto-Marrow* or Dr. Williams' *Little Pink Pills*, among dozens of others. You have to work to find the real news submerged in a sea of bold squares touting bogus drugs in the largest allowable type. All make the most absurd claims: the same remedy cures anemia, headaches, impotence, sterility, venereal disease, and, of course, *worms!* How am I supposed to let people know about the real cure when I am surrounded by such stupidity on all sides?"

Rafi turned back to the keyboard and crossed hands, knocking out a rippling passage in four-part polyphony. "Cheer up and remove those thoughts from your head. Your leave is around the corner, and you'll have a chance to restore your energies far away from your critics. Maybe working on your journal report will help."

"Yes, the results from our first patients are almost ready for submission to the New York *Medical Journal*," Ashford brightened slightly, though his instrument still hung loosely at his side. "I have requested expedited publication given the importance of our discovery here in Puerto Rico and the high likelihood that it applies to other countries."

Rafi signaled Ashford to resume playing. "I certainly don't see why hookworms could not be found anywhere the conditions are right."

Ashford tucked his violin back under his chin. "I grew up in the South, where you will often hear the expression '*poor white trash.*' There are large swaths of the United States bordering the Gulf of Mexico where anemia outbreaks resurface every spring. Maybe those poor white folks have hookworm disease."

"Maybe so," echoed Rafi.

Ashford began to play again, and then the biggest smile came to his face. "By the way, Rafi, I almost forgot to share my joyful news. Mrs. Ashford is expecting!"

"Ha! A tiny Ashford! Teach him the cello and you are halfway to a string quartet!"

"Or *her*."

*****

Ashford and María Asunción returned to San Juan the week prior to leaving for the mainland. Before their departure, María Asunción's father offered *La Correspondencia* as a platform for Ashford to describe his findings. Ashford demurred, not sure if a civilian newspaper was the appropriate venue for a military doctor to defend his discovery. But he thanked don Ramón, explaining that he would publish in a prestigious journal very soon.

Vacation started for the Ashfords when they boarded the steamer *Philadelphia* in San Juan, hoping to be in time to celebrate Christmas in Washington, D.C. Ashford was looking forward to a brief vacation in his hometown and to spending more time with his wife. At the same time, he was worried that efforts against the hookworm were going to stall in his absence, due largely to his failure in convincing more doctors of the importance of the parasite.

Under his direction, the *Hospital Militar de Ponce* had treated several dozen anemia patients successfully, while losing less than a handful, whom Ashford suspected were too sick to survive the process anyway. For those poor unfortunates, severe anemia had wrecked their systems for so long that no matter how many worms were killed, it was too little, too late. But in spite of his distress at the losses, he was fully aware that when deploying a new discovery in the clinic, occasionally losing patients was the price for getting many others well.

When the couple arrived in Washington, they found housing in the army barracks for married officers. After two years in the tropics, Ashford thought winter in the District of Columbia to be unusually gloomy, whereas María Asunción considered the cold and snow a novelty. Generally, there was not much for a lieutenant to do on a temporary leave from the Medical Corps. Try as he might, Ashford could not get anybody interested in the precious hookworms he was carrying around in fixative. He wrote twice to Professor Stiles but received no reply. After a month, Ashford ran out of patience and went to visit his former professor.

Out of deference to his teacher, Ashford had included Stiles' name in the paper he had submitted to the *Medical Journal*. He had decided to mention Stiles to lend credence to the publication, but somehow had neglected to let his professor know of the arrangement. To correct his oversight, Ashford thought he would give the worms to Stiles to describe the tiny creatures in a separate article. To Ashford's chagrin, his *Medical Journal* article had not appeared yet, despite the request for expedited publication.

Upon arriving on the Georgetown campus, he realized why the professor had not yet replied to his letters. Charles Stiles was not in the city. Instead, Ashford was greeted indifferently by his assistant, Albert Hassall, a large man with a disarranged mop of curly red hair and a pipe continuously in his mouth. Hassall could not recall Ashford the student, but at least had the courtesy to ask for his name. The assistant asked the purpose of his visit, and Ashford produced the jar with the floating worms. Hassall leisurely turned the container over and over. Finally, he removed the lid, placed one of the tiny worms on a glass slide, and scrutinized it under the microscope. After only two minutes, Hassel looked up and stared intently at Ashford, as if looking straight through him.

Ashford stared back, pointing at the slide. "It is the *Ancylostoma duodenale*. I have submitted a report on twenty successfully treated cases of anemia caused by this same hookworm for publication in the New York *Medical Journal*. Listen, Hassall, I do not wish to present myself as an expert on parasites. In fact, we only identified the hookworm by matching it to the illustrations in Manson's *Tropical Medicine*. I thought it appropriate to turn these specimens over to Dr. Stiles for him to publish a description, should he wish to do so."

"And exactly why are you giving these to Stiles?"

"I've just told you."

"But if they are simply hookworms, why do you give them to him? Is there nothing else? He has dozens of *Ancylostoma* specimens from Europe and South Asia."

Ashford was growing exasperated with the stonewalling. "Well, yes, there is something else. These damned things have no teeth, and being *Ancylostoma*, of course they should have teeth. So why is that?"

"And because of that you want to give them to Stiles, do you?"

Ashford turned crimson with anger. "I think that I have said that several times."

"Look here," Hassall snapped, taking the pipe out of his mouth for the first time. "Why don't you describe them yourself?"

Ashford could barely restrain himself from striking the assistant. With great effort, he finally managed to say, "I am quite satisfied with having discovered the cause of anemia in Puerto Rico. I don't want to presume to be a parasitologist. These worms have no teeth, but they should, and I am not sure why. If there is anything funny about them, let the professor describe them and get the credit. The big thing is settled, that they are the agent of a fatal pandemic of anemia."

"Very well then," said Hassall dryly, and the pipe went back into his mouth.

Ashford headed back to the barracks in a foul mood. The haughty assistant had trivialized his discovery, and the growing number of unbelievers was wearing on him. His leave was about to expire, and he couldn't be happier to return to Puerto

Rico and renew the fight against the hookworm. Luckily, it seemed to him that his superiors felt the same, for waiting at the barracks was a letter from his unit commander. He was to report at 0900 for orders.

The next morning, the head of the Medical Corps greeted Ashford in his office at the requested hour. It was his old commander from the war, Colonel Robert O'Reilly.

"Lieutenant Ashford, it is good to see you once more. It has been, what—eighteen months or so, since Mayagüez?"

Ashford nodded, his hands folded neatly behind his back. "Yes Colonel, more or less that long. Those were quite the times, simultaneously fighting the Spanish and typhoid fever. I would take on the enemy before typhoid, any day."

O'Reilly smiled at his recollections. "The Spanish were gallant adversaries; they were simply undermanned and overwhelmed. The people of Mayagüez certainly do not seem to miss them."

"I agree, Colonel. In fact, I recently married a young woman from Mayagüez. She looks forward to our return so we can await the arrival of our first-born."

The colonel grew quiet, and slowly stood up from behind his large desk.

"Lieutenant, it is precisely of that matter I wished to speak to you this morning. Not too surprisingly, the Filipinos have decided to form their own nation, and very much sooner rather than later. They are angry at the United States for not immediately granting them independence, and have started a revolt. They are ferocious fighters, our casualties are mounting, and our soldiers need surgeons." He handed Ashford a single sheet of paper, which the lieutenant read with mounting dismay and utter disbelief.

His voice full of regret, the colonel spoke as Ashford scanned the neatly printed letter before him. "You must be disappointed, Ashford. Truth be told, during the war you proved yourself to be a good clinician and a talented field surgeon. Colonel Hoff admired your work in San Juan and recommended you as the very embodiment of the ideal physician soldier." Ashford could not disguise the stark cynicism that crossed his face.

"There are also many words of praise," O'Reilly continued, "regarding your treatment of that general illness of the islanders, the one that leaves them idle and lazy, a condition I had mentioned to you on our voyage and then personally observed."

"I understand, sir."

The colonel looked straight at Ashford. "We cannot spare you from the Philippines at present, Lieutenant. I can, however, personally commit to bringing you back after one year, without fault, perhaps sooner if the Aguinaldo forces can be brought to the table."

"Thank you, sir," Ashford said, his tone bleak. Then he saluted, and left, his footfalls as heavy as his heart.

He walked to the barracks through a cutting winter wind, lost in thought.

> *There are many plans in a man's heart,*
> *Nevertheless, the decree of the LORD—that shall prevail.*

But the Bible's words brought him little comfort in the face of his disappointment. The trees were bare and the sky overcast in muted grays, the cold as flat and oppressive as Ashford's mood. That day, there was no consolation from nature as he headed back to María Asunción with his orders in his pocket. The crestfallen physician walked into their apartment, handed her the paper, and stared silently at the floor. María Asunción's color drained from her face as she read the orders.

A full minute passed before Ashford again looked at María Asunción, whose eyes were now welling with tears. "As you can see, I have been assigned to the Philippines," he murmured. "I leave within a week for California, and from there to those islands rebelling against us, their liberators, without even waiting for the ink to dry on their transfer from Spain."

Ashford had never felt so dejected. Here he was, the discoverer of the cause of a disease that affected two-thirds of the inhabitants of Puerto Rico, still only a first lieutenant, and now assigned to a post 7,000 miles away from his work and his wife, who was to give birth in a few months. He could not challenge the gospel that when he joined the Army as a physician-soldier, he was first a soldier, then a physician, but for the very first time, he now wished the order of those words could be inverted. But they could not, and the Philippines it was to be. Glumly, the couple started packing for different ends of the globe. They could be apart for up to a year, with no guarantee that they were to see each other again.

Chapter Twenty-Five

RETURN TO LARES, FEBRUARY 1900

With Ashford's departure from Puerto Rico in late 1899, the treatment of the anemic patients came to a halt. The field hospital had been built to feed and shelter those displaced after San Ciriaco, and the Army considered the discovery of the *Ancylostoma* and the subsequent treatment of a few dozen people to be nothing but a sideshow. With conditions normalizing, people left the hospital and started rebuilding their lives. Most of the peasants headed back to their old homes, hoping to somehow reassemble their lives working in the devastated coffee plantations and among the ravaged food trees that had once sustained them. Many others left the mountains permanently to take their chances on the coast, for the golden age of sugar cane was arriving as fast as coffee was passing.

Rafi and Sister Mary Elizabeth found themselves back where they had started so many months previously. Sister Mary Elizabeth returned to the Asilo de las Damas. She resumed her nursing duties, now with the added frustration of knowing what most of her patients needed to get well, but being powerless to provide it. Meanwhile, the local doctors continued their mockery of the whole hookworm episode. No one risked prescribing thymol to a critical patient when a bad outcome could easily be blamed on their treatment with a dangerous drug.

The Army no longer needed Rafi Moore, so he remained in Ponce, living on a handsome allowance from his father, whose fortunes were soaring under the American flag. But Rafi was a scientist at heart, and his time under Ashford had shown him his future. He looked forward to fighting the anemia of his countrymen, alone if necessary. But he could not prescribe or administer the little balls of thymol, and with no local doctors willing to cooperate, it was impossible for him to continue treating patients with anemia. As the month drew to a close, both Rafi and Sister Mary Elizabeth began to look forward to the day when Ashford's leave would end and he would return to Puerto Rico's shores.

Only a few days before Ashford's expected return from his leave, Rafi received a letter from the doctor.

Mr. Rafael Moore
16 Bertoly Street
Ponce, Porto Rico

February 8, 1900

My dear Rafi,

I hope this letter finds you well. Unfortunately, I have no good news for you. I have received orders to proceed to the Philippines after my leave is over. Mrs. Ashford will return to Porto Rico, but it appears that I will not. I regret not having had more success convincing our local colleagues of the importance of beginning an island-wide campaign for the treatment of the hookworm, which I hope will continue in my absence. I am afraid that much misery that could have been so easily prevented will now come to pass.

Only last week, I left our worms with Stiles' assistant to pass on to him to examine. I have not heard anything yet and do not know if I will. All I can ask now is that you continue our labors in any way you can, for your fellow countrymen. Take good care of yourself and take good care of our little island. I close, for suddenly, I feel very fatigued and not very well. Give my warm regards to Sister Mary Elizabeth.

Your friend,

B. K. Ashford

Rafi spent the night at the piano, trying to deal with this

disappointing news and thinking of a way forward. The next morning, he woke up with the germ of a plan: if he could not fight the disease with thymol, then he would fight it with education and prevention. The few months he had spent studying the hookworm convinced Rafi that preventing re-infections and breaking the infection cycle was the first step toward improving the lives of his countrymen. It might take more time than deworming treatments, but it would be the cornerstone of any campaign going forward.

The next day, Rafi went to visit sister Mary Elizabeth, as he had been doing once a week. Sister Mary Elizabeth was very surprised when a tired-looking Rafi walked into the *Asilo* and silently handed her the letter from Ashford. She read it slowly and returned the sheet to him. With a smile that hid her intense disappointment, she said, "We will have to do what we can without him, at least for the moment."

Rafi leaned forward. "We already started educating the patients before the doctor left. We will simply continue bringing the simple message that shoes and latrines save lives."

Sister Mary Elizabeth drew her brows together. "How will you do that? The vast majority of the *jíbaros* can't read."

"Very true, but in every *barrio* there is always some person who is literate, a local leader, the one that responds to the *alcalde*. It will be a lot of work, but I plan to visit as many of them as possible. With their help, we could call a meeting of the community, provide food and drink to attract them, and then address the importance of wearing shoes everywhere and always. Many of these *jíbaros* have at least one pair of shoes, even if they only wear them to special occasions. Equally important, we have to convince them to dig latrines and then use them."

Sister Mary Elizabeth clasped both hands in front of her tunic. "That...could work. We can try to do the same here. The Sister Superior is a big fan of Dr. Ashford's work. She was the one who put me in contact with him in the first place, at the *Hospital Militar*. The doctors at the *Asilo* refuse to use thymol, but at least we can talk with the patients about the importance of basic hygiene. They listen, whether out of courtesy or true interest, I don't know, but they do listen."

Rafi rose to leave. "Very well, Sister. For my part, I plan to start next week in Lares. I have some connections there with a *barrio* chief named Ernesto Pérez and his brother, don Eugenio, the *alcalde*. I may be able to gauge from their reaction what we may face with a larger campaign in the mountains."

Sister Mary Elizabeth accompanied her colleague to the steps of the *Asilo,* and gently grasped his shoulders with her hands. "Good luck, Rafi, and don't neglect to tell us how you are coming along."

Rafi headed home to plan his visit to Lares. He expected the trip to take four days each way, and he hoped this arduous journey would not be wasted. In his favor, Ernesto and Eugenio Pérez listened when the bilharzia flatworm was identified in their *barrio* of Pezuela. But, on the other hand, the trek was very long, the last twenty miles or so being on horseback over poor mountain trails and crossing country that had not yet been tamed. Rafi removed his Colt revolver from its drawer, spun the chambers and checked that it was fully loaded.

The Ponce to Yauco line was by far the shortest of the island's four train routes, and for twenty cents, Rafi traveled the twenty miles in a little over an hour. In Yauco, Rafi bought a horse, one of the improved island stock that had appeared since the American conquest of the island. He then continued his journey on horseback, first to San Germán for the night, then one more day to Mayagüez, where he had spent several months alongside Ashford at the *Hospital de San Antonio.* There, Rafi spent some precious days resting, visiting old friends, and enjoying the comforts of civilization before continuing his journey into the mountains.

The next leg of Rafi's tour took him to Las Marías, well into the rugged interior and near the site of the last Spanish defeat of the war. This was the heart of coffee country, isolated and restless, and its inhabitants were struggling mightily to recover from the ravages of the hurricane. The people who had returned had rebuilt their huts rather quickly, but food was scarce and work impossible to find. Times were bad, and bad times make for desperate people.

The last day of the journey found Rafi following the Añasco River toward the Lares border, then proceeding south along the Guaba River to the *barrio* of Pezuela. By early evening, he was starting the turn to the *Guaba* when hushed noises made him rein in his horse. There were voices coming from the riverbank ahead, carried downstream by the current and the echoes of the canyon. Leaving his horse to investigate, Rafi found that the voices belonged to several men about two hundred yards away, hidden around a slight bend in the river. What this group of men was doing there, haunting an isolated mountain pass at nightfall, Rafi did not know, but their presence was likely a problem. This was desolate mountain country; the nearest hacienda was more than two hours away and there were no towns or *barrios* for miles along the narrow mountain paths.

Rafi deliberately walked his horse back a few hundred yards and tied its bridle to a mountain palm. Before he could safely resume his journey, he had to approach the men, assess whether they were truly up to no good, and if so, somehow bypass them on a parallel trail.

Going on foot, Rafi carefully picked his way along the southern slope of the valley and pressed forward, searching for a place where he could safely observe the group. Progress was slow—he constantly scanned the ground for branches that could snap, or snags that could trip him. Finally, he arrived at a perch above the river where, hidden by a granite boulder, he could observe the men from about fifty feet above the riverbank.

In the fading light, he could see several figures, most of whom appeared to be drunk out of their minds. Several rifles and machetes lay on the ground nearby. Rafi counted eight men who were sitting, talking vociferously among themselves; the ninth was apparently dead, lying still with his face turned toward the sky.

His pulse quickening, Rafi watched from his hiding place. The corpse lay, limbs splayed beside the path—a tall white man with blondish hair and mustache, dressed in good clothes. Rafi was close enough to distinguish the delicate features of aristocracy. As to who led the group, there was no question. Standing by the fire was a very tall, muscular, light-complexioned man with a bushy mustache and a menacing, deep bass voice. When he talked, the others listened, and no dissent was allowed. Nor could it even be attempted, for the leader was the only person sober and in full possession of his faculties.

Rafi felt his blood freeze in his veins. He had seen this man's likeness in posters hanging in both Ponce and Mayagüez, even in the Yauco train depot. There was no question: this chief was José Maldonado Román, known to many as El Águila Blanca, the legendary White Eagle of the mountains of Puerto Rico. Rafi had known of him even as a teenager in San Juan, where the bandit was lionized by the clientele of the low-life bars Rafi played in the Old City.

A confirmed outlaw who had been in and out of jails since he was eleven, El Águila had always vocally condemned Spanish rule, and cultivated an image as a liberator to justify violent attacks on wealthy landowners and merchants, whom he portrayed as collaborationists. The astute Maldonado shared some of his take with the *jíbaros,* many of whom hid him from the authorities out of equal parts gratitude and fear. The change from Spanish to American rule had done nothing to reform the bandit, who, if anything, had become more ruthless than ever. The American civil government in San Juan had finally put a bounty on his head. Maldonado, also known as "don Pepe" to his friends, then disappeared deep into the mountainous interior. From there he had escalated his attacks, as the dead man at his feet now proved to Rafi.

A drunk underling was getting in Águila's face. "Pepe," he slurred, what are we going to do with this Roig *hijo de puta* now?"

Águila pushed him back, his nose wrinkling at the pungent smell of alcohol.

"We'll send a message to don Arturo asking for a ransom. He doesn't know that his son is dead, only that he is missing."

The man wiped some bloody snot on his sleeve and staggered away. "*Esto sí que nos va a joder.*" (This is really going to screw us up.)

Unruffled by this, El Águila started to clean his revolver. "Not if we do this right. We may have to disappear completely, at least for a short while. I am going south to visit family in Juana Díaz for a few weeks. Nobody bothers me in my town.

The *alcalde* is my uncle, and I keep his coffers well supplied."

Another bandit sat up with difficulty. "Too bad *Señor* Roig decided to fight. He never had a chance, the poor *pendejo*, one against eight."

Don Pepe narrowed his eyes. "Yes, it would have been much cleaner to rob him and then hold him for money, but not all our projects go according to plan."

The gang had positioned themselves in such a way that they dominated the only path accessible by horse that led to Pezuela. No rider was going to get through without their knowledge. Since there were no alternative trails to bypass them on horseback, Rafi either had to give up and turn back, or walk the rest of the way.

He decided to press ahead. But as he was about to retreat from his spot and free his horse, his boot slipped and a small avalanche of gravel and rock bounced noisily down the mountain.

In a split second, the men were up. Pepe cocked his revolver while the others grabbed rifles and *machetes*, looking warily around.

"*¿Qué carajo fue eso?*" (What the hell was that?) The White Eagle surveyed the slope, his eyes glinting in the firelight, but saw nothing in the growing darkness.

Rafi broke into a cold sweat. He reached for his revolver and waited, a straitjacket of fear compressing his chest. Luckily, he had chosen his post well; to get to him, the men would have to climb steeply and gain fifty vertical feet in elevation. Drunk as they were, except for their leader, it was possible that if Rafi could lie still, he might be able to wait until dark and escape up the mountain.

He spent the next minutes in pure, unadulterated agony, hardly daring to breathe while those below him noisily argued. The inebriated men showed no desire to move, much less to climb the slope to investigate. Rafi dared to hope that they might have missed him entirely. But his heart sank when he heard them agree to send two armed men to search in his direction.

The selected bandits shouldered their rifles and slowly began the difficult climb, their feet sliding on broken rock and fighting exposed roots. Rafi held his breath and remained perfectly still, pressed close to the ground, his right hand grasping his revolver. The drunk bandits had progressed about a third of the way to his perch when one of them slipped on the sludgy clay and tumbled violently down the hillside. That ended the reconnaissance. The men turned back to the camp and reached for more rum. They lounged about the camp loudly blaming each other for their misadventure, while Rafi crouched a mere fifty feet above them with his heart hammering in his chest.

The moon set around midnight. In the deeper darkness, Rafi began to retreat up the mountain on all fours. Down by the river, the men slept heavily except for don Pepe, who zealously kept watch. Rafi's progress through the inky blackness was agonizingly slow. At last, he reached the crest and made his way north for a while, before once again descending the steep incline to his horse. Freeing his mount from the tree, he led it up the path for half a mile. Then, with a firm slap on the rump, he sent the animal back toward Las Marías.

Rafi climbed once again, passed over the ridge, and descended into the next valley to continue south toward Pezuela. When he felt he had put enough distance between himself and El Águila, he rested for the night. With the first rays of the morning, Rafi resumed his trek, again reaching the Añasco River and following one of its tributary creeks to the *barrio*. He arrived around noon, famished, thirsty, and covered in insect bites, but happy to be alive. He stumbled past the site of the erstwhile dam and its swimming hole, now an overgrown meadow, and pushed into the small village.

The people did not know what to make of Rafi's return. Last time they had seen him, this man had come on horseback with armed soldiers at his side to take away their precious lake. Now, he was alone and ragged. What possible reason could he have for visiting them like this?

They took Rafi to don Ernesto's house, who greeted him warmly. "Rafael Moore, it is good to see you again! It has been well over a year, has it not? I didn't expect to have you back so soon, and on foot, no less! Please come into my house and recover."

Rafi passed his forearm over his face to clear sweat from his eyes. "I left Mayagüez two days ago on a beautiful trail horse. Half a day out of Las Marías, I ran into the Águila and a band of seven men. They had just killed someone, a young white man who looked well-to-do." Rafi described the victim as well as he could.

Ernesto listened raptly, then gestured Rafi to a chair. "Rafael, you are very fortunate to have made it here. That is indeed Pepe Maldonado. He has been reported in the area for the last two weeks. We heard word that don Arturo Roig's son, the heir to Las Alturas, was traveling with two foremen to Las Marías to look into purchasing ruined coffee farms. He never made it there. Now we know what must have happened."

"If so, the foremen must have escaped."

Ernesto nodded. "Yes. By now, surely they have returned to Utuado and relayed news of the attack. It's odd, usually, the rich victims are ransomed."

Rafi quickly drained a glass of water Ernesto's wife had brought him. "The bandits said young Roig was killed trying to escape."

Ernesto let out a long sigh. "It will be a blow to don Arturo. And to his hopes for rebuilding Las Alturas, and on all who depend on him for work, as well. These are dark times, my friend. My brother Eugenio will need to hear of this...."

Rafi drew himself up in his chair. "Don Ernesto, before you speak to your brother the *alcalde,* I will tell you why I have travelled all the way from Ponce. When we discovered the bilharzia problem in the creek here at Pezuela, you and your brother did a courageous thing. It required great leadership and authority to drain that pond and free the river."

Ernesto gave a lopsided grin. "The common people here still cannot understand how some strange and invisible worm could have been killing their families, and even less why they had to destroy their precious dam simply on the word of some *yanqui* doctor."

Rafi gently grasped Ernesto's arm. "You and your brother were able to get the *jíbaros* to listen and go along for the greater good of the community, even though they could barely grasp the reasons. I respect what you did, especially since you had recently lost your son to the bilharzia parasite. Now, we need your help to fight a much deadlier enemy—the hookworm."

Ernesto Pérez stared at the younger man. "Rafael, we have heard that somebody at the *Hospital Militar* in Ponce has discovered a medicine which supposedly cures *la anemia*. Nobody believed the rumors at first, but now, three of my neighbors actually know someone who has taken this medicine. Many people here wish to receive this treatment. Even doña Inés, the *curandera*, says she will take the *bolitas de cristal*."

Then Ernesto softened, looking at Rafi with concern. "But I refuse to hear anything else until you have changed into fresh clothes and rested from your harrowing journey. I will send word to Lares requesting to meet tomorrow with the *alcalde*. I will not mention your reason for coming."

"Yes, I'd rather not say much more until tomorrow." Rafi sighed with relief. "But I will be grateful for a place to rest and a shot of *ron*."

"Now that, I can take care of," Don Ernesto said with a laugh, sliding Rafi another glass.

The next day, Rafi and don Ernesto rode the four miles into Lares. After lunch, the meeting with *alcalde* began over a strong brew of Lares coffee. Don Eugenio opened the conversation.

"So, Rafael, my brother says you have come from the *Hospital Militar*. Please, tell us what is happening in Ponce with this anemia treatment, and what you want from us here in Lares."

"*Señor alcalde*, at the *Hospital Militar* in Ponce, Dr. Bailey Ashford has identified a parasitic worm directly responsible for the pandemic of chronic anemia so widespread in Lares and most of the other towns on the island."

Don Eugenio coughed into his cup, spilling hot coffee down his bright white shirt. The *alcalde* stared incredulously at Rafi. "*Surely you can't mean another worm?* You must be referring to the same damned creature as last time, the worm that supposedly hides in rivers and lakes?"

Rafi vehemently shook his head. "No, this is most definitely a different worm. In Spanish, we call it *la uncinaria*. This hookworm lives in soils instead of water. It enters the body through people's feet when they walk barefoot on ground soiled by infected human excrement."

Eugenio Pérez could not believe what he was hearing. How many different killer worms were prowling around Lares anyway? It seemed fantastic—a saga of the doctor knights against the dragon worms.

The *alcalde* narrowed his eyes. "Infected ground, you say?"

"Yes, sir. The ground is continuously being contaminated by eggs deposited in the droppings of those with infectious anemia who relieve their bowels wherever they get the urge. The eggs hatch into young worms that attach to a person's foot when walking barefoot. The number of people fouling the soil is so high that the entire countryside is covered in hookworm eggs and young."

For Eugenio, the story was getting more far-fetched with every word that came out of Rafi's mouth.

Oblivious to the *alcalde's* skepticism, Rafi continued, "When the worm enters the skin of the feet it circulates throughout the body until it ends up in the intestines. There, the worms grow and mature, and then they start feeding on people's blood."

As crazy as that sounded, the Pérez brothers knew that animals like bats, leeches and, of course, common mosquitoes fed on blood. But those animals lived on blood that they got from outside the body. What Rafi was describing was a legion of minuscule vampires that sucked victims dry from the inside out.

With a look of skepticism, don Eugenio encouraged Rafi to proceed. "Hookworms cut into the wall of the intestines with mouth plates as sharp as the razor-like *navajas* you attach to the ankles of fighting cocks to slash their opponents. The parasite then laps up the blood oozing from the tiny wound. When that site dries up, it moves to another spot, where it cuts the lining again. All the while, every female hookworm is pushing out eggs she manufactured with nutrients from the ingested blood—twenty thousand of them, *every day*."

"If there are so many worms waiting to ambush us, then, tell me, why do I feel well, as does my brother and our families?"

Rafi leaned toward the *alcalde*. "Because you put on shoes when you step outside your house, and you defecate into a latrine."

Don Eugenio's brows shot upward. The simple truth of this statement completely disarmed him. Wearing shoes outside the home every day was a symbol of status and authority. In addition, he had built his family a privy years ago for the very reason that fouling up your cozy family farm with your own turds was something only the common and ignorant poor did. Like putting on shoes, not shitting all over his own backyard like the chickens meant that on some level, he was better than the common *jíbaros*.

Ernesto interrupted his brother's thoughts. "How much blood can you lose to an animal you can barely see with a magnifying glass?"

Rafi sensed his moment. "There lies the key to the problem. If only one generation of worms latched themselves onto hosts, then the losses might perhaps be surmountable. But the number of larval worms crawling on the ground is so ridiculous, so outrageously high, that peasants are constantly getting infected, *and reinfected*, conceivably acquiring several new worms every day. At the hospital in Ponce, we found that our average patient hosted in excess of a thousand hookworms at a time."

The image of hundreds of tiny hookworms writhing together, incessantly biting his gut raw made Eugenio cringe. Ernesto turned a shade of pale green and wiped his brow. The two brothers quickly downed some rum and seemed temporarily restored to health. Next, they wanted to know exactly what were the mysterious glass capsules that people swallowed.

Rafi explained, "Dr. Ashford decided to use a medicine derived from the thyme bush, what you sometimes call *orégano* here."

At this, the brothers nodded together in comprehension. Herbal cures were something they could understand, and probably better than those foreign doctors in Ponce.

"The drug itself is called thymol," Rafi continued, "And we deliver it in soft capsules that look somewhat like very tiny glass spheres, the *bolitas de cristal* that people are talking about. Enough thymol kills all the worms, which are then expelled by a cathartic. One, two and, rarely, three of the thymol capsules is all it takes."

The brothers exchanged knowing glances once more. Eugenio declared, "Well then, what we need here is some of these *bolitas de cristal,* as our *jíbaro* neighbors call them."

"That is a problem," Rafi admitted. "Dr. Ashford has not been able to convince the other doctors in Ponce to begin using thymol. Then he was called back to the United States, so our project, at the present, stands still."

"We can make teas of the thyme, or have people eat the twigs and the leaves," Ernesto suggested.

Rafi held up his hands. "I am not sure that will work well. And the bigger problem is that even if we could kill all the hookworms in a particular person, as soon as they step barefoot on infected ground once again, the parasites will come charging back."

The brothers looked straight at Rafi, their eyes searching his for answers.

"What we need to do right away is, first, get everybody to wear shoes all the time, and second, have every family build a latrine they will actually visit. Then, when thymol becomes available once again, we will use it. But for now, it will have to be shoes and latrines."

"Very well Rafael," said don Eugenio, rising from the table. "We will consider this information, and your requests, to the fullest. Nothing can be lost if people wear shoes and go to the bathroom in designated holes, at least for a time, until we see what happens. Don't you agree, Ernesto?" His brother nodded, and the meeting drew to a close.

Two days later, Rafi was ready to leave Pezuela. He had a mount once again, this one borrowed from his host, with instructions to leave it in Yauco for someone to retrieve. He shook hands with Ernesto, climbed onto a diminutive rathorse, and pointed his mount toward Mayagüez. He was just passing what little remained of the Hoyo pond when he heard a young voice hailing him from behind. It was a *jíbaro* boy, about ten years old, carrying a rusty spade on his right shoulder. Rafi turned and waved a greeting.

"*Hola hermanito. ¿Cómo te va?*"

"Not so well, *señor doctor,*" the youngster said, his chin stuck out defiantly. "I was trying to get your attention to complain in person that thanks to you, we already lost our swimming place, and now I have to dig a hole for my whole family to use *para cagar*. At least they will still let me pee on the trees," he grumbled.

Rafi looked down at the grimy figure, so short and impossibly thin, and noticed that the boy was wearing shoes. Smiling broadly, Rafi turned his mount back up the trail. Only after five minutes had passed did it occur to him that the boy was digging the latrine half a mile from his hut.

Chapter Twenty-Six

SUBTERFUGE, JULY 1900

Without the cataclysm of San Ciriaco, the link between the parasite and the anemia pandemic might have gone unnoticed. The hurricane had killed thousands, but it had also provided an opportunity to save thousands more. Although the Báez family had lost their home in the hurricane, they had quite literally been given a new life by the capsules of thymol. Three months after the discovery of the hookworm egg on November 24, 1899, Simón would not have been recognized by his former employers at Las Alturas. Now that the parasites were gone, he felt about as well as he could remember. Carlos and Ana were also healthy. Meanwhile, Juan provided them all with new clothes and shoes, and continuously reminded the family of the dangers of hookworm infection and the simple measures they must take to prevent it.

After weeks of recovering and rebuilding in Ponce, the time came to decide on their future. For Simón and Josefa, the mountain had nearly been their death, but it was also their life. The mountain was all they knew—it was where they had been born, raised, and where they lived together. They knew the trees and the streams; they reveled in the cool air and the frequent refreshing rains. There was work available in rebuilding the plantations, which they could now perform with knowledge of the cause and prevention of the disease that had hobbled them before.

Regarding Carlos and Ana, the answers were not as clear. Josefa wanted the children with her, the youngest two members of her brood, most of whom the parasites had taken from her much too soon. But the men refused to listen to her. Juan firmly ended the discussion. "There is nothing in Utuado for them except a life of struggles and ignorance," he said. "Even if they kept the hookworms at bay, a life of picking coffee as poor peasants who can't read or write their names will cloud their future. No, the children will not return to the mountains. They will remain with me, go to school, and make a new life in Ponce." Simón and Pepa reluctantly agreed. They packed their mule, and one fine morning in February of 1900, they headed up the trail to Utuado—Pepa gimping with her corrective shoes, Simón proudly wearing his new ones, and both wrestling with the uncertainty of leaving their two young children behind.

In Utuado, the process of rebuilding Las Alturas promised to be long and arduous. Don Arturo Roig had saved enough capital to purchase new coffee plants from Martinique and hire displaced workers, like Simón and Pepa, to plant them under the shade of surviving nurse trees. Beyond the restoration of the trees, the large, elegant plantation house was proudly rebuilt from its stone foundations over the next year. Roig ordered latrines built along the perimeter of the hacienda and made their use mandatory. Some *jíbaros* followed his directives, many others did not. Most had heard of the discovery of the hookworms, but this did not necessarily influence their habits. Thus, while Simón and Pepa remained healthy, conscientiously using the new facilities and never going outside the home without shoes, the majority of the other *jíbaros* returned to the same life they had known before the hurricane, once again facing defeat from the same economic problems and social stagnation exacerbated by the chronic illness that had plagued them before.

With their banked capital, the Roig family also planned to purchase several smaller, struggling coffee operations at bargain prices. Ruined by the hurricane, the more modest haciendas faced long odds against rebuilding compared to larger operations like Roig's, and selling out to him offered them an easier solution. But in the course of a trip to evaluate one such potential acquisition, a disaster of unequaled proportions befell the Roig family. Sebastián Roig's bloated body was found floating face down in the Añasco River by *jíbaros* coming to do their wash. The young man had been shot and mutilated with machetes. In addition to the heartbreak this brought the family, his death greatly complicated the rehabilitation of Las Alturas.

Sister Mary Elizabeth, for her part, settled back into her work as a nurse at the Asilo de Damas in Ponce. Just like before the hurricane, she treated the usual mix of the sick and the infirm. Many suffered from tuberculosis, others from heart failure, while yet others found their way to the convent with typhoid, diphtheria, rheumatic fever, smallpox, and measles. And over half of the patients that came into the *Asilo* clearly suffered to a greater or lesser degree from the infectious anemia she had treated with Ashford at the *Hospital Militar*.

When such patients arrived, she offered them a simple but precise explanation of the cause of their anemia, educating them on the importance of hygiene and wearing shoes. For her pains, she often got mixed reactions. For many, living with anemia was simply part of their life, and they refused to consider changing their habits. Others listened with interest, primed by outrageous stories such as the one saying that so and so's second cousin had perished from anemia, but that the doctors had miraculously raised her from the dead with tiny magical balls they had forced down the throat of the corpse. She had then been seen walking around the farmer's market the following Sunday.

Nevertheless, Sister Mary Elizabeth's focus changed one morning in mid-April when an Afro-Puerto Rican woman about twenty-five years old walked into the *Asilo* carrying in her arms the limp figure of a girl of about six or seven. She stopped the first nun she saw, and in a low voice dripping with fear, said, "I am looking for *Sor* (Sister) María Isabel, the worm doctor."

The nun had no doubt who she was seeking. "Please, wait here, I will get her right away."

The woman sat down on a bench, cradling her daughter's head in her arm, looking anxiously into her drawn face. She knew her child was dying. She had been ill for a long time—maybe a year or even longer—slowly wasting away as her mother sought the advice of family members, *curanderas*, the local doctor and the priest. All of them had different opinions, all which were useless. She had tried feeding her child better, sometimes going without food herself for the sake of her daughter. Nothing helped, and for this week it seemed that the end was near. But the previous day, her partner's supervisor, a man by the name of Juan Báez, had listened to the story of the sick girl. Juan knew Ashford had left the island, and that in his absence, the thymol treatments had virtually stopped. The military hospital on the small hill to the north had gone back to caring exclusively for army personnel, and sick Puerto Ricans once again sought help at the civilian hospitals. Juan had pointed the couple to the *Asilo* and Sister Mary Elizabeth, the one person he knew might help.

Sister Mary Elizabeth walked into the corridor where the young mother was seated and introduced herself. The mother spoke, desperation in her voice.

"My name is María Elena Vega, and this is my daughter Teresa. She has been ill for many months, and I think she is dying. Please help us, *doctora*."

Sister Mary Elizabeth looked at the frail body with its pasty, waxy color, labored respirations and sunken eyes of the purest black staring blankly back at her. She immediately thought, *"Dear Jesus! This child is dying from advanced anemia."*

"María Elena," she said, "I am glad that you have come. I am not a doctor, but I will try to help you in any way I can. I will talk to my superior right away."

Sor Juana Inés, the Sister Superior, was a kindly woman of fifty, whose entire life was devoted to nursing the sick with a dedication that often led her to disregard her own health. She had survived typhoid, diphtheria, and malaria, and thirty years prior had barely avoided contracting smallpox during a severe epidemic by volunteering for inoculation. She had followed Sister Mary Elizabeth's work at the military hospital with great interest.

So, when Sister Mary Elizabeth walked into *Sor* Juana Inés' stark office and explained the situation, she immediately set aside her work to listen. Sister Mary Elizabeth explained the young girl's dire condition.

"And I want your permission to draw her blood to take up to the *Hospital Militar*," she added. "I think they will let me use their instruments."

Her superior frowned. "If the child is so ill, what could we possibly gain by that?"

"I am not sure." Sister Mary Elizabeth's voice betrayed a slight tremor. "But there is clearly nothing to lose. As it is, the child probably has less than one week to live."

Sister Juana Inés thought for a moment, and then gave her permission.

Sister Mary Elizabeth returned to María Elena and explained what she proposed to do. She retrieved a slide and coverslip from her room and, drawing two blood drops from Teresa's diminutive index finger, expertly prepared her blood smear. She asked her colleagues to care for the guests, then headed up the hill to the military hospital.

The nun was greeted with affection and respect, and was ushered to her former laboratory. The idle microscopes had been set under covers on the counter, as if waiting for an old friend. Sister Mary Elizabeth did not pause to reminisce; she immediately improvised a blood stain as best she could with the dyes available on the shelf and processed the slide. In the space of two hours, she was looking under the microscope. The smear was much as Sister Mary Elizabeth expected: it showed a marked decrease of the oxygen-carrying red cells, to 1.5 million per cubic millimeter, 30 percent of the normal value. But then came a glimmer of hope—scattered around the red cells, their bright scarlet granules dressed in the crimson dye, were untold numbers of eosinophils. They abounded throughout the slide, the beautiful diminutive orbs announcing that Teresa might possibly have a chance.

Sister Mary Elizabeth backed away from the microscope and stared off, thinking about the dilemma before her. If the child was going to survive, the nun would have to act boldly and quickly. She found Sergeant Moretti and pulled him to a quiet corner of the courtyard, where they spoke in low voices. Sergeant Moretti soon excused himself, rapidly crossed the courtyard and, looking around cautiously, entered a room at the other side. Within two minutes he returned to his visitor, discreetly slipping a small vial into the pocket of her tunic.

By early afternoon, the nun had returned to Sister Juana

Inés. The head nun fanned herself in the cramped, baking-hot room as she inquired about the visit to the *Hospital Militar*.

"The soldiers allowed me access to the laboratory where I once worked," Sister Mary Elizabeth began. "It remains exactly as Dr. Ashford left it four months ago. Teresa's blood smear shows that she has end-stage anemia with a red cell count less than a third of what it should be."

"It is, then, a desperate case." The Sister Superior inclined her head, her face falling with a familiar grief. "Another beautiful child will soon be lost to this disease. The mother will be crushed; the pain is too much to bear. Sister Mary Elizabeth, you have seen so many cases since last summer, is there anything that can be done?"

"Last year, I might have said the girl is beyond saving. But now…" The diminutive nun hesitated, her hand inching toward her tunic pocket.

"Please continue, Sister."

"The blood smear has given me something to work with," Sister Mary Elizabeth said haltingly. "Although the red blood cells are fatally depleted, there is also a marked abundance of eosinophils—forty percent, to be exact. That is a very elevated proportion."

The superior leaned forward, starting to understand. "So, this means…?"

"Exactly, Sister Superior. Teresa's bone marrow is still vigorous, desperately manufacturing blood cells to overcome its losses to the parasites. It cannot make up for all the lost red cells, but it can still manage to overproduce eosinophils. We do not know exactly why this happens, but as long as there are elevated eosinophils in the blood, thymol is virtually always effective. Once the bone marrow becomes so exhausted that eosinophils disappear, the chance of survival falls steeply."

Sor Juana Inés began to pace the crowded room. "If we could only get one of our doctors to prescribe the deworming medicine! Our doctors here in Ponce are kind and careful, but they are obstinate. They seem to think that some part of being Puerto Rican is to live and die of *la anemia*." The head nun leaned her arms on the desk. "In any case, this child needs more than shoes and a latrine."

Sister Mary Elizabeth stared at her boss in silence with a guilty look.

Sor Juana Inés looked intently at her subordinate. "Sister Mary Elizabeth, is there anything you would like to add?"

Sister Mary Elizabeth gave a wry smile. "It may be that all is *not* lost."

The head nun sat back down and leaned forward, resting her elbows upon the desk. "What more is there to do except to make the child comfortable?"

Sister Mary Elizabeth stood in the center of the oppressively hot room, her right hand playing with something in her pocket. Sister Juana Inés suddenly realized what was being silently hinted at.

"Sister! Have you—?"

"I'm afraid so, Sister Superior. I am complicit in a theft." Reaching into her tunic, the nun brought out a glass vial filled halfway with white granular crystals. "One of the soldiers borrowed this from their pharmacy stock."

"Borrowed?"

"Yes, Reverend Sister."

The head nun stared at the vial in disbelief. It could only be one thing.

Sister Mary Elizabeth pleaded, *"By all that is holy!* This is the girl's only chance."

The Sister Superior frowned at the half-oath and looked at the ceiling in consternation. What Sister Mary Elizabeth was implicitly proposing was that they give a medication with potentially lethal side effects, acquired under dubious circumstances by a soldier with no medical background, to a dying six-year-old wasted to half her normal weight, and without a doctor's permission or supervision. And yet, the alternative course was far worse, and to the head sister, impossible to contemplate. The nun's sharp mind quickly ran through all the angles and permutations contained in the situation. She made up her mind.

"We will treat the child."

The vial was opened, and the unmistakable odor of thymol escaped into the room. At the very least, Sergeant Moretti had apparently procured the correct medication. Within the vial, the two Sisters had about 30 grams of thymol at their disposal. For a child of Teresa's size, they needed less than one gram for the first treatment. Deliberately, they measured and weighed the intended quantity of the drug, and with a tiny metal scoop, carefully placed the substance into a small gelatin capsule and closed it firmly. Then they went to see the girl and her mother, waiting in the children's ward.

Sister Mary Elizabeth began, "María Elena, your daughter suffers from a very advanced case of anemia. Without the right medicine, she will not survive."

The mother broke down, and through her sobs answered, "Yes, Sister, that is why I came here. Nobody has been able to do anything for Teresa, and there is no one left for us to see."

Sister Mary Elizabeth placed her hand gently on María Elena's shoulder. "This treatment has risks—the medicine itself could make her worse, and no doctor will help us give it to her." She did not add that they were breaking rules by doing this.

The mother was desperate and hardly heard the warnings. She only wanted her daughter treated. Sister Mary Elizabeth opened her right hand, where the capsule lay.

María Elena gasped in awe. "*!Una bolita de cristal!*"

To spare the young child the use of the cathartic, Sister Mary Elizabeth had adjusted the dose of thymol as high as she dared, to three quarters of a gram. She speculated that without the gut-cleansing effect of the sodium sulfate, the higher dose of thymol might be needed to attack the hookworms. It was pure guesswork, and it carried quite a bit of risk. But all the same, she placed the capsule into the child's mouth. With a sweet, soft voice, her mother encouraged the child to swallow it.

The expression on the girl's face changed from indifferent to bewildered as the thymol slowly burned down her throat and into her stomach. There was a sudden change in the girl's coloration to a sickly shade of green as the nuns prayed fervently that the medicine would stay down. They offered her sugar water and after ten anxious minutes, Teresa settled down and fell asleep. Sister Mary Elizabeth had always been struck by how the smallest children were the bravest patients and grown men the biggest cowards, a theory that the emaciated child curled up before her had proven once again.

Sister Mary Elizabeth stayed with the family, observing the sleeping child for any change in her breathing or pulse, watching uneasily as the girl's pounding heart refused to slow. Since no purgative had been used, there was a rather long wait for results, but these were finally collected in a ceramic pot, washed in a preparation of weak brine, and then filtered slowly through paper. The filtered material was resuspended and poured into a small jar, which Sister Mary Elizabeth then carried into the office of Sister Juana Inés. By then, it was completely dark outside, so she held up the jar to examine it by the light of the oil lamp illuminating the room. The two women gasped as one. There in the jar, barely visible by the flicker from the lamps, were dozens, if not hundreds, of tiny filaments. Like minuscule fragments of white thread, the dead worms drifted aimlessly around the jar.

Sister Mary Elizabeth removed a tenth of the fluid—and counted no fewer than fifty dead parasites in a small glass dish. With a handheld loupe, she demonstrated to her superior the characteristic shape of one of the parasites. This creature had been rather well preserved, having managed after its demise to avoid serious damage from the host's digestive enzymes. It was most likely a female *Ancylostoma*: one centimeter long and impossibly thin, but a champion egg producer and the consummate killer. Toward one end, the head of the animal bent sharply forward in the unmistakable shape of a tiny hook. The two nuns had their culprit.

This time, the subsequent days brought no surprises to defeat them. Once the girl recovered from the first dose of thymol, the sisters administered a second one two days later, expelling the last few remaining hookworms. Only then were they able to relax and admire the miracle of the treatment unfolding before their eyes. With an uncontrollable appetite, the child began to replenish her stores of iron and her marrow automatically corrected the proportion of blood cells needed for a complete recovery. Within three days, she was walking, within five, she was playing dolls with the holy figurines, and by the tenth, she was running around the courtyard in shoes the nuns had procured. Her skin color was quickly returning to the rich tones of a healthy Puerto Rican of equal African and European extraction, subtly enlivened by a touch of the *Taíno*—her rich inheritance restored to its full splendor by the expulsion of the hookworms that had been feeding on her.

With every day that passed, the two complicit nuns breathed easier. Meanwhile, most of the thymol remained un-used in the contraband vial, carefully hidden away in Sister Mary Elizabeth's room.

Chapter Twenty-Seven

FAR FROM THE ISLAND

Two days before Ashford was to depart for California, a late winter snow blanketed the capital with a thick cover of the purest white. Lieutenant Ashford was in the grip of a dark depression, thoroughly miserable at the prospect of being separated from María Asunción and missing the birth of his first child. Moreover, the unpredictability of a life in the armed forces meant that he might never return to Puerto Rico and his campaign against the hookworm. To make everything worse, he was not feeling particularly well.

Immediately after lunch, he found himself alternating between rapid waves of burning heat and freezing chills. When he lay down to rest, a sudden, violent shaking overtook him. The bed rattled as if caught in a giant earthquake. For five minutes, he trembled without relief before breaking into a cold sweat, turning clammy and nauseous. María Asunción looked at her husband's condition with growing concern.

As many doctors are apt to do, Ashford immediately diagnosed himself—it must be a relapse of the malaria he had first contracted in Mayagüez. He had felt equally miserable then with very similar symptoms. His one consolation was that being an otherwise healthy man in his prime, he knew he should quickly overcome the relapsing illness. He knew exactly what would happen next: his doctors would confirm his self-diagnosis and again prescribe the ubiquitous quinine, after which, he would get well and be on his way to the Philippines.

But Ashford was impatient in matters of his own health. He decided that instead of relying on the opinion of others, he might as well go ahead and treat himself. There was no need to incur the condescending pity of his colleagues, grinning with amusement while his teeth chattered noisily in the throes of a malarial attack. He went to the drug cabinet, and with hands shaking from the high fever, carefully measured and prepared his own solution of quinine. María Asunción took the glass from his unsteady hands and guided it to his lips in order to swallow the bitter drug, which had been dissolved in sweetened water. Overcome by exhaustion, Ashford lay down to rest.

He awoke two hours later suffering from a splitting headache and the worst sore throat he could ever remember. He examined himself with a mirror and a light, and found the inside of his throat was a bright scarlet red. He prepared a diluted solution of phenol and applied it gently to the inflamed areas of his throat with a cloth rag. The burning was severe, but not intolerable, and in a minute the phenol eased his discomfort. But he could not eat anything for dinner, and in the midst of another violent attack of shaking chills, much to the horror of his wife, Ashford passed out on their bed.

Well before sunrise the next morning, it became clear to María Asunción that this illness was far worse than any malarial attack she had ever witnessed. Ashford could hardly talk because of severe hoarseness, and only with a supreme effort could he swallow his own saliva. With drool slipping down from the corner of his mouth and onto his chest, Ashford hastily scribbled a note and handed it to María Asunción, asking her to get help to transport him to the infirmary.

The sudden appearance of the lieutenant, harshly wheezing, hoarse, saliva running from his mouth and blue around the lips, frightened the young medic at the desk into immediate action. An orderly was sent to find the duty physician at once with a simple message: come immediately and bring a colleague. Two surgeons, a captain and a lieutenant, arrived within minutes. By then, Ashford was having difficulty breathing. The lymph nodes in his neck had swelled to the size of lemons and his fever had climbed to 104 degrees, causing him to slide into delirium. Through a thick kaleidoscopic haze in his brain Ashford heard a distant voice saying, *"Lieutenant... can you hear us? We have to look in your throat..."*

Summoning all his strength, the feeble Ashford tried his

hardest to comply. The captain used a mouth-gag to assist his patient, and then, with a broad metal blade, depressed Ashford's tongue while his assistant provided a light. The surgeons took turns examining their patient's throat; each pulled back in horror. There was no mistaking the foul-smelling, thick gray coating all over the lieutenant's tonsils and palate.

The captain spoke to his semiconscious patient, nearly shouting. "Lieutenant Ashford, you have contracted diphtheria and are in danger of your life. We need to move you to the hospital immediately. If you worsen, a tracheotomy may become necessary to save you." María Asunción turned white with fear. She understood enough English to know that her husband faced a potentially fatal outcome. María Asunción did not know about diphtheria's cause or treatment, but she had heard of the disease, and what she knew was not reassuring. She sat on the bed with a blank stare while the doctors prepared to move her husband to the hospital, visions of widowhood and a child orphaned before birth passing grimly before her.

The doctors removed some of the obstructing material from Ashford's throat, which improved his breathing. Then, they reapplied the solution of phenol and sprayed some more of the chemical throughout the room to sanitize the air. Without waiting for the transport service, the doctors rushed the stricken patient through the corridors to the main hospital building, where they placed him under continuous observation. The surgeons planned to remain at his bedside to intervene surgically, should their patient grow worse. As the night wore on, his high fever persisted along with his delirium.

An animated debate then took place between the two attending physicians. They had both seen numerous cases of diphtheria of various degrees of severity, and both had lost and saved a number of patients with this deadly infection. They immediately set up a Lister sprayer to sanitize the air with its fine plume of carbolic acid. But there were few other weapons in their arsenal to combat the disease. They knew about using papayotin, a milky sap extracted from certain plants. If touched with a 5 percent solution of its extract, the diphtheric film sometimes disappeared rapidly, relieving the obstruction to the breathing. The captain brought up the use of turpentine—he had some experience preparing a solution for inhalation by pouring the oil into water kept boiling by an alcohol lamp. This charged the air with the supposedly beneficial vapors. But nobody knew how turpentine worked for diphtheria or, indeed, if it worked at all.

The junior surgeon turned to his superior and said in a low voice, "Captain, our patient faces some very uncertain and critical hours. Unless I am mistaken, the diphtheria has already invaded his trachea."

"I agree. We should be ready to intervene and support his breathing. If he requires either a tracheotomy or intubation, his chance for survival would decrease to one in three."

"Perhaps we should seek Major Reed's opinion on using diphtheria antitoxin."

Major Walter Reed was the top infectious disease expert in the Army, who, by pure chance, happened to be a friend to Bailey Ashford. The 49-year-old Reed had supervised Ashford when the lieutenant had joined the Medical Corps two years before. He was a brilliant investigator and an insightful clinician who had fought yellow fever in Cuba with the same enthusiasm with which Ashford had battled the hookworm in Puerto Rico, and was now stationed in Washington.

Major Reed hurried to the hospital and examined his friend.

"There is no question that your diagnosis of diphtheria is correct," Reed said to his colleagues. "And as you can undoubtedly see, the obstructive process is starting to affect his breathing. I agree with the immediate need for antitoxin, not only for Lieutenant Ashford, but also for Mrs. Ashford."

The three physicians approached María Asunción, and Reed addressed the distraught wife. He explained that her husband's best chance was to receive injections of diphtheria antitoxin. The antitoxin was prepared from the blood of horses that had received low doses of the poisons produced by the diphtheria microbe until they built a tolerance to those toxins. The serum from this process had been given to thousands of people with advanced cases of diphtheria and could potentially double or even triple his chances for survival.

"Furthermore," Reed added, "it is important that we treat

you as well, Mrs. Ashford. We should assume that you have been exposed to a great number of these microbes, even before your husband showed any symptoms of the illness. With your consent, we will give you the antitoxin as well, at lower doses."

María Asunción nodded. She had understood enough to give permission to treat her husband.

In the several years the antitoxin had been in use, Reed had seen it work miracles on several occasions. He also happened to know precisely where to procure several doses expeditiously. Being that the Medical Corps was a close fraternity of officers who jealously looked after their own, the antitoxin serum was procured within an hour. Ashford immediately received an intramuscular injection of 10 units. The dose was repeated three more times at intervals of eight hours.

In the end, Walter Reed was proven right; the serum saved Ashford. Twenty-four hours after the first injection, the worst of the disease began to subside, and the diphtheric membrane threatening to obstruct his breathing began to disappear. For the next several days, Ashford endured a few minor challenges—swelling in his joints, a bothersome rash, and occasional fevers—but overall progress was rapid, and he soon recovered completely.

After ten days, the lieutenant was discharged to the barracks, back to the waiting arms of María Asunción. To his great relief, he had been assigned to Fort Slocum in New York, where he could be kept under observation during his recovery. It was not exactly Puerto Rico, but it was far closer than Manila. Unbeknownst to Ashford, as he had languished in that hospital bed so close to death, another army physician had been assigned to the Philippines in his place.

Fort Slocum was a large military post located near the city of New Rochelle, at the extreme western end of Long Island Sound. The fort dated back to the Civil War, but since then had undergone extensive renovations, including new officers' quarters, enlisted men's barracks, mess halls, and large modern hospital buildings. It was maintained to provide coastal artillery defense and protect the eastern approaches to New York City.

Ashford and María Asunción could only think of Puerto Rico; she of her family, he of the hookworm problem. His last letter from Rafi Moore had described the sorry state into which the anemia campaign had fallen in his absence. The military governors of the island had been replaced by civilians appointed by the President, but unlike the Major Generals, the civilian governors of Puerto Rico had never heard of Lieutenant Ashford or of his discoveries. The civilian physicians still opposed treating with thymol. The educational campaign Rafi had organized progressed slowly. Rafi related how he had made inroads in Lares with Ernesto and Eugenio Pérez, who had supported his preventative efforts. In Pezuela, failure to use the latrine got a *jíbaro* fined one chicken for a first offense, two for the second, and so on. Wearing shoes was encouraged, and relief organizations had begun to provide for the many who could not afford them.

Unfortunately, the large distances over rugged terrain slowed the free flow of information. Ashford found some of the news encouraging, but it also inflamed his desire to return to the island and organize a well-funded deworming campaign. He had shown that anemia patients got well very quickly with thymol—now all he needed was for someone with deep pockets and great influence across the island to see it his way. Curing patients would encourage others to seek treatment and embrace preventative measures. He had to return to Puerto Rico as soon as possible.

*****

The Ashfords spent many long months in Fort Slocum. The tedious routine was broken by caring for their baby son Mahlon, who had arrived just before their departure from Washington.

One scorching day in August, regimental commander Robert Lee Howze found Ashford staring in silence at the distant horizon over Long Island Sound. Howze was a big, plain-spoken Texan who had earned a Medal of Honor for bravery during the Sioux Wars in South Dakota. The two had become good friends mostly because their marked disparities greatly amused one another.

"Ashford, if I catch you brooding on this seawall one more time, I am going to report you for morale detrimental to the joviality of the post!" Howze proclaimed, leaning his elbows on the seawall.

Ashford replied listlessly, "Another suffocating day on Long Island Sound, Major. I don't know how you can stand it."

Howze cheerfully slapped Ashford's back. "Come now, Ashford. I've seen worse in the Philippines, and having the city nearby for leave isn't bad."

Ashford gazed absent-mindedly out into the water. "Right now, my wife could not care less about New York. She has been a good sport about coming here, but I can't see her waiting much longer to return to Puerto Rico. Her parents have yet to meet our baby. It is tearing my wife to pieces."

"It must be difficult for your gal," Howze admitted, turning to look out at the water. "It is bad enough for other wives, who are from this country. It must be that much worse for any young lady with a newborn, foreign-born, and so far from family."

Ashford sighed longingly. "It is hard on both of us; I am fond of that little island."

Howze volunteered that the medical officers were familiar with Ashford's paper on the hookworm from the New York *Medical Journal.* "I've heard several of the officers say this discovery could be a trail-blazer, if only folks paid closer attention."

Ashford shook his head slowly. "We could not convince the local medical establishment to listen. Not even the government showed much interest."

Howze stood silent for some moments. "Don't give up— any dent you could make against that dang illness would have big consequences."

Ashford shrugged. "Unfortunately, the deaths will go on," he said, sounding resigned, "until someone can compel both the Puerto Ricans and the Americans to take action. I was starting to make progress when the Army found another post for me. Imagine this—not long ago, I was headed to the Philippines, probably to serve in your regiment."

Howze put his bear's arm over Ashford's shoulder. "Your abilities are being wasted here. Puerto Rico is where you're needed."

Ashford gave a bleak chuckle. "Supposedly, I am due to be reassigned to Ponce, but there's been no news for a while. I am beginning to think the Army brass have forgotten about me."

Howze tapped his barrel chest. "I know some people at the War Department who might listen to me. You don't belong in this hole, treating colds and hemorrhoids. Where did you say you were stationed when you worked on the pandemic?"

"In Ponce, on the southern coast."

The other man smiled and nodded. "Leave this to your man Howze."

*****

The next week brought a surprise letter from Washington, D.C.

Bailey K. Ashford, MD
Fort Slocum, New York

August 30, 1900

My dear Ashford,

I hope this letter finds you well. Thank you for your generous gift of the hookworms from Porto Rico which you so kindly left with Hassall several months ago. I admit that at first, I was at a loss as to why you wanted me to examine more Ancylosotma *worms. Hassall seemed to think you wanted me to write on the morphology of your specimens. Not being sure of what you meant and unable to locate you, the specimens sat untouched on my shelf for months. It is a credit to your meticulous preservation techniques that they were not lost. By the purest chance, I very recently came upon the specimens again, and had almost disposed of them down the sink, when I decided that not having come across* Ancylostoma *in some time, I should make its reacquaintance.*

I was doubly surprised, therefore, that when examining your worms, I noticed them to be decidedly odd-looking. I then retrieved some of my better hookworm specimens and became even more surprised. Your worms looked decidedly small, but with that fact I could live. What I could not abide was their bizarre mouthparts. I yelled for Hassell, who remembered your mentioning as much. I looked again: There was no question that these Porto Rican worms lacked the claw-like teeth of the other specimens. As you well know, these worms of yours access the lining of the intestine by way of sharp plate-like structures. In every other way the hookworms are identical. Even the eggs appear indistinguishable.

Suddenly it came to me. You had found a completely new species! One so similar to the older hookworm as to produce the exact same disease, and yet different enough to warrant its own classification. I thus intend to write a paper for the presentation of this new species, to which I have assigned the name of Necator americanus. *I thank you for the specimens and your kind offer to let me describe them. I will forward my fees for consultation to the War Dept., etc.*

I remain, yours,

Charles Wardell Stiles PhD

Ashford felt his heart was going to burst through his ribs. A new species of hookworm had been described from his efforts in Puerto Rico! And furthermore, it was one Stiles agreed could be responsible for the same disease as the older specimens. But his joy was short-lived as the realization came to him that if he did not make it back to the island soon, he was likely to learn about the eradication of the killer parasite from the newspapers, his due credit going to some local doctor who finally decided to accept the undeniable facts as described by a distinguished researcher.

He had fallen on his bunk more miserable than ever, when María Asunción bustled into their bedroom and handed him a second envelope, this one with the familiar markings of a posting assignment. With shaking hands, Ashford opened the envelope and read that he had, at last, been transferred to the post at Ponce, Puerto Rico. With this new posting, the Ashfords should be back on the island by early winter. He immediately began a letter to Rafi relaying his good news. They would soon be together, working on the anemia campaign again.

Later that day, Ashford found Howze lounging in the mess and dropped into the seat beside his superior. "Major, today I received orders transferring me back to Ponce. I don't know how much you had to do with this, but María Asunción and I wish to thank you."

Howze slapped his subordinate on the back, pushing aside his plate. "Darn it Ashford, that is great news indeed! I have only one request from you."

Ashford smiled. "What can I do, Major Howze?"

"Keep me informed of your progress fighting the hookworm infections," the other man ordered, folding his napkin. "By goodness! I only hope that you'll receive the support your work deserves."

Ashford nodded, "I will be delighted and honored to do so, sir."

Howze broke into a broad grin, and with a glint in his eye, said, "Excellent! I also want to tell you that I've made it that much easier for you and María Asunción to keep in touch by getting myself transferred to Puerto Rico as well! Y'all made the place sound like such a paradise that I just couldn't stay here. I've been named commander of the Puerto Rico Provisional Regiment of Infantry, starting in October. New York's dad-gum fog and snow are not for me. From here on out I will spend my off-days on the beach."

"Yes, Major, why not do that?" Ashford said with forced levity, swallowing the jealousy of knowing that while Major Howze would likely find himself in the tropics within the month, the Ashford family would not be leaving Fort Slocum until December, at the soonest.

Chapter Twenty-Eight

CHARLES MOORE

R afi received Ashford's letter after he returned from yet another trip to coffee country. Over the past year, he had met with *alcaldes* and *barrio* leaders alike regarding the hookworm and the anemia illness affecting farm laborers, to mixed results. Some chieftains responded like the Pérez brothers in Lares, immediately encouraging the use of latrines and shoes in their villages. Many others, however, simply did not believe him, accusing Rafi of secretly working for the usurping Americans to undermine their way of life. Rafi strongly suspected that these uncooperative politicians had ulterior motives, rooted in their fear of losing influence and economic control.

Ashford's letter fired Rafi with a new enthusiasm. He decided to secure the cooperation of important people in San Juan and to start with his own father. Luckily, Ponce and San Juan had recently been connected by a macadamized highway known as the *Carretera Central*, which greatly eased such travels across the rugged and mountainous terrain. Otherwise, Rafi might have made a sea-voyage; but even then, a stretch of prevailing easterlies and unpredictable weather could lengthen the trip.

Even the central highway route was not easy after the first twenty-five miles, which led to the town of Coamo in the foothills of the *cordillera*. It then began a steep climb around the endless hairpin turns of the island's central spine of mountains to the pass at Cayey. Countless treacherous switchbacks followed until at last, the road slowly descended into the valley of Caguas, and followed the river valleys into San Juan. A straight-line distance of fifty miles became ninety difficult ones on the horse trail. Still, given that it was the dry season,

Rafi chose to go by land.

Arriving late in the afternoon on the second day of his journey, Rafi finally embraced his parents in their colonial house in the Old City. After dinner, father and son went to the balcony to smoke cigars. The two men closely resembled one another, except that the younger man was somewhat taller and thinner, and lacked his father's closely cropped beard. Finally together after so long, they paused in silence for a minute to enjoy the view over the expanse of San Juan Bay. Rafi spoke first.

"Father, I have come to ask for help with some delicate matters. Some involve political concerns, and you know how to handle politics better than any person I know."

"Very well, tell me what this is about."

Rafi breathed some of the magnificent sea air and began filling in his father on the upcoming return of Ashford.

"He has been reassigned to his old post in Ponce. He comes back with the hope that he will be allowed to continue fighting anemia in the *jíbaros*. Since his departure, our work has ground to a halt. When the War Department was running the island, they had a vested interest in the success of one of their own officers. But now that there is a civilian government, I am not sure how much he will be allowed to do."

Charles Moore stared pensively at the dark waters of the harbor. Finally, he turned to Rafi.

"I am afraid you are right, son. Our island administration is quite new, and it seems unlikely that it would wish to spare much time for Lieutenant Bailey Ashford and his worms. It's a pity."

The elder Moore took a deep drag from his cigar, then continued. "I believe Dr. Ashford is a good man and a hard worker, who, without being from this island, has selflessly thrown in his lot with the poor of Puerto Rico and deserves the fullest support of the island government. From what I have read in your letters, you have already had significant successes."

A fleeting bitterness then crossed the elder Moore's face, the glitter of his eyes hazy in a wreath of smoke. "And keep in mind that if this disease were affecting Portsmouth or Poughkeepsie instead of Ponce, we would have seen vigorous government action already."

"True," Rafi said carefully. "But he need not be alone when he returns. And perhaps he could earn the new government's support, if...others were to vouch for him, either in word or deed or funds." His father nodded absently, now glancing up at the glittering stars above. Rafi prompted, "Ashford arrives in less than two months."

The elder Moore paused, taking a long drag from his cigar. "Then, there is no time to lose."

The next morning, Charles Moore requested a meeting at the governor's mansion of *La Fortaleza*. As a wealthy American citizen who had resided on the island for almost thirty years, Moore's views were often sought out by the fellow countrymen who led the government. The current Governor of Puerto Rico was forty-three-year-old William Henry Hunt, a brilliant lawyer who had served as the President of the Executive Council of Puerto Rico under the previous governor. Coincidentally, Hunt had started his tenure on the same day that his patron, William McKinley, succumbed to an assassin's bullet in Buffalo. A committed Republican, Hunt was a fierce defender of American interests on the island, but never at the expense of the common people.

Governor Hunt was glad to receive his good friend and compatriot. "Charlie Moore! I am delighted you have come to visit. Your timing is impeccable, as there was something I wanted to ask you."

"Governor, it is good to see you again. How are you liking the *Fortaleza*?" Moore asked, following Hunt into his study.

"Truly a wonderful place, I wish I could buy it and retire right here." The governor laughed, waving at the crystalline blue sea and sky beyond his window. "But alas, I don't believe that is possible! In any event, I am glad to see you. I wanted to know whether you might be interested in serving on the Executive Council. There may well be a vacancy very soon, since Jim Harlan is thinking about resigning as Attorney General. He says that the climate doesn't agree with him and he wishes to return to Washington. We could easily move some of the posts around to make room for you."

Moore smiled. "Thank you, I believe I could be talked into

that."

"On trade matters, we pretty much follow your guidance anyway, so we might as well make it official." The governor chuckled, proffering a small glass of brandy. "And what did you have in mind for me today, Charlie?"

"Governor, my son Rafael has come to see me from Ponce—" Moore began, accepting the glass, "—about a request which may significantly help your administration in the eyes of local leaders."

"Rafael is your Yale boy, correct?" Governor Hunt poured a glass of his own, and the two men ambled toward the expansive windows framing a view of the bay.

"Yes, he hopes to start a microbiology degree next year. He tells me that Dr. Ashford, the young Medical Corps lieutenant who studied parasites in peasants, is headed back to Puerto Rico."

"This is the worm doctor, Ashford, you refer to?"

"Yes, sir. It seems that the Army will be sending him back to his old haunts in Ponce as a communicable disease specialist to fight typhoid and malaria affecting the soldiers from time to time. Rafael knows him well, and says Ashford wishes to continue investigating the anemia problem."

"I thought the local experts had decided he was on a wild goose chase." Hunt raised an eyebrow at his friend. "They all seemed to agree that the anemia was due to malnutrition and something about the air in those damned hills where they grow the coffee."

Moore turned away from the window to face Governor Hunt.

"The local experts did, yes. But Rafi is rather convinced that they are on to something new and important."

The governor began to pace the room, calculating. "The Puerto Ricans currently serving in my administration will want us to cooperate. Moreover, when we consider the impact Ashford's claims had two years ago, I think it is best for the majority of Puerto Ricans if we support him. It may ruffle some feathers in Ponce, but so be it. Now, Charlie, what do you think it will cost?"

"Rafi says they can treat each patient for a just under a dollar," the businessman answered. "The drug they were using seems to be very effective at killing the hookworm and can be easily obtained for pennies per dose. The rest of the expenditures go to cover a minimal staff and the facilities from which to operate. The Army is willing to give Ashford the time he needs to complete a formal clinical trial, and if he succeeds, then he will be permitted to expand its scope."

"Well," Hunt declared, "it seems to me that there is nothing to lose, given that the disease is nearly always fatal—as long as the treatment is relatively safe. We can easily appropriate up to $500 to fund a trial. In Ponce we have a strong ally by the name of Dr. Luis Aguerrevere, who seems fervent in his support of the United States. He has recently been appointed to head the Tricoche Hospital for civilians in central Ponce, and I believe he could provide some space for Doctor Ashford—particularly if it gives him an opportunity to embarrass the local Spanish supporters on his medical staff. He also tells me that most of the nurses at the hospital are old-fashioned nuns who think all Americans are Protestant heathens! It will be quite a thing to see," he said with a chuckle.

The two friends parted warmly, each having achieved his own goal for the meeting. But even as Moore departed the governor's office, he saw conflict coming: one that would pit progressive Americans supporting Ashford's theory against local conservative Iberophiles defending the time-honored ideas of malnutrition and noxious humors. Moore did not think the Ponce physicians were purposefully malicious, but Rafi had convinced him that those views were mistaken. Their stubbornness must be rooted in hubris and fear of losing prestige. Underneath it all ran strong, clashing cultural undercurrents: Protestant versus Catholic, Anglo-Saxon versus Latino, all battling over a disease that killed hundreds every month. For his part, Charles Moore would do his part to resolve potential conflicts in favor of the Ashford camp.

Rafi, buoyed by news of the governor's promise of support, returned to Ponce by the commercial steamer, which for only $4 took him on the overnight journey in first class.

Chapter Twenty-Nine

THE TRICOCHE HOSPITAL, 1902

Shortly after docking in Ponce, Rafi stopped at the Asilo de Damas to see Sister Mary Elizabeth.

The tiny nun came to greet him. "Rafi Moore! What a pleasant surprise! Come, sit here in the courtyard and have some coffee."

Rafi clasped her hand, relieved to see her again. "Sister, I am sorry it has taken me this long to come see you. I have been traveling to meet with *alcaldes* in the mountains, and most recently to San Juan to see my father."

Sister Mary Elizabeth dismissed Rafi's apology with a wave of her hand. "You have been doing your part to educate the town leaders. That is about all we can do in Dr. Ashford's absence."

The two sat down at a small wooden table. Rafi gave his friend a knowing look, grinning broadly. Catching his look, Sister Mary Elizabeth hesitated, her eyes narrowing with suspicion.

"Rafi, is there something you have to tell me?"

Rafi's eyes gleamed. "Dr. Ashford has been transferred to Ponce. He arrives in a few weeks."

Sister Mary Elizabeth let out a small, delighted cry and embraced Rafi, beaming, a wide smile of joy and relief on her face. Then her smile faded. "I will burden you with a small secret, Rafi. Sister Juana Inés and I have been treating anemia patients here at the *Asilo* for the last several months. Several patients arrived so near death that they were clearly not going to survive without thymol. We acquired a small supply of the drug, but it's starting to run out. Every time we treat, we rejoice in the life we restore while thinking of the possi-

283

ble repercussions with abject horror. If we were to get caught treating patients on our own, or worse still, if we were to lose a patient…"

Rafi took her hands in his. "Sister, your actions are heroic, and well justified."

Sister Mary Elizabeth felt her throat tightening with emotion. "As God is my witness, come what may, expulsion from the order, arrest, jail—saving a child makes it all worthwhile."

"Dr. Ashford may be able to treat anemic patients from the Tricoche Hospital just up the street. Governor Hunt is pursuing arrangements on his behalf. Soon, your dilemma will be resolved."

The two colleagues paused to let their emotions settle.

After the coffee was gone, Rafi rose to leave and grasped his friend's hand. The nun's eyes moistened. "I pray you are right. I don't think we can continue this way much longer."

Rafi left and walked the few blocks to the hospital. Rafi was delighted because the eastern side of the building faced his lodgings on Bertoly Street. This location was far more accessible than the military hospital 300 yards uphill, where the anemia treatments had started after the hurricane. Nevertheless, it remained to be seen if they were granted the space they had been promised.

*****

It was with some trepidation, but infinite excitement, that Ashford finally set foot on the pier at Ponce in January of 1902. Rafi was there to meet him, his smile as bright as it had been when he had last seen it two years ago. As Rafi escorted the couple and their baby to their lodgings, Ashford noticed that during his absence the city had almost completely recovered from the effects of San Ciriaco. The vibrant nightlife had returned, the plaza had been restored, and everybody seemed to be in fine spirits. The Ashfords settled into a small house on Calle Guadalupe, courtesy of the Army, not far from the center of town and about two blocks from the Tricoche Hospital. As before, the bulk of Ashford's work would consist of caring for Army personnel out of his old command at the former

Spanish military hospital, though he was also available for the occasional consultation on civilian cases at the Tricoche.

Once settled, Ashford began to rebuild his network. He had already made contact with Rafi, who headquartered his educational efforts from a house around the corner from the Ashford home. He visited Sister Mary Elizabeth at the Asilo de Damas and was pleased to learn about her surreptitious treatment of the more desperate cases. Finally, he visited his old friend Dr. Zeno, who had been one of the few local physicians encouraging Ashford to continue his investigations, although he freely admitted not being fully convinced of their validity.

Ashford and Rafi celebrated their reunion over drinks at the Bar La Perla, where Rafi reviewed the status of their campaign. He was crestfallen by the limited progress of his educational efforts but reported the encouraging news that Governor Hunt was willing to support an initial trial for civilians.

"I have some encouraging news of my own, Rafi," said Ashford. "Walter King, the new Public Health Officer for the port of Ponce, is an old friend. He is sensible, honest, and calm. He has proven his courage by ostracizing himself from his Spanish-speaking colleagues as well, who have been calling us 'the Don Quixote and Sancho Panza of worm doctors.'"

Rafi broke into a grin. "They've been calling you *what*?"

"Never mind that," Ashford waved dismissively. "Anyway, King wrote to say that at the port, he had met a certain Juan Báez, who relayed the story of his father's cure by a certain Lieutenant Ashford. Upon hearing this, King almost came out of his shoes and said that the fight against the hookworm had to be renewed immediately. He stated in his letter that he wants to join the treatment team as soon as one is assembled."

Rafi took a sip of his brandy. "I look forward to meeting Dr. King. He would be pleased to know that Governor Hunt has contacted Dr. Luis Aguerrevere, the new Director of the Tricoche Hospital, to request space for the exclusive treatment of anemia patients. He expected a favorable decision, given the director's staunch support of the American administration. We were to go see him after your arrival."

Ashford nodded his assent. "We will request a meeting for tomorrow morning, and I will ask King to come along."

The day following Ashford's arrival began with a warm, beautiful morning, the likes of which he had missed over the last two years. The sun shone brightly, and the oppressive blanket of humidity which usually covered the island appeared as though it would stay away. The Tricoche gleamed in the sunlight. The hospital had been named after Valentín Tricoche, a local philanthropist who had bequeathed a large sum of money for the building's construction. Its official name was the Albergue Caritativo Tricoche, but to the townspeople it was simply known as the Hospital Tricoche. The institution's mission was to provide the best medical attention, completely free of cost, to the poor and needy of Ponce. The eye-catching structure was designed in neoclassical style, consisting of a single story built around two identical interior courtyards. The façade was organized around an entrance portico articulated by flat Tuscan pilasters and three arches, the central one slightly protruding to the front. Over the portico, separated by cornice and parapet, the name *"Tricoche"* was carved into the stone. It was a grand old building, occupying an entire city block north of the plaza, and the exquisite architecture reflected the superior quality of the institution.

Rafi waited for Ashford under the central arch of the entrance. They stood together until Walter King joined them shortly before ten o'clock. He was a young man of twenty-six, somewhat paunchy, of middle height, with dark hair, brown eyes, and a bushy mustache. Perched on a Roman nose, a pair of thick spectacles gave him an owlish look. Behind his retiring façade was the mind of a brilliant and innovative thinker, well-suited to complement Ashford's relentless drive.

The trio walked into the hospital director's office. Dr. Aguerrevere greeted them enthusiastically in perfect, though heavily accented, English. "Just a few days back, I received a telegram from Governor Hunt announcing your return to Puerto Rico."

"I am very pleased to meet you, Doctor." Ashford shook the man's hand. "I understand the hospital is doing very well in your capable hands."

Rafi suppressed a smile. The 44-year-old doctor was known as an autocratic manager. He had taken over running the hospital from an order of nuns who had stayed on as his nursing staff. His acid remark to the Sister Superior, that he found "more cleanliness of soul than of body" in the hospital, had been reported in the local press and had elicited both furious denunciation and wild applause from contending factions—which bothered the director not at all. He was not ashamed to voice his rabid support for the pro-American faction, and was the first person in Ponce to display the U.S. flag from his balcony, which, not infrequently, he found pelted by rotten eggs.

Aguerrevere gestured his visitors to seats in his spacious office, and leaned forward over his desk.

"As a fellow physician, I have followed your treatment of the anemic patients with great interest," he continued. "Your article in the *Medical Journal* of New York will become a seminal piece in parasitology, and it is past time we began deworming again, this time on a much bigger scale. I would have started already, but the pharmacies will not sell us thymol because of pressure from local doctors. I am surrounded by reactionaries, even on my own staff. They would rather continue all the medical nonsense we had under Spanish rule."

"Procuring thymol will no longer be a problem for the Tricoche," said Ashford reassuringly. "We will obtain our supply from Army stores. If the local doctors want to do battle, we will meet them head on."

Aguerrevere seemed pleased. "The nuns staffing the place are also up in arms over your coming here," he warned, "but I believe they will come around. Nothing like a good controversy to get the blood going. We will fight all the unbelieving doctors, nuns, politicos, and hookworms until they stand no more!"

"Does this mean you will be able to provide Dr. Ashford with space to begin his work?" King asked.

"The sooner, the better!" The director escorted them to a large patient room immediately off the entrance, facing the eastern side of the courtyard. "You can base your work out of this ward, where you can keep any patients too weak to be dismissed. I will provide you with nurses and orderlies, Dr. Ashford—if you would please provide the thymol."

"Consider it done," replied Ashford with enthusiasm.

"When can you open this anemia ward?" asked Aguerrevere when they had returned to his office.

"Mr. Moore and I plan to begin the trial by treating a group of a hundred people as soon as we can find them," Ashford replied. "We will keep detailed records regarding their vital statistics, response to treatment, hookworm load, coinfections, and any other data of potential interest."

Dr. Aguerrevere agreed with this process, and the discussion turned to the planning phase. They agreed that the trial should focus on patients for whom they could do the most good. They would look particularly for patients that met their criteria for severe anemia, since favorable outcomes in terminal patients would lend prestige and energy to the campaign.

King spoke up: "We cannot simply advertise in the newspapers or put up placards around town since practically all prospective patients can't read. And it would take too long for news to spread by word of mouth. I think we will have to actively reach out to potential patients and convince them to come in for treatment."

Aguerrevere looked puzzled, "How do you propose to do that?"

Ashford turned to Rafi, "Do you think Juan Báez would be willing to help us?"

"He would be perfect. His father Simón is living proof of the efficacy of our treatment, and to his friends and neighbors, he is no less than a walking miracle. With Juan and Simón's help, we might convince the *jíbaros* of the Utuado to come here."

"You might even have to turn some away," the director said.

Ashford's lips pressed into a thin line. "I certainly hope not. I hate to think of sending away someone we can treat."

"So do we all," Aguerrevere replied, his voice a touch gentler. "But you may not have a choice."

"If that does happen," Ashford said, rising, "we may have to look at opening additional anemia wards." The foreman shook hands, and the director signaled them to follow him out. Nearing the hospital entrance under the elegant portico, they ran into the Sister Superior. She narrowed her eyes and turned up her nose, seamlessly conveying her condescension and suspicion.

"Buenos días, Sor Castigos," Aguerrevere addressed the nun with a devious smile.

"Good day to you, *Señor director*. Are we turning the hospital into army barracks? I am afraid I can't allow it. I can't trust these soldiers around my religious sisters… You know how army men are," the woman sniped, sending them all a scathing glare.

"We were only thinking about treating some *anémicos*, if that will suit you, Sister," the director replied lightly, the picture of innocence.

"What?" The head nurse stiffened. "Why, there will be no end to the filth and dirt those *jíbaros* will bring here. What a cross to bear!"

"Oh yes, Sister, since you have raised the subject of filth, there should be no shortage of soap in the convent's stores. It doesn't appear to get much use." Aguerrevere's words were as sharp and wicked as a knife. The nun's cheeks pinked with a livid rage.

With that, Aguerrevere stepped around the glaring *Sor* Castigos and continued escorting Ashford and his group. The director would hear about his cutting comments from the governing board of the hospital, but little did he care. He loved a good fight and he had picked his side.

Chapter Thirty

RECRUITMENT AND SETBACK

J uan Báez had continued to prosper in Puerto Rico under the flag of the United States. He was promoted to assistant administrator of the port, as his employers took note of his abilities and his integrity. Walter King and Rafi invited him to lunch to tell him about their plans for expanding the anemia campaign.

"We have good news, Juan," Rafi said as soon as they had ordered. "We are planning to start deworming treatments again. The director of the Tricoche Hospital has granted us space and generous staffing."

"*Excelente!*" Juan replied.

"Now that Dr. Ashford is back on the island," Dr. King said, "we hope to pick up where he left off."

"Rafi should also be proud of his crusade in the mountains for shoes and latrines—" Juan began, but was interrupted by Dr. King.

"Education is well and good, but we need to start curing people. The preventative measures are effective, but simply too slow. We can save more lives if we kill the worms first— then, the hygienic practices will work better on populations that have been made free of the parasites already."

"Is there some way that I can help?" asked Juan, trying to figure out why they were meeting.

"Your family is living proof of the power of the same old treatment. The people of Utuado, and particularly those around Hacienda Las Alturas, have seen its curative effects on them. They also know your family's history of sad losses to the disease, as well as those of many of their own family members, who unfortunately were never treated."

Juan quickly grasped the point. "You think that more of our *jíbaro* neighbors may come to Ponce for treatment if it is offered once again."

"Yes, that is precisely what we hope will happen," King said, tapping loudly on the table for emphasis. "We would like to ask you to be our agent to Utuado, to inform the *jíbaros* that we are treating for worms again, this time out of the Tricoche hospital."

Juan considered for a few moments. "I would be more than willing to help, as long as I can make arrangements for my younger siblings and a few days off from the port."

Juan accomplished both tasks without problems and left that Friday morning. With a good Army horse that had been procured by Ashford, the trip home took eight hours. By sunset, he was sitting with his parents in their new rebuilt hut, this one constructed of sturdier cedar planks and pitched under three guava trees that had survived the hurricane. Juan's parents looked exceedingly well, particularly his father, who had remained remarkably healthy after the exorcism of the devil worms the previous year. He did continue to suffer from relatively mild heart failure as a consequence of his longstanding anemia, but that was improving with the digitalis prescribed by the Army doctors in Ponce.

Simón listened to his son with great interest, as Juan sat both him and Pepa down at their table and gave them the news of Dr. Ashford's return to Ponce. "Dr. Ashford is anxious to know whether some of your friends and neighbors might consider treatment, *Papi*."

Simón thought for a moment. "My neighbors see my cure as nothing short of a miracle, and I often hear their regrets about not getting to Ponce while they could to receive the magical balls of glass. They talk about those *bolitas* all the time, you know."

"I am glad to hear that the *jíbaros* have not forgotten Ashford," Juan said.

Simón gave a sad smile. "Most people around here are still sick. Sure, a few of them have built latrines and have begun wearing shoes, but most are not convinced that this will make them well, or they are simply too set in their ways. However, if people knew that the *bolitas de cristal* with the magic medicine were once again available, they might be willing to go. You know how the *jíbaros* are about magic cures—the stranger the better."

"It is worth a try," Juan replied. "There is certainly nothing to lose."

They agreed on a plan to visit some of the huts the next morning. They would start with the *bohíos* of Iván Acosta, Manuel Mercado, and Gaspar Reyes—who all suffered from anemia, as did their wives and their adult children. Their huts were scattered over a square mile of the rainforest.

Father and son were welcomed at all the *bohíos* with enthusiasm. *Jíbaros* lived in a tight-knit society linked by an intricate network of godfathers and special friendships, the *padrinos* and the *compadres,* which stretched throughout the mountains in a web of adoptive kinship, bonds that were as strong as those between blood relatives. Juan hoped that the families' systems of *compadres and padrinos* would elicit a widening group of potential patients willing to take thymol.

When the *jíbaros* were reassured that the treatment involved the same *bolitas de cristal* they had heard of, many enthusiastically agreed to go. But it remained to be seen whether they meant to go to Ponce *mañana,* or next week, or next year. Time was a flexible concept for the *jíbaros,* who approached life at their own pace. When an event was planned, it was only in the loosest of terms. When it happened, if it happened, then it would happen and no sooner.

Juan left twenty silver *pesos* for his family, and twenty more for those who needed to hire horses or mules to travel. He embraced his parents tightly, mounted his horse, and started back toward the coast.

Meanwhile, Ashford, King, and Rafi worked on the preparation of the special ward at the Tricoche. Happily, few of the nurses from the religious order turned out to be as stubborn and as obstreperous as their superior. Many nurses had heard of the cures at the *Hospital Militar* and looked forward to providing care that was efficacious. Cots for thirty patients were brought into the ward. Three hundred grams of thymol were procured from the Army's supply, to be released in smaller amounts as needed. Microscopes were prepared, two new hemoglobinometers arrived from San Juan, and dyes needed to prepare stains were procured. This time, Ashford chose the new staining method developed by his friend, Dr. James Wright, whose unpublished formulation promised to become the new standard. Aguerrevere assigned them his best staff.

Then the team waited.

Almost a month passed with no patients seeking help for anemia at the Tricoche Hospital. They came seeking help for rashes, colds, diarrhea, or sore throats. Many patients had some degree of anemia, but since it was not the main reason for their visit to the hospital, they remained untreated. For the most part, these urbanites suffered from what the team considered a mild case of the disease, in large part because they were not exposed to the continuous reinfections of the mountain dwellers. The hookworms simply did not thrive as well inside the city with its paved streets, sidewalks, and relatively low rainfall. These patients were treated for their main complaint, informed of preventive measures against the parasites, and sent on their way. If they complied, they might overcome the hookworms without the need for thymol.

*****

In contrast to Ponce, the mountains of Utuado remained heavily infested by hookworm eggs and larvae. Several weeks after Juan's visit to the mountains, the *bohío* of the Reyes family became a focus of interest for the community. Gaspar Reyes' six-year-old grandson, Esteban, had always suffered from anemia, yet his pallor and fatigue, shared by so many others, had been largely viewed with indifference. But whether due to slightly less dietary iron or a less vigorous bone marrow, Esteban had entered the same downward cycle that had killed little Rosa and come within an eyelash of killing Teresa, if not for the nuns at the *Asilo*. Over the course of three months, Esteban had become increasingly languid and lethargic, his skin acquiring the appearance and texture of wax paper.

His parents argued back and forth about going to Ponce, weighing the missed wages, travel expenses, and difficulties of a long trip against the health of their child. However, when his grandparents came to visit and found the child eating the palm fronds that covered the floor of the hut, the discussion was over. They declared that they would take Esteban to Ponce themselves, and if it was over the dead bodies of his parents, so be it.

Gaspar had heard about the aid money Juan had left with Simón, and obtained a few *pesos* from him to hire a mule to help carry the child to Ponce. Gaspar and Esteban were joined by the boy's father, Domingo, and Simón and Pepa Báez, who meant to visit Juan, Carlos, and Ana. The travel was awful, with the trails and roads washed out by the near-constant rains. Rivers were high and crossing them proved slow and difficult. By the time the bedraggled group arrived in Ponce, the adults were exhausted and the boy was critical. Simón and Pepa headed to find their family, while Gaspar and Domingo took Esteban to the Tricoche, in search of the doctors and their promised cure.

As soon as they arrived, a nun triaged the family and immediately sent an orderly to track down Ashford. He was also asked to find *Señor* Moore at his lodgings across the street and bring him back. By pure chance, Rafi was walking down Bertoly Street toward the plaza, and at the messenger's arrival, immediately turned back toward the hospital. It took another thirty minutes to find Ashford, who was having coffee with Walter King.

Meanwhile, a nurse had prepared the boy for examination. Esteban presented the classic picture of profound anemia: he was pale and delirious with a weak, thready pulse and fluid in his lungs. A drop of blood was drawn from his thumb, from which Rafi prepared a smear. They abbreviated the stain protocol due to the emergency, and in slightly over an hour's time, the three men were taking turns at the microscope. Esteban's red cells were below one million, their discs small and pale under the microscope's eye, and his eosinophils remarkable only by their complete absence. It was, once again, the picture of a terminal patient.

Ashford glanced at King with concern. Esteban was so ill that his death was almost a certainty, with or without treatment. If Ashford withheld treatment and the child died, he would be guilty of neglecting his oath and ethics. That would be bad enough, but if he treated Esteban and he died *after* receiving thymol, he could be seen as a reckless experimenter, determined to prove his methods at all costs with blatant disregard for the suffering of his patients. And yet, he could not stop dispel the wisdom of the Proverbs 3: '*Withhold not good from them to whom it is due, when it is in the power of the thine hand to do it.*' As bad as treating the boy could turn out, not offering him thymol was indefensible. Ashford and King decided to carefully present the situation and the two available alternatives for the family to consider, but their final recommendation would be to deworm the boy.

Aguerrevere arrived at the ward. Ashford notified him of the risky plan, and he silently nodded his approval, fully aware that the reputation of his hospital was also at stake. Ashford, King, and Rafi went to see the Reyes men in the waiting area. Rafi stepped forward to explain the nuances of their options in their native tongue. He described Esteban's dire condition and how, without thymol, there was no question that he would succumb to anemia within the next several days. The only chance for Esteban's survival was to administer the anthelminthic, and Rafi carefully emphasized that even then, the child might not survive. The two men deliberated only briefly before asking Rafi to convey their desire to proceed with the treatment. The orderly was sent out to find Juan, who, as a friend of the family, could provide much-needed emotional support. Then, a nurse brought the family into the ward to see their boy.

Several decisions now faced Ashford and King. First was the question of whether they should administer the cathartic of sodium sulfate to clean the boy's bowels and make the thymol more effective. The sulfate would allow them to use a lower dose of thymol, but it also carried its own particular risks, and these were not negligible in a critical patient who was severely dehydrated. Alternatively, they could forego the purgation of the gut, but that would mean increasing the thymol dosage, or having to use it twice. Ashford felt the sweat covering his brow and beginning to soak his shirt. There was nowhere in the building to hide from the high temperatures outside, and wet towels with ice had to be applied to relieve the stress the oppressive heat was putting on Esteban's heart.

At last, the doctors decided to proceed with purgation and then treat their patient with one gram of thymol. In the early afternoon, as the two Reyes men, Juan, Rafi, and the doctors watched in tense anticipation, a nun gently administered 15 grams of sodium sulfate, about half of the adult dose, to Esteban. The boy opened his expressionless eyes for only a moment, and slowly swallowed the medication. Now, they would wait eight hours for the purge to work before administering the antihelminthic later that night. The patient was carefully laid in his cot while all others looked on, watching his laboring chest rise and fall in spasms as he slept. The ward was empty of other patients, and completely quiet.

No one budged from the patient's bedside. The first two hours passed quietly enough. Then, as the shadows began lengthening in the late afternoon, the sulfate began to take effect. Esteban's body began to cleanse itself, slowly at first, but then with increasing violence as the medication took effect. A concerned nurse silently performed the cleaning tasks, while the doctors encouraged the child to drink a solution of essential salts. The cathartic ravaged the child's body with its full power, and as his fluid losses mounted, his mental state deteriorated further until he lost consciousness. Now, the doctors could no longer continue rehydrating Esteban by mouth, leaving him at the full mercy of the sodium sulfate. The tension in the ward was palpable, with time seemingly stretching into an eternity, until finally, Esteban's evacuations slowed and he settled onto his cot, his breath rasping through the empty ward. His family was sent outside to rest, and the sisters brought them something to eat.

Meanwhile, inside the ward, the concerned physicians consulted one another. The cathartic had hit the boy hard, much harder than Ashford had seen in any of his previous treatments. Doubt crept in—could the boy survive what came next? But by then, they were fully committed. The patient's only chance of survival was the thymol. They would have to wait for him to return to consciousness to administer the capsule, which only an alert patient could swallow safely. If he did not awaken, they agreed they would administer the thymol through a tube passed from the nose into the stomach, in which case it would have to be suspended in water and flushed through the tube into the alimentary tract. These were uncharted waters for both Ashford and King, but if necessary, they would not hesitate.

Toward eight in the evening, the full veil of night had descended upon the hospital. Outside, the happy cackling of people could be heard heading toward the plaza. Esteban finally opened his eyes, looked around the room, and managed a wan smile directed at the Sister nursing him through the ordeal. Ashford immediately produced the capsule—*la bolita de cristal* about which the Reyes men had heard so much, but never seen. They gently guided it into the back of the boy's mouth, who reflexively swallowed the strange object, like the time he had accidentally swallowed a marble. He took some water to send the thymol on its way and gave a slight cough as a small amount of fluid spilled into his airway. Once again, he was laid down to rest.

Within the hour, it became clear that the protocol had been too much. Tipped over the edge by the cathartic, Esteban's dehydrated body was operating at the edge of its limits, and could not tolerate the thymol. As Ashford and King worriedly looked on, the nurse urgently summoned the two Reyes men back to the room. They arrived barely in time to witness the weak convulsions of the boy as he began entering the final stages of his journey. There was a general shudder, the languid face twisted into a grimace, and then, as his father and grandfather watched, grief-stricken, Esteban's lips slowly turned blue around the edges, his face became dusky and the child was still.

Everyone in the room went as perfectly still as the wasted body on the cot. The doctors looked at the floor with blank expressions while the nurses wept silently, fists to their mouths, biting their fingers to suppress their sobs. The father and grandfather began to collapse as they realized that Esteban was dead at last, gone for good after years of suffering. They requested that the body be released to them as soon as possible. Acquiescing, Ashford completed the death certificate through eyes moist with tears of frustration and helplessness. The health inspector gave approval for the eventual release of the body, and Juan Báez took the Reyes men back to his house for the night.

Ashford, King, and Rafi headed out of the hospital for a long walk. No one spoke for the first half mile. King finally broke the ice, murmuring, "Bailey, you know we did right by that boy. We cannot torment ourselves forever if we are going to continue to do some good for these people."

Ashford replied, his voice low and tremulous, "The sulfate, it was too much, we should have stayed away from it. It was the wrong decision."

"All we can do is to apply our knowledge and experience to each particular circumstance as it comes. Your protocol has cured several dozen patients, and I am of the opinion that we have to continue treating aggressively."

"By morning the news will be all over the city that we lost a patient—not to the hookworms, but to the thymol. I wager there won't be much talk about how terribly ill that child was when he arrived from the mountains. Instead, they will blame the drug, along with its prescribers. We can expect to be vilified for our efforts, and this may well be the end of our treatment trial."

"Maybe so," King said, "but maybe not. Come now, there's no use despairing over what has not happened yet. Yes, we should grieve the loss of our patient, but we should also not doubt our purpose here. Our mission is good, it is anchored in solid science and backed by good preliminary results. Thank the grace of some benevolent higher power that your first patient was Simón Báez, and not Esteban Reyes."

"We have done some good," Ashford replied heavily. "For a long time, patients have borne the death of their children with little more than a stony resignation—its daily occurrence numbs their senses. I only hope that we will still have a chance to change that attitude into a thing of the past."

Later that evening in Juan's house, the members of the household and their visitors heatedly discussed the events of the last two days. At one end of a long table sat the five members of the Báez family, all healthy, three of them cured by Ashford two years before. At the other end sat the Reyes men, both sick, with another family member dead at the hospital, lost to anemia. Many tears of sorrow, and many of guilt, were shed by all. Family and friends shared some recriminations and some consolation. After two hours, the elder Reyes stood up and asked for silence. Slowly and deliberately, he made an announcement. The Báez clan all stared at the patriarch with astonishment, while the younger Reyes silently nodded his assent.

Shortly after daybreak the next morning, Simón and Juan left for Utuado with a mule-driven cart in which Esteban's body lay, wrapped in a blanket. It was of utmost importance that the child have his *velorio* before too much time had elapsed. The Báez men would convey the circumstances of the child's passing to his family, as well as the reason his father and grandfather had remained behind in Ponce.

Chapter Thirty-One

REDEMPTION

The morning following Esteban's death, a dejected Ashford began taking the daily sick call at the *Hospital Militar*. The day brought the usual smattering of mild orthopedic injuries, two recovering typhoid victims, the odd laceration or two, and a mixture of general ailments which made up the routine fare of a small Army clinic. Ashford and Moretti had always taken a certain devilish pleasure in announcing a diagnosis of "the clap" to some poor embarrassed soldier, who was then left to imagine what was to happen to him next. But on that day, there was no delight in anything they did. Ashford was moody, depressed, and short with everybody. In his mind's eye, he kept seeing Esteban's face as he died.

Close to the midday break, King approached Ashford in the clinic.

"Young Báez came to see me very early this morning," King said, "just before he left with Esteban's body for the mountains. He said the Reyes men have requested to meet with you at the Tricoche Hospital later today, before they head home for the *velorio*. Juan either couldn't, or wouldn't, say more."

Ashford swallowed hard. Now he had to prepare himself for the inevitable and severe dressing-down he would receive from the relatives of a dead patient. It promised to be unpleasant, and moreover, he believed that he thoroughly deserved it. His mind whirled with second thoughts: maybe they should have refused to treat the boy, or given him less medicine, or perhaps forgone the cathartic. Maybe they should have waited longer between the thymol and the cathartic, or used a modified cathartic instead. Pulling himself out of his downward mental spiral, Ashford let out a long sigh. He had been counting on taking several weeks away from the Tricoche to gather his thoughts, but he could not shirk this meeting—he owed the grieving relatives no less. King agreed to join him, and they asked Rafi to come as well, so that none of the subtleties of either language were misunderstood.

The parties began arriving in the small waiting area outside the anemia ward: first Ashford and King, followed by Director Aguerrevere and then Rafi Moore. The last to arrive were Gaspar and Domingo Reyes. Aguerrevere motioned for everybody to sit on the wooden benches, but the Reyes family declined.

Ashford began to speak words of sympathy and condolences in his best Spanish. "I wanted to express to the Reyes how sorry I am about Esteban's death. We did our very best to save him. I think that his body was already so weak from advanced anemia that…"

The senior Reyes held up his hand and called for silence. He fixed his eyes on Ashford and spoke deliberately in a strong voice that still trembled with emotion, as Rafi translated.

"Today we weep for our dear Esteban, taken from us at six, so very young and yet so knowledgeable in the bitterest offerings of this world. But though our tears are heavy, I know that sorrow is not our exclusive property. I see anguish in the eyes of Dr. Ashford and Dr. King, and in those of their nurses and their staff, and finally, in the honorable Director. We all share this grief, and by our sharing, the burden is made lighter. I will soon be fifty years old, and by all accounts, I should have died long ago. I should have perished of the poorly named 'natural causes' which, since last year, has had its name changed to 'epidemic infectious anemia.'

"My son and I brought Esteban here for treatment, hopeful of a cure, against what surely must have been insurmountable odds. If there is blame for the death of our boy, then it must fall on me. On me, on my son, and on our families who have come to accept this disease as our companion through life, like our grinding poverty, our backbreaking labor for a scant few cents, and the ignorance that clouds our brains. We could see that Esteban's life was coming to a close months ago, and yet we did nothing. We heard that sick children could be secretly treated at the Asilo de Damas by the two brave sisters, and still we did nothing. When the poor child resorted to eating dirt and chewing palm fronds, we should have known that it was probably too late to save him. And yet, we came here with our desperate hopes.

"When I look at my *ahijado* Juan and his family—Simón, Carlos and Ana—all sickened in the worst way and now completely well, I know that what the doctors proposed to do for Esteban was good. These treatments must not stop because we have lost a darling child that heaven was determined to receive regardless of our plans." Gaspar then walked up to Ashford, and gently taking him by both shoulders announced, "Domingo and I have come today to request that you please treat us as well."

Ashford and King stood there, speechless. Rafi's face was wet with tears, fallen while he was translating. Finally, Aguerrevere nodded, silently accepting the men's offer, then solemnly escorted the prospective patients into the ward. The doctors soon followed, still in a state of shock. Rafi drew a small amount of blood from each man while Ashford and King performed their examinations. Next, a small amount of fecal material was examined under the microscope. Finding one egg sufficed to confirm what everybody already suspected: both men were diagnosed with parasitic anemia secondary to the hookworm. Stiles had recently renamed the worm *Necator americanus*, "the American killer," which Ashford considered rather grandiose.

The two Reyes men may not have been as badly infected as their neighbor Simón, the team's first cure, but their anemia was certainly severe enough to warrant immediate treatment. Rafi examined their blood smears and reported slightly under two million cells each, as well as markedly elevated eosinophils for both men. But although seriously ill, unlike Esteban, these two patients at least had a functioning bone marrow. They were also alert and fully cooperative, unlike their boy, who had been neither. Still, to prevent their previous error, the doctors began by vigorously hydrating the two men. Gaspar and Domingo received almost two liters of lightly salted water over the course of four hours, during which the two men recounted tales of their lives in the mountains, their hardships, and the coming of the hurricane. Domingo proudly volunteered that he had been among the very first to build his latrine, as Simón had suggested. His father countered that it might have served better if he hadn't dug the hole a half hour's walk from his hut.

"That was on purpose, so the odors stay far away," said Domingo.

"Yes, and the people also stay away, it is so far from anything," retorted his father.

By early evening, their hydration was complete, and the cathartic of sodium sulfate was administered at its full strength of 30 grams. The patients knew what to expect and soon retired to the area designated as a lavatory, there to spend the night manning their chamber pots, and passing them off to an unflappable orderly for disposal. By the following morning, their diarrhea had largely resolved, and by eight, the nurse handed them each a thymol capsule. The men took their medicine without ceremony, washed it down with sweetened water, and waited. Almost immediately, they felt the characteristic burning in their throats, which they compared to swallowing the strongest fraction of rum from the *alambique*. The burning proceeded to trail the capsule all the way down to their stomachs, forcing the men to hold their mouths closed to keep from regurgitating the medicine. They endured moderate nausea and their skin turned the slightest shade of green over the next fifteen minutes, but they kept the thymol down. Within thirty minutes, they could feel the burning passing into their abdomens. Being no worse for wear, after two hours they were given a second capsule with half the dose of the antihelminthic, and two hours after that, the last dose of the sulfate purgative. This time, the patients were not allowed to go to the lavatory. For twelve hours, their post-purgation waste was duly collected by the nuns, and turned over to the physicians.

The doctors had more than enough material for study. Ashford believed that generally, patients passed 80 percent of the hookworms within the first twelve hours and therefore, these samples should give them a fair idea of whether their effort had been successful. The clinicians went back to the small lab, where the diluted and filtered feces were run through the special black counting trough. Rafi transferred the material with a large dropper while Ashford and King tallied the parasites. By the end, they had each counted well over 900 dead organisms from both patients.

One of the largest hookworms was carefully selected with forceps and placed under the microscope at low power. Right under their eyes, magnified into all its macabre splendor, lay a large, plump female *Necator* hookworm. The telltale bend at the neck was clearly visible along with the fearsome cutting plates, sharp as razor blades and slightly agape, as if protesting the untimely eviction from its bloody banquet. The drug had accomplished its mission; now the physicians had to accomplish theirs by ensuring that their patients survived the treatment.

The Reyes men were asked to remain in the hospital for the next three days. They were fed well, and kept fully hydrated. No adverse effects occurred, and by the morning of their dismissal five days after the death of Esteban, there was no doubt that the treatment had been a complete success. Virtually all their worms had been expelled, and their healthy bone morrow, fed by the riches of a balanced diet, jazzed by iron supplements, and, at long last, unopposed by an army of parasites, rapidly began to replenish their blood.

In four days, the men's red cell counts surpassed three million, their eosinophils began to fall in number, and they felt a new and unfamiliar energy building inside them. It was a new vitality to face life, along with a new clarity in thinking. Ashford assured them that this was only the beginning, and that they could expect even more improvement, as long as they avoided reinfection. The team reemphasized the two simple tenets of effective prevention: limiting soil pollution to a few designated areas, and wearing shoes outside the home, without exception.

Three days later, Rafi walked to Ashford's house to pick him up for breakfast. Ashford would then proceed to the sick call at the *Hospital Militar*, while Rafi would travel to one of Ponce's mountain *barrios* to meet with local leaders. The pair had begun to walk up Bertoly Street toward the military hospital when they stopped suddenly.

Coming toward them down the steep road from the Utuado mountains marched a crowd three dozen strong—men and women, old and young. They were dressed uniformly in ragged white clothes, the men wearing straw hats, the women with their hair up in buns. As the group approached, Ashford could see they were all barefoot and their faces bore the unmistakable pallor of anemia. These were *jíbaros* from the mountains. As they got nearer, Rafi walked toward them and addressed the nearest person.

"*Buenos días compadre,* may I assist you in some way?"

"*Sí señor,* we come from Utuado, near Hacienda Las Alturas. We are headed to see Dr. Ashford at the Tricoche."

Ashford moved forward. "I am Dr. Bailey Ashford."

The lead *jíbaro* shook his hand, saying, "We had news in Utuado from our *compadre,* Simón, that the doctor with the magic *bolitas de cristal* has come back to Ponce. We also know that young Esteban sadly did not survive, despite the best efforts to care for him."

The lead *jíbaro* explained how at the *velorio,* word had spread that Esteban had arrived in Ponce unconscious, and died despite the doctors' efforts. They had also heard that despite this tragedy, Domingo and Gaspar had decided to remain to be cured regardless of the loss of their boy. "We have come seeking treatment for the worms living inside us, as they did," the man said.

Staggered, Ashford asked Rafi to guide the *jíbaros* to the hospital while he hurried to the port to get Dr. King. Rafi led the crowd of sick peasants to the front portico of the Tricoche Hospital and asked them to wait outside for a moment while he went to find the hospital director. Aguerrevere quickly mustered a handful of nuns to stay with the *jíbaros.*

As soon as Ashford and King returned, they made a hurried plan for collecting information from their new patients' physical exams and bloodwork. Sister Mary Elizabeth was summoned to assist as well. The group of thirty-three patients were divided into three groups, triaged by apparent severity of illness. Ashford and King began by treating the palest and gauntest of the group, while the rest awaited their turn in the ward.

The first group of eight patients was admitted and examined. Their examination showed that all were deathly pale, suffering from heart failure and fluid in their lungs. Malnutrition was rampant, all were exhausted, and many were disoriented. The team treated them that very day, and planned to keep them in the hospital until they got well. The next day, they would evaluate the next group, expanding treatments until they could attend to all persons.

The nurses aggressively hydrated the first patients until their urine became copious and dilute. As the *jíbaros* rested in the ward, Sister Mary Elizabeth and Rafi reported the values from their laboratory studies. All were in the late stages of the disease.

The treatments began that evening with sodium sulfate. With assiduous care and some luck, Ashford and King expected all to have favorable outcomes. The next morning, they found they had been proved correct, and so all the patients could proceed to the next stage of their treatment. They administered two doses of thymol, two hours apart to each patient, and at noon, they gave the final dose of cathartic. While this group recovered from the treatments, the doctors went on to examine the next set of patients.

After the first day, the activity in the ward escalated to a near-unmanageable level. Everywhere nurses were treating and encouraging patients, orderlies rushing about, people retching and others reaching for bedpans, doctors listening to chests with and without stethoscopes and administrators emptying chamber pots, all in a nonstop frenzy of interweaving action amidst a cloud of the most nauseating stench. Shifts came and went, but Ashford and King couldn't sleep. Another lieutenant physician came to help, and even the dour *Sor* Castigos joined the fray. Some patients were discharged after two days, others after three, and yet others remained too weak to leave after four days or more of recovery.

Gradually the tide began to turn, and the ward came under a semblance of sanity and equilibrium. By now, other people not part of the original group from Utuado were seeking treatment as well. Ashford was granted complete leave from his military duties for eight weeks to deal with the influx of cases. Rafi functioned as another physician, directing treatments and examining patients. Three days after treatment, the red cell count for any given case showed an average improvement of 30 percent. With this initial increase, most patients already felt decidedly better and were able to vacate their beds, just in time for a new batch to come stumbling through the hospital doors.

Over the next two months, they treated one hundred patients. As their work progressed through the summer months and into fall, a curious phenomenon emerged. The severity of the patients' illnesses seemed to diverge into two very different groups, based on their initial presentation and the treatment they would require. First, there were the patients with mild to moderate anemia who were treated as outpatients. Their hemoglobin levels were all above 50 percent and red cell counts were typically over 2.5 million per cubic millimeter. They often came early in the morning, were administered the purgative, and then brought back in the afternoon for the two doses of thymol and the final cathartic. Most of these patients went home in the evening with instructions to return to the hospital if they felt unwell. Many of them, feeling well soon after treatment, went back to their *barrios* and never returned to the hospital for follow-ups.

On the other end of the spectrum, as word of their successes spread, the two doctors began to see a larger proportion of patients who were within days, perhaps even hours, of dying. Many of these were borne by improvised human ambulances, conveyed for miles by a rotating team of *jíbaros*. Two in the front and two in the back would carry a crude canvas hammock suspended from poles of sturdy *guayacán* ironwood. In this way the patient was delivered to the entrance of the Tricoche *in extremis* and often unconscious. Luckily, the physicians had implemented improvements and refinements in their protocols, begun after Esteban's death, which gave them a fighting chance to save even these patients. Some of their laboratory values could hardly be believed, with several patients showing red cell counts that numbered below one million.

As time wore on, the trend toward more severe cases accelerated and the team began to lose more patients. As the ward began to swell with critical cases, two of the hospital's younger nuns approached Ashford and King. One of them, Sister Marcelina, could not have been much over twenty years old. With her colleague encouraging her, the young nurse addressed Ashford.

"Last year, I spent six months training at the Santo Spirito Hospital in Rome. There, the doctors occasionally employed what they called '*heroic resuscitation*,' a last-ditch effort to save critical patients who were so dehydrated and delirious that they could no longer drink the fluids needed to keep them alive. The idea was simply to deliver the fluids they desperately needed directly into their circulation."

Ashford and King exchanged glances; they had never heard or read of this technique. Sister Marcelina went on to explain how the doctors performed a very brief operation to expose a vein in the forearm. Then, they made a tiny opening in the vein and would insert a small rubber tube that had been boiled in salted water. A nurse put pressure on the forearm to stop the bleeding, and then, if fluid was passed into the vein fast enough, the blood would not clot inside the tube. After the procedure, many of these desperate patients had regained consciousness and could drink again.

In answer to their questions, the nun provided more details about the fluid and its preparation. To Ashford, the whole process sounded labor-intensive and rather unorthodox. But the science behind it was solid, and the condition of many of their patients warranted trying these methods. The doctors agreed to try the intravenous technique on extremely ill patients, who stood a minimal chance of survival without rapidly receiving large quantities of fluid. The nuns devised an effective method of preparing the sterilized salt water needed for rapid rehydration, and under the direction of the opinionated yet highly competent *Sor* Castigos, they varied the proportions of salt to water, refining the process as they worked. The team's use of intravenous fluids, experimental and nearly untried, likely saved over twenty of their sickest patients.

As the Tricoche anemia ward became a smooth-running machine for treatment and research, Sister Mary Elizabeth compiled their findings regarding the presenting symptoms and treatment of the first one hundred patients who had passed through their doors, and submitted it to the hospital's governing body for review. The level of disease severity the hospital had seen had been off the charts, but the anemia team had saved eighty-nine of the first hundred patients. In Ashford's opinion, by any measure, this first organized trial against the hookworm was a triumph, and anybody who disagreed with this assessment had to be a fool. Eleven patients had unfortunately died, but Ashford believed that any careful and unbiased evaluation of his care would have concluded that all would have perished independently of their contact with his team.

Those eleven deaths nevertheless produced heated discussion among the governing board of the hospital, which was dominated by pro-Spanish conservatives who took every opportunity to denounce the American physicians as proponents of harebrained schemes. The minority pro-American faction, in turn, defended the overall results as impressive in light of the patients' acute state of illness. The animosity grew so fierce among the board that, at one meeting, their shouting could be heard echoing from inside the board-room all the way to the anemia ward. The two sides might have come to blows, had Director Aguerrevere not calmly stood up and declared that, "Yes, eleven out of a hundred have died, but before Ashford arrived, they *all* died." That blunt statement swiftly brought the conference to an end.

Chapter Thirty-Two

SURPRISES

The statement by Dr. Aguerrevere cut both ways. Ashford and King had their supporters and these were no longer so few in number. Their detractors, however, were also many, ruthless and, as it turned out, very cunning. Word of the contentious meeting of the governing board of the Tricoche Hospital soon leaked out, distorted and exaggerated, and was relayed completely out of context. Malignant voices soon whispered through Ponce that there had been deaths, and that moreover, the *gringo* doctors had been observed experimenting on the sick, recklessly putting tubes into their hearts through which they pumped some mysterious fluids, surely some poison. These whispers grew to grumbles, then shouts—these pernicious practices must be made to stop. If the foreign doctors wanted to experiment, then let them do it on their own soldiers, those undesirables who only served to harass virtuous *ponceños* and spread venereal disease.

As the rumors spread like fog creeping in from the bay, the number of sick people waiting for treatment outside the hospital steadily multiplied. Meanwhile, the board of governors dragged their heels, deliberating the same arguments over and over. Finally, barely a week after the contentious meeting, a divided hospital board ordered the Director to close the anemia ward for the foreseeable future. Ponce became the eye of a political hurricane whirling around the island's public health system.

Word from San Juan came that Governor Hunt was becoming increasingly impatient with the wrangling in Ponce's largest hospital and was growing dismayed by the local doctors' skepticism over the hookworm. As a non-medical person,

Hunt could not grasp why Ashford could not garner more widespread support if his results were as impressive as he claimed. With a sinking heart, Ashford saw the political shadow that the governor's hesitation cast upon his work. Rumors that Hunt's impatience could negatively influence his support would prove a severe blow to reopening the operation at the *Tricoche*. The governor may have had some shortcomings, but his initial interest in defeating the anemia pandemic had been sincere and unwavering. Ashford knew that to lose his full support might spell the end of his campaign.

Ashford and King waited with growing frustration, their hands tied week after week, as their plans to reopen the anemia ward stalled. The room for the anemia patients sat empty while dozens inquired daily as to when they might be admitted. The impasse had lasted for well over a month, with no end in sight, when the two doctors met for evening drinks at the *Hotel Ponceño*.

Ashford greeted his colleague and dropped languidly into a rickety chair.

"You know, King, we've been sabotaged. Dr. Zeno has told me in strictest confidence that several *Tricoche* board members have accused us of wholesale experimentation on people too ill to refuse treatment. Furthermore, we are supposedly engaging in all this reckless behavior under the convenient cover that our patients are going to die anyway."

King shook his head in dismay and waved to a waiter. "Sadly, sometimes advances are made slowly in the face of the tyranny of prejudice. Most of our detractors decided to fight us well before they had seen a single cure."

"The Tricoche board is about as useful as a trapdoor on a johnboat," Ashford snapped, ignoring the glass King slid before him. "We've got to do something to get the trials moving again. It may be necessary to bypass the Army chain of command altogether and complain to the federal government directly."

"Bailey, the Army no longer has any right to interfere in civilian affairs," King warned, his eyebrows nearly creeping to his hairline. "The repercussions could be severe. You could be court-martialed."

"I know, King, *but this gets my goat!*" Ashford practically snarled, his eyes narrowing as he tightly gripped his glass without touching the liquor within. "The hookworm disease has been fully described for over three years now. You would think that those in charge would have jumped on board. Yes, we received some money and some space for the trial, but now that it's been an unqualified success, we are met with vilification and disdain. And meanwhile, people suffer. We have to act."

King let out a long sigh, bracing his elbows on their table. "What do you propose?"

Ashford leaned closer to his comrade, his voice sharp and intense. "We forge ahead, publish on our own. We can send our paper to *American Medicine.* You know Gould, the editor, don't you?"

King leaned closer. "I do indeed, quite well."

Ashford's eyes gleamed. "Then we will submit our data, and an opinion letter to publish alongside our paper. Even if Dr. Gould doesn't print the letter, he might be willing to pen a supporting editorial instead. The data speaks for itself, loud and clear. If it's released to the public, then it can no longer be suppressed."

King smiled at the cleverness of Ashford's plan. "We are asking for one hell of a lot of trouble."

Ashford beat his fist against his hand. "I don't care a rat's ass about trouble! The only way we will get anywhere is precisely by getting in as much hot water as we can. The Army may dismiss me when it finds out that we have been treading in civilian muck, but in any trial the truth will have to come out. I'd rather be dismissed from the Army than allow these deaths to continue because I kept my mouth shut."

The next day, the two partners started work on their journal submission, with the working title of *A Study of Uncinariasis in Porto Rico.* Each of the one hundred cases from the Tricoche Hospital would be individually described by age, sex, occupation, region of residence, symptoms on presentation, laboratory results, and outcome. They also decided to include additional comments on any peculiarities relevant to each case. For example, if a patient had been found to suffer from advanced tuberculosis of the lung, they noted this in the margin next to the patient's initials, which served to identify the case. Similarly, they noted the many patients who suffered from simultaneous infection by other species of parasitic worms, particularly the high numbers co-infected by a relatively harmless species with the common name of the giant intestinal roundworm, which the islanders referred to as *las lombrices*. They hoped their manuscript would be nothing less than a comprehensive medico-sociological study of the Puerto Rican lower classes at the start of the new century.

Day after day, the authors labored over the content and presentation of their data. They exchanged drafts daily between their offices, sent back and forth by couriers—generally impoverished young men hired to walk the four miles between the port and the *Hospital Militar* several times a day. By the third week, Joaquín, their main courier, began covering the route on a new Rover bicycle, the only one on the streets of Ponce. Ashford congratulated him on this flashy method of transport, and the young man gladly agreed to let him try out his bicycle. When the doctor jokingly pointed out that the sleek machine must have cost him a year's wages, Joaquín merely replied, "Business is good."

The two scientists were blissfully unaware that, thanks to Joaquín, their confidential correspondence was no longer private. Surreptitious summaries of the writings that Ashford and King had been preparing made their way to Governor Hunt. They were among the hundreds of reports he received, as supreme magistrate of the island, regarding a wide range of issues from the extraordinary to the mundane. The reports delivered to Hunt invariably contained alarmist commentaries panning the physicians' risky clinical methods and their supposedly unsubstantiated conclusions. In the latest report, the governor had received information that the two American investigators planned to publicly criticize his newly appointed Puerto Rico Board of Health by means of a journal article.

At this news, Hunt became alarmed and resentful at such presumptuous interference by a junior Army officer. He decided to act. A letter from the Governor's Office was soon on its way to the War Department in Washington, D.C.

Governor Hunt had always advocated most unapologetically for the full assimilation of the island into the United States, and within days of assuming office, he had decreed that the residents of Puerto Rico were to observe Thanksgiving in the tradition of their parent nation. Whether by coincidence or not, the Ashfords received an invitation to celebrate this new official holiday in Puerto Rico with the high Army brass in San Juan. A fabulous party was held at the *Casa Blanca*, the original fortified house of the first governor, Juan Ponce de León. Its name derived from the stark whitewash which had covered its outside walls for nearly 400 years. The imposing three-story structure dated to 1520, and its reinforced masonry walls overlooked the bay from the highest point in the Old City. Numerous balustraded balconies opened to breathtaking views of the harbor from far above the city walls.

The Ashfords wandered through the crowd in the large open salon on the main floor, where the grand party featured an American-style spread with a dozen turkeys, yams, squash, green beans, and cornbread. María Asunción enjoyed herself thoroughly, having left Mahlon at her parents' house less than three blocks away. This was certainly far better than the dreary parties at Fort Slocum.

After the meal, Ashford was invited to share the dessert wine in private with the recently installed U.S. military commander for the island, Colonel James Buchanan. A corporal led Ashford into a spacious side room and closed the huge ebony double doors behind him, muting the raucous sounds of the party to a soft murmur.

Buchanan welcomed him with a firm handshake. "Lieutenant Ashford, welcome once again to San Juan. What a fabulous time we have all had today! If there is one thing I miss while deployed, it is the sumptuous and delicious meal on Thanksgiving Day. The island can keep their roast pork and plantains, I say give me a nice turkey and corn, any day! That, and a good game of golf. You know, Ashford, I've been thinking about constructing a full-sized golf course on the Army's sixty acres in front of the *Morro* castle."

Ashford cringed, knowing it was unlikely that Buchanan had invited him solely to discuss his love of golf. All the same, he wearily replied, "That will be a spectacular setting for the sport, sir."

Buchanan chuckled and clapped the younger man across the shoulder. "But enough of these pleasantries. I asked you to come all the way from Ponce because I wish to share some official news, which I hope you will find, well… agreeable."

Ashford squirmed, memories of a similar meeting in Washington the year before coming to mind. The colonel straightened.

"The War Department proudly recognizes your exemplary services to the island. I am happy to inform you that you have been promoted to the rank of captain, retroactive to November 6. I believe that this was perhaps quite overdue."

Ashford remained silent, expecting the price of the promotion to be named next.

"Along with the promotion in rank, you will be assigned to the Army hospital in Washington to help lead the section of infectious diseases as Associate Surgeon. You may not have heard that its former head, Major Walter Reed, passed away unexpectedly five days ago."

The news fell upon Ashford like a pile of bricks. He stood speechless. In one brief instant, he learned that the mentor and friend who had once saved his life was dead, and worse yet, that he was slated to leave the island to take his place. Desperate, he threw aside the conventions of rank and authority and spoke up.

"Why am I being removed from the island, where you say I've rendered such great service? Why now, when we are finally beginning to succeed in our fight against the *Necator* anemia?"

The commander raised his eyebrows at Ashford's unwelcome candor. "There are powerful figures in San Juan," he answered, "and you have alienated them. Make no mistake, the Army, and I, personally, enthusiastically support your work and accept your theories. In fact, the War Department tells me there is mounting evidence to suggest that this New World hookworm also exists in large numbers in Florida and Georgia, and possibly elsewhere on the mainland. I agree with you that this war against the hookworm must be vigorously prosecuted and won. The question is whether you are the best person for the job."

Ashford shook his head in resignation. "Is there anything that might be done to keep me in Puerto Rico?"

Buchanan paused for a long minute before replying. "I suppose you can argue your case to the top man himself. Inviting you to San Juan for the holiday was *his* idea, actually. He is coming to join us very shortly, along with the President of the Executive Council." Buchanan turned to the attending soldier and asked him to see if the guests of honor had arrived. A few minutes later, the corporal returned to the room followed by Governor William Henry Hunt himself, along with his thirty-year-old right-hand man and head of the Executive Council, Regis Post. The two made a formidable pair—both men young and athletic, perceptive and intelligent, and radiating an authoritarian air born of aristocratic upbringing. Ashford overcame his initial surprise, and immediately rose to his feet.

Colonel Buchanan introduced him to the two men as "Captain Bailey Ashford of the Army Medical Corps."

Hunt greeted the newly-minted captain with a firm handshake and a serious look. "So, this is the young officer who has been making waves down in Ponce?"

Ashford was taken aback, but managed an embarrassed reply, "Yes, sir, I believe you are referring to me, sir."

Hunt and Post sat down in the comfortably stuffed chairs, followed by Buchanan and finally Ashford. The four sat in silence as the new arrivals were served their drinks before Councilman Post spoke.

"Captain Ashford, Governor Hunt and I have been somewhat troubled to learn that you are planning to publish a research article that could be construed as critical to our government, particularly in how we have addressed the health of its people."

"Forgive me, Mr. Post," Ashford replied, working to keep his voice calm. "My only interest has been to seek what I consider best for the islanders."

A red-faced Hunt forcefully interrupted. "I assure you, Captain Ashford, the health of the islanders is the top priority for us as well. What we cannot understand is why, if your conclusions are correct, so few of the doctors agree with you. We keep hearing from them that the poor health of the laborers working in the coffee plantations and sugar cane fields results from a combination of malaria and malnutrition. The doctors are asking for funds to purchase more quinine, not pursue vampire worms."

"I believe," Ashford replied, "that their opposition is a combination of stubborn reliance on old ideas and methods, augmented by an arbitrary dislike for Americans. Even after four years, many of them still consider themselves subjects of Spain, and see us as invaders."

Governor Hunt threw his hands in the air. "I should've known. One thing I'm sure of is that politics drives most decisions, including misguided ones that may hurt many people."

Post's eyes narrowed. "Dr. Ashford, only a few weeks ago, Governor Hunt asked me to write to the War Department and express our displeasure at the Army's inappropriate meddling in civilian affairs. The day after the letter was posted, we received a letter from Mr. Arturo Roig, owner of Las Alturas plantation in the municipality of Utuado. Mr. Roig is held in the highest regard in San Juan—the governor went so far as to send a high ranking official to his son's funeral following his tragic death. In his letter to Governor Hunt, Mr. Roig expressed his most sincere admiration for you."

Ashford looked quizzically at Post. "I do not recall having met anyone named Arturo Roig."

"You may not know of him, but he knows of *you*," the governor said. "He commended the efforts that you and Dr. King undertook to solve the longstanding health issues plaguing his workers. Apparently, many of his workers have been your patients in Ponce. Hunt pulled a neatly folded letter from his coat pocket, and unfolded it. "Mr. Roig even included the names of some of the workers that you treated and cured: Simón Báez, Carlos Báez, Gaspar Reyes, Domingo Reyes, José Miguel Reyes, Iván Acosta, Manuel Mercado…the list continues. I believe he mentions over sixty employees by name. He goes on to say that the workers' recovery turned his hacienda's slow, arduous rebuilding process into a veritable beehive of activity almost overnight."

Ashford shook his head slowly. "I am afraid I don't fully understand you, Governor Hunt."

"The point Roig makes is this: before these workers arrived at your hospitals, they could barely saw a plank or drive a nail. Now, it's as if they could build the Great Pyramids up there in Utuado. The *jíbaros* come to work every day and labor well for ten hours. They no longer need to stop and catch their breath or recover from paralyzing fatigue. The rebuilding of the coffee plantation now proceeds at a furious pace, and Mr. Roig says he plans to increase the grounds under cultivation and expand his workforce provided he can continue to get healthy laborers." It suddenly occurred to Ashford that many of the patients they had treated at the Tricoche Hospital had come to Ponce at the urging of their co-worker Simón Báez, the very first person that they had cured of infectious anemia. At long last, those efforts had begun to bear fruit.

Colonel Buchanan rose from his chair and began to pace about the room. "A few days ago, I received a cable from the War Department ordering your immediate promotion, something you were already due, and then asking me to approve your transfer from the island while offering you a prestigious post as consolation. I have always thought that you were on the right track and your problems were the result of politics and petty jealousies. When Governor Hunt approached me with the letter from this prominent coffee planter, I spoke to him plainly. The time has come for you to really show us what you can do, and I think the most appropriate thing will be to put your transfer on hold for now, if the Governor agrees."

Ashford's eyes lit up, and he turned expectantly toward Hunt.

The governor added, "I came here today to meet you and link a face to the name of Ashford, allowing me to judge what should be done. The recent letter from Utuado has made me think twice. Please tell us how you would proceed if you were allowed to stay."

Ashford could feel his heart pounding inside his chest. "Governor," he began, "I would be lying if I said that I haven't hoped for this possibility many times, and I am grateful beyond words to have the opportunity to share my ideas with you. I believe that the next step in our campaign against the hookworm should be to create a core group of medical professionals properly equipped to treat dozens of patients every day. During our best days in Ponce, we could not care for more than a handful of patients."

"True enough," Post said. "Treating only ten patients a day will not get you very far."

"Exactly," Ashford replied. "I propose to start a treatment center in one of the most severely affected rural areas, and build a local clinic with the sole purpose of treating anemia patients. It will be organized to serve the maximum number of patients by following the model of the tent hospital at the *Hospital Militar* that we set up after the hurricane. My goal would be to treat no fewer than a hundred patients daily. That is the number I estimate we would need to reach to eradicate the hookworms."

The governor asked, "Where would you build the first center?"

"We have had good results with the people of Utuado, so we might consider starting there. Our efforts there have become widely known. With government support, and a good word from former patients among Mr. Roig's workers, then I believe that we could have a successful clinic operating relatively quickly. We could be very busy within just a few days."

Post shook his head. "There are also drawbacks to Utuado. The *alcalde* and his council lead a vocal anti-American faction. Yes, Roig recognizes the good that you have done for him, but many of the *barrio* leaders will likely oppose us. They could use the press to argue that anemia results from hard times, or worse, from bad treatment of the locals by the American administration in San Juan. It may be unwise to risk failure at such a crucial period."

"That is possible," Ashford replied. "On the other hand, when we succeed under adversity in Utuado, as I have no doubt we will, our detractors will have to assume that we can succeed anywhere. It could bring the doubters over to our side."

The governor looked at the others in the room. "The power to appoint the *alcalde* in Utuado falls solely to the Office of the

Governor. I think the time has come to become more involved in the politics of that town. It would be relatively easy to appoint a new mayor, one with a more favorable opinion of the United States."

Post nodded, "I see what you are getting at, Governor. We remove the current mayor and then name someone we can convince that anemia is preventable and curable."

Hunt looked deliberately at Post. "Or better yet, name somebody who already agrees that anemia is preventable and curable."

Post suddenly understood. "You mean Arturo Roig?"

Hunt smiled deviously, and replied, "Well, why not? He's well known and highly respected in Utuado. Roig would make an excellent mayor."

Ashford interrupted, "I propose that we officially name the medical team the Puerto Rico Anemia Commission, to give it full legitimacy. This Anemia Commission would consist of three or four physicians supported by a specially trained group of technicians, nurses and interpreters. When we are successful in Utuado, then we will move to another location and begin the process once more."

Post drew himself up toward Ashford, "We are counting on you to be successful, Dr. Ashford. We cannot have it any other way."

"I have no doubt that we will succeed," Ashford declared with assurance. "I have great confidence in Dr. King, and I think we can recruit other prominent physicians, such as Dr. Agustín Stahl, who practices very near here in Bayamón."

Governor Hunt asked, "What do you envision by way of a budget? Specifically, Dr. Ashford, how many patients could you treat for, say, $5,000?"

Ashford was taken aback by the offer of such a generous sum. He calculated silently for an instant before presenting a number he considered wildly optimistic. "I believe for that amount we can staff a rural clinic and treat between five and six hundred patients."

"Very well, Dr. Ashford, that sum can be procured for you with no difficulty. I will say that for $5,000, we expect to see five hundred cures, no less," said Governor Hunt, his tone suspended somewhere between light and dead serious. The four men rose from their seats and cordially shook hands. Dr. Ashford was to remain in Puerto Rico. Now, it would be up to an unborn Puerto Rico Anemia Commission to see that all this came to fruition.

Chapter Thirty-Three

THE ANEMIA COMMISION, 1903

Ashford's immediate concern was recruiting and then organizing the physicians who would form part of the Puerto Rico Anemia Commission. He spent the weeks after the Thanksgiving holiday in San Juan doing just this. The capital held more promise than Ponce, where opinions had already hardened. As soon as it was formed, the Commission would proceed to Utuado to organize their first rural clinic. Walter King and Rafi Moore immediately agreed to join. Ashford then contacted Agustín Stahl, his old acquaintance from Agaudilla, and quickly convinced him to serve. This core of physicians constituted the heart of the Commission, to be joined by a small army of nurses and orderlies.

Just after the start of the new year, the recently constituted Anemia Commission arrived in the municipality of Utuado. They installed themselves in a picturesque old country house near the banks of the *Río Vivi*, perched in a large clearing surrounded on three sides by a thick forest of tropical hardwoods and royal palms. All around them stood the tall green peaks of the island's central mountainous spine; about two miles away across a deep valley, the picturesque town of Utuado nestled among the greenery.

The Sunday evening following their arrival, the physicians walked into town to enjoy an evening in the old square, dominated by its large yellow stucco church. As in so many other towns around the island, the central plaza was full of young people flirting and mingling to the sounds of the municipal band, their parents and grandparents discreetly watching from a long line of rocking chairs.

The next morning, Ashford began the work of constructing the field hospital in the large open space in front of the house and stretched for ten acres in all directions. The complex would consist of thirty large tents, graciously provided by the Army, and set up in a square formation. The medical personnel were just beginning to raise the cumbersome tents when they saw a group of twenty men coming down the trail from the direction of the coffee plantation. As they drew closer, Ashford and Rafi recognized the leader of the group as their old patient, Simón Báez. Next to him was his son, Carlos, followed by Gaspar and Domingo Reyes, and a number of other former patients from either the Tricoche Hospital or the *Hospital Militar de Ponce*. All the men looked strong and in good health. Gone from their faces was the sickly pallor and gauntness which had once marked them as victims of the hookworm.

Simón and the others walked up to Ashford and warmly shook his hand. Ashford could now understand their Spanish without difficulty as Simón spoke.

"Doctor Ashford, don Arturo informed us that you *americano* doctors were coming to Utuado to treat sick people with the *bolitas de cristal,* and that you might need help putting up the field hospital. We asked don Arturo if he could give us a day to assist our doctor friends in building the camp, for we all want you to begin your work as soon as possible. Don Arturo agreed, and he is paying us our wages, just as if we were working at the hacienda."

A broad smile came to Ashford's face. "I am very moved that your group has come here today. It seems fitting that now that you are well, you can help us build this small hospital where we can reach many more of your neighbors. We are grateful for your assistance."

The men began to work, and the tents were raised by the early afternoon. The workers then talked amicably with Ashford and the other members of the Commission for the better part of what remained of the day. Finally, as the sunlight deepened into its pre-evening orange, the *jíbaros* began the walk back to Las Alturas, two hours away on the other side of the *cordillera*.

Don Arturo, the new *alcalde* of Utuado, kept his promise to refer fifty patients to the new clinic. This activity on the part of the mayor aroused the curiosity of the *jíbaros*, who began sending in their gravely ill friends and relatives on their own. Word quickly spread of the one item required by the doctors before they saw anyone as a patient: each person had to bring a sample to be examined for hookworm eggs. From all over the 150-square-mile municipality of Utuado, men, women, and children arrived in all stages of anemia, each carrying a small specimen in a matchbox. The handy container easily opened for the purpose of access and also easily closed for the purpose of modesty. Every so often, a man or woman learned about this somewhat unorthodox requirement *after* they had already joined the long line waiting for treatment. In that case, they resolved their dilemma by borrowing part of the sample belonging to another *jíbaro* in the line. In this manner, everybody entered the clinic with the required fecal sample, even if it was not truly their own.

The activities of the Anemia Commission closely resembled those at the military hospital in Ponce. The tents served as patient wards, while the old country house became the outpatient clinic and the laboratory. Outpatients—those less severely afflicted—were given sulfate and thymol at appropriate intervals and then sent home with instructions to return to the clinic in a month for re-evaluation. People suffering from more severe anemia were kept in the tents as inpatients under careful supervision. These inpatients had their blood smears and hemoglobin levels checked on admission, and then daily during their stay.

The first four weeks proved hectic for the Anemia Commission. During that time, they managed to successfully treat almost two hundred patients, of whom fifty were severely anemic, ill enough to need hospitalization. Some of their laboratory values proved as shocking as those from the sickest patients at the Tricoche Hospital.

Then, after the initial rush of patients, people suddenly stopped coming. Ashford could not understand what had changed to keep them away. In the space of one day, the team had gone from treating twenty new patients each morning, to none. Ashford became concerned as a week passed without any new patients. The governor had already provided the promised $5,000 with the understanding that the Anemia Commission was to treat and cure approximately five hundred patients. If the current trend continued, they would fall short of their agreement. Ashford suspected that a few hostile *barrio* leaders had targeted the Anemia Commission, exactly as Governor Hunt had predicted.

Mayor Roig travelled to the field hospital to speak with Ashford and King. He explained that Utuado was plagued by a vocal faction of small-time politicians and religious figures, who were painting the Anemia Commission as a ploy to exonerate the United States from responsibility for the worsening pandemic. Before long, the team saw evidence of the opposition for themselves. One evening, the town priest and his red-robed altar boys were seen leaving the church in Utuado carrying crucifixes, burning candles and chanting loudly as they crossed the valley to the hospital clearing. From across the valley, Ashford kept a close eye on their progress, sure that the pomp and circumstance was meant to identify his clinic as an unholy place in need of a priest's assistance—and this could hardly be encouraging to new patients.

When the procession arrived at the clinic, the priest began to administer the final rites of the Church to the patients *en masse*, proceeding systematically from tent to tent and collecting fees as he went. But after a half hour of this, the solemnity of the ritual evaporated out of nowhere, as a crusty and desperately sick old man began to curse the priest in the most vivid and colorful language. This same priest had, apparently, once refused to anoint the man's dying wife unless he was paid an exorbitant amount of money. The incensed man called for the skies to open and release a bolt of lightning to split the priest in half. Everyone in the tent, patients and staff, found the exchange hilarious, except, of course, for the priest, who was never again seen anywhere near the hospital.

But interference from one priest could not account for the clinic's lack of patients. Soon after the incident of the last rites, another occurred which exposed the source of their difficulties. Very late on an evening that storm clouds and an absent moon had made especially dark, a *jíbaro* orderly raced up the back staircase in search of Ashford and Rafi, who were up late mixing stains in the upstairs laboratory. Agustín was a jaunty, hard-working, and scrupulously honest man whose mother Ashford had cured at the *Hospital Militar*. She had risen after two weeks at death's door with a normal blood count and restored to good health. In appreciation of the care given his mother, Agustín volunteered at the tent hospital; he was ferociously loyal to Ashford.

The frightened orderly burst into the laboratory sweating and out of breath, whispering hoarsely, "Doctor, come quick. A man is approaching who is a wanted criminal. He is known to have killed at least a dozen men!"

Nearly dropping a full bottle of tissue stain, Ashford gasped, "Agustín, what on earth are you talking about?"

"I am saying that there is a known murderer coming up the outside stairs! You should hide. I am sure he means harm!"

Ashford and Rafi cautiously followed Agustín out to the veranda in time to witness a most peculiar sight. Slowly climbing the external stairway leading from the lawn to the upper balcony was a tall, muscular, rough-looking individual, holding a portable kerosene lamp in his right hand and, slung over his opposite shoulder the limp figure of a child of five or six. Rafi let out a gasp. Not ten yards away, his features revealed by the faint flicker of the lamp, was the all-too-familiar face of Pepe Maldonado Román, the White Eagle of the mountains of Puerto Rico.

Rafi pulled Ashford inside the laboratory. "Dr. Ashford, the man coming up the stairs is the leader of the bandits that murdered don Arturo's son on the trail to Lares. There is a bounty on his head."

Rafi had barely finished his warning when into the room walked Don Pepe, carrying the languid figure in his arms. He lovingly placed the child on a chair, respectfully removed his hat, and spoke to them in slow and deliberate Spanish. "My name is José Maldonado, and I am a fugitive wanted for murder. This is my only child and the light of my life, Adela. She is five years old and dying of anemia. Can you please help us?"

Ashford and Rafi stared at the man in silence. He was in his late twenties, powerfully built, with abundant dark hair, a bold mustache, and intelligent brown eyes. He normally would have commanded a fearful presence, but at that moment, he was a helpless father consumed by grief.

"Please know," Maldonado continued, "that during the time I spent hiding with my family in Juana Díaz, I heard of the miracles taking place at the hospitals in Ponce. My beautiful Adela has become progressively worse this last year, and the *curanderas* have not been able to help her. I was unwilling to take her to any doctor, for fear that they would betray me for the reward money. But last week, Adela became extremely ill, and so we have come here to beg for the curing medicine that only you possess. I am willing to risk my freedom and my life to see that my child lives."

Ashford listened, dumbfounded. He walked over to the sleeping child as soon as the man finished, then looked at her for a minute, deep in thought. She was a lovely child with thick brown curls framing a pretty face, her smooth skin marred only by the specter of anemic pallor.

Looking up, Ashford signaled to Don Pepe, saying, "Please, follow me."

Don Pepe took Adela in his arms and followed Ashford and Rafi into one of the examination rooms. Agustín brought three large portable lamps, and by the shimmer of light they provided, Ashford and Rafi conducted their examination. The child exhibited all the features of profound anemia so familiar to them. In English, Rafi asked Ashford what they should do. Theirs was a terrible dilemma: Not treating the child would be unethical, but if they treated her and she died, there was no telling what Pepe, a violent criminal, might do.

Don Pepe clearly did not understand their exchange. Ashford thought for a moment, and then switching to a heavily accented but correct Spanish, addressed the father. "*Señor* Maldonado, my name is Dr. Bailey Ashford and next to me is my assistant, Mr. Rafael Moore. At this time, we don't care who you are or how you make a living. Your daughter is innocent of any wrongdoing and is in danger of losing her life. There is no time to search for hookworm eggs. We will study her blood, and if she has anemia, we can treat her with the medicine. Will you give me permission?"

With a trembling voice, the bandit gave his assent.

"Very well." Ashford nodded, pushing back memories of the last time the parents of a seriously ill child had come to him in the dead of night, begging for help. "Rafi, will you please prepare the blood smear, while I procure the hemoglobinometer? Agustín, we will need far more light if the microscopes are to work properly."

Over the course of the next two hours, they completed the necessary blood studies. Adela's tests brought no surprises. The blood studies confirmed a case of severe anemia, with 15 percent hemoglobin, markedly reduced, pale red cells, and only the occasional eosinophil. The case was truly dire, threatening a replay of the fatal outcome for Esteban Reyes.

Ashford turned to Maldonado and said, "As you know, Adela is extremely sick. Her anemia is so severe that her bone marrow is failing and quickly running out of iron. Treating Adela could possibly precipitate her death, but not treating her will ensure that she will die within the week."

Tears filled the eyes of Don Pepe, a man used to getting his way with bullets and threats, now reduced to abject helplessness. "Dr. Ashford, Señor Moore, I understand perfectly. If there is a higher power looking down upon my family today, may it judge us by the innocence of my daughter and not by the blackness of my actions. I place my daughter entirely in your hands."

"Then there is not a moment to lose," Ashford said. "Rafi, we will apply the heroic resuscitation protocol we learned at the Tricoche Hospital. Are you confident that we can repeat it here? I do not believe Adela will survive her treatment without direct rehydration."

"Yes, Dr. Ashford. Between Dr. King, Dr. Stahl, and me, we can have fluids ready in about two hours."

"Good. We are fortunate that she is a small child, that will reduce the volume of fluid required and the risks of contamination. One liter of resuscitation fluid should prove more than enough."

"And after that?" asked Rafi.

"I am tempted to forego the first dose of the cathartic and proceed directly to a slightly higher dosage of thymol. What we cannot avoid is the final dose of the sodium sulfate to clear her system of any remaining drug."

Once the procedure was agreed upon, Agustín was sent to gather the rest of the team. Out of compassion for the girl's father, he was allowed to stay in the room, standing silently to one side, hidden in the shadows. Through some unspoken agreement, neither Agustín nor the doctors shared his identity. Within two hours, the child was ready to receive intravenous fluids via the contraption *Sor* Marcelina at the Tricoche had shown them. Adela was given half a liter of fluid over two hours. The fluid revived her, and encouraged the team to proceed with the thymol.

Ashford turned to Maldonado and showed him a gelatin capsule that had been filled with one half-gram of thymol. "This capsule contains the medicine which will kill and expel the hookworms." Ashford extended his arm to give the capsule for the girl to swallow, when suddenly Maldonado stepped forward and held back the doctor's hand.

Looking straight at Ashford, don Pepe spoke in a voice charged with emotion. "Dr. Ashford, if you will permit it, I prefer to give her the medicine myself. For, if something were to go wrong, then all the blame will fall on Pepe Maldonado, the one responsible for bringing upon her the suffering that Providence meant for me."

Ashford handed the tiny capsule to Don Pepe. The father looked at his darling girl and, speaking softly, said to her, "Adela, here is the *bolita de cristal* that I promised to find for you. Your *Papi* will help you take it." Don Pepe put the capsule up to Adela's mouth and encouraged her to swallow it with some sugar water. The girl appeared puzzled by the burning sensation passing from her throat into her stomach, then frowned as she experienced the usual nausea for a few minutes. But she kept the drug down without vomiting and soon fell asleep on the cot with her father watching over her. Two hours later, Don Pepe gave her a second dose. That seemed to go well, and two hours after that they administered the final medicine, ten grams of sodium sulfate, to purge any remaining thymol from her gut.

The collection of the girl's fecal matter began shortly after that. By now, Ashford knew that a majority of the dead hookworms appeared within twelve hours. But the girl was by no means out of danger yet. They gave her another half a liter of fluid intravenously, and soon after that, she was alert enough to take more fluids by mouth. For the next twelve hours, stretching through the rest of the night and well into the following afternoon, Adela's waste was collected and filtered. Rafi, King, and Stahl counted 700 worms, a heavy load for such a small patient. Ashford told Don Pepe that the child had to remain in the hospital for at least one week before they could be certain of her survival. During this period, they planned to provide the best recuperative care for her, including nutritious food and iron supplements.

Over the next week, Don Pepe disappeared into the forest by day and returned to his daughter late at night under the cloak of darkness, varying the time of his visits and staying for no longer than ten minutes. At the times when Don Pepe emerged silently from the shadows, Ashford and Rafi never failed to meet him by Adela's bedside. The child proved to be cut from the same sturdy cloth as her father. She was strong, stubborn, and full of life, one she evidently wanted to live to the fullest. The little girl was soon feeding herself, and by the third day, a pinkish hue could be discerned on her cheeks and lips. By the fifth day, Adela was beginning to act like any other normal, healthy five-year-old.

The transformation of the child stunned her father. The fifth night after treatment, Don Pepe asked Ashford to release Adela from the hospital. He had received word that the authorities in Ponce had been notified of his present whereabouts, and he could be found and arrested at any moment. Don Pepe had repeatedly pressed his luck by coming into camp, and the time had come to take Adela away. At first, Ashford insisted she stay longer to regain more strength, but her father's occupation made that impossible.

That night, the wanted man and the doctor walked together to the small clearing in front of the tents. Don Pepe again thanked Ashford for saving his daughter, and Ashford offered his well-rehearsed sermon on shoes and latrines. With those words, and with the night at its darkest— moonrise was still three hours away—José Maldonado took Adela by the hand, and with his daughter now walking effortlessly beside him, led her into the shadows of the nearby forest.

The days passed and no new patients came to the anemia clinic. The only patients now keeping the Anemia Commission busy were the few remaining inpatients left in the tents, and most of these were almost fully recovered. Here they were, fully installed and funded to treat hundreds more of the *jíbaros,* and not a single one had come to their door in almost two weeks. The project appeared to be in danger of collapsing.

One foggy morning, about ten days after Don Pepe had taken a healthy Adela back into the mountains, Ashford was sitting on the porch of the old house trying to enjoy his coffee in the company of Dr. King, Dr. Stahl, and Rafi Moore, when a slow crescendo of approaching voices reached their ears. Looking up, the physicians gazed dumbfounded as a parade of thin, pale *jíbaros* materialized from the mists, slowly descending the steep mountainside along the narrow trail. The caravan of specters had returned. This time, instead of coming to Ponce in search of shelter, they were approaching the hospital in search of treatment. On each side, four men escorted the group. Their appearance told Ashford that these men belonged to Don Pepe's band.

Ashford and Rafi descended to the lawn to meet one of the men escorting the procession. The man approached Ashford, respectfully removed his hat and handed him an envelope with a folded letter. The letter was written in the unorthodox Puerto Rican Spanish of the mountain country, and Ashford handed it to Rafi to translate out loud. The letter read:

"Doctor Ashford, My band has been responsible for keeping patients away from your hospital. Shortly after your group arrived in the mountains of Utuado, I was approached by one of your detractors, asking me to sabotage your campaign. It was the former alcalde who approached us for this purpose. He paid us 500 pesos from funds collected by your enemies and threatened to turn us in to the authorities if we did not disrupt the flow of patients seeking treatment. My men and I shamelessly intimidated prospective patients and spread villainous rumors about your treatments, knowing full

well that these were lies invented by politicians. Then came a miracle and my child was saved. We have come today so that other children like Adela may have a chance at a healthy life. After today, you will no longer see us, but rest assured that my men and I will be protecting the patients who come to receive care in this clinic. Word will spread very quickly of your successes, and your Commission will be buried in work within the next few days. While you remain in Utuado, my men and I will make sure that you are not bothered again."

Rafi looked at Ashford and added, "It is signed—José Maldonado Román, *El Águila Blanca*."

In the space of a day, everything had changed. The hidden forces that opposed the Anemia Commission's work had been completely supplanted by those wishing them success. Ashford could not bring himself to shake the messenger's hand, but he did manage to say, "Please tell *Señor* Maldonado that I cannot pretend to judge any man, or what has brought him to lead a certain kind of life, but I can confidently say that today he has done a great good for his island." Ashford's favorite proverb suddenly came to his mind.

I have fought the good fight, I have finished my course, I have kept the faith.

Many times, he recited this mantra in gratitude as he watched patient after patient begin to stream into the clinic once again. He looked on in astonishment as day after day, people came from all locations, Utuado, Adjuntas, Lares, and beyond; patients of all ages, from a year to eighty years old. They travelled long distances over dangerous trails, under the broiling sun and the driving rain, up and down steep hills and tall mountains, all of them seeking the doctors who cured people with the magical *bolitas de cristal*. More tents had to be set up as the number of patients seeking help swelled from ten to fifty to a hundred per day. Every one of them had a fecal examination, received a short talk on the importance of wearing shoes and using latrines and were provided with the tiny capsules that did the magic. To add to the daily flood of new patients, there was still a full contingent of sick inpatients requiring daily visits, blood counts and treatments, constantly filling their beds. After six weeks, when Ashford finally tallied the number of people his Anemia Commission had treated so far, he arrived at a count of well over five thousand patients.

Chapter Thirty-Four

CONCLUSION

With only a few exceptions, people who had originally opposed Ashford's campaign soon fell in among the believers, including the Utuado priest, who every Sunday now raved endorsements from his pulpit. The clinic's daily load continued to swell to proportions that were truly overwhelming. The Commission started their work at daybreak, labored all day without lunch and continued until the late evening, when they could no longer see and were forced to turn away patients. These last *jíbaros*, rather than give up their place in line, gladly slept on the ground until morning. In this way, Ashford and his Anemia Commission in Utuado gathered a staggering amount of data regarding blood values, symptomatology, prevention and the response to treatments, all critical to completing the first scientific study of epidemic anemia.

The final salvo in their war against the detractors of the hookworm discovery came with Ashford and King's article on the first hundred cases from Ponce's Tricoche Hospital, published in the September, 1903 edition of *American Medicine*. The article was accompanied by a scathing editorial attacking the failure of local doctors to embrace and implement the efficacious deworming treatments:

"**Uncinariasis, an economic question for Porto Rico.**—The frequent appearance of references to uncinariasis in medical journals shows that the profession has at last awakened to the vital economic importance of the disease. First brought into prominence by the St. Gothard epidemic, it has been generally slighted, except in a few countries. We have been accustomed to look upon it in a pharisaic attitude as something far away of no special interest to the United States. Various reports have come to us as to its prevalence in South America and the West Indies, especially Porto Rico, while Dr. Charles Wardell Stiles, zoologist to the Public Health and the Marine-Hospital Service has unequivocally demonstrated its presence in the Southern States...The article, completed elsewhere in these columns, and written by Drs. Ashford and King, is the result of careful study and further investigation in a series of one hundred cases, chiefly in Ponce, P. R...It seems almost incredible that this disease should have existed in Porto Rico for so many years (as undoubtedly it has) without its true nature being investigated by the local physicians. It is easily diagnosed and easily cured. The Superior Board of Health has published and distributed to every physician and nearly all druggists, a pamphlet in Spanish, explaining clearly the nature and treatment of this tropical anemia in Porto Rico. But the seed seems to have fallen on stony ground, for as yet little or no effort has been made to either cure or prevent, and we have the spectacle of a naturally healthful island menaced with a severe check to the physical and moral development of its people, and secondarily a source of danger to the United States. Now that their Superior Board of Health reports that nearly one-third of the deaths may be due to this cause, the time for talk is past. Four years are more than sufficient to waste in fruitless discussion and unwarranted indifference to an epidemic comparable to cholera in its results, if not in sensational rapidity. The prosperity of a country depends largely upon the laboring classes. We cannot expect much from a workman with only 10% to 20% (*sic*) of hemoglobin and 1,500,000 to 2,500,000 red cells in his blood. All credit is due to the few who have begun treatment directed against the parasite, but the majority, and unhappily, the municipal physicians, have given the matter little thought and with few exceptions, no trial. Thymol and iron are cheap remedies, and more necessary than quinin (*sic*) the consumption of which is large in Porto Rico. Opposition or indifference to this matter is the most unpatriotic attitude for those having the interest of the country at heart. The anemia is of undoubted parasitic origin, and the profession of Porto Rico will find itself alone against the best judgment and rapid advances of modern medicine should they fail to realize this demonstrated truth."

The *American Medicine* editorial blew the lid off any attempt to keep the hookworm and the anemia pandemic it caused as a local matter. A prestigious journal had endorsed Ashford's discovery, and there would be no going back to improbable and unprovable theories. Now the whole world knew about the health crisis on the island and the barriers placed in front of the discoverer of its cause.

Ashford always believed that the success of the initial campaign should be attributed to self-interest on the part of people in their own salvation. Although the majority of patients could not read or write, it was the spoken word, not pen and paper, that proved the best way to disseminate his discovery. First came thirty or forty timid souls, always suffering from terminal anemia. Then came their sensationally rapid improvement, and within a month, the field hospital was running to capacity, treating from 600 to 800 patients a day. By the close of the first phase of the Commission's work, thousands of people had joined in to spread the news in every direction: the anemia in the *jíbaros* was being cured by certain mysterious little balls of glass and their magic medicine. The island Ashford had come to love was free from the shackles of parasitic anemia, giving its people a new lease on life and license to enjoy the many gifts Puerto Rico had to offer.

But all of these successes were tempered by events out of Ashford's control. On an early January day in 1905, Ashford once again stood on the docks of San Juan Bay, a fresh ocean breeze tugging at his jacket as he looked out to sea. The life of a soldier is never quite his own and now Captain Bailey K. Ashford found himself transferred back to the mainland. It made no sense to him—he had only recently been named Associate Director for the Department of Infectious Diseases at the army hospital. But the Army had at long last decided that the time had come to apply Ashford's abilities on the mainland. The surprise of his promotion and the new and greater responsibilities it brought with it paled in comparison to the deep dejection he felt at his departure. No degree of protestations or supplications on Ashford's part had changed his orders.

The last few days in Puerto Rico with his wife and his little boy had been exceedingly gloomy, counting the hours as the dreaded day inevitably approached. The morning of the departure had finally arrived, dawning clear and bright, giving rise to one of those beautiful December days so commonplace at these latitudes. Numerous bags were piled around his feet. By his side stood his wife María Asunción with young Mahlon in her arms, her father Don Ramón, and a few other close family members. The glory of the warm, beautiful day made his departure that much more difficult. People came and went, the boilers from the ship let out a whistle of impatience, and Bailey Ashford prepared himself to say goodbye to Puerto Rico.

Already waiting for him at the port was his good friend, Juan Báez, now, at only twenty-two years old, the deputy collector for the port of Ponce. Juan took Ashford's shoulders and held them firmly with his hands. Looking into the physician's eyes, he said, "Dr. Ashford, there are no words to express what my family and I owe you. I only wish Providence had sent you sooner. You saved my father, my brother, my sister, and many of my friends, and for that I will never forget you."

Ashford could feel a knot forming in his throat. "Juan," he said softly, "I have not told anyone else, but I have never felt so downhearted. This island is my home and I cannot bear to leave it now, especially knowing that there are still so many sick people who need our help."

Juan smiled broadly. "I have heard from my superiors in Ponce that, even without you asking, the island legislature has appropriated an additional $50,000 for anemia relief in the coming year. Have faith, Doctor. Things have a way of sorting themselves out in the end, you will see."

Ashford stared out at the vast expanse of the bay. "I hope you are right, Juan. I can say for sure that my life is better for having known your family. Not a day will pass when I won't think of you."

With a warm handshake, Ashford turned toward the companionway with María Asunción and their son by his side. A refreshing breeze blew from the east and pushed away any incipient humidity as if by sleight of hand. Above the pier rose the dark hull of the steamship *Ponce*, by curious happenstance named for the city where he had blazed his path to success after many initial struggles. By the side of the ship, other passengers had gathered, most of them looking forward to boarding for the four-day journey to Philadelphia, from where they would continue to their final destinations.

From beyond the slip, where San Juan's docks met the Calle Marina, someone called from afar. The voice was unmistakable, and looking up the street, Ashford recognized his good friend and special colleague, Rafael Moore. The ever-loyal Rafi had come to bid him farewell, accompanied by his father, and trailing not far behind them, the familiar figure of Walter King. The trio turned from the street into the pier and approached the waiting Ashford. Rafi threw his arms around his boss, who had been his best friend and teacher for over three years.

Putting on a semblance of happiness while furiously fighting back his tears, Rafi managed to stammer, "Dr. Ashford, my island owes you a debt I am afraid we can never repay," as his voice failed him completely.

Ashford passed an arm over Rafi's shoulder, as they turned together to walk toward the ship. "You know, my dearest friend, who would have imagined just four short years ago that it would have come to this: a proven cure conveyed by a dedicated medical taskforce which has treated over 100,000 patients, representing nearly 1,000,000 visits to the clinic stations."

Rafi smiled. "And each person cured at the cost of what… a pound of sugar, a sack of flour?"

Ashford held up a finger, "By my latest calculations, for sixty cents a patient."

Rafi replied, "We have indeed come a long way since that trip to Aguadilla. It was all an unfathomable mystery back then."

Ashford took Rafi's hand in his own for the final time, saying, "Now we know the cause and successful treatment of a killer that preyed preferentially on poor laborers. A killer that destroyed people piecemeal, taking away their desire to live, to prosper, to improve themselves and their children.

But much remains to be done. As of now, the pandemic is still killing hundreds each month. Over one-third of all the deaths reported last year were blamed directly on infectious anemia. It remains a staggering number."

Rafi tried unsuccessfully to hide his heartache by looking away. "We'll conquer the disease. We'll get there soon, thanks to you."

Ashford looked into his colleague's saddened face. "Rafi, I have come to realize that a friend is truly special when you have attempted to say farewell a thousand times and still you cannot find the words that allow you to go."

The men embraced while their families looked on."

Hoisting their son on her hip, María Asunción made her way to the gangplank. Suddenly realizing she had done so on her own, she turned back to her husband. "Are you coming, love?"

Startled, Ashford broke from his reverie and looked up at his wife, the golden morning sun spilling across her face. She looked at him quizzically, but with the same intelligence and gentleness that had so struck him when they first met at her father's party, seemingly so long ago. He hesitated as a pang of sorrow gripped his heart and twisted to survey the docks one more time; the bustling of the workers, the citizens of the capital strolling along streets hemmed in by mansions and workhouses, markets and bars that leaked music into the streets, the crash of the surf, all against the backdrop of the verdant mountains in the distance. Puerto Rico was no longer a dream of battle and glory, nor a medical mystery to solve. It was his home. And he would return.

"*Estoy justo detrás de ti, mi amor,*" he smiled, taking pleasure in how easily Spanish tripped off his tongue now. María Asunción extended her hand and Ashford took it, her palm warm in his, and they boarded the ship together.

The steamer gave a shrill whistle, and with a billow of smoke from its single stack, retreated slowly from its moorings and eased along the waterfront facing the city. From the starboard rail, Ashford gazed at the landmarks of receding wharves, muttering under his breath:

The Lord bless thee, and keep thee,

The Lord make his face shine upon thee, and be gracious unto thee:

The Lord lift up his countenance upon thee, and give thee peace.

Before long, with the turn around the craggy, southern spit of San Juan known as La Puntilla, the governor's palace came into view with its white crenellated towers dating back to the early sixteenth century. Next in line was the small gap in the fortified wall that served as the lone entrance to the city from that side of the bay, and finally at the very tip of the city, the proud fortress of San Felipe, which had fired defiantly on the American fleet at the start of the war with Spain. The magnificent structure high atop the bluff of El Morro, had guarded the entrance to the harbor with its many batteries for almost four centuries. As the ship gradually negotiated the narrow channel, Ashford looked at the castle fortress and thought what a magnificent embodiment it was of this island, proud as its people, facing silently forward toward a new future. As the ship slowly steamed past the fort and toward the empty sea to the north, the distant hills dissolving into the blue sky conveyed the sad farewell of a grateful nation. And far, far away, over the highest peaks to the south, a diffuse and dark gray streak bore witness to a fresh rain falling once again on the coffee trees.

Author's Note

"The story of the reconquest of Puerto Rico from the tyranny of the hookworm is one of the most thrilling accounts to be found in the history of the island."

Bailey Ashford's statement is as true today as when he first shared it a hundred years ago. I first heard the name of Bailey K. Ashford from my grandmother. She was fond of recounting repeatedly and most enthusiastically how her sister, Luz María Dalmáu, had helped discover the cause of endemic anemia in the Puerto Rican *jíbaro*. When we drove by Ashford's attractive house at the corner of *Avenida El Condado* (now Ashford Avenue) and *Calle Cervantes*, my mother never failed to remark that the great doctor once lived there. But other than those few observations, I knew little else about Ashford. The celebrated figures in Puerto Rican history are almost exclusively politicians and musical artists, and the accomplishments of this American doctor from the southern United States were not the subject of common discussions or island holidays. In fact, I cannot recall Ashford being mentioned at all in the extensive Puerto Rican history required from every high school student on the island for graduation.

I am not sure why this is so. Perhaps nowadays, we take our health increasingly for granted. Or maybe the reason is that the discovery belonged to a lowly Army lieutenant of twenty-five. In any event, ample evidence suggests that even after widespread acceptance of his momentous discovery, recognition was slow to come Ashford's way. Some bitterness is evident when he describes how, at least initially, inordinate credit went to his former Georgetown professor, Charles Wardell Stiles, undoubtedly because he was much better connected. The results of the Puerto Rico Anemia Commission led directly to the organization of the Rockefeller Sanitary Commission for work in the American South, exactly along the lines that had been laid down in Puerto Rico. After phenomenal successes following this approach, it did not take long for the Rockefeller Sanitary Commission to evolve into the International Health Commission.

To put Ashford's achievement in perspective, imagine an often-fatal disease that affects 60 percent of our current population. This figure greatly exceeds the current incidence of heart disease, cancer, COPD, cerebrovascular disease, kidney disease, and dementia *combined*; a disease so common that people had resigned themselves to living and dying with it, or helplessly watching many of their loved ones succumb to its effects. Then, imagine a rookie medical graduate stating that by simply taking a few pills, thousands upon thousands (millions, if we extrapolate to today) of people can be restored fully to health in a matter of days. This is exactly what happened in Puerto Rico in late 1899.

No island holidays are named after Ashford, and his humble tomb in Bayamón is not a site for pilgrimages. Ashford's discovery of the hookworm at the *Hospital Militar de Ponce* seems to have passed from Puerto Rico's common consciousness. I do not overstate the case by saying that the events of November, 1899—the discovery of the *Necator* egg, the corresponding hookworm, and the subsequent implementation of thymol—changed the course of history for the island, completely and forever. At the time, an unimaginable proportion of the population struggled to earn a living while their bodies starved for oxygen, as if they labored high up in the Himalayas, and with the added burden of an incomprehensibly poor diet. And then, through serendipity born out of the *San Ciriaco* catastrophe, Ashford uncovered a single hookworm egg, *and immediately realized what it meant*. From that point, the island had its laborers gradually restored to her, after more than three centuries of near-absence.

Ashford returned permanently to Puerto Rico in 1908 and remained in the Army for the greater part of his life. His many scientific and humanitarian accomplishments cannot be adequately described in a few words. He practiced almost until his death from prostate cancer in 1934, treating not only soldiers but also countless civilians. He founded Puerto Rico's celebrated Institute of Tropical Medicine with former colleagues from the Anemia Commission, and traveled around the world educating medical communities. Ashford dedicated much of his later investigations to the problem of tropical sprue, investing great efforts in trying to link the condition to various yeasts. His conclusions were met with mostly lukewarm reactions from the scientific community.

But, as I eventually discovered, this was where my great-aunt Luz María came in: she had been his mycologist, his yeast expert, never having been involved in the anemia discovery at all.

Acknowledgments

I wish to express my deepest gratitude to Miriam Seidel and Alex Keenan for their patient, repeated readings of the manuscript and providing numerous invaluable and insightful suggestions for improvement.

I am grateful to Jordan Virtue of Stanford University for reviewing the final version of the novel and providing the feedback that finally made it all come together.

A very special recognition goes to my daughter Cecilia García for her vital help with our website, publicity, securing the cover art, drawing the historical map of San Juan, and numerous editorial recommendations.

This book would not have been possible without the early encouragement and feedback I received from my wife Lisa Wortman García, my daughter Sofía García, and my son Charlie García. They never let me give up, even when the Muse went missing for extended periods of time.

My brother Dr. José Antonio García was the first person to read the manuscript and encourage me to go forward with the hard work required to get the book to its current form.

Thank you Gabe Palma for the amazing cover art watercolor depiction of 19th century rural Puerto Rico.

And most of all, thank you to my dear departed sister Ana Isabel Garcia Saúl who first taught me to love history so many years ago. We miss you every day.

About the author

Carlos García Saúl is a native of San Juan, Puerto Rico. He graduated *summa cum laude* from Harvard College with a B.A. in Biology in 1985. His medical degree is from Yale University and his surgical training in Head and Neck Surgery was completed at the Harvard Medical School. He practiced medicine for 28 years in Massachusetts and Kansas. Dr Garcia Saúl's academic interests include the history of medicine and its responses to the political climate of the 19th and 20th centuries. The story of the conquest of the parasitic anemia in Puerto Rico has been of particular personal and professional interest. He considered the defeat of the infectious anemia agent in Puerto Rico to be socially and economically on par with the remarkable advances of the 1940s and 1950s and the economic miracle of Operation Bootstrap. Dr. García Saúl's other interests include art history, traveling, and collecting rare orchids and Taino artifacts. Since retiring, he has resided in Saint Petersburg, Florida with with his wife, Lisa.

Made in United States
Orlando, FL
16 September 2024

51604144R00207